The Princess Thieves

Written by Alexander Shaw

Other books by Alexander Shaw

The New Century Multiverse
Let Them Go
Secret Rooms
The Cartographer's Handbook
Arlington
Tiger's Eye
The Princess Thieves
The Christmas Thieves
SteamHeart
Uncivil Outlaw

Movie A Day
Movie A Day Vol. 1
Movie A Day Vol. 2

This is a story from THE NEW CENTURY MULTIVERSE. Each of these tales is self-contained, with a beginning, a middle and an end. You don't need to have read any of the others to enjoy this one, but every subsequent volume you take in will add a piece to the grand unfolding tapestry of alternate Earths, lost in time.

THE PRINCESS THIEVES takes place in two different Englands, over one May week of an alternate 1883.

Across the Atlantic other stories are happening.

Contents

Part 3: Hanging Heavy

Part 1: London Town

"Just a minute. Robin Hood steals money from my pocket, forcing me to hurt the public… and they love him for it?

That's it then. Cancel the kitchen scraps for lepers and orphans, no more merciful beheadings, and call off Christmas!"

-Alan Rickman

Prologue

(Delivered by the Moste Anciente Wizarde Merlene)

A thousand years ago, the Duart, short, proud and cunning, first made their home on the island of Britannica, in the realm of Celador (that's pronounced with a hard C, from the Celtic, darling). More recently the Akka, green-skinned and monstrous (although I personally would have chosen a less negative descriptor like "powerful") came to Celador from the realm of Hannoth, demanding a new home from the Duart people (again, that's a half-truth, deeply coloured by the dominant race dictating the narrative). They lived, uncomfortably, for some time.

Then a decade before this story begins, a gateway opened, north of the Duart city of Londinium, a passage to another Earth, one which you might have read about in *The Cartographer's Handbook*, *Secret Rooms* or *Arlington*, though prior knowledge of these is not essential to this story. The two races ventured through and emerged into the new realm (which I am calling Centrum; with a soft C, like the Latin century) and the city of London in their year of 1873.

As with the rest of this world, the British Isles had recently been beset by a terrible plague, and many of the people had been reduced to savage, infected beasts, spoken of in hushed whispers as the Barghest; aggressive and feral hunters who preyed on humankind and snuck in the shadows. Queen Victoria had fled to the North, and the city had burned. But the Londoners still living in this broken place were hardy folk, with a talent for survival, and formed allegiances with the newcomers.

Soon the Duart Firecasters were patrolling the counties of Britain hunting down the creatures, their stout bodies mercifully immune to the infection. They were fascinated with the technology encountered in this world and asked the humans to teach it to them in exchange for their protection. An uneasy balance was struck across the country and the industrial revolution, which had been briefly stalled, was begun once more.

Most people live in poverty, and Barghest still roam the fens and forests from Suffolk to Warwickshire. In the absence of a queen, the Duart Archduke Coriolanus was appointed Regent of the throne of the British Empire. His place is to guard over the only remaining member of Victoria's Saxe-Coburg bloodline; the young Princess Gwendoline. Now, today, ten years after these worlds collided, all of London is abuzz with excitement for the wedding of Gwendoline to the Duart Lord Aaron of Britannica.

This is the story of the days leading up to that fateful wedding, and the disreputable outlaws who buggered up the whole affair.

Chapter 1: The Duart and the Akka

London, 1875

We should really start a few years ago, actually, when a female duart named Viola came to Buckingham Palace one morning to apply for a job. As she walked the lavish halls accompanied by the butler, she passed a nanny in a state of sheer, exasperated apoplexy. The woman was heading from the master bedroom, rearranging her pinafore, which had been torn at the shoulder by some kind of rabid beast. She also sported a black eye.

"Good luck with that one, little madam. She is quite beyond the help of normal folk," the human snapped.

Viola did not remark upon this but curtsied and continued her walk of determination. The willowy butler towered above her, unruffled but apprehensive. She was led into the bedroom of a red-faced chubby little girl of nine who had just flung a vase at the wall. The whole room was in disarray. Clothes everywhere, bedsheets on the floor, furniture pushed over. The girl's eyes flashed, her hair was an unruly bird's nest and her little fists were clenched tight as she shook with fury.

"Hello, Princess," Viola said calmly.

"I suppose you're here to caper for me with your bright clothes and silly hair," the girl snarled in response. "Well I don't want a jester today. I don't want anything!"

Viola locked her purple eyes on the girl's and did not move.

"Did you hear me? Are you deaf as well as hideously ugly?"

Viola said nothing. She walked to the side of the room and hopped up nimbly upon the dresser.

"What are you doing?"

Viola picked up an equally expensive looking vase and flung it down on the floor, where it smashed into a thousand pieces.

"You're for it now! Hey, stop that!"

Viola had kicked several perfume bottles over. The precious liquid inside glugged out and dribbled onto the white fur rug.

"That's mine," the Princess said, petulantly.

"It's *all* yours," Viola replied. "But if you're going to treat it like this we may as well smash the lot."

"Oh, you disgusting thing. Simpson! SIMPSON!"

The butler entered once more.

"Yes, your Royal Highness?" he said, with a well-concealed sigh.

"Take this pink and purple thing away. Have her stuffed, or something."

"I'm afraid the Archduke has placed Miss Viola in charge today," Simpson replied.

"But… she's smashing my things!"

Simpson ignored her and addressed Viola in deadpan fashion. "I must abscond from this. Let me know if she screams enough to make herself vomit."

They watched the man leave, closing the doors behind him, and while Gwendoline gawped in surprise, a little smile settled upon Viola's face.

"You will not push me around," the Princess insisted through clenched teeth.

Viola made a great leap and landed squarely against the girl's chest, propelling her backwards and down upon the bed with a squeak of pure rage. The little duart then settled calmly upon a cushion while the Princess screamed bloody murder.

(Personally, I would have punched her square out, but that's why I'm not a nanny - MORTIMER)

Viola instead waited until the girl rose up to grab at her with a surprisingly strong grip. The duart performed a quick, intricate finger-dance with one hand and whispered an incantation. A thin trail of blue smoke passed across the child's features as she tasted lavender; her eyes rolled back, and she fell into a light slumber.

"Naptime," Viola hummed. She opened a pouch at her waist and fished out a barley sugar sweet, sucking on it to recover a little energy from the spell expenditure.

***

Twenty minutes passed and the girl eventually stirred, awaking to find those strange, intense eyes watching her from the foot of the bed.

"How dare you?" Gwen exclaimed blearily.

"Princess," said Viola, her tone firm. "I didn't want to do that and probably shouldn't have. I'm sorry to tell you this, but it's become common knowledge that you're a miniature tyrant. Your nannies have all fled or been banished by you."

"Well, why don't *you*? Why don't you leave me as well? I don't need you!"

"Because, Gwendoline, I don't want to. And I'm not scared of you."

"You should be," Gwen said sharply. "I could have you executed if I wanted to."

"I know, but you're not going to."

"You want me to be a good little girl? Tidy my room? Wear a pretty dress?" The Princess' voice dripped with sarcasm.

Viola looked hard at her. "I'll settle for just looking after yourself and wiping your nose. Here… have my hanky." She retrieved a small square of fabric from her pocket and held it out. Gwendoline glared at her and defiantly blew her nose on the bedsheets. Viola returned the hanky to her pocket with a shrug. "I'm not going to be gotten rid of easily, but I'll make you a deal. If you still hate me within one week from this point which is…" She glanced at the clock on the mantelpiece. "Ten forty-five next Wednesday, then I shall leave. But if you don't hate me, I shall stay."

"How did you do that… thing you did? You made me sleep. I've not seen that."

"I have a whole bag of secrets, my dear Princess. Best not to tell anyone about them, though."

Gwen's eyes lit up. "Hah! Now I've got you. I shall tell Simpson right away that you're using some kind of forbidden maajik."

"Yes, you can do that at any point," Viola said, "but then you'll only have known one of my secrets. Now who's this?" She turned in the direction of a plaintive meow coming from under the rumpled bedsheets.

"That's… that's Sebastian," the Princess said hesitantly.

"And is he your favourite?" Viola asked, holding out her hand.

"Yes… Oh…" Gwen stared as a rotund calico cat emerged from between the sheets and rubbed his cheek against Viola's fingers. "He likes you."

"Is that good?"

"He hasn't liked any of my other nannies."

"Well I'm… going to be more than that, I think." Viola smiled.

"Can you make Sebastian sleep?"

At this, the pink-haired duart studied the new excited look in the child's eyes and recognised the traces of a dangerous curiosity. She decided to put her straight immediately. "Sebastian isn't going to hurt himself, or me," she said. "I used that spell because you were beyond your own control."

"Can you make Simpson sleep?"

"No, I won't. Same principle."

"I see…" Gwen was manifestly disappointed that this avenue of potential mischief was to remain closed, but she tried a new line of questioning. "Are you going to be my bodyguard too?"

"Very astute, Princess. That may indeed be the case, although officially speaking, I was retained as your jester."

"If I don't hate you," Gwen remarked, airily.

"If you don't hate me. Now, are you hungry? I notice a destroyed breakfast there on the floor."

"I... am... a bit."

"Then can you call for second breakfast please. I'll have two poached eggs and toast. Then we'll see about tidying up this disaster area."

Gwen was silent for a moment, somewhat taken aback at the conclusion of this conversation. Evidently Viola had impressed her. She finally said in a small, contrite voice, "I'm... I'm sorry I said you were ugly... you're pretty."

"And tea as well, please."

"Alright."

"'Yes, Miss Viola'," the duart pressed in a singsong voice.

"Yes, Miss Viola..." Gwen's eyes narrowed. "You haven't beaten me, you know."

"I'm not trying to, Princess."

Gwen became emboldened once more. "You're not even that much older than me. Why, if you were a boy, you'd be barely out of school yourself!"

At this Viola came down harder, her accent slipping as she did so, to something rougher, far more common than her genteel mannerisms up until now. "Listen, Princess, I've had to fight for everything my whole life; I reckon I'm tough enough to handle you."

Gwen smiled, triumphantly. "That remains to be seen..." she retorted imperiously. Then with a little tremble of excitement, she added, "Are you going to tell me some more of your secrets?"

Viola composed herself and brought her accent back under control, raising her chin authoritatively, and wondering how long it would take for this human to grow far taller than she. "Well… that really all depends on your behaviour."

Neither of them knew at the time, but what had begun at that moment was a bond that would endure through the brightest and darkest of times.

Chapter 2: Outlaws and Awakening

London, 1883

Eight years later and London had slowly and subtly transformed. Its rows of brick factories were now augmented with the trappings of Duart architecture, all colonnades and archways and statuary with beautifully painted detail. Repairs had been carried out with the new occupants of England in mind, and naturally, with the Akka towering seven feet tall, the Duart ranging between 3'6" for the females and 4'6" for the males, and the humans stuck with an average somewhere in between, nobody could agree on the right size of door frame. This meant Akka kept knocking their skulls periodically on English oak, reminded each time of their awkward, too-big stature, and whenever a duart stepped into or out of a room they felt a pang of anxiety that everyone else was bigger than them.

To this end it became the fashion for the Duart gentry to adapt the front entrances of their purloined homes to be shorter, so humans would have to stoop to enter and Akka would be put off altogether. The servant's entrances round the back stayed the same.

You might wonder why the humans didn't rise up and toss these diminutive new oppressors back to their own world. Well, there were three chief reasons: one, the Duart Firecasters were, as has been said, exceptionally good at dispatching the infected Barghest, which made them a formidable fighting force to contend with, tough and stubborn. Two, even if they were somehow shoved back through the gateway to Celador, the humans had no idea how to shut it behind them. It was, to all intents and purposes, a permanently open fixture to the north of London that would lead to the strange, parallel island of Britannica. And three, after ten years of being hungry, oppressed, miserable and choking on black chimney smoke, things were much the same as when humans were in charge.

However, that didn't mean there wasn't a strong resistance gathering beneath the streets. For when you push people too far, revolution is inevitable.

(At least I've always found that to be the case, but what do I know? I'm a horse - THE NAG).

***

We begin again with two key players in the resistance, and neither of them was human.

Picture a gilded carriage, drawn by four beautiful, dappled white mares. Now picture the occupants, the Marquis of Chiswick, a title that had to be invented for him, it's important to note, along with his wife and daughter. Recall, if you will, the kind of bewigged, powdered regency fashion that gripped England and France during that lengthy Marie Antoinette era that had eventually ended round about fifty years previously, with the less pompous and actually quite sensible King William IV. Well, as it turns out, the Duart gentry were rather fond of it, and the look had been experiencing something of a resurgence *(along with those dashing Napoleonic band-leader jackets favoured by Sergeant Pepper and Freddie Mercury).*

The brigands were wearing this style of coat that morning, adapted with hoods and bandanas to conceal their faces.

The shorter of the pair hopped up against the side of the carriage, brandishing a pistol through the window, aimed lazily at the Marquis, and declared in an ostentatious fashion; "Okay, thin white duke, prepare to have a thrilling story of a brush with death to tell all your high society friends, because you are, as of now, being held up by Robin of the Hood."

"You blackguards," spluttered the Marquis, his chins aquiver. "How dare you. Do you know who I am?"

"Of course we know who you are," the bandit retorted. "We've been planning this for days. I'll have the ring and the pouch… no not that one…" The hooded man's eyes widened. "The one in your underclothes."

"How do you know about that one?"

"London has eyes at every window and ears at every door," came the smooth reply. "You remember that when you're scrimping on the wages of your next round of servants."

"Turn over our purses, Tarquin," the Marquis' wife squalled at him, fanning herself feverishly. "Can't you see this fine, rough gentleman is in control here?"

Robin glanced slyly at her and smiled beneath his mask. "Smart lady, and fairer than you deserve, *Tarquin*."

"Are you really Robin of Loxley?" the Marchioness asked, as the outlaw held out his hand, clad in a brown leather fingerless mitt.

"Yes, I certainly am. Necklace and earrings please, ma'am," he pressed.

"But by your frame, surely... you're a duart? I thought he was a human." She divested her neck and earlobes of the jewellery and handed it over.

"*I* thought he died a thousand years ago," piped up the extravagantly attired duart child sitting in the corner of the carriage. She held an expensive-looking human doll, as gaudily over-decorated as she was, and almost as big. "*This* fellow's an imposter."

"What an adorable child," Robin said, glancing at her. "What's your name, sweetheart?"

"Imogen, you rapscallion," she replied snootily.

"Well, Imogen," he said in a covert whisper. "You tell all your little friends... Robin Hood is back."

Imogen raised her eyebrows, unimpressed. "You're going to get sloppy and you're going to get caught."

"Yes, Robin," her mother interrupted, leaning in front of her. "Can I call you Robin? Aren't you afraid they'll catch you?"

The outlaw cocked his head and stood a little more jauntily against the carriage, twirling his pistol. "Me? No, I'm quick as a fox and twice as cunning. Now, if you'll excuse me and my partner, Little John here, we shall bid you good day and assure you that we really *would* have murdered you all horribly on the spot if you'd put up even the slightest bit of resistance." Robin winked and bowed theatrically.

"Watchmen coming, Robb," warned his considerably larger companion.

"Urgh, yuck, it's a filthy great akka," Imogen whined. "Daddy, make it go away faster."

"We're going," the akka growled, narrowing his eyes.

The little beast was not going to be silenced. She hopped up on her seat and exclaimed loudly, "My Daddy says all *you* people do is steal anyway, so I suppose I shouldn't be too *very* surprised."

"Is that so?" John stared at her for a moment, then snaked his enormous, green arm into the carriage window and snatched the doll out of her little fists.

"Hey!" she shouted indignantly. "Daddy, he took Veronica!"

"Give it back," Robin sighed.

"No."

"I want to see his head on a spike!" Imogen spat.

"*Don't* give it back," Robin corrected.

"I wasn't gonna."

"Quiet, Imogen," hissed the Marquis, his face turning pale imperceptibly behind the powder. "He's a seasoned cutthroat who will kill us all, didn't you hear him?"

"You two I'd kill..." John glared at the adults and then nodded towards Imogen. "This one I'd probably eat."

"You vile brute!" Imogen's mother moved in front of her once more. "Stay away from my daughter." She leaned away from John's glowering masked face and re-engaged the duart highwayman, plaintively. "Robin, how can someone as charming as you associate with such a repulsive creature?"

23

"Madam, I might ask you the same question…" Robin glanced at her husband and child, as his tone became icy. "Twice."

"Filthy, thieving *greenskin*," Imogen sniped, peering around her mother's sizeable dress. At this slur John roared at them all, shaking the timbers of the carriage and causing the whole family to shriek in fright.

Robin realised as he looked into their aghast faces that there was no sticking the landing of this one. "Right… well… that's us…" he said, shrugging and touching his forefinger to his head in a mock salute. "Good luck… raising *this* one."

"We're off," John said, elbowing him, as a sharp whistle could be heard not too far away.

The two highwaymen, one considerably less dandy than the other, beat a hasty escape, drawing pursuers as they did so.

***

There were three kinds of Watchmen to be found in this London of 1883. Firecasters were the most intimidating, as being the gifted, chosen and empowered they were actively encouraged to reiterate on a daily basis the awe-inspiring Maajikal supremacy of the Duart race. What this boiled down to on most days was the bullying of shopkeepers, turning out the hiding places of undesirable types and setting smallish freestanding structures on fire to keep the locals frightened and thus in line.

London had already partially burned down in a second great fire which had still been raging when the Duart first appeared, so it was seen as somewhat portentous; the sons of flame, summoned to this world to be its rulers – but what this equated to was that after ten years of rebuilding nobody wanted everything burned down yet again. This was why these lawmen rarely set light to one of the houses, shops or factories that connected down a line of similar buildings, lest the blaze carry itself beyond the control of the Firecasters present at the scene. It was possible, when concentrating hard, for a Firecaster to withdraw enough heat to extinguish flames, but it required a level of focus and serenity that was difficult to attain, so they often needed several working together with the larger conflagrations.

This exalted, military police force wore intricately detailed armour of deep maroon and iron grey. It was forged with caronite, an alloy from their own world, resistant to all but the most intense heat, and though natural-born firecasters were somewhat flame-proof, they still had to watch out for their own clothes and hair when igniting and casting firebolts.

The second kind of Watchmen were the Heavies. These fellows also wore armour of the sort England had not seen in use for centuries, only their suits took those ancient designs to new heights with complex, overlapping plate layers to allow for greater protection and freedom of movement. Topped with aggressively forward-pointing helmets, it made each Heavy a formidable fighting unit.

Heavies also carried a variety of hand weaponry; short-swords, cudgels, studded gauntlets for greater punching and occasionally bows and crossbows. The Duart, by and large, had deliberately avoided the rifles and pistols that the humans employed in Celador. This was partly because their armour deflected the majority of oncoming bullets, so this semi-imperviousness, combined with their own indifference to guns, discouraged human dependence on firearms. It was also out of respect for their maajik users whose *literal* firepower they saw as being far superior. Guns, after all, had not saved the human race from the Barghest… fire had.

The third group wore wool coats and were considerably more swift. They were a relatively new measure introduced to a city where sneak-thieves, pickpockets, footpads and cat-burglars were commonplace. The Heavies could not catch these criminals, and the Firecasters could not hit them without collateral damage, so units were trained in sprinting, climbing and navigating the labyrinthine streets, alleys and rooftops of London.

Their greatest weapon was communication over medium distances, drawing more support to their position with coded whistle-blows. Once several had set upon a single fleeing target, that person would be intercepted and stopped very quickly. The small, thin batons they wielded were reinforced with caronite and when employed sharply against the bones of hands and knees, their quarry soon found fast foot-travel not only immediately impossible, but a serious unlikelihood in the long-term. These Duart were initially dubbed the Street Response Squads, but over time a new name had sprung up that had eclipsed this one and held fast, so now even their official city authority term was 'Grabbers'.

It was several of these Grabbers that broke from the Heavy patrol in the Ravenscourt Park area where Robin and Little John had been conducting their daring holdup and gave chase through the afternoon sun.

The outlaws knew better than to charge down the middle of the street in broad daylight – that would get every authority figure and well-to-do onlooker unified in a grand effort to cease their escape – so they wove and threaded their way through back gardens, mantling over fences and shimmying up drainpipes. When they crossed roads it was done under bridges after trotting alongside carriages, tipping imaginary hats to the disgruntled passengers.

London was fine this afternoon and the extensive puddles of rainwater from last night's downpour, which collected in the pitted and uneven streets, reflected a blue sky upon their gravy-brown surface. The walls of the surrounding buildings were brick, mottled and patched with mortar and blackened with soot, the wood of the shutters was old and frequently repurposed from older constructions, painted with sharply pungent tar to keep out the damp. Shop fronts and doors bore faded paint in green and red, with stencilled lettering in brash yellow or filthy white and at the middle and end of every street stood an unlit lamp post of black iron. Barrels and crates were piled high and the ropes from cranes for pulling stock to higher floors hung down above the street like the vines of a slate jungle.

The people dressed in thick layers of wool, linen, cotton and leather, mostly in dark colours which hid the dirt better. Clothing was designed to last and protect, though cut in a manner that in many ways mimicked the fineries of the rich. Waistcoats were popular, along with long coats, jackets, braces, shirt-sleeves, shawls, ties and sturdy boots or shoes. Nearly everyone wore a hat, from a selection of flat caps, bonnets, bowlers and bedraggled toppers.

They were now far from the beautiful plumage of the highborn Duart gentry that might traverse the streets of Mayfair or Westminster, those now occupying the former houses of the mutton-chopped masters of the fallen Empire. Instead these places were peopled mostly with humans. Here and there those few Duart of severely meagre means walked among them, and towering over both species lumbered the Akka, grim-faced heavy labourers who were almost always found living and working only in the poorest areas.

Those with a keen eye might spot pieces of ancient or tribal jewellery, items of clothing made from the hide of animals not of this Earth and metal fastenings hewn in exotic fashion. The air was laden with snatches of conversation in rough Cockney tongues, and the aromas were resplendent of tannery lime, flood damage, glue rendering, fish deliveries, chimney smoke and engine steam.

Robin and Little John made their way southward to the banks of the Thames, seeking out the louder industrial areas which might mask shrieking whistles, always aware of the movement of dark blue, pursuing smudges in the periphery of their vision. They alternated as they went, between a pantomime of casual behaviour within small crowds and moving off at angles down side streets when the herd thinned out. This was obviously easier for Robin who could disappear below the neckline of humans standing close together, whereas Little John loomed many feet above them. Robin snatched a towel off a washing line, and later a tablecloth, to drape over his companion and obscure that lofty, green-hooded head.

Finally they had scattered the Grabbers enough so that taking refuge in the opening of a coal chute drew their closest pursuer in. He landed quietly in the rear yard, his sharp eyes searching. He was only a little older than Robin and his clipped moustache danced as he detected a trace of sweat on the breeze. Robin leapt out of his crouch in the darkness and snatched away the whistle as it neared the fellow's lips, elbowing him in the gut to knock the wind from him immediately before he was yanked into the darkness of the coal chute. They left the chap unconscious after relieving him of his wallet, uninjured save for some heavy bruising. Robin always declined the temptation to mete out the kind of life-altering damage their potential captors would gladly and enthusiastically inflict upon the outlaws. He considered this practice… distasteful.

One by one, they trapped and overcame three more of the Grabbers, stowing them deep and dark around the dockyards and the gardens of the rowing club. They slowed to a walk by the bank of the Thames, as the hundreds of slow-moving barges crawled past and off into the distance, sliding through the grey, torpid waters. Finally, under Hammersmith Bridge, satisfied that their getaway had been clean enough, they inspected the spoils of the day.

"Next time, less of the theatrics and more of the intimidation," John announced. "I'll take the lead. I can put the guy's head in my mouth, and you shake them down." Robin began to retort but John held up a large, green hand. "We use the fear and mistrust of the Akka to our advantage. You took far too long there."

"For the practical necessities of a robbery, yes, but not for building a legend," Robin protested.

"That's just what I'm worried about, Robb." John's tone was concerned now. "You keep focusing on building this image, and that little brat will be right, you're going to let your heart run places your head ain't goin'. You're gonna get caught."

"I'm not giving up the Robin Hood persona, you can forget that," Robin said firmly.

"You scare me with this kind of talk, Robb. You ain't him."

"They never caught Robin Hood, they never killed him and most of all... he was beloved." Robin had given this speech many times before. "The name and the reputation built on centuries of mythology has already greased all kinds of wheels. It will make the people we rob from fear us and be more obliging, and the more we give back to the poor, the bigger our support network." At this, his companion frowned. Robin held up his hands ostentatiously. "It's not 'money, power, women' like those other clumsy oafs in the outlaw game imagine, it's 'money, generosity, status, women and a whole city of the downtrodden who think we're the dog's bollocks'. They cheer for us, you've heard that. Were you ever cheered for prior to this?"

John was adamant. "But that's just it, this seems to be more about you. Piss the authorities off enough and they'll come after you with everything they've got. There's already a fifty gold reward on your head."

"Fifty gold…" Robin exclaimed. "I shall have to drive that up a bit; soon it shall be a hundred and we will be infamous!"

John glared at him. "Not at all what I want. Can we just go incognito for the next few? Let the heat die down a little?"

"My dear John… the heat is the sharp, opposing edge of everything we're doing this for." Robin stared at him for a moment. "All that ire we're causing, that just means those in charge are getting angrier and the people have more to be hopeful about. It means we're doing something right."

"Right?" The akka threw up his hands. "We must have different dictionaries."

"Look, if you want to talk sloppy, what was taking that girl's doll?" Robin's heroic tone became somewhat more exasperated.

"You heard her." John turned away.

"Yes, I did," Robin replied. "She was a tiny little hate-filled sack of racist rhetoric with a face that looked like a scowling, white testicle, and she deserved to have her dolly stolen, but I'm trying to figure out if that was your pride acting out or your kleptomania." His eyes narrowed as he studied John's reaction.

"It's *not* the kleptomania." John said, uncertainly.

Robin started rifling through John's knapsack, arranging a collection of oddments from their travels upon the flagstones beside them. "We've got plenty of things of genuine value here and…what's this?" The duart pulled a particularly incriminating item out into the light.

"It's, uh…" John hesitated. "The handle off the door of the carriage."

"Did you tear this off in a rage?"

"Will you be less mad at me if I say yes?"

"Yes. And I'm giving you my best piercing stare right now…" Robin gestured, waving his finger at himself. "Look at my face, this is it."

John's head drooped. "No, you're right; I stole it."

"Why?"

The akka shrugged and did not look up. "I don't know."

Robin's expression softened. "I'm worried about you too, old chum. I don't know how else to say it or how many repetitions until it really sinks in." He took a breath and searched for the best response he could. "Look, the next time you feel like you're going to take something that we can't use or just plain don't need, can you give me a keyword or something? To let me know what you're thinking, feeling, I mean."

"It's such a shameful habit," John admitted.

"I know, but on the other hand, we *are* thieves," Robin said, patting the enormous hand in a vaguely reassuring way. "We take things. Your average person won't search deeply into your motivation for doing so."

"No, I mean for *me*."

"Oh, you mean as an akka." This was a far thornier issue. Robin chose to address the larger scale of it. "God, you know how much I hate that stereotype. I would never-"

John now looked at him. "But you can see why it would bother me."

"Yes, I can see, and I do understand. Well then, the code word is 'handle'."

"So, you want me to somehow slip that into conversation if I feel like I'm weakening?" John asked, somewhat incredulously.

"And I'll help you, John. I'll… play for time or something. Improvise."

He nodded. "Okay."

"Really okay?" Robin asked.

"Yes, I want to get better…" John began, then paused. "But that's another thing right there, I want you to call me 'Oberon' when we're out of earshot of the public. I get the whole alias thing, but I don't need to live it every minute."

Robin looked at him kindly. "Certainly, 'Oberon'."

"Thank you… '*Robin*'," he replied, pointedly.

Sunday Morning (Seven Days Left)

The next morning, at Buckingham Palace, the Princess, now seventeen years of age, was awoken by Viola with some semi-exciting news. Not overmuch had changed in this room over the past eight years, but a few things that will prove to be very important for this story had developed.

"I'm opening the curtains to let in the sunlight, your Royal Highness," Viola said loudly, sweeping the heavy fabric aside and flooding the room with brightness. Gwen yanked the covers over her head and made a sound that was half groan, half growl. "You can't lay there all day, slothful and indolent," Viola continued, ignoring her protestations. "The Lord Aaron craves an audience with you."

Gwen groaned again, more intensely, and burrowed further into the bed.

"I'm going to open a window," said Viola, wrinkling her nose. "It reeks like nine different cats in here." She lifted the sash and heaved it up as far as she could.

"Ten," Gwen corrected her in a muffled voice. "Sebastian is under here with me. And one doesn't feel like visiting with Lord Aaron today, thank you very much."

"If it helps, I think he brought a present," Viola sang.

"What shape was it?" asked Gwen suspiciously.

"Ahhh, well get dressed and come with me and you'll find out."

"Was it egg-shaped?"

34

Viola paused, calculating the likely responses she'd get from both truth and further stalling. "It was… on the eggy side, yes."

"Oh, buggeration!" Gwen threw the covers aside and sat up. "How many of these rotten things does he think I want?"

"The other aristocracy love them," Viola told her. "They're specially made, one of a kind. And for goodness sake, don't talk like that around him."

"But the eggs don't DO anything!"

"Not true," Viola said defensively. "One of them had a little horse and carriage inside when you opened it up."

"Ooh, I forgot about the horse and carriage," Gwen cooed sarcastically. "That bumps it up from completely bloody useless to rather extremely pointless." She sighed and flopped back down onto the pillows. "Throw it on the egg pile then."

"He hasn't given it to you yet," Viola reminded her.

"You know, if he got me a real horse and carriage with a boiled egg in it, that I would like. Provided I could ride my egg anywhere, of course."

"Get dressed," Viola said, changing the subject and pulling clothes out of the gilded wardrobe.

"I don't want to," Gwen responded petulantly. "I'm just going to lay here all morning with Sebastian on my chest and smell his smelly cat breath." She pulled the patchy white, black and orange cat, now even larger and more cuddly, out of the tangle of blankets and held him up to her face. He closed his eyes contentedly and his lower body hung like a great, furry bell. "Isn't that right, Sebastian? Yessssss." She nuzzled him affectionately.

"We don't want to go and hear tales of the tedious court and legislation and wotnot. And we shall have cake. Cake please, Viola!" She waved an imperious hand.

"Now, listen," Viola said firmly, but Gwen ignored her.

"Angel Cake… and Devil's Food. I feel undecided as to my moral compass this morning."

"Right, you spoiled little twit. Come here!" The duart launched herself at the Princess and landed squarely on her chest, knocking the cat out of her arms in the process. Sebastian burbled, most affronted, and rolled quickly off the bed to flop upon a nearby chaise longue.

"Agh, get off me! See, you scared him off with your meaty frame!"

"I think I'll lounge on your ample décolletage," Viola said, leaning back. "Oh, it's quite comfy up here!"

"I said get off my knockers!" Gwen tried to push her, but the Duart were heavier than their height suggested, and Viola was sturdy enough to keep her position.

"No, you're right," the nanny said. "We'll call for cake. Make a morning of it."

"I can't breathe," Gwen huffed.

"Yes, you can."

"I'll scream."

"Nope." Viola waved her hand in a complex manner and muttered some words that Gwen didn't understand, but she recognised them from previous squabbles and was not surprised when her shriek came out as a muffled protest, as if Viola was holding a soft glove over her mouth.

"How dare you!" Gwen tried, but what came out sounded more like someone shouting "Oww Air Ooo" inside a small bottle.

Viola folded her arms. "There. The spell is cast. Now you can't say a word. Oh, this *is* peaceful."

"Ake iss off ee a unff!" Gwen mumbled again, trying to throw Viola off her by heaving her body upwards.

"Hey! Be careful with me, I'm only little!" Viola protested, but it was mainly in jest; Gwen's efforts were in vain.

"Ett off ee oo iffle tvolluff!" Gwen tried again, followed by a string of very unprincesslike swear words when she still could not make her voice louder than a soft squeak.

"What's that? 'You're right, Viola, now I'm up out of bed and I'm about to choose a dress'?"

Gwen gave a muffled scream of frustration.

"You want your voice back?" Viola asked. Gwen nodded. "Say please." Gwen mumbled something that would probably have made a docker blush. "And down on one knee," Viola added.

Gwen got up and took a knee, grumbling as she did so. "I aan eleev I ooing iss," she growled as she got to the floor.

"Say, 'Please Miss Viola, may I have my voice back, and I promise I'll stop acting like such an obstinate little gobshite'," Viola said primly.

Gwen repeated it back to her as best she could without her voice, her face displaying far less contrition than her words. Viola decided it was good enough.

"Now…" She ran her fingers over Gwen's head. "You have cake in your hair," she said, kindly but firmly. "You look like a royal nightmare. We'll leave Aaron waiting a while longer, but you need a bath." She whispered a few more unintelligible words, lifting the spell.

Gwen gasped. "You would never have been this bold when I was younger."

"Yes, well, when you were younger you were cruel and spoiled rather than just spoiled. You might actually have had me sent away. Now you realise my inherent value."

"Well, I'm out of my bed. I suppose I must have my bath. And those silence spells of yours always leave me craving bacon for some reason…" She trailed off. "But I so wish I didn't have to breakfast with Aaron this morning." Gwen paused again and turned to Viola. "There's a snap in the air," she said, her tone conspiratorial. "Can you smell it?"

Viola stared at her. "No, just cat," she said brightly.

"I caught it when you opened the window," Gwen continued. "Out there, my darling, out there, adventure is waiting for us."

Viola glanced out of the window in the direction Gwen was gazing. "In Saint James' Park?"

"Further," Gwen said excitedly. "Through the cobblestone streets of London, past dark alleyways where skulduggerous plots are hatched every minute."

Viola's voice became sharp. "We've talked about this. We agreed that last time really would be the last. You could have been seen, kidnapped, killed!"

Gwen shook her head. "I'm not talking about sneaking out to the fights. Though I could really use getting into a proper walloping right now. I mean to go beyond the alleyways, sneak further, to the outskirts of London and beyond that and further still, out into the wild countryside." She took a deep breath as though longing to fill her lungs with unfamiliar air. "There we shall find the real world and the real people far from these boring courtiers, silk sheets and poxy jewelled eggs. That's where I want to roam."

Viola shook her head and that rougher accent trailed back into her voice. "You're forgetting, Gwen, I came from the real world, as you put it. I know exactly what sort of person lives there. It's nobody you want to meet." She turned back to the bed and started straightening the covers. "Out there you'll find hairy, grotty little Duart with unsavoury thoughts on their minds, humans who don't give a flying fornication that you're royalty, and worst of all, lumbering green-skinned Akka with those protruding tusks and caveman foreheads. Hulking, baseborn savages all, and if they caught one glimpse of your succulent, Rubenesque figure they'd surely gobble you up in a trice…" She paused and looked back over her shoulder at Gwen with a glint in her eye. "Well… if there were two or three of them and they were VERY hungry."

"You cheeky sod!" Gwen cried, unable to suppress a smile.

"Sorry, that was mean-spirited and oddly satisfying," Viola grinned back.

"I do like being called succulent, though."

"I meant truculent."

Gwen turned back to the window, still caught up in her own wanderlust. "Viola, I know that you don't like or trust... anyone, but I dream of being out of this palace. I know I shouldn't and I'm supposed to be a good little girl, but all the best intentions, warnings and reprimands in the world... can't stop my mind from wandering." She broke off, and her voice dropped to a delicate whisper, this time of her own doing. "It betrays me, you know. My mind, as I sleep. In my dreams I fly over the fields of England, through the night sky, with all laid out before me like an embroidered blanket. I wish I could take you up there, Viola, flying onward and upward with the wind whipping through my hair; truly free." There was a catch in her voice as she gasped to herself, visualising it clearly. "I wake up with my heart beating so fast, afraid I'm going to fall, but so excited... it takes me a moment to remember who I am." She turned away from the window again, seeming suddenly smaller, and stared sadly at Viola. "And then I'm in here again. And my whole life is laid out before me like an exquisitely crafted, one of a kind china tea set." Her shoulders slumped as she surveyed the clothes laid out on the bed. "Complete with a jewelled egg cup."

Viola nodded gently. "Princess, someone has to bring you back down to earth... and while I hate seeing that look on your face when I do, it's best if it be me. Come on, you can put on some riding clothes instead; those will be acceptable for breakfast. That way you can make an excuse to take out Trumble this morning."

Gwen sighed. "Yes, I suppose I can."

Chapter 3: Breakfast Brawl

Buckingham Palace

At breakfast, Gwendoline *did* behave herself. Aaron sat across from her and they exchanged formal chit-chat. He was tall for a Duart and nearly came up to her suprasternal notch. Put a big hat on his head and he'd be touching her chin. He had neatly groomed red hair, pale blue, serious eyes and a clipped moustache. At one point he extended across the table a thick-fingered hand to her. Gwendoline took it, feeling the warm, grip and its intentions of reassurance, even if that goal was not reached.

"Only seven days to go. So exciting, wouldn't you say?" he remarked. "But of course, no doubt you're also nervous."

Gwendoline glanced over at Viola, who was daintily eating porridge. Her companion nodded, barely perceptibly.

"Becoming your queen," Gwen replied, searching for the very best words. "And you becoming King… it's always been an awful lot of responsibility… quite a bit of transformation, too."

"Do you not think you're ready yet, sweet-pea?" he looked concerned. "You know everything that has to be done. And I promise your day-to-day routine will not be transformed overmuch."

"But I'll be Queen of the Empire."

"Yes, you will." In the long pause after this pointless confirmation, Gwendoline let her eyes rest on the wrapped gift that sat on the table beside her breakfast.

The doors at the end of the hall opened and Coriolanus, the Archduke of Buckingham, strode in, his bootfalls echoing around the magnificent room, his armour clinking. This duart's face had been a permanent fixture in Gwendoline's life.

The majority of people who have ever existed shall never have statues or busts crafted in their likeness. Particularly significant figures of royalty or office or historical importance are bestowed this honour. In most cases, the artist must overlook the human frailties, blemishes, double or absent chins or generally ordinary appearance of the vast majority of this fortunate minority. The focus must be on capturing their importance and status for the ages.

(Rather than their… for want of a better term, fugliness – ROBIN)

Coriolanus was a rare beast indeed, in that he not only had a face and form seemingly designed to be chipped out of stone but may in fact have been some kind of animated statue himself. It was not that he was perfect; his brow was furrowed, his skin mottled and scarred from battle, his gait slightly leaning due to an injured knee. No, it was that when beheld in his entirety he was a truly splendid and fearsome sight to behold. Gwendoline, Viola and Lord Aaron raised themselves from their seated positions and bowed to the Regent. He set down his helmet and seated himself.

"I shall savour these last few bows," he said with a tight smile. "Next Sunday I will have to bend my head to both of you."

"You shan't have to if you don't want to, Father," Gwen ventured.

"The bow is not about what one wants, child, but of what is expected." The Archduke inclined his head and studied the girl, whose glances darted from Viola to Aaron to her breakfast.

"She has pre-wedding jitters," Aaron said, with an indulgent expression.

"Understandable." Coriolanus turned to Gwen. "How are the pains?"

"They have been bothering me more of late," she admitted.

"And have you seen Doctor Marcus this week?"

"No… in fact I don't think I've seen him for… oh…" She broke off as she attempted to work out how long it had been.

"Three weeks and two days," the Archduke informed her.

"Yes."

"I have been too busy with the arrangements to see to your comings and goings on a daily basis; that was the charge of… other… people who look after you." At this he glanced over towards Viola who, despite her diminutive size and boldness, visibly shrank. "Gwendoline, my dear, your sickness is not going to go away," he stated. "It must be maintained and kept in balance, or you shall have these hysterical fits and furious outbursts for the rest of your life. A queen shall not be of any use to her subjects if she cannot keep her temper, or if the rampant discomfort in her head and body overcomes her good nature."

"Yes, Father," Gwen replied, her voice contrite.

"You will see him tomorrow at the first convenience."

"Yes, Father."

"And again, on Saturday, the last thing you must do before you are wed. I want your mind clear, your head held high and your crown shining." He smoothed her hair away from her forehead with his gentle rough touch. This unusual physical contact made Gwendoline tremble and her heart race.

"I don't like him," she whispered, keeping her eyes down.

"I know. He is not a likable man... but he is keeping you well." The Archduke's eyes were unmoving. "Let him."

"As you wish, Father."

"Now, I must speak with Lord Aaron. You may go and play with your pony." He stared at the nursemaid. "Viola, be sure she does not come to any harm whatsoever."

"Yes, your Grace."

Gwendoline raised herself and then with all the daintiness she could muster conveyed her ample frame to the end of the hall, Viola jogging alongside her. As she finally cleared the doors she was able to speak.

"Bugger," she hissed. "Bugger, bugger, bugger, bastard, bollocks!"

"Are you quite alright?" Viola asked.

"Yes," Gwen snapped, sounding anything but. "Come on." As she walked she waved over a nearby guard, a tall and muscular human named Simon. "Gym, please, Simon."

She strode through the palace with Simon and Viola in tow until they reached the area in question. As the doors opened, Gwen unbuttoned and unlaced her riding dress, letting it fall to the floor as she walked. Viola scooped it up, and the petticoat and the boots... and Simon's coat... and Simon's boots and shirt, until you could no longer see her pink hair behind the teetering pile of clothing.

Gwendoline stopped at the end of the slightly raised wooden platform in the centre of the gym, and with her naked feet clutching at the boards, she turned, in her underclothes, towards Simon. He stood, lightly, flexing his back and arms. His eyes lowered and respectful.

"Begin," said Gwen.

Simon stepped in and swung a hard punch towards her gut. Gwen intercepted and countered, yanking the arm to one side and pulling him off-balance. His knees came up and one of them collided with her chest. She gasped and turned forwards, sending him crashing to the ground with her on top. He pulled back and away but her legs were locked around his waist. She felt him struggle and smiled to herself, punching him in the chest and shoulder, hard enough to bruise, hard enough to let out the aggression, not hard enough to break his bones. His arm flailed and caught her in the side of the face and Viola started forward, seeing the sudden look of panic in Simon's eyes.

Gwendoline grinned and shook her jaw out, twisting into a leg-lock and pushing Simon uncomfortably face-down into the wood. She heard him grunt and felt the tension, felt him push harder and harder and ultimately give. She picked herself up and let him get back to his feet.

"Two gold, Viola," she ordered.

"Thank you, your Royal Highness," said Simon.

"You let me win, though," Gwen frowned.

"Begging your pardon ma'am, but I didn't," Simon insisted.

"A real attacker would have hurt me far more," she replied.

"I do as I am instructed to the best of my abilities, with concern for your safety paramount in my mind, your Royal Highness."

Gwendoline looked at him carefully. "Is that so? Viola, three more gold for Simon please. I want to go again."

She pounced. By the end of the fight Simon was nursing sore fingers, Gwendoline had been winded by a sharp jab, and her head was ringing from an accidental crack against the floor.

From where she stood Viola very subtly cast a mind-numbing spell on Simon. His fingers would still be in pain, but he would notice it less. She stared up at Gwen who was wiping a thin trickle of blood from her nose, observing the tiny splash of red triumphantly. Viola breathed deeply and steadily and tried to control her pounding heart.

"We need to get you another bath before we ride Trumble, and some makeup to cover those bruises. It won't do to let people see you like this," she said primly.

"No more baths," Gwendoline insisted. "To the stables. Thank you again, Simon. Viola, can you tip him an extra gold – and tell him sorry about the head-butt."

"I'm really very sorry, Simon," Viola said quietly. "She's got a lot to work through right now. Your pains are deeply appreciated. I'll double that tip."

"I really *didn't* go easy on her," said Simon earnestly.

"I know, I could see. But she can't be told anything."

Sunday Night

Robin and Oberon were hugging the wall at the eastern edge of the Manfred Rope Factory in Putney. Robin stole a glance through the open window and beheld three dozen workers sitting in rows, much like the pews of a church, each with a coil of rope fibre in their lap and weaving away diligently. He could imagine the callouses on their fingers, the multitude of cuts upon their hands, the strain of their foreheads as they squinted in the lamplight. Not one of them was older than eleven years.

The enforcers walked the stalls, hardened men with batons, occasionally prodding or striking the children whose speed and productivity dropped below the minimum required. Always on the legs and backs; the hands needed to be kept as functional as possible and if the heads were struck, their work would deteriorate inevitably anyway. Robin's lips were pursed, his teeth ground together, his moustache twitched, and his brow lowered to his nose. His laboured, tight breathing was audible and Oberon had to hold up an enormous hand to caution him.

Robin quietened himself and marked the lamps; four of them. They would all have to be put out for this to work properly. The pair would need total darkness to overcome five enforcers. Unfortunately, they both knew he wasn't the best shot in the world. His short-bow was clutched in his hands, but practice every week though he might, under duress like this his aim was dicey at best.

Nevertheless, he eyeballed the lamp on the far left of the room and nodded Oberon towards the one at the opposite corner. They would get those dealt with and then see to the two in the centre when the panic began. Oberon moved over to the far window and Robin saw him nod in readiness. He took aim at the lamp, but an enforcer with a half-chewed ear blocked his shot. The burly fellow walked casually down the line to where a little girl was crying and nursing a cut under her thumbnail which was making weaving exceptionally difficult tonight. Half-Ear leaned down and tapped her in the mouth with his baton. Not too hard, not enough to badly injure her. But she gasped in pain and fright and a tooth fell to the ground. Robin's temper flared and Half-Ear suddenly had an arrow in his bicep. He stared at it in wonder for the first few seconds before the pain of his pierced humerus bone set in.

"Sir," Robin called from the window as all eyes trained upon him. "It is time you picked on someone your own size… I mean two thirds your own size… I mean, we're about the same thickness, but... Oh, bollocks to it!"

Robin vaulted through the window and Oberon grimaced with frustration, following him. The room was now in uproar; children were screaming and leaping to their feet and the enforcers were bellowing at the intruders. The lamps were knocked over, a lot of rope caught fire and the two outlaws tried their level best not to give the children nightmares regarding how their thuggish overseers were dispatched. Robin left Oberon to finish off the last two and hurried the children from the factory, now filled with smoke and flames.

They assembled in the back lot, and Robin kept them out of view of the street as the akka emerged from the building, cradling the frail girl who had been hit in the mouth. A tall boy stepped up eye to eye with Robin and shouted.

"What are you doing? Why did you do that?"

"We're sorry," Robin said hastily. "That wasn't how it was supposed to go... but we're freeing you. Now we have to move."

"What do you mean, freeing us?" the boy yelled. "That was our home, they fed us! Now where are we supposed to go?" His beady eyes flashed and several of his co-workers seemed in agreement.

Robin looked at him for a moment and then turned to the rest of the group. "Hands up who wants a job? An *actual* job." There was a pause, and then a widespread raising of hands. Even the tall boy opted in. "Right, then stop your yapping and follow us. Quick and quiet."

"Oh, like that was?" Oberon muttered sarcastically.

"Don't start!" Robin replied. "Okay, move down this way. Are you okay, girl?"

"Yes. Thank you, Biggun," replied the child who was missing a tooth.

"'Biggun,'" Robin snorted. "Hah, I'm keeping that one. What's your name?"

"Lavinia."

"Well, I'm Robin Hood, That's Little John."

"But... he's big." She seemed puzzled.

"Yeah, I know, that's the... joke," said Robin, sheepishly. "It's British understatement."

"I'm Latvian," the child replied, looking unimpressed with his explanation.

"I don't get it, and I'm British," put in the boy who had shouted at them.

"I'm calling you Biggun," Lavinia insisted.

"Here kid," said Oberon, genially. "Have a dolly." Oberon passed her the toy he had liberated from the rude girl in the carriage.

"For me?" Lavinia took it, breaking into a huge smile. "Thank you."

"Hey, how come she gets a doll?" the tall boy asked indignantly.

"You want a doll?" Robin asked him.

"No," he said with a sneer. "But what about a cup and ball, or a stick and hoop?"

"Look, we're not Father Christmas here," Robin pointed out. "We just had a spare doll."

"You can have this door handle to play with," said Oberon, holding it out.

"What am I supposed to do with this?"

"Hey, how come he gets a door handle?" called another lad.

Robin rolled his eyes. "Ohhhh, shut all of your cake holes or we'll drop you off at the next factory and there will be no dolls or door handles for anyone."

"I've never eaten cake in my life," the second boy objected.

"Shhh," hissed Robin.

"Me neither," agreed the tall kid.

"My grandmother used to make such wonderful honey-cake," Lavinia said, dreamily.

"Shhhhhhhhh," Robin said again, louder this time, and scowling.

"My grandmother was a good cook too," Oberon told her with a smile.

"Gah! Shut your gruel-holes!" Robin snapped.

"That's more like it."

Robin and Oberon led the children through the foggy streets, taking the back ways and secret paths and steering well clear of the Watchmen. Eventually they came to The Thirsty Hog Inn and were led around the back to the basement door. It was warm and dry inside, and the bartender had set out a small cask of brandy and some wooden cups. The children warmed themselves beside the fire and sipped the brandy, blowing on their stiff fingers and trying to contain their shivers of shock at the upheaval of their lives.

Eventually the basement door opened and a female akka dressed in red descended the stairs and stood with a slight stoop beneath the low ceiling.

51

"I'm sorry for how frightening the events of your exodus were," she said. "But I can promise you that you are in a better, safer place now. May I start by asking who among you has ever earned a wage before?" Around a quarter of the hands went up, but it was slow and tentative as the memories took a while to be uncovered. "That seems about right. Well I can tell you all now, that outside your workhouse the average male, human factory worker in this city earns eight silver a week, female humans, four silver and children two." She paced across the front of the group, as though talking to a roomful of adults who understood her completely. "Akka are paid on a lower scale, an adult female like myself would be lucky to get three silver a week. You were working there with no pay at all, correct?" The children nodded. "Yeah, well, your masters were getting labour from you ten times the value of housing and food. You were being exploited and I want to give you the opportunity to choose what you do next. Now, you could go and compete for that low-paying work I just talked about, or you can consider my factories. I can offer you four silver a week, the same as an adult, human female to work in my places of business. You can tour them first and inspect the conditions, talk to the other workers. You can live with them or find your own place, though that may be costlier from your wages."

"Excuse me, Akka lady," said the tall boy.

"My name is Scarlet Wilhelmina."

"Excuse me, Scarlet, but what are you hiding? Why are you doing this?"

"I am doing this because I value fairness Mr...?"

"Jack," he replied.

"Mr Jack, everybody deserves to be treated with what you call humanity. As for what I am hiding, have any of you heard of the Hoods?" Several of the children nodded. To demonstrate their point, Scarlet, Robin and Oberon all drew up their hoods. "You are looking at three of the most important members of that gang. That is what we are hiding, Mr Jack, our business fronts and our activities therein. We are spread all throughout the city. Some of you may even get to be my eyes and ears on the street. This is all done in aid of slowly unclenching the grip of the Duart and freeing London from the imprisonment and degradation of the soul that poverty entails."

"Aren't you afraid someone is going to betray you to the Watch? Tell them where this place is?"

She gazed at him, unwavering. "You know, Jack... I'm not afraid. Because we've been operating like this for three years now and it hasn't happened once. I have given no worker and no associate of mine cause to want to betray me. Would you have that cause?"

"I..." He hesitated. "No."

"Then we have an agreement?"

"Alright... we'll take a look," he said grudgingly.

"And the rest of you?" Scarlet asked.

The children nodded vigorously. None dared approach this immense, fearsome looking akka, but Lavinia's hand reached up to clutch at Oberon's finger. He glanced down in surprise.

Chapter 4: Desperate Measures

The Thirsty Hog

After the children had been moved to new lodgings Robin felt a broad finger on his shoulder. Scarlet was bearing down on him. She nodded to her chambers and lightly pushed him, still with the same digit, into her private quarters.

(Not like that. Wash your minds out, this is supposed to be serious – VIOLA)

Inside, Robin nonetheless hopped up on the bed with a broad grin.

"Shall we begin?" he asked.

(Ugh, he's just as bad as you are)

In response, Scarlet

(whom I like)

frowned at the Duart and patted him on the head theatrically.

"This is serious, Robin," she replied. "We are running out of money."

"Still?" At this, Robin seemed honestly shocked.

"Yes," Scarlet said, with controlled exasperation. "Surprisingly not all that much has changed since yesterday when you brought me the pickings from the Marquis and I told you 'Thank you, more like that and definitely no more workers please. We can't afford them!'"

"You may have been speaking into my bad ear," the outlaw replied dismissively.

"Stop being a prick and grow up," retorted Scarlet.

"I'm not apologising for bringing you those children," he said, firmly now. "I couldn't let them spend another night in that place."

"I know." Scarlet's temper flared. "Do you have any idea how wretched I feel having to say this to you? How counter to my nature it is? You get to go play hero while I'm left frantically spinning plates, trying to give these guttersnipes a life worth living."

"Yes, it's almost like we're married." Robin raised an eyebrow at her.

"It's not at all like that, and take your boots off my bed." At this, she perched on the room's only chair and leaned towards him, gesturing to make herself clearer. "Today we had to kill two members of the Knives who were infiltrating the Hackney wool mill disguised as our workers. They were sniffing around for information. They've started to copy our moves and their factories are outstripping ours. If I keep giving these children a decent wage we remain at a permanent, tactical disadvantage, and we need to balance it. I've got my eye on some shipping contracts, so we can move more product, but if we're looking to pounce on them before the Knives do, we have to act fast, and that is going to cost."

"So we need a sudden, large cash injection," Robin replied.

"That would be *very* nice."

"And if we don't get it…"

"A lot of hungry children, a lot of our factories close down, and the Knives get the contracts AND our factories."

"Right… that *is* bad," Robin agreed.

"We need something low-key but high yield."

"Rather like your good self."

Scarlet narrowed her eyes. "I swear, I could crush your skull like a melon." She indicated the appropriate motion with vigour. It was manifestly true.

"Relax, Scarlet, I have a particular love for big ladies."

"You kind of have to from down there," she observed. "But last I checked you weren't that fussy."

Robin cleared his throat, sounding slightly hurt. "You have something lined up?"

"Of course I do. Look here." She opened up some papers on the table. "Sophia Beaverbrook, Duchess of Wellington."

"Ah, the human duchess, very nice," Robin commented.

"She's at the Ambassador's Ball in Kensington this coming Thursday between eight and midnight. Word from her personal dresser is she's chosen not to wear the White Hart."

"You want me to steal a necklace," Robin said flatly.

"With a diamond the size of a gonad."

"Who are you going to get to fence that?"

"Actually, nobody," Scarlet responded, with a sly smile. "Jewels I can normally move, but this thing is so special and so recognisable that it makes it too dangerous to sell on. The only person who would want it to the tune of what it's worth is the Duchess herself."

"So we ransom it to her?" Robin sat up and took notice at last. "I suppose if she doesn't pay up we can start shaving bits off and sending her engagement rings."

"Oh, she'll pay," Scarlet said confidently. "And I have a network we can pass it through that will ensure it's not traced to us. I can trust every one of these people."

"If she has the means to pay for it," Robin interjected, "why not just cut out the middleman and steal the gold directly?"

"Because you'll need to be swift of foot and quiet as a mouse, and you can't do that if you're jingling and jangling," she replied. "You will be in and out inside of three minutes and you will leave the gold. The Duchess can deliver that to a place of our choosing herself later. We won't be greedy. We just need enough for the shipping contracts and a little extra to keep our workers going for three months. Give us all some breathing room." The akka sat back and sighed at this. "And if she or that oaf of a husband attempt to follow the trail back to us, we will subtly imply that her priceless collection of perfumes are going to be snatched from her bedroom and poured out over her prizewinning roses."

"Check bloody mate." Robin sounded impressed. "You really have thought about all of this, haven't you?"

"It's all I do. Plan, think and organise. You're my hands," Scarlet told him.

"And what do you like to do with your hands when you're tired and aching from a hard day's organizing?" he asked, smoothly.

"Like a melon, I swear."

"Sorry."

She leaned forward again and began raising powerful green fingers one by one. "Diamond. Ransom. Shipping contracts, we stay afloat. Happy, busy children. Me, relaxed. You, head intact. Everybody got that? Good."

"Alright then," Robin agreed, gathering up the slips of paper she had laid down throughout her diatribe. "I'll take all this and get to planning and preparation and I'll run it by you before Thursday night."

"Good. Oh, and Robin…"

"Yes?"

"Don't bring Oberon… please," Scarlet asked solemnly. There was a silence as Robin met her meaningful gaze. "We can't afford to have him snatching things that will slow you down or trace back to us." She was deadly serious.

Robin shook his head. "I'm working on that, we have a code. Please don't ask me to exclude him."

"If you can spend some time getting his impulses under control, we might be able to trust him at a later date. Right now things are precarious and there's too much that can go wrong here. We can't take the risk." The firm resolution in her expression was unsuccessful in concealing the lengths of boundless crappiness Scarlet was feeling at saying these words. As Robin's mouth drew into a tight, imperceptible line behind his moustache, she relented just a little. "Let him be your getaway driver, don't let him go in with you."

What she was saying made sense, and Robin knew it, but his reply was threaded with reproach. "Alright, Scarlet. You really do know how to make a fellow feel special."

"I know," she said dryly, and not a little sadly. "It's one of my gifts."

***

As Robin walked despondently from Scarlet's room, wracking his brains for the best terms to couch this personal rejection to his closest friend, Oberon approached him with a tiny companion.

"Lavinia... what's the problem?" Robin asked her.

"I don't want to work in a factory," she replied firmly.

"She doesn't want to work in a factory," Oberon repeated.

"I had heard," Robin told him. "Why not?" he asked the child. "It's honest work, you can provide for your family." Something occurred to him as he said this, "Do you need help finding them again?"

"They are dead, Mr Loxley," she told him, flatly.

"Oh..." He trailed off, and cast about for options. "Well, what about the other children? It's a nice bunch they have here."

"I miss my own family," she folded her arms. "I miss Latvian food. I will work, yes, I will find a job. But I do not wish to stay here." Her voice shook a little, but her face remained stubbornly fixed.

"I think I see what you mean, Lavinia. Do you want to know if there are any Latvian families that might take you in?"

"Yes."

"I was thinking of the Dragushas," Oberon suggested.

Robin frowned. "They're Albanian."

"Close enough," the akka replied.

"Those countries are on opposite sides of Europe."

"They're kind. And they lost a son to cholera last November."

"Ah, yes," Robin sighed, "poor little Edon."

"Can you think of anybody else?" Oberon asked.

"Fair point." Robin turned back to the girl again. "Lavinia, do you mind going for a bit of a walk? There's one lot who might take you in. No promises, but we trust them."

"I would walk a thousand years to have my family back. What's a walk through London?" Lavinia said, and she meant it.

"Well… quite," Robin nodded.

***

The duart, the akka and the human child stole through the quiet, lamplit streets, dodging the Watchmen and staying in the shadows. Eventually they reached a point on the Thames occupied by many moored barges. They located the one painted with bright yellow mountain flowers and Robin lightly rapped on the hatch.

"Hape deren."

A female voice sounded from within and after a moment the hatch opened and a man with a salt and pepper moustache and a quizzical expression stood in the lamplight.

"It's the short guy and his monster friend," he said cheerily.

A woman hove into view and stood with her arms folded, glaring at them. Her face was worn and lined and her hair was greying, but her eyes were bright.

"Have you reprobates any idea what time it is?" she scolded.

"I know, and we're awfully sorry, Dashurie, but this couldn't wait. You see, this girl…"

"Is getting cold, same as I am," the matriarch interrupted, gesturing to them to come in. "All of you, inside now." She paused and looked pointedly at Oberon. "You, watch yourself. My ceiling is still cracked."

"Yes, ma'am," he replied obediently.

"Now, we need to get you some grosh. Here you go, girl, and some bread and cheese." Dashurie's tone was immediately softer, though still insistent.

Lavinia took the offered bowl gratefully. "Thank you."

"You two want?" the woman asked the outlaws.

"What is it?" Oberon asked.

"It's bean soup," she replied, handing him a tureen and ladling a sizeable helping into it.

"Well, what is it now?" he said, with a wry grin.

"Oh, hah," Dashurie said, clearly unamused. "You are a funny big thing that breaks ceilings. Eat your soup and keep your funny big mouth busy." He obliged.

"This is Lavinia," said Robin, accepting a bowl of soup. "Lavinia, if I recall correctly this is Skender…" He nodded at the man who had opened the door to them. Skender looked up and smiled at her.

"Hello. Miam broma kuka," he said.

Robin pointed with his spoon to one of the older children. "That is… don't tell me… Jetmir…?"

"Correct. Mireseerdhe, Lavinia."

"The beautiful young lady over there is Teuta…"

"Hi there," she said with a grin.

"And we should keep our voices down because Ahab and Annabel are sleeping in those bunks," Robin finished with a flourish, sending flecks of soup across the cabin.

"Very good party trick," Dashurie said, unimpressed.

"And Dashurie here is Teuta's even more gorgeous little sister," Robin added, grinning at her. Dashurie tutted and shook her head.

"I am her mother, child." She laid a hand gently on the girl's shoulder as she ate. "Now what do you want?" She turned back to Robin, smiling despite herself.

It looked like Lavinia's presence alone was doing most of the work, but closing the deal was going to require tact and charm. Robin pressed on. "Dashurie, thank you for inviting us into your home. I shall get straight to the point. Lavina here has just found herself short of a workhouse."

"I see." She pushed a plate of bread towards the girl, an expression approaching sympathy on her face. "Have some more."

"She doesn't wish to continue working in factories."

"What do you need, girl?" Dashurie asked her, blanking Robin.

"I need… sky." Lavinia held her hands out, palms up, gesturing to signify open space.

Dashurie raised an eyebrow. "You work on boat before?"

"No, but I can learn."

"You help sell in market?"

"Absolutely," Lavinia nodded enthusiastically.

"She's really very hardworking, I saw," Robin put in.

Dashurie scowled at him. "Ah, enough from you, Mr Talky. Let the girl speak."

"I'll shut up," he agreed.

"You are Albanian?" Dashurie asked Lavinia.

"Latvian," the girl replied, her face falling.

Dashurie shrugged. "Eh… it will do. You can have lowest bunk."

"Really?" Lavinia gasped.

"Of course, zemra," Dashurie said kindly. "Your eyes are tired, so finish your soup and get yourself to sleep. Tomorrow we have much work for you."

"Paldies… thank you." The child put down her bowl carefully and embraced the woman's midriff. Dashurie nodded to Robin.

"This one will be alright," she estimated.

By the time the thieves left the barge, they had eaten twice their fill of white bean soup, and Lavinia was curled up under a wool blanket, listening to the waters lapping against the hull and still cradling Veronica, the purloined doll, in her arms.

Flashback 1875

Eight years previously, young Gwendoline roamed the hallways of Buckingham Palace, creeping as stealthily as she could in and out of rooms. As she passed the staff she held a finger to her lips. They must not give her location away. The only time she permitted them to intervene was on the occasions she descended the stairs, when she was obliged to hold the hand of an adult. This of course caused her some consternation, but the indoor sled incident with the large serving tray had prompted this firm order from Coriolanus. It was intended, of course, for her protection, though it felt more like a punishment.

She sidled into the library, extending her toes to creep across the carpeted floor, lowering her head to scan under tables and peer behind chairs. Eventually she sank into one of these and closed her eyes, breathing in the scent of the rich leather and the hundreds of thousands of old pages that surrounded her. Then she caught it. The tiniest traces of an exotic perfume. One eye opened and she rose once more. Viola was definitely in this room.

Gwendoline didn't have a particularly well-developed sense of smell but she had a head on her shoulders and used what clues were available, and as she had traversed the halls the thought occurred to her that out of sight didn't necessarily preclude detection through her other faculties. What she wasn't, was patient. Several minutes more of circling the library and no sign of Viola, and she found herself standing in the centre of the room.

"I'm going to go down to the kitchens and see if they might make me a little smackerel of something," she stated in a matter-of-fact voice. "You carry on hiding."

Viola's exasperation could no longer be contained. "Oh, for goodness sake," came the muffled sigh.

"I knew it," Gwen shouted triumphantly.

"I'm over here," Viola conceded.

"Where?" Gwen looked around the room, trying to locate the source of the sound.

"Here," Viola said insistently.

"Behind the books?"

"In a manner of speaking."

"Is it… are you in a secret room?"

"Yes."

Gwen gasped. "I don't know whether to be furious with you for cheating or tremendously excited."

"Can't you be both?"

"Yes…" Gwen thought for a moment. "It would appear I can."

"Anyway, it's not cheating," Viola pointed out. "We said anywhere you could reach."

"Well, how can I reach you?"

"See the fireplace?" Gwen moved closer to inspect. Viola continued, "Lower skirting board panel. There's a catch back there. You wouldn't see it if you looked or if you were cleaning but slide your fingers into that alcove on the right."

"How did you find this?"

"I was lying under that chair, waiting for you, and the sunlight fell on the fireplace," Viola explained. "I saw the catch in the shadows down there."

"Is this it?" Gwen clicked the switch and the bookcase unlatched and swung open, revealing Viola in the shadows behind.

"You found me."

"Oh, that's wonderful," Gwen said, thrilled. "Can I get in there too?"

"Yes, come on in. I had a bit of a fright when I tried to pull the case mostly shut and it properly shut. Fortunately, the inside lever works fine." As Gwen squeezed through the doorway, Viola pulled the bookcase closed behind her.

"This isn't a room," Gwen realised.

"I know," Viola replied. She pulled the lever and the bookcase clicked open again.

"It's a tunnel," Gwen said.

Viola struck a match and peered as far as she could into the darkness. "We need to come back here with a lamp," she said, decisively.

Gwen glanced at her in surprise. "That isn't like you, Viola. You should be scolding me and sending me back to my nice, safe bedroom."

"Are you completely out of your mind, girl? This is a secret tunnel!" The excitement in Viola's voice was evident.

"Secret tunnel…" Gwen echoed. "What's this little plate here? Look, there's words; 'Franz Nordstrom, 1823'."

"The architect," Viola breathed.

"Oh, Viola…it's just like *Journey to the Centre of the Earth*. I don't think I've ever been more excited and scared of anything in my whole life." In this moment of peaking fervour, she closed her eyes and grasped her head. "I...ugh..."

"Is it hurting again?" Viola moved quickly forward to take her arm. "We should go and rest."

"We shall do no such thing. We need a lamp right now." Gwen shook herself, making things worse in the process.

"No, you're in pain."

"But..." Gwen's failed attempt at imperiousness faded into frustration.

"I have a job to fulfil," Viola said, her tone implacable.

"Viola!"

"Gwendoline! Don't make me Sleep you. It's dusty in here."

"You..." An indignant protest was on the tip of Gwen's tongue, but she thought better of it. "Alright..." Her shoulders drooped and she pressed her hand against the worn, varnished wood of the heavy door, looking at her companion earnestly as they stood half-shrouded in darkness. "When I'm better, can we come back in here please?"

"I promise," agreed Viola. "We shall pack a lunch and bring two lamps and I will take you as far as we can go while I am convinced you are not in immediate danger, but you must do as I tell you and if I say we go back, we go back. Deal?"

Gwen smiled through the throbbing pain in her head. "Deal."

Chapter 5: Shadows of London

Sunday Night

(The following is to be read in a thick Devonshire accent. Think Hobbits. – THE NAG)

"I am The Black Shuck. The twilight streets stretchin' from Twickenham to Gallows Corner are my stalking ground. This city is a broken woman, beaten, battered and savagely violated, crying out for salvation through bloodied teeth, and only I can hear her plaintive call.

"I prowl high above cobblestone streets wet with rain and shinin' like the tears on a weepin' woman's face. Every dark alleyway hides a thief or a murderer, burrowed in like… burrowin' insects. I watch them go about their foul nights' work with 'ungry eyes. I wait for them to enact their unholy sins and then I swoops in, like a black angel of retribution, and I clobbers every one of 'em.

"Tonight, I sees a fine woman walking the street, 'er pale dress positively glowin' in the moonlight. Slender shoulders wrapped in a shawl, a basket of food under 'er arm, no doubt for 'er kindly but broken grandmama. Only a matter of time, thinks I, before this pretty maid is dragged into one of the oozing crevices in the stonework by one of the grubs that slides through the underbelly. I watch 'er walk and know she has only moments left of this fragile purity, before it is taken from 'er.

"We walk for many streets until I am almost out of rooftop and have to scramble down to the gutter in order to pass to the next. This is my city, and yet architecturally speakin' it's really *quite inconvenient sometimes… you know, when you're stalking the night as its dark bringer of justice. Almost immediately, after about twenty minutes, she is approached by a Stepney sub-creature."*

"Lovely evening, miss," said the young man as the tall woman in the pale dress passed him by.

"It certainly is," she replied. "Spring's in the air."

"Retribution will not suffice tonight. If there is even the tiniest chance that the man down there will fall upon this maiden and drag her into his sewer then I must act. It is the duty I swore at my parents as they was leavin' London cos of all them monsters.

"Knowing in my mind that her virtue stands upon the precipice I swoop in from up on high, crushing the hooligan to the pavement beneath my hobnail boots. He screams in pain and tries to escape, but my reflexes are simply too fast. I clobber him with my fighting stick while the lady cowers in a puddle. I turn to her, my imposing frame shrouded in the shadows, I watch her with my eyes."

The woman watched the shadowy, muttering figure carefully, eventually concluding that his lengthy monologue was not directly addressed to her.

"You can go 'ome now, miss," he finally said in a louder, rougher tone. "There's dodgy folk abroad."

"Thank you, sir," she replied. "How can I repay you?"

"Justice is its own reward…" he began.

"You're very kind," she interrupted, but he ignored her and continued.

"But if you really wanna thank me I suppose we can go down that alley there for a bit of how's your father and then afterwards…" He broke off, suddenly afflicted with a sharp, erratic fit of shaking and shuddering before dropping to the ground, drooling slightly and wincing rather more.

"There we are," the woman said briskly, lowering the large, intricately designed copper rod with the black leather grip back to her side, but maintaining a stance that suggested she could raise it again at the slightest provocation. Her tone had become business-like and elegantly rude. "Now don't worry, the twitching will stop in a bit. Yes, it's horrible, isn't it? Alright, I'm just going to bind your hands. You'll need your legs free so I can walk you to my carriage. And really don't struggle or try to…"

He shouted across her hoarsely. "What have you done to me?"

"Oh, this is a device of my own invention, Mr Shuck," she replied, twirling the rod in her hand. "Its effects aren't permanently harmful, but you really don't want another jolt from it."

"Who are you?" he asked her. "How did you know my secret weakness?"

"Shush, now," she replied, stowing her weapon under her arm, before pulling the cord she had wrapped around his wrists tight, and knotting it firmly. "We're going to take a trip to the nice people at the Tower of London. You've been causing the Watch quite a bit of exasperation."

"Once you make yourself more than a man," he recited loudly, "you becomes a legend!" He sprawled back, shuffled his feet underneath himself and staggered unsteadily to an upright position. She stepped back and gave him space as he hobbled down the alley away from her. Rolling her eyes, she followed him at a walking pace.

"Oh for goodness' sake, settle down. Your legs aren't even working properly yet…"

"It's not who I am under this mask," he maintained to the night, "but who I am when I'm in the mask when…" The rest was gibberish, and he fell to convulsing and collapsing again as she caught up to him and poked him firmly with the sparking copper rod. Mercifully, he kept control of his bowels, as she continued in a clipped tone.

"I can sense that you are going to be a peculiar nuisance to me tonight."

"I am the stalking black dog, harbinger of doom for the wrongdoer!" he wailed from the ground. She was not convinced.

"Now, I'm just going to help this fellow down here. You gave him quite a nasty bump on the head there with that broom handle." She paced back to the young man on the cobbles who had managed to get to his knees and was nursing the side of his head. "Get up now, Sonny Jim, are you tickety-boo? What's your name?"

"Simon, and I'll live," he muttered, "but frankly, since you ask, I feel a bit more afraid to walk the streets now." He scowled at the now-face-down and wriggling caped figure with the tied hands.

"Fear… fear is my weapon!" the Shuck yelled. "Against the cowardly and the superst…"

"Here's three silver pieces. Get a doctor to look at that, would you," she ordered.

"Bless you, ma'am," he replied.

"Do you live near here? You're alright getting home? This *is* actually quite a rough area."

"Just round the corner. I'll be alright."

"Ta-ta, then," she said, waving her fingers at him as he limped off around the end of the alley.

The Shuck tried again. "Hey, why isn't anybody paying attention to me?"

"Oh, I will," the woman replied, watching Simon disappear and then stalking back towards him. "It's important you know who just handed you your wretched arse, so I'll introduce myself; my name is Mortimer. I've been hunting you for some time, and the bounty should just about pay for the sheer mind-bending annoyance of having to trap and transport you."

"I should have never have trusted a woman," he growled. "You weren't a defenceless virgin at all, you were a lying, vicious 'ore."

"That's disgusting language," she scolded. "Now let's get you to the Watch, you narcissistic shitpile."

He squalled in a piercing fashion, long and indignantly, as she took hold of the cord around his wrists and yanked him in the direction of the carriage.

Monday Morning (Six Days Left)

Gwendoline and Viola stood in the courtyard of the palace, in the morning light, surveying the lines of Duart Firecasters that proceeded through the front gates.

"Look, Viola," Gwen whispered. "There's your next career choice, for when you're done with me."

"Shut up, Your Highness," Viola retorted.

Captain Baltus, at the head of the party of Watchmen, strode up, clad in full armour. Though it could not be seen, both Gwen and Viola knew that his hair matched the helmet above it; a black brush stripe down the middle of his crown. A clipped black moustache and small, square, black beard on his chin gave the impression he had engaged in battle with a cartwheel that had travelled the circumference of his head, only for Baltus to emerge the victor. The marching Watchmen behind him halted and parted, and down the centre of the line for Gwen to behold crouched four Barghest, secured with iron rods and wire snares. They were straining at their bonds and gasping, eyes flicking back and forth madly across the assembled troops.

Captain Baltus spoke. "We caught them sneaking around the streets of Croydon." His voice was hard and grim, like being kicked down some stairs.

With that, the Duart Watchmen holding the iron poles marched the frantic creatures over to the far side of the palace yard and secured all four to a metal contraption. The front gates had closed, but dozens of Londoners who had been following the Watch procession now crushed up against the railings, their eyes on the Barghest. One of the creatures pulled its frame upside-down, spiderlike, in an attempt to escape; one howled over and over; one was choking itself, straining at the wire, and the last collapsed immediately, clearly beyond the ability to fight any further.

Gwendoline surveyed the captives. She had seen their like before, several times and knew exactly what was coming next, but usually they frightened her. There was still that unsettling feeling from the movements, their lithe, animalistic bodies, those orange eyes and the sounds they were making, but when she searched for the familiar hate, it just wasn't there. These monsters that had once been human were now a cause for pity.

The Firecasters lined up twenty yards from the Barghest, and as one unit readied both hands. Two dozen glowing flames snapped into life with domino timing. All of a sudden, a pang struck Gwendoline and she glanced down at Viola.

"Is there… can we…?" She broke off, wanting to ask if there was anything they could do to stop this, knowing what Viola's answer would be.

"Shhhh," her bodyguard replied.

"I'm just so tired of watching this."

"Listen to your nursemaid, Princess," Captain Baltus advised her. "This is man's work, and entirely necessary."

"Do you mean to say you managed to catch all four of these rabid creatures with only thirty men?" Viola's voice dripped with sarcasm. "Sir, your bravery and acumen in battle is peerless."

The Captain's eyes narrowed. "Tell the buffoon to fall silent. I do not like her tone." Gwen scowled at him.

"Viola, I implore you, *don't* fall silent, whatever you do."

"FIRE!" Baltus screamed. The Firecasters flung out first their right hands, then their left. Two volleys of flame sailed through the air and entirely engulfed the Barghest. The heightened, hysterical, anguished screaming lasted for seventeen seconds. In that time, Gwen had gone from a scowl to staving off angry tears. Her body shook. Captain Baltus regarded her. "You see? Not one of my men is delicate. Not one of them fears violence. Not one of them would hesitate to act. We bow to your graciousness, your Royal Highness, and take pride that we can protect you and your lands." This last part did not seem at all sincere.

"Exactly what does it take to become Captain of the Watch?" Viola asked. He glanced down, as though just remembering she was there.

"A spotless career record, a drive to succeed at any cost… and an endowment which you do not possess, pretty thing."

"And what an achievement owning one of those is," Viola replied icily.

"Not having one entails that you should be birthing our next generation." His words were cold, flat, merciless. "I wonder why you linger here and do not set yourself to the duty of our noble females."

Viola flushed crimson. Baltus sneered victoriously and marched past the two of them, approaching the Archduke who stood with his gauntlets clasped behind his back, surveying the scene as the charred skeletons of the Barghest collapsed into black ash, which partially dissipated into the cold, morning air. Viola whispered something, fluttering her fingers, and Baltus caught his foot on the steps, stumbling on his way up.

"Are you alright?" Coriolanus asked, as the Captain recovered his balance and hastily straightened his breastplate and collar.

"I'm fine." He smoothed his ruffled dignity and looked straight ahead.

"Very good show, Captain Baltus. The people are pleased." Coriolanus spoke without warmth or generosity, merely stating the facts.

"We shall find the rest of the remaining infected and cleanse them all in time, your Grace."

Coriolanus let his grey-green eyes rest on the chattering crowd at the gates. Some were open-mouthed, some were cheering, some were crying.

"No rush," he reassured Baltus. "Besides, you have much to attend to on the streets of London. The Hoods, the Knives; these organised gangs are making a mockery of our esteemed Watchmen. You must tighten the noose around the boldest of them. Show the people what defiance truly entails."

"It shall be done, your Grace."

"I'm sure it hasn't escaped your attention that last night a particular thorn in your side was plucked out at last. The Black Shuck was apprehended, not by one of your men…" His tone grew darker. "But by a freelance bounty hunter… and a female at that."

Baltus' eyes flicked slightly to the right, but he maintained his stance. "I am aware of this turn of events."

"We have standards to maintain," the Archduke reminded him.

"Yes."

"Find the heads of the gangs," Coriolanus reiterated, looking past the Captain to Gwendoline and Viola.

"Yes, sir."

"And Gwendoline, I trust you have not forgotten your appointment with Doctor Marcus this afternoon."

Gwen responded without emotion. "I shall be there as you ask, father…" Her eyes brightened momentarily. "Though I should say I rather like the sound of these Hoods. I mean they must be devilishly cunning if they can run rings around the Watchmen."

Baltus fumed at her words. "A combination of blind luck and the treachery of the less desirable people of London," he replied, venomously. "Make no mistake, the hammer of justice is poised above these Hoods. Whatever their next nefarious deed is, it shall not go unpunished."

Monday Lunchtime

Oberon threaded his way through the Hogwell Smotes textile factory. Without America to provide cotton, the British Isles had gone back to wool and linen. Wales and several of the middle counties were now enormous sheep farms, and flax was being grown up and down England. Sheffield provided the steel, Newcastle and Yorkshire the coal. Ships were departing for France and beyond every day, and to everyone's intense relief, tea was finally being brought in from India once more. There was even talk of making contact with the Colonies, once the Duart army was strong enough to contend with the potentially millions of Barghest thought to be still running rampant over there.

Next door was the Hogwell Smotes timber mill. Now the human workers had given way to Akka and their muscular frames, in their many shades of green, were busy hauling and splitting the wood. Oberon paced between the whirling saws and clanking machinery until he reached the dock area and found a brawny fellow pulling logs from a barge. The akka's eyes glanced up and met his. A glimmer of recognition formed.

"Hello Ajax, it's me, Oberon. I'm a friend." The glimmer took hold and Ajax nodded slowly as the memories were unpacked. "Are you doing okay here today?" Oberon continued. "They're not pushing you too hard?"

"Yes… uh… no…"

Oberon collared the human foreman.

"Evans, what hours is he pulling this week?"

"Fourteen a day for the past few," replied the man.

"That's too much, he needs more rest. Cut it to eleven. Are you checking his pay?"

Evans nodded firmly. "Absolutely. He's getting every hour accounted for."

Oberon turned back to Ajax. "Did you break for lunch today?" he asked.

"He's just got back…" Evans began, then saw the look on Oberon's face. "I mean, he's just going."

"I'll bring him back in thirty minutes," Oberon growled. He reached out a hand toward Ajax. "Come on, friend, let's go and eat."

The two Akka sat on the bank of the Thames devouring hunks of bread with dripping. Oberon quietly chewed and regarded Ajax, who stared off at the barges passing them by.

"I, uh…saw a pretty big dog today. A Bull Mastiff," Oberon ventured. Ajax looked across, suddenly aware that Oberon was there, and nodded enthusiastically. "You like that? You know what kind that is?" Ajax drew a large hand up to his own face and traced the fingers over, indicating the darkened jowls of this breed. Oberon nodded back. "Good, that's right. What's the biggest you've seen this week?"

"Scottish Deerhound," Ajax replied, looking pleased with himself.

"Big?"

"Three feet high." He indicated with his hand.

"Yeah, that's pretty big," Oberon agreed. "Was that the same one as last week?"

Ajax looked at him with a slightly pained expression. "Yes… no…"

"Probably," Oberon soothed. "Are they still treating you well? You getting enough rest?"

"I sleep enough," Ajax shrugged.

"Good. You doing anything else when you're not working? Remember I gave you that whittling knife?"

At this Ajax brightened and reached into his waist pouch, pulling out a small, carved wooden dog. "Kuvasz… from Hungary," he said softly. "Biggest dog." He laid it in Oberon's hand and then gently closed the akka's fingers around it.

"For me?" Oberon breathed quietly for a moment, feeling the object inside his fist and studying his companion's eyes. "Thank you, my friend. This is lovely." Ajax nodded and went back to his lunch. Oberon stowed his new treasure away and straightened up. "Now, I have to get back. You're coming with me."

Ajax rose to his feet, swallowing the last morsel, and glanced down, a little surprised as Oberon gave him a quick and rough embrace before leading his brother back to work.

Monday Afternoon

Gwendoline was shown into the offices of Doctor Marcus. Everything was dark brown stained wood. Marcus was sporting a clipped moustache and hair slicked over to the left. He wore a smart, three-piece suit with steel-rimmed spectacles and a fine gold pocket watch, and as he walked to the door to meet her, he leaned on a beautifully carved cane of Australian snakewood.

"Ah, your Royal Highness, it's been far too long. Come in, sit down." He crossed back to his desk and gestured to the chair in front of it. Gwen, despite her obvious unease, did as she was told.

"Thank you," she said in a small voice.

"Now, have the pains intensified?" he asked. Gwen suppressed a shudder but raised her eyes and forced herself to look at him.

"A little, yes," she admitted.

"And why have you been having them?" he asked in a lightly patronising tone.

"Because I haven't been coming to see you," Gwen replied quietly.

He shook his head in a manner possibly intended to convey exasperated fondness. "I really won't bite," he said. "Now, let's begin, shall we?" He turned to the mantelpiece and set a large metronome in motion. Gwen felt her stomach churn as the too-familiar tick – tick – tick – tick sounded throughout the room.

"Before we do…" she interrupted, "I'm not feeling well. Do you have a bucket nearby just in case I…?"

"You are never sick in my office," he said firmly. "I catch your problems very quickly. Now let's set to work fixing you, Princess."

"I really do feel…" Gwen attempted again.

"Shhhh, let me work," he insisted.

***

Thirty minutes later, Gwendoline emerged from the office, clear headed but scowling. Viola, who had been sat in the waiting room reading the Times, hopped down and approached the Princess with watchful eyes.

"Are you alright, Gwen?"

"I'm fine," Gwen snapped in reply, then acceded, "I need bed."

"Let's get you home, then."

***

Back in Gwendoline's room after she was undressed and put into her nightgown by the maid, Viola paced about, questioning further and putting out the lamps.

"You're not still nervous about Sunday, are you? No, of course you are, how silly of me. Is your nose hurting from yesterday? Did you eat enough? That might be why you were feeling faint. That or concussion from that crack on the floor. I really wish you would just…" She trailed off.

"What? Viola, you wish I would what?"

"Be happy… no, that's not right. I mean, I want you to be happy, but you don't have to be. Oh, I'm rubbish at this; I should just stick to my tasks."

"Well, you are still my jester. Isn't it your job to make me happy?"

Viola sighed. "What can I do for you, Princess?"

"I'd like a story, please," Gwen asked politely.

"You want us to finish *Pride and Prejudice*?"

Gwen shook her head. "Tempting… but I think… not tonight."

"*Journey to the Centre of the Earth*?" Viola suggested.

"Perfect." Gwen smiled.

Viola moved to the book shelf and glanced back at Gwendoline sat in her bed, all cats save for Sebastian shooed away. The girl had such a forlorn look in her eye. Just one more week, Viola thought. One more week until what? The same exact situation, only with a crown far heavier upon her brow.

***

After she had read for an hour with Gwen, the girl's eyelids drooped and she fell into a slumber. Viola fondly stroked her hair, adjusted the quilt and before she realised she was doing so, had prepared a moderately powerful Sleep spell to nudge the girl far down into a dreamless healing rest. Viola held her hand out, her fingers tingling inches from the Princess' face, before slowly drawing it back in. Despite having done this many times in the past during Gwen's most troubled nights, this evening it no longer felt right.

Viola turned back to her newspaper, spreading the human-scaled sheet out across her own bed and settled in for the night, mug of cocoa in hand. Her eye fell on the report of a brazen daylight coach robbery of the Marquis of Chiswick and she tutted to herself. Things would surely be better in the morning.

Chapter 6: The Fox and Bear

Monday Evening

Gwendoline wandered the misty courtyard in the pre-dawn chill, feeling the wet ground under her toes. Shivering in her nightdress, she approached the immense gates, knowing that as usual they would be locked and guarded.

But there was no sign of another soul. The red-coated guards, both Duart and human were gone, their boxes empty, their posts abandoned. Gwendoline glanced behind her, wishing for Viola, knowing the harsh words her companion would say and how soon she would be ushered back inside. But she heard no sound.

She reached the gates, painted black with golden prongs, adorned with her family crest and bordered by ornately sculpted, tall, white square pillars. Experimentally, knowing the familiar locked resistance, Gwendoline pushed… and to her astonishment the gates swung open. Electricity danced up her spine. London lay beyond that cold whiteness. Her heart thundered in her chest.

The mist began to part and she paced forward eagerly only to come up against a force that terrified her to the core. A balefully familiar curtain blocked her way. Its icy touch made her gasp and recoil, clutching at spasming fingers. There was no colour or edge, and for all Gwen knew it was boundless, but the veil held back the mist in such thick clouds that nothing could be glimpsed beyond.

Her head throbbed and she turned, walking as smartly as she could back towards the front doors of Buckingham Palace. She felt movement behind her and her breathing quickened as she conjured it might be following her. Those doors would be unlocked; surely, she could get back inside. Any second now.

And if they were locked?

Gwendoline awoke with a scream and lay panting in her bed, sheets soaked in sweat, her head and heart pounding in tandem. Viola was up and beside her in moments.

"It's alright, you're here. I'll protect you." She put a hand on the Princess' shoulder.

Gwen's voice trembled, her face was ashen. "V… Viola. I… I need to fight. I need to."

"I'll go and see if one of the guards is up for it. I know Simon's already gone home."

"No." Gwen looked at Viola, her expression defiant. "A real fight. I need… the truth."

Viola shook her head. "It's nearly ten, the fighting rings will all be closing soon."

"Not all of them; the one beneath the Fox and Bear goes on until one in the morning."

"We have talked about this a hundred times, Gwen." Viola folded her arms and frowned. "Don't make me say yes. I could lose my job, or far worse. You would be in terrible danger. Please stay."

Gwendoline reached out her trembling hands in the dark and found those of her friend.

"Viola, look at me. I need this," she pleaded, squeezing tight.

"Ohhhh, I'm going to get charged with treason," Viola muttered, shaking her head.

"Darling Viola. I will destroy any man who dares suggest that you have anything but my best interests at heart," Gwen assured her, with a weak smile.

"Well, you may have to," her companion sighed. "Can we at least make this quick? Wear the good disguises, get out, get back, nobody shall know."

"You'll have to be handy with the spells."

"Alright, you have three minutes to get dressed." Viola agreed reluctantly.

In three minutes and thirty seconds the pair were stealing through the darkened palace, evading detection. In the library, Gwen found the familiar catch under the fire and the bookcase swung open. Lighting their lamp, they stole inside.

They passed behind walls and in between rooms, stealthily navigating their shadow halls. There was nowhere else in the palace with this smell. Dust and damp pervaded the air, infusing it with an odour part way between an ancient well and a ruined church, as they picked carefully across mahogany boards which creaked with endurance. They were aware that what had been built sixty years ago, unattended as it was, would not last forever. Eventually, no matter how well-preserved the tunnels had been, they would begin to succumb to the expansion and contraction of heat, the pervasive moisture and the erratically moving weight of the two explorers.

On this night, both of them stepped carefully over the hole which Gwen had created with her foot last spring. Back then, once she had extricated her knee and calmed down they had peered through the splintered gap, the lamplight casting faint traces of gold down into a passage which neither of them recognised and which they had never found the way into. The winding steps at the end of every corridor had more of a permanence about them, and hand rails which suggested these might have been part of the original design of this place, walled off and repurposed. They were too grand to be for servants alone, but uncarpeted and rough.

The Princess' favourite point was coming up ahead of them now. The tall archway in the western wall, decorated in black tiles, was briefly illuminated, bricked up solidly. As a child Gwen had been determined to break through and see what was on the other side. Viola had deterred her and shot down every wild speculation, but still had not been able to come up with sufficient evidence as to which room or place it led to. No amount of hunting round the palace side could turn up its counterpart. So, there it lay in Gwendoline's mind, ever beckoning further investigation, ever offering new possibilities. She brushed a cracked tile with her fingers as they passed.

The pathway sloped down as they descended into the catacombs below. It was chillier here, and the smell of earth seeped through the stone foundations. Here and there the water had accumulated and risen to the level where in certain tunnels it drew up to Gwen's waist and

Viola's shoulders. There was a swift return to bed and two baths on the night they had discovered that.

But the way out was mercifully still dry and they were grateful for their dark, warm coats, headscarves and tricorn hats. Eventually they emerged, blinking, into the night, from the unfolding statue of King George IV in Green Park, far north enough to avoid being spotted by the guards.

London really did lie before them now. Clenching and unclenching her gloved fists, Gwendoline strode forth, with Viola keeping a watchful eye upon her.

This was not the first time Gwendoline had ventured out into London. In point of fact, it was her fourth.

1879

The first time, aged thirteen, she had been so giddy that she contented herself with wandering the moonlit streets for three hours, Viola fending off those Londoners who approached with confusion and darkness spells. They had ended up in Covent Garden, sat on a bench, Gwen staring up at the lit windows and the stars, an enormous grin plastered across her face, breathing in the intermingled scents that lingered from the previous day: roasting goose, the rain on the pavement, a man being copiously sick in a nearby alley. Some of these odours would certainly have been repellent to you or I, but to Gwendoline that sharp stench meant new, it meant different, it meant danger, and that was what she wanted. It was two in the morning before Viola managed to get the Princess back to her bedroom. But the way the girl kept sighing told her tiny guardian that this was of course not going to be the only time.

1880

On the second occasion, Gwendoline had made a beeline for a particularly seedy-looking establishment they had passed before – the Mad Bull Inn. After an intense and hushed argument outside, Viola paid the four ten-copper pieces for their entry and they descended into the bowels of an underground fighting ring. That night had been purely spectating, watching as a tall, skinny man went up against a string of opponents, none of whom seemed able to shift him from his winning streak. Gwen watched the man, whose name was Colin, studying his approach to combat carefully. She worked out that it wasn't how hard he hit, but his fine control when blocking. Because of his awkward frame his opponent was always slightly off-balance and their fists and feet tended to come into contact with his bony arms and knees, which were always in the way.

The human hand has 27 bones. Duart have only 23 and Akka have 25, but there are still a lot, all held together with muscle, cartilage and connective tissue, making for one of the most delicate and complex instruments at the disposal of our bodies. Just one little bone out of line, fractured or broken, and it doesn't work properly. Much like the ear, only people don't tend to punch with their ears.

The human elbow, forearm and knee have a lot fewer, less complex bones, and the human skull has developed as armour for the brain, with some extremely hard, protective plates. It is thus when the complex collides violently with the simple that things go wrong for the complex.

All Colin had to do was ensure that when a beefy chap made a punch to his ribs that those delicate finger bones connected at an obtuse angle with an elbow and in that one blow, Beefy would find himself subsequently unable to safely punch with that hand. Stinging pain would attack his central nervous system, making it harder to judge his next move. A lunging kick and suddenly his leg was going numb as Colin moved to the side. Half of Colin's opponents actually gave up after a few moments in the ring with him. It hurt too much and there didn't seem to be many options.

What proved his undoing was Galash, an akka of exactly the same height but extremely thick build. Galash was an enforcer for a low-level gang boss and didn't mess around. The akka didn't bother punching, he just edged Colin into a corner and enfolded him in a powerful bear hug. An awkward knee to the knackers didn't faze Galash; he was wearing an iron codpiece, and now suddenly Colin's knee had encountered even less complexity. Gwen watched and smiled. This was something she could do.

1881

The third time Gwendoline was out of the palace, at the tender age of fifteen, she somehow convinced Viola to let her fight. Her face and body obscured behind scarves, a hat, and a long overcoat, she entered the ring trembling, the cacophony of shouts eclipsing the sound of the out of tune piano playing in the corner of the establishment. The floor was disgusting, caked in dried blood and mucus. The walls around her were dull whitewashed brick, and the lamplight flickered cold and green.

Not only was she out of her depth, she could no longer even see her depth.

Gwen's first opponent was a cruel, hard looking man with grey hair, who immediately swung at her gut. As the girl turned her body away from this, his other fist cracked against her jaw. Suddenly they were very close, engaged in a frantic pushing-away of one another's faces. She was hit several more times and found herself on the floor being kicked.

All of a sudden, Grey swung his foot too far up and found himself off-balance. From the floor, Gwen could see Viola whispering in the crowd, her fingers weaving away. A combination of indignant fury and intense relief flooded Gwen and she was up in a flash, ramming her knee sharply against the man's back, grabbing his head and tumbling down to crush him with her weight. His body spasmed and he struggled a moment before going limp.

This was different. He had not pulled his punches and now she hurt badly all over. Breathing was painful, and she suspected a rib had cracked. Viola, with her spell, had helped Gwen get over the initial shock and fear of being hit, and she had won.

The difference between this and her confrontations with the palace guards was that Gwen knew that Grey did not care at all about hurting her. All he cared about was winning. He brought a simple, cold truth to the ring with him. The punches and kicks had felt horrible, but they were real. In effect, victory didn't matter; the important thing was that she had fought.

Drunk on this revelation she went up against an immensely fat, bald man, named Gareth, who incidentally was a keen participant in the local theatre scene, and on the side of his shipyard job had spent many nights in minor roles on Drury Lane. Gareth was on top form tonight, having just killed it as Aslak in Peer Gynt, so Gwen got slapped hard to the head and went down like a sack of potatoes in six seconds. As they left the establishment, she could not stop shaking and laughing.

The next day they had applied liberal makeup to cover the bruising. Later that morning she had taken a controlled tumble from her pony, landing painfully but at least being able to explain the damage to her body, allowing her time to heal without arousing suspicion.

1883 – Monday Night

Now, tonight, she wanted to fight once more. Winning was not important. Fear was coursing through her and she wished to meet it head on. To take the punch and keep going.

Under the considerably less grotty establishment of The Fox & Bear, Gwen fought three opponents in a row. The first was a muscular red-haired, well-kept duart who reminded her of Lord Aaron. He had hit hard, but she countered with an unexpected ferocity. In the end she was chasing him round the ring kicking at him frantically, ending it with a sudden, about face which had him collide with her shoulder. The duart crashed backwards onto the boards and lain groaning and immobile as she kneeled on his chest.

Gwen was already flying on her first victory. She glanced up at Viola suspiciously. Viola shrugged with a genuine glimmer of pride in her eyes. Gwen squared herself for her second opponent, and her eyes widened. It was Colin. She watched him carefully as they moved around one another in the ring. She did not make the mistake of attacking, and clearly Colin was wary of another bear-hug. In the end the fight happened slowly and in ungainly fashion, with the two of them grappling. Colin seemed to know the best places to put his arms to give her less purchase.

Gwen recalled reading about how a Burmese Python overcame its prey, the example on this particular occasion being a piglet. Now they were on the floor with his bony coils around her she struggled hard against this unfavourable comparison. Things started to go blurry as she felt herself drifting. Hoisting her legs up into the air, crunching her body double, Gwen attempted to set him off-balance. Inadvertently Colin's head became trapped between her immense, muscular thighs and as she felt him panic she squeezed and rolled over. Colin's shinbone came up and clocked her in the side of the face but she grabbed it and locked her arm around, holding the other up to guard against his remaining flailing limbs. Eventually, mercifully, he went limp and she stood, once again victorious.

Her third opponent was an enormous green akka. She was now exhausted and by all rights, should have quit whilst she was ahead. Instead, once again, she kept pushing, testing her limits, which were swiftly found.

Back at the palace, whenever she fought, she would hit her natural limit and then stop. She would get tired or bored and go off to do something else, ergo her strength improved at a steady rate, as did her skill, but her stamina and ability to pace herself was absolutely rubbish.

Now here she was testing those limits and finding them unequal to the task. The akka charged ferociously, roaring at her, and she tripped over her own feet trying to find a stable position.

Oberon, for naturally it was he, slammed his arm against her chest as he passed and in a spiralling instant she was over, the wind knocked out of her. More alarmingly, her scarf had slipped, which made her heart lurch as her lips met the air. She rolled and hastily pulled it back on, but almost nobody in the room was looking directly at her, instead marvelling at the akka who thrust his fists in the air and roared. A second or so after Gwen was unmasked the lights dimmed, or at least that was what appeared to happen, and by the time everything was clear the scarf was back up, though through their watered-down ales, everybody could taste boot polish for some reason.

But Robin had seen her face.

This is why when she exited the ring, greeted a female duart with pink hair and left the cellar laughing, Robin collared Oberon who was collecting his winnings.

"Well done, old boy." He clapped his friend on the arm, as high as he could reach.

"He was tired. I just went in with the sudden shock tactic. This is why we should be doing that more often on the job."

"She," Robin corrected him.

"What?"

"She was tired. Didn't you make out that figure of hers through the coat? Did you see her face?"

Oberon stared at him. "You thought that was a woman?"

"Is it only me who has an eye for these things? Come on." Robin turned to go, gesturing eagerly to Oberon to follow him.

"What are we doing?" Oberon asked, ducking his head as they went through the door.

"Well, that wasn't just any woman," Robin informed him. He pulled himself up close to Oberon's ear. "It was Princess Gwendoline."

Oberon stared at him. "You're out of your mind."

"You think I'd mistake a face like that?" asked Robin, shaking his head. "I've looked upon her a hundred times at the National Portrait Gallery."

"You've gone there a hundred times?"

"I appreciate art, especially the shapely kind. But that's not important right now. I know it doesn't make sense but somehow… somehow she's out and about in London, and she likes a fight." His eyes sparkled with the prospect.

"Oh no." Oberon drew back, holding his hands up, eyes tightly shut, shaking his head with exasperation. "I can't believe you're about to say… what I'm pretty sure you're about to say."

"I'm definitely about to say it."

"I can't believe it." Oberon clutched at his forehead and breathed out. By now the pair were outside and pacing along the street several hundred yards behind Gwendoline and Viola as they headed back to the statue of George IV in Green Park.

"Royal kidnap," Robin confirmed in a hushed whisper. "She's right there for the taking. Have you any idea how much gold we could get? Scarlet and the Hoods would be at a tactical advantage for once."

As they paced along, Oberon stared at him for a moment, realised he was right, considered their predicament, weighed up the worst outcomes, and then shrugged. "Okay, let's do it."

"Really?" Robin looked surprised.

"Yes. Quick, before I become sane and change my mind."

"I'll pull the old dashing hold-up and tell them both to stay quiet and come with us. You hold her while we walk. We'll need some swiftly acquired transportation. And watch out for that little duart toddling along beside her," Robin added, gesturing to the Princess' companion. "She looks like trouble."

***

Meanwhile, not far ahead, Gwendoline and Viola were engaged in a dispute of their own.

"Did you see that?" Gwen gushed, ecstatic. "*Did you see that?* I beat Colin. I beat the gangly one!"

"And that akka nearly tore your face off and wore it like a bonnet," her nursemaid grumbled.

"Your amazing mind." Gwen shook her head in frustration.

"I didn't like seeing him touch you."

Gwendoline rolled her eyes. "Oh, but the ginger duart was okay? Colin was okay when his slender, sinewy arms were all around me?"

"No," Viola admitted.

"Then why all this special mistrust of the Akka? That one seemed like a ferocious warrior to me. Someone to be feared and respected, but not hated."

Viola raised her chin defensively. "They're squatters and thieves. I don't like saying it, but it's the truth."

"Have you ever met any?"

"I've met plenty of them," Viola replied indignantly.

"No, I mean actually talked to one," persisted Gwen.

Viola shook her head with a snort. "They have nothing to say. The savage ones are the worst. Mindless brutes."

"I only ask because there's one following us right now," Gwen told her quietly.

"I know," Viola whispered back. "It's the one you fought."

"Do you think he saw my face?" Gwen asked.

"I was quick with the Darkness on the room, but there were a lot of eyes and I don't know if it had full effect on everyone." Viola stopped, suddenly terrified. "Princess… look at me, if someone did see you, then this game is up. I mean it. We've had an exciting time, but there are too many things that can go wrong when you fight. I've been a fool letting you do it. Terrible at my job, and I deserve to be relieved of my post and no longer your friend."

"Nonsense; dear, sweet Viola, you've performed admirably."

Viola shook her head firmly. "I could have cast all sorts of spells on you, clouded your thoughts, brought you home gentle as a lamb."

"Get those spells ready," Gwen advised.

"Yes, I have a dreadful feeling you're about to be kidnapped." Viola glanced at her with determined eyes, adjusting her gloves and crunching down a fistful of butterscotch. "Do exactly as I say, and if it comes to a fight, you take on the duart."

Chapter 7: Crossed Pathways

Regent's Park

Robin pulled out a pair of pistols and proffered them with a flourish at the two young ladies.

"Excuse me, your Majesty," he said, with his most charming drawl. "Frightfully sorry to do this, but I'm going to have to ask you two to come with me."

"We have no idea what you're talking about," Viola said quickly. "We're fishmongers on the way home after a long day of mongering fish and… fighting." She trailed off, then added, "We don't have any money."

Robin sniffed. "You don't smell of fish at all, which is odd for a brace of seasoned fishmongers."

"We clean up well," Viola snarled.

"You certainly do. Now, your Majesty…" He turned back to Gwendoline.

"Your Highness," she corrected him.

"*Brilliant*," Viola muttered.

"Sorry?" Robin was confused.

"You call a King or Queen 'your Majesty'," Gwen clarified.

"Thank you," Robin smirked. "Drop the charade please, Princess Gwendoline, I know your lovely face very well."

What happened next was fairly fast. Viola whispered something and Robin's fingers turned to figurative jelly. He dropped his pistols and Oberon realised that the female duart was responsible. The akka's eyes widened;

he made a grab and flung her across Regent's Park and into a large Cypress tree. As she sailed through the air, Viola managed a pinpointed Sleep spell upon Oberon who obligingly crashed to the ground leaving Gwendoline punching at the empty space where Robin had been.

"Stand still!" she shouted at him.

"No," Robin retorted. "You'll hit me."

"You little rat," Gwen snapped.

"That's hurtful," he reproached. "Honestly, this isn't going at all how I planned." As Gwen dived and lashed at Robin he sidestepped and wove around her. "I never knew you could do this. I was watching you fight earlier. You're amazing… I mean, for a girl."

Gwen roared at him and made another lunge towards his head. "Come on, calm down, I promise I won't kidnap you," he said reassuringly. She looked at him with an expression of sheer disbelief. "I can't! I mean look at my friend down there. How am I supposed to move you and him at once?" He ducked under her fist and darted away again.

"Come here!" she yelled furiously.

"You've won, Princess, you can escape now," he assured her.

"I don't want to escape, I want you brought to justice, mister…?"

"I'm not sure I want to tell you. I have a reputation to maintain," he said primly. "And bungled kidnappings really don't help that sort of thing."

"I *know* who you are," she panted.

"Really." He sounded curious.

"Well, you have a hood, you're a duart and you won't stop bloody talking, so… HAH!" She had caught him by the collar and pinned his right arm behind his back, and said, without betraying reverence of any kind, "I believe I'm in the presence of the dashing brigand Robin of the Hood."

"Let go of me," he demanded.

"No."

"Please?"

"Oh… alright."

"Really?"

"NO!" She tightened her grip on his arm and they both looked up at the sound of a whistle. Running footsteps could be heard, and two Watchmen came speeding round the corner.

"Alright, what's going on here? Are these robbers?" asked the taller of the two.

A voice carried across the darkened park. "Can someone please help me down out of this sodding tree?"

"Yes, please help her down, Officer," Gwen added, easing up on Robin's arm just a little, but still keeping him held firmly in front of her.

"Jump into my arms, miss…" The head Watchman reached up towards the tree and Viola slipped off the branch and squeaked as he caught her firmly. "There." He set her down, glaring at Robin and the unconscious Oberon. "Smith, bring the wagon around. We've got an akka and a duart, thieves for the Chokey."

"Actually," Robin stepped forward as much as he could. "*They* were robbing *us*."

The Watchman's face twitched in confusion. "What?"

"What?" Gwen echoed. She let go of Robin's arm and took a step backward.

"We tried to run, but the duart girl there tripped my companion over and this ruffian mercilessly beat me into submission," Robin explained. "And she took my friend's wallet," he added, pointing at Gwen.

"I did nothing of the sort!" Gwen cried indignantly.

"I think you'll find she did," Robin insisted, ignoring her expression and directing his remarks only to the Watchmen. "It has something like twelve silver in it. Brown leather." The Watchman who had caught Viola nodded to his companion, who moved behind Gwen and went swiftly through her pockets.

"Why, I…" Gwen was too astonished to even object.

"He's correct, sir," the second Watchman said, withdrawing a large purse from Gwen's coat and holding it up. "The girl does have it, right here. Twelve silver, like he said."

"He must have slipped it into my coat just now!" Gwen exclaimed.

"What about the pistols?" Viola demanded, only a little less confused about what exactly was happening here than Gwen.

"Are you going to arrest me for armed *donation* to this woman?" Robin asked, again addressing the Watchmen.

Oberon chose that moment to come around from his maajikal sleep. "Oh, my head…" he groaned. "What happened?"

"You fell asleep and these two took us for everything we have," Robin told him, with as much dignity as he could muster.

"This is absolute balderdash," Viola said loudly, stepping forwards. "Officer, you are speaking to the…"

Gwen poked her sharply in the shoulder. "Shhh!"

"What?" Now it was Viola's turn to look thoroughly baffled.

"Shush now, Vio-uh… *Vanessa.* The game's up. They've got us bang to rights."

Viola folded her arms angrily. "No. It's time we faced the music. I have to tell them." She turned to the Watchmen and gestured at her companion. "This is Princess Gwendoline, you fool! Look at her face."

"Er… it's pretty swollen and filthy," said the first Watchman.

"She's been fighting," Viola pointed out, as though to an idiot.

"Which we all know princesses do," Robin put in, helpfully.

"Who are *you* then?" the Watchman asked Viola.

"I am Miss Viola Heartstone, official bodyguard of the Princess. Take us to Buckingham Palace, immediately. Everybody in there tonight will vouch for us."

"What do you think, Smith?" The Watchman turned to his partner.

"Probably best to at least check before we take them to the Tower," the duart officer mused. "Something about this smells fishy."

"No, it doesn't," Robin muttered. He'd glanced quizzically and surreptitiously at Gwen when she had admitted to this manifestly false culpability, and when Smith was talking, she had returned the look.

"*Nothing* about this smells right," said the head officer. "I don't trust a one of you shifty bleeders."

"What did I do?" Oberon asked, holding his ringing head.

"Shut your face, akka. Smith, pick up them pistols and take the bow off of the duart, and the blade off the big one. Right, into the wagon, all of you. We're making two stops."

***

Inside the wagon Viola and Oberon scowled. Robin and Gwen, however, were experimenting with catching one another's eye. She kept smiling which made him smile back, and their companions frown more deeply.

"What about '*do exactly as I tell you*' did you *not* get?" Viola hissed at Gwen with frustrated annoyance.

"You didn't tell me to *do* anything," Gwen reminded her. "You just said we were fishmongers, which he didn't believe for a second, did you?" she asked, turning to Robin.

"I didn't," he agreed.

Viola scowled at all of them. "How are we going to get out of this?"

"Leave that to me," Robin replied.

"You're rather confident for a highwayman in chains," Viola said.

"First of all," Robin said, hopping up on the bench he and Oberon were chained to. "I wouldn't have much of a career as a thief without being a good lock picking artist." He crouched down and felt at the back of his boot, retrieving a pair of angled metal rods. "I'll confess I'm not much of a good shot at all with the bow or the pistols, I'm not a brilliant fighter, though I'm fairly good at avoiding getting punched, but lock picking... that I *can* do." He deftly palmed and resituated the rods and began to work them into the padlock on Oberon's shackles. "Now these are Mandelson locks, which are tricky but not impossible. If they were Strode locks we'd be in trouble." There was a click, and Robin bent his wrists with some difficulty to reach the bindings around them. With his hands now free he tended to first the akka's ankles and finally his own. He glanced around, rubbing at his aching extremities and continued, slyly, "This isn't my first police wagon escape. Now, we need a distraction, and if I'm not mistaking that building there, we're currently riding down Charing Cross Road. Which means..."

Robin trailed off and pushed his face up to the window bars, his eyes wide open. Mercifully, among the people on the street at that late hour, there was a gaggle of green-attired hoods. He whistled two sharp notes that meant a great deal to them, and in response they clocked the wagon and began to quietly pursue it down the street. Robin sat back down again, grinning broadly, and glanced at Viola who angrily and deliberately held up her cuffed hands.

"Just wait a moment." Robin responded, gesturing to her to put her hands down.

"No, you unbind us now," she barked.

"Hush up a moment, Pinkie."

Viola lowered her eyebrows threateningly. "Call me that again and I'll addle your brain so much with spells, your eyes will never uncross."

"And then where would we be?" This was becoming more fun for him by the minute.

"Back at the palace," Viola said.

"And that's where you really want to be, right?" He leaned in and rested his head on his hands. "I notice you haven't exactly been crying out for help since I started this escape attempt." He looked into her purple eyes with mocking curiosity. "You don't want a big song and dance made of this, do you?"

"We would *like* to be able to sneak back inside quietly if that's possible," Gwen admitted. He turned his attention to her as she continued. "We'll be in awful trouble otherwise. And if my father finds out she has been accompanying me outside the walls, Viola might lose her situation."

Robin nodded. "Well, we can't have that."

"What are you going to do?" Gwen asked.

"Let's go back to Plan A, shall we," Robin decided.

The duart looked first from Gwen, then to Robin and Oberon, then back to Gwen again and that strange, hungry look on the Princess' face. Viola inhaled sharply to scream.

"OFFICERS!"

Quick as lightning the akka leapt forwards and covered the bodyguard from head to foot in his knapsack. At this same moment, the wagon ground to a halt as the Hoods caught up with it and struck from the shadows. And there was much thumping. Then the back door opened and a lady of Punjabi descent, adorned in a Lincoln-green headscarf, was holding it. Robin stepped out gratefully and clapped hands with her.

"Latika, you are an absolute star, thank you."

"You okay there, Robb?" she asked, scanning the other inhabitants of the wagon with sharp, bright eyes. Oberon waved to her and placed his palms together in a gesture of gratitude.

"I'm fine," Robin said, "but I'll need you to bring those Watchmen to Scarlet, along with a message from me. Give them the old bag-on-head treatment, they have to be out of the way and in the dark for at least a week, and for God's sake don't let them find out where they are or we shall have to kill them, because this is quite a… provocative endeavour."

"Sounds complicated," Latika said thoughtfully. "We need to get you all away from this wagon."

"Absolutely," Robin agreed. "Do you know where we can get something a little more low-profile?"

***

Six minutes later they were passengers on a cartful of hay and agricultural supplies. Oberon had hopped up into the driver's position and raised his hood, placing his kicking knapsack down gently on the seat beside him.

Gwendoline and Robin lay huddled inside a trunk in the back of the cart.

"Where are you taking us?" Gwen demanded.

"Relax, we're not going to hurt you."

"*That* I'm not scared of, but you didn't answer my question," she said, an edge to her voice.

"Ever been to Britannica?"

"Yes," said the Princess, "on diplomatic trips."

"Well, we have a hideout there," Robin explained. "We're going to plan a ransom for you. And hopefully everything should go smoothly."

It was musty in the trunk and within its confines they had naturally adopted a spooning position. Gwen realised she was trembling at the thought of venturing out into new lands, but also that she had not been this close to a member of the opposite sex before whom she wasn't actively punching. Robin spoke softly to her and kept his hands to himself.

"May as well talk a little to pass the hours, get to know your abductor," he said.

"Have you been doing this long?" Gwen asked.

"What? Princess thievery? No, only about forty minutes."

"You surprise me. You're very professional."

"That's sarcasm, isn't it?" Robin noted. "You humans invented that."

"It's French."

"We have it too. Your Duart employee seemed pretty adept at it."

"She's my *friend*," Gwen corrected him.

"She said she was your bodyguard."

"Technically she's my jester."

"Does she make you laugh?"

"She makes me scream sometimes," Gwen replied with a smile.

"Yeah, but I've got a feeling you really care about her," he said. "You two are close, right?"

"She's... she's my only friend," admitted Gwen, haltingly.

"How's that? You're a comely girl. You must have had all sorts of opportunities to rub shoulders with the cream of the crop."

"Less than you'd think. I have difficulty finding like-minded people in my line of work."

"It's easy making friends," Robin said, airily. "You just remember things about people, their names, their likes and dislikes, you kind of... you mirror them. Don't force them to come to you. Be fun and assertive, but not controlling."

Gwen was quiet for a moment. "And you count all these acquaintances as your friends?"

"They know I would go out of my way to help them. That usually inspires *them* to feel the same."

"But do they *really* know you?" she asked. It was Robin's turn to be silent.

"Ahhh... the akka does. Maybe one or... yeah, one more."

Gwen sighed. "Well, your technique's sound," she conceded. "For somebody so annoying, you are rather approachable."

"I'll say the same about you."

"Not many would share your views. I *am* rather a handful."

There was another, slightly more nervous silence, which Robin eventually broke. "Ah… So tell me what it's like being a princess. I mean I've never taken that much interest in the royalty game myself beyond robbing the minor gentry. I know you're getting married this Sunday to-"

"Lord Aaron of Britannica," Gwen finished for him.

"Is he nice?"

"He's lovely."

"So you get hitched to him and become Queen of both realms. That means you need to get back for Sunday?"

"Mmmm."

"What's 'Mmmm'?" Robin asked. "Don't you *want* to marry him?"

"Of course I do. I just… well… I kind of needed a holiday first. Looks like one fell in my lap. I get to be a hostage in sunny Britannica."

"Yeah, kind of wish I could have taken you somewhere more pleasant."

"Where would you take me?"

"I hear France is nice."

"The sarcasm is *splendid* this time of year."

"We're getting off the point," Robin said. "You really are the last heir to Victoria?"

"She was my grandmother. Edward VII was my father. He was her eldest, married to Princess Alexandra of Denmark," Gwen qualified. She had recited all this family history so many times, it was reflexive.

"Was that your Mum, then?"

"No, actually, thank you for asking," Gwen said frankly. "Apparently sometime around 1865 he was carrying on with Lady Anne Hathaway. It was a few years after he married Alexandra, so naturally the scandal was hushed up."

"I'm shocked," he said, reassuringly. "But you know, I'm glad it happened, all the same. It means you're here."

"But of course," she continued. "In early '72 when the Barghest hit Europe and spread up here so awfully quickly, all the royals fled, except for little me... I got left behind. You know, I was seven years old and left in London. They never write, they never visit."

Robin pondered at this parentless childhood. "Seriously, are they still alive?"

"I don't know, some of them might be. Balmoral was attacked pretty heavily that year. As far as we know, I'm all that's left." She broke off, and then added with resignation, "You're all stuck with me."

"Is your mother still around?"

"No, she... OW!" Gwen screwed up her face as though prodded sharply with a needle. "She died."

"I'm sorry," Robin said sympathetically. He could not see her expression in the darkness of the trunk, but he felt her tense up. "Are you alright?"

"Yes, I'm fine," she sighed. "You Duart turned up not long after that, when the gateway opened, and I was rescued and raised by the Archduke of Buckingham."

"Oh... Coriolanus," Robin said, with a hint of reservation in his realization.

"Yes, the war hero," Gwen said pointedly. "This whole situation is going to make him furious. I don't fancy your chances."

"I know how to handle nobles. He'll be no different," said Robin, a little too confidently.

"You're handling me pretty well,"

Robin reached into his bag of smooth responses and pulled out a handful of nothing. "I…uh."

"Can I take off this coat, please?" she asked.

"What?"

"This coat. It's roasting under here and it smells of some kind of animal."

"It's sheep, I think," Robin replied. "And yeah, of course."

Then followed a lot of shoving and heaving as Gwen divested herself of her thick outer layer, resettling against Robin who now had to actively place his hands behind his back in order to maintain being a gentleman.

"Can you move your hair out of the way of my face, please?"

"Your moustache is tickling the back of my neck."

"Well… I suppose." He tried to move his head back a little.

"Here. I don't mind." Gwen pulled her hair forwards over her shoulder, so that most of it was tucked under her chin. Robin shifted position and ended up with his hands in front of him, the back of his fingers lightly touching Gwen's bare arm. She trembled slightly.

"Ahhh," Robin pulled away, politely. "Are my hands cold?"

"No."

"Do you mind if I rest them here?"

"No, please do."

"Thank you." He managed to shuffle his arms so that he was lying more comfortably, no longer at risk of cutting off the circulation.

"So how about you?" she asked him. "What's it like being a thousand years old?"

"You know I'm not the original Robin Hood."

"I suspected."

"I do alright, it's an important responsibility. The name, I mean. We rob from the rich and we really do give to the poor, me and Little John up there."

"Who *were* you?"

"What's that?"

"Before you started calling yourself Robin Hood and Little John," she pressed. "I mean. I assume you're Duart gentry; you certainly seem to speak as someone with an education."

"My father was a nobleman, yes."

"Who? I'd probably know of them."

Robin interrupted. "Shhh, we're approaching the gate."

Gwen smiled to herself. "You realise when we get to the gateway they're going to search the cart? Your Little John is going to be left completely exposed and they're going to take me and Viola back to the palace and execute the pair of you."

"Do you want that?"

"It's not about what I want. It's still going to happen."

"But do you *want* that?" he asked again.

Gwen thought for a moment. "…No," she conceded. "Okay, just don't scream when they start sniffing around."

The cart halted and there were voices. The guards were talking with the akka. Gwendoline could see through a crack in the trunk a sight she had beheld before. A billowing aperture that stretched above them many feet up and off to either side. They were sitting now at the gateway to another world. Gwen could hear the sound of rushing as the air from different atmospheres moved through and wind currents blended.

Right now, she could scream. No matter what Robin said, she had time before he clamped those strong hands over her mouth to cry out for help. Her eyes flicked back to him, his face faintly lit by the worlds outside. He had clever blue eyes framed by long, blond hair, a cavalier moustache and a pointed beard. He set that mouth of his to as serious manner as he was able, but that crooked, lopsided grin just kept pulling it out of line.

The lid of the trunk was thrown back and a craggy Duart face glared at them, his eyelids drooping a little. Robin and the Princess were only partially covered by Gwen's coat. Recognising familiar behaviour, she held the outlaw back as they looked up at this intruder. Neither of them breathed.

The guard sniffed and wrinkled his nose, before slamming the trunk. A few more muffled words outside, and their cart began to move again.

Robin gasped. "Holy jumping cats, he didn't see us!"

"Viola," Gwen whispered.

"Your friend? Was she working some kind of maajik from up there?"

"Yes, did you see his eyes? I'll bet you ten gold he thought he was looking at farming equipment. She must have used Befuddle."

"Ahhh."

"It's a variation of Confusion.

"Oh yeah, Confusion, right."

"Wow, this really isn't a well-known ability, is it?"

"No."

"She always told me to keep absolutely quiet on the matter. In fact, you're lucky to still be here, she's not very good at Befuddle."

"I'm more intrigued by the fact that she used it at all," Robin breathed. "Doesn't she want to get caught and taken back to the palace?"

Gwen shook her head. "No, it's like you said, she's very worried she'll be held accountable for this. It looks like you have an accomplice... at *least* one."

She smiled back at him and wriggled a little closer. Robin sighed quietly as he began to realise what an enormous catastrophe he had now set into motion.

Chapter 8: The Crone

Celador

The cart left one world and entered another, proceeding from the portal and up a wide, mostly empty road. Back in London, while some streets had been cobblestone, the majority were covered with granite slabs or wood. In the upmarket districts where Gwendoline had conducted her shopping, her carriage had rolled over jarrah, a hardwood originating in the Antipodean colonies. The area Scarlet operated in the Thirsty Hog Inn was laid with Swedish yellow deal, which tended to absorb horse piss like a sponge and squirt it back out over one's boots. On wet days, the sprayback and mud would make navigating the streets a stomach-churning endurance run.

However, as they passed into this new old world, the track they were on switched to a hardier mix of cement and flagstones. They had crisscrossed the land for a long age, and if every Duart and Akka were to remove themselves from Celador, and millennia were to elapse, the remnants of these roads would remain.

The travellers were now shrouded in a different kind of darkness, a different night sky overhead; one Viola was familiar with, having been born under it. In the light of their hanging lantern, fields of barley disappeared on either side, and beyond them, far off, could be seen pinpricks of orange as a few nearby villages kept vigil. It was past midnight now, and this was not a land where it was prudent to wander as the witching hour approached.

"Hey, tiny," Oberon said to the bag beside him. There was no response. "Hey…" Still nothing. "Hey, you grumpy, pampered little champagne macaroon!"

"What?" came Viola's muffled, indignant voice.

"Are you going to behave if I let you out?"

"Do I have a choice?"

"I guess you could start flinging that maajik crap around and attempt to take control of the situation, despite being way in over your head."

"It's not maajik crap, you oaf," she snarled. "What I weave is a series of spells so delicate and nuanced you couldn't possibly comprehend their complexity. When I work I'm performing mental surgery, you hammer-fisted bone-sack!"

Oberon snorted in response. "Okay, first of all, my hands are pretty dextrous, I'm a thief. That takes subtlety!" He dropped a light, leather object beside the sack. "Here's your hat when you want it back. Second of all, that wasn't supposed to sound derogatory, I was actually kind of impressed at how you handled that inspector. I thought I was going to have to tear him in two. You saved us an unpleasant confrontation… and I wanted to thank you."

"You're welcome… Greenskin."

Oberon clenched his thieving mitts in frustration. "You know what? Stay in the bag. I'm throwing your hat away now." There was a different noise coming from the bag, and Oberon gritted his teeth and set his gaze forward, trying his level best to ignore it.

At the point where the other vehicles wheeled around and turned south, joining the main thoroughfare back toward Londinium, this cart moved onto the road north, which had fewer carts still, and eventually turned off onto a dirt pathway which had none. Ahead, a vast, black shadow loomed into the starlight.

After a while Oberon muttered, "We're approaching Camelot Forest. I just thought you'd like to see it." Through an opening in the hide flap of the akka's bag the proud little duart watched as the trees drew nearer. Sure enough, the clouds had parted and the valley into which they had ridden was bathed in a pale glow. The forest was dense and tall, and as they passed the threshold and found themselves under its leaves, a sound not unlike an enormous breath was let out.

Viola trembled, her mind traveling through childhood stories. These had fascinated her brothers and sisters but only served to horrify Viola; tales of child-snatching demons and half-men who had given their souls to beasts. All of them resided in the dark bowers of the forests outside the safety and lamplights of the villages; all of those creatures that King Arthor had driven up to the Northlands so long ago. The stories told of their slow, creeping journey back down south to where the brightness drew them forth. It occurred to Viola that monsters need people, as a shadow cannot exist without a light.

Now the moon came in shafts and bolts, pushing through the gaps in the whispering trees as their cart made its way along the old paths. Viola tried not to scream and for one wild moment considered that the akka would protect her.

She dismissed this thought immediately. He would in fact present the greatest danger to she and her Princess. No, what was needed right now was a plan. Let these two thieves talk until it became apparent where their weaknesses lay and how she might return to Buckingham Palace, somehow not the treasonous witch who gravely endangered the future queen of two realms. She would have to actively *save* Gwendoline in order to survive this.

On went the cart, drawn by a brown and white Shire horse mare named Carrots. Carrots was none too pleased with their surroundings and kept her eyes down as she proceeded through the darkened woods, ignoring as best she could the sounds coming from all directions. They did not resemble animal calls of any kind she was used to, being born and raised in London. If anything, they sounded like voices from beings without mouths. Carrots pondered this contradiction, thankful of the lamp mounted on the cart behind her and trusting that should any of these mouthless beings turn up, the akka would protect her.

Within the trees ahead lay a craggy expanse, the monolithic edifice of an ancient fortress, now a half-unformed ruin of its former glory. As the cart and its passengers passed under the hanging portcullis the resignation of majesty to years of abandonment was palpable. Buckled pillars leaned this way and that like inebriated giants; torches dangled, devoid of purpose upon crumbling walls, their blackened heads long bereft of flame. There was an absence to the place, a sense that the air had been threaded with laughter and shouts of joy on countless occasions, now far beyond living memory.

But it was not a place of death. The forest had made its home here, now that the original occupants had departed. Ivy clutched at the stonework, the boughs of trees snaked through the openings to the world outside and every flagstone was framed with wild grass pushing through from beneath. The air hung with damp, woody odours and the sounds of the night birds and insects reminded all who were there to listen that life goes on in some form, whether we interfere or not.

Oberon stopped the cart and dismounted.

"Okay, we're here. You two get yourselves out." The trunk opened and Gwendoline and Robin emerged into the darkness.

"Where's Viola?" Gwen asked, looking around her.

"Still in the knapsack," Oberon replied. "She wasn't being very nice."

"Can you let her out, please?" Gwen asked. "If we wait for her to be nice we could be here rather a long time."

"Keep your voices down," Robin hushed, "we'll wake *her.*"

"We *want* to wake her," Oberon said pointedly.

"Viola's sleeping?" Gwen asked, confused.

"Not Viola," Robin said. "We've come to see someone who dwells within these walls. She's positively rancorous on the best of days, and we're going to ask for a favour so I want you all ten times nicer than pie."

Oberon unfastened his bag and turned it upside down, dropping the duart inside onto some moss. She glowered up at him but refused to speak.

A light flickered behind a window and the grumpy quartet could see more clearly that they now stood within the front courtyard, beside the gatehouse. A door, made of far newer wood than the decayed surroundings contained, opened up to reveal a tall old woman leaning on a gnarled staff and dressed in blue-grey, ragged robes that matched her peppery hair. She held up her lantern and glared at them.

"It's two in the flipping morning!" she bellowed, her rough voice clattering off the stonework. "What the bloody hell do you think you're playing at, Loxley?"

Robin was contrite. "Megan, I apologise for our appalling timing, I know we woke you and this can't be at all convenient."

"No, it's not," she snapped back, lowering her brow angrily. "I was having a luscious dream about a strapping farmhand with eyes like the sea after a storm asking me to help him shave and then you bunch of bastards come blundering into my house, and I am never going to see that fellow again!"

"We cannot apologise enough," Robin assured her. "Whatever we can do to make the place conducive for sleep as soon as possible we will. Just tell us where to go."

"I'll tell you where to go," the crone retorted. "The barn. Your beds of hay are unmade where you left them." She paused, catching sight of Viola and Gwendoline. "And who, may I ask, are these two?"

"Well, that's the reason we woke you, and why we're here," Robin began.

"On the run again?"

"Yes, you see…"

"Will you *please introduce* us, Loxley?"

Gwen stepped forwards and curtseyed. "I am Princess Gwendoline Amelia Gertrude Victoria of the house of Saxe-Coburg and Gotha," she said elegantly.

"Do you need all those names in case you lose one?" the old woman asked.

"It's so that the records can tell us apart from one another," Gwen explained. "My family were very keen on reusing first names. It's a pleasure to meet you, madam…?"

"I'm just Old Meg," she replied. "Nice to meet you too. Unfortunately, my house is not prepared for guests of such fanciness since nobody warned me you'd be coming…" She glanced pointedly at Robin. "But I've got a spare bed you can sleep on." She squinted at Gwen. "You look knackered."

"I am," Gwen nodded. "And thank you. Could my bodyguard sleep there too, please?"

"Why not?" Meg agreed, gesturing to them both. "Come inside, you two. Spit spot. You other two. Barn. Loxley, do you have a pocket watch?"

"Yes." He retrieved one from his coat and held it up.

"Good. Don't bother us for seven hours. The Princess needs to sleep." She bustled Gwen and Viola into the house and started to close the door behind them.

"Thank you again," Robin called. "Sleep well."

"Be off with you," she snapped back over her shoulder. "Stable your horse and don't mess with the other one."

"We won't," Oberon assured her.

Old Meg led Gwendoline and Viola into her home, the lantern throwing warm, orange light over stacks of old books as they passed. There were writing papers piled within leather folders, bottles of substances with labels in a strange language that neither of them recognised, and a fireplace in which embers were still glowing. She turned a corner and pointed to a doorway, leading into a small bedroom with a single bed which smelled of cats. Gwen thanked the old lady and obediently lay down with Viola who was still scowling. They were the oldest bedsheets the Princess had ever been wrapped in, and as the lantern was taken away and the door closed behind them, darkness enfolded the pair once more.

"Explain all this to me in the morning, I have a dream to recapture," Meg called out as she walked away.

"Viola…" Gwen whispered as the footsteps died away. "This is something of an adventure, wouldn't you say?"

"Goodnight, Princess," her protector said firmly.

Tuesday Morning (Five Days Left)

The morning light played across Gwendoline's eyelids and she awoke with an immense grin on her face to see Viola, arms folded, sat at the foot of the bed.

"What?"

"Sweet dreams?" Viola asked, one eyebrow raised.

"I… don't remember," Gwen lied.

"You were hugging me pretty tightly in your sleep," Viola informed her. "Gave the back of my neck rather a lot of attention too."

"Oh, I…" Gwen suddenly froze.

"*And* you were muttering names," Viola added sharply.

"It's probably just all the stress of the kidnap," Gwen said quickly.

Viola gave her a hard, warning stare. "*Stay away from him.*"

"I will… No, wait, hang on a moment, why?" Gwen was indignant. "He's actually kind of sweet when you talk to him. He's got this whole act he clings to, but…"

"I don't care," Viola interrupted. "He landed us in all of this. He's the one we have to overcome to get out of it. He's nothing but trouble."

Gwen looked at her companion carefully. "Are you… are you jealous, Vi?"

"Of that brigand? Not in the slightest."

"He has something neither of us have."

"A death warrant?"

"Freedom."

Viola snorted. "Hah! Oh, you're *serious*. Princess, he's days away from getting caught and executed."

"But he could go anywhere right now, and I… I want to go with him, Viola. I do. I think I *really* like him, and what he stands for."

Viola shook her head. "This is preposterous, you're just about to inherit everything."

"I don't want it. I don't want to be Empress of Europe and Britannica. I don't think I ever did." Gwendoline's head sparked with pain and she clutched at it. "Ow!"

"They're never going to stop looking for you," Viola said with utmost resolution. "It will have begun already. They will hunt us down, kill him and drag you home."

"And you…?" Gwen gasped. "Oh, Viola, what will they do to you?"

"I'll probably be executed along with him for collusion," the duart replied nonchalantly.

"I won't allow it," Gwen said firmly. Viola glared at her with icy reproach.

"Well, won't it be fun finding out if that makes any difference?"

"You're ruining this," Gwen said, her face falling, along with her shoulders.

"I'm ruining your kidnapping?" Viola's voice was an incredulous squeak.

Gwen shook her head. "My… my chance of a real life."

They stared at each other for a moment, then looked up as they heard Old Meg bark from the kitchen. "If you two are up already, I've got breakfast on!"

Gwen collected herself. "Bacon… Come on." The Princess stood and studied her companion. "Just, please give me a little time, as a favour," she pleaded. The duart sighed deeply, but would neither acquiesce to this, nor even look at her, as they went to breakfast.

***

Meanwhile in the barn, Oberon was feeding carrots to Carrots (*not literally, that would be hideous – THE NAG*) and trying to talk some sense into his companion.

"She's going to bring all of London down on our heads, Robb, she's nothing but trouble."

"Ahh, but she's so much more *fun* than you'd think a princess would be," Robin countered. "You should talk to her."

Oberon scowled. "This ain't about fun, you scobberlotcher. You're playing with fire, figuratively and literally – they'll have the whole army combing two countries."

"So I suppose…" said Robin in a distracted tone. "We just figure out how to get the ransom conveyed as quickly as possible, get the gold to Scarlet, get Gwendoline to the church on time and say goodbye?" He shrugged. "It's a sound plan. Everybody's happy."

"Consider sneaking her back *near* the palace and then just cheesing it," pressed Oberon. "We don't need attention like this. Far beyond just your life and mine, it could ruin our whole enterprise. Lot of people tied up in that. Lot of heads on the block."

Robin shook his head. "It's not as easy as that, old boy, we're already on the ropes. The Hoods, I mean; the factories. We need a lot of money very quickly and there's no way of getting it without making somebody very rich, very angry. I'd say with their assistance we may have… well, not the *perfect* crime, but one with fewer victims, more goodwill and a pretty sizable reward… for Scarlet, I mean."

"Speaking of which, we're jumping to Scarlet's tune, not to mention jumping for that crazy Albanian woman."

"I think jumping is what wrecked her ceiling."

"Now we're jumping for Old Meg. I'm sensing a pattern here." Oberon folded his arms.

"I *do* like strong women," Robin admitted.

"Yeah, but you're rolling over for them each time they raise their voice to you. It feels like you have no control over what's happening to us. It's all driven by their iron whims. And if *they* are your conscience, and your impulses are the deciding factor when one of them isn't around, Robb… who are *you* in all of this?"

"What would you have me do, dear John?" Robin asked in a strained voice.

"*Oberon!*"

"Barge in here in the dead of night," Robin continued, ignoring his mistake. "Take over the place? Set it up as our base of operations, do things the old-fashioned way and start barking out orders to our Merry Men? Depose Scarlet, trample everyone with a lick of sense that we're involved with to get what *I* want?"

"What *do* you want?" Oberon shouted in exasperation.

"I want…" Robin trailed off. "Bacon… smell that?" The akka gaped at him, and then shook his head.

"What time is it?"

"Nine," said Robin, checking the pocket watch. "Let's go." Oberon followed him, still amazed at how his very serious line of questioning had been so deftly cast aside in favour of fried pork rinds. This was, he assured himself, not at all over.

***

Around that same time the Archduke paced in a palace hall, the Captain of the Watchmen standing before him with grim intentions.

"Baltus," said Coriolanus, his tone insistent and agitated. "This is not a matter of discussion nor a call for subtlety or moderation. Gwendoline is either alive or she is dead. If she is alive then no matter her condition we may still pluck her from the jaws of calamity. If she is dead I want those responsible punished in ways that haunt the nightmares of all who learn of their fate." He turned, his expression resolved. "This is our binary course. You have five days to bring her back to us. Do whatever you believe is necessary."

"Yes, your Grace." Baltus saluted his commander with respect, and unflagging certainty that this hunt would reach a fruitful conclusion.

"Send in the female on your way out," ordered Coriolanus, his attention shifting away from the Captain

128

to a stack of reports upon a nearby table concerning his next visitor. Baltus' brow furrowed at this and he bowed curtly and stalked to the end of the hall.

As he opened the magnificent double-doors, before the words had left his lips, the human lady waiting in the reception chamber had moved past him, sashaying towards the Archduke, her boot heels clacking upon the marble floor. She was clad in a long, purple leather coat, under which various weapons and devices would usually have been stowed away in holsters. Right now, those were in the purvey of the palace guards at the entrance, but that did not make the woman who approached significantly less lethal. Her shining black hair hung in a pair of French braids which ran all the way up to the centre of her forehead, though this fact was obscured by an elegant bowler hat. She cut an imposing figure that was notably a foot taller than Baltus, and as he spoke she kept her golden eyes locked upon Coriolanus.

"Mortimer," Baltus spat contemptuously to her back. "The Archduke will see y…"

"Well, obviously," she said quickly, smoothly, and without a trace of respect. "Go join your little army and good hunting."

"Watch your tone, woman."

"You just wasted four seconds gawping at my rear," she called back without turning. "Toodle-pip."

"Hiring you is foolhardy and a waste of time," Baltus snarled. "I shall be the one who succeeds."

Mortimer finally glanced at him over her shoulder. "Of *course* you will. The Archduke has total faith in your extensive connections and abilities. That is, naturally, why I'm here."

"Why are you shouting in my chambers?" Coriolanus asked loudly from the other end of the hall.

"Greetings, your Archness," Mortimer said sweetly, Captain Baltus now invisible to her, as the doors closed.

"You will address me as your *Grace*," Coriolanus advised, still examining the papers closely. He glanced up at her. "And have a care with your words."

"A thousand pardons, your Gracefulness," she corrected herself.

The Archduke narrowed his eyes and glared. "I would like to remind you that I am currently undergoing the most upsetting day of maybe my entire life, and bear in mind I have led armies into wars. Couple that with the fact that I was also not blessed with an abundance of humour. It is only your track record that keeps you from being at the very best ejected from this palace in the next few moments." He pointed to the doors. "The very worst involves defenestration and is more of a… height modifier of the very best." He gestured in a direction some way above the doors, towards the upper floors of the palace. "Now speak quickly, time is a precious factor."

"Understood, your Grace," Mortimer replied, a smidgen more deferentially. "And while that ejection would be quite a bother for me, *you* don't want to have to spend today locating the second-greatest bounty hunter in London." She tilted her head. "I can tell you right now my services are worth the impropriety and indignity of conversing with me, besides which Second-

Best Smithson is unremittingly flatulent, due to his diet of chicken livers, so it's swings and roundabouts. *Some* part of you is going to feel assaulted meeting with either one of us, but I assure you that despite my abundance of character quirks that I am most dashedly professional about what I do, so what say we get to the point, Archibald?"

His reply was a growl. "What do you know already?"

"A missing princess, disappeared from her bedroom last night," said Mortimer, not deterred by his repressed fury. "No signs of forced entry, so it's presumed she has either run off of her own accord or been spirited away by persons unknown. Can you give me any good reason, other than that she's about to get married and become an almighty Empress, as to why she might run away?"

"Her mind is often addled," Coriolanus stated. "She has fits of temper and delusion. She may, in fact, not come quietly at all."

"Which is why you don't just want to send that flaming rhino out to get her," Mortimer observed.

"Correct. Baltus is a sledgehammer and will beat his way through two worlds until all is flattened," conceded Coriolanus. "That response serves more than one purpose for me. But for this I need a scalpel." He stepped back and sat upon his ornately carved, golden throne, tapping his gloved fingers against the arm. "Root out those who may have been involved. Use your connections, your underground networking to locate her and whomsoever she is with." He stopped and calculated. "I can offer you two thousand gold."

"Two thousand gold? Why, that's almost a king's ransom."

"I will add a bonus multiplier depending on the girl's state of mind," the archduke explained. "If she is horribly traumatised by the whole affair you get less. If she is ultimately relieved to return you get more. This is contingent on your methods and approach. Do you need weapons? Men?"

"Both, every single day," Mortimer admitted, "but I can acquire the ones I need without help."

"One more thing," the Archduke said, leaning over and speaking quietly. This information is for your ears only. Gwendoline will most likely be accompanied by her bodyguard, Viola Heartstone. She is a duart, and capable of some exceptionally strong Mind maajik. I discovered this, long after she had proved herself capable to her tasks. For better or worse, I decided to trust her to use these abilities to continue to protect the Princess, keeping this maajikal aberration a secret so as not to… unsettle the palace staff, the gentry, the people of England. I am now wondering whether I shall regret that course of action. Though Viola has proved dutiful and has helped my daughter immeasurably, she may have broken our bond of trust."

Mortimer pursed her lips thoughtfully as his brow furrowed. "She's a Mindmage, you say? So what if things get *very* difficult?"

"You are my contingency for Captain Baltus and his methods," he restated. "I have no contingency for you… So you must do what it takes to recover Gwendoline above all else. The conspirators who took her may be dealt with as you wish."

"The Princess and her bodyguard, are they friends?" Mortimer asked.

Coriolanus nodded. "She has none closer."

"Leverage, then," Mortimer concluded.

"For both of us," the Archduke agreed. "This shall be your last resort, though. And your intuition is sound. Gwendoline will most likely do anything to prevent harm to her companion. Listen to me carefully, if Viola has become treacherous and looks to harm Gwendoline or keep her from returning... *kill* her." He paused for a moment to impress the gravity of the situation on the bounty hunter. "Find my daughter, bring her back to me." The last word was spoken with an imploring inflection that any who knew him would find uncharacteristic. "Please."

Part 2: Camelot!

Chapter 9: The Stone and the Sword

Camelot!

Breakfast with Old Meg was a meaty affair, with eggs and three kinds of sausages to go with the bacon. Gwendoline, who had never eaten black pudding, found herself a new least-favourite food, but the rest she declared to be delicious. Old Meg attacked her own meal noisily and remained mostly silent. Viola would not speak to Oberon or to Robin, Oberon would not speak to Viola and both Robin and Gwendoline found themselves a little shy all of a sudden.

Gwendoline solved this awkward silence with periods of explaining to the room how different things were to her here. She had hoped this would put them at ease and perhaps get them talking. By the time the eggs were being mopped up with the last of the crusty bread she had trailed off and just allowed everybody to chew in peace.

Now full and slightly less anxious Gwen inclined in her seat. She had been regarding Old Meg's kitchen, and through doorways, the rest of the home this woman had made here. Certain artefacts had caught her attention including a globe, a telescope and roosting on a perch in one corner, a particularly grumpy-looking owl. Old Meg watched the Princess lick the grease daintily from her fingertips as her eyes roved around the house.

"Do you know where you are, girl?"

The Princess rose from the breakfast table, crossed to the front door and opened it to take in the morning sun falling upon the ruins that surrounded them. Little bolts of lightning danced up Gwendoline's spine as she stood silhouetted in the doorway and found the words.

"Camelot!"

"Yes."

Gwen turned at this confirmation, to find that the entire table was looking at her expectantly. Her breathing quickened. Her cheeks flushed. She was on the brink of tears, though she could not pin down the prevailing cause.

"Viola told me about the Duart version of the Camelot legend after she read me *The Idylls of the King…* by Tennyson," she began, by way of explanation.

"I do like the way he tells it," Meg remarked. "Though his take on femininity leaves a lot to be desired."

"But if we're in Camelot right now," Gwen continued, "and if what Viola told me was actually true, then that means… the sword is here."

Meg nodded slowly. "Quite so." Robin glanced at her with a strange expression that Gwen could not place. In a flash it was gone and his breezier demeanour returned.

"May I see it? Please," Gwen asked with trembling enthusiasm. Meg smiled dryly.

"Course you can, luv. It's the first thing most people go to."

"Lead the way."

Old Meg sighed and hefted her staff, stalking through the front door with the rest following her out among the crumbling stonework. Robin moved to the front and turned to the group, nimbly walking backwards as he spoke.

"You see, *your* King Arthur was an ancient, Roman-era tribal leader who, while charismatic, seasoned in battle and a born leader, was sadly far less maajikal in real life than Tennyson, Sir Thomas Mallory and that fellow Geoffrey of Monmouth built him up to be." He hopped over a portion of collapsed wall without looking. "You see, it all came down to the *sword* he was bestowed. In your world it was a length of metal with a pointy end used to martial the tribes to his aid in defeating the Saxons. Your scribes and poets speak with reverence of Excalibur, and its symbolic nature was romanticised and made all the more epic in the retelling." His face darkened as he layered on more import. "But like Beowulf before him, Arthur was ultimately just a man holding a well-crafted steel sword. Throughout time, across worlds, swords of significance have emerged and become legends, along with those who wielded them, but the one in Celador… the one we approach right now… was never really *only* a sword…"

And as he said this they emerged into a quiet courtyard, into which shafts of sunlight shone through the thick canopy of a glade of trees, arrayed within its stone walls. The air hung with tiny, glowing, orange motes of dust and before them, not twenty yards away, up at the top of a flight of steps with a sunbeam drenching it, stood The Sword. It was wound with ivy, its blade dull and corroded, its handle faded gold. At the base of the blade, just above the hilt, a blackened sphere was inset. Below these were symbols not unlike hieroglyphics. It was, just as Gwen had been told as a child, firmly driven into a stone tablet, the side of which was engraved with more words in that same unfamiliar language.

Robin continued. "What stands before you is the *Archenblade*." He pronounced the first syllable to rhyme with "march". Old Meg shook her head.

"Ark-en-blade," she corrected.

"Sorry. Do you see that orb below the hilt?"

"Yes," Gwen nodded.

"That made this artefact so much more," said Robin, reverently. "When he held it, King Arthor was a demi-god, capable of astonishing feats of strength and endurance. Since his passing the sword has waited, entombed in stone, many long years for the return of someone suitable enough to be its bearer."

"Meg," asked Gwendoline. "What would happen if, say, I walked up now and tried to pull it out?"

The old woman shrugged. "Go ahead."

Gwen did not move. "Viola told me that many have tried already," she said, warily.

"Countless," Meg confirmed.

"Arthor left no heirs," Robin said, his voice flat now. "That royal bloodline ended with him."

"What's binding the sword in place?" asked Gwen. "Do you have to be a rightful king... or a queen?"

"I guess we could have a debate about what the word 'rightful' means here," muttered Oberon. Viola glared at him, sharply.

"Hmmm," Meg stroked at her chin and looked at Gwen. "Can you read the writing etched in the stone at the base?"

"No."

"That's a shame," said Meg, "I was hoping you could tell me what it says." Viola climbed the steps and squinted at the wording before shaking her head.

"Akka?" she asked, turning to Oberon, who shrugged.

"I already know I can't read that." His tone was indifferent and he ignored the glower of triumph in the duart's eye.

"Well, should I give it a try anyway?" Gwen asked, of nobody in particular. "I mean, it can't hurt… it didn't hurt the others who tried, did it?"

"I heard some of them broke their arms pulling too hard," Viola remarked, "but no, there aren't any curses, as far as I know."

Gwendoline glanced at her companions and gingerly climbed the steps to stand behind the sword. She flexed her fingers and reached out her hand grasping the hilt.

In a breath-taking flash…

Absolutely bugger-all happened.

Gwen grunted a few times and pulled until her arm hurt before angrily giving up.

"Oh sod it!" she cried in frustration. "I thought that would work."

"Maybe if you come back when you're a queen?" Oberon suggested, brightly.

"I don't see why that would make any difference," Robin frowned. "All the legends say Arthor was just a stable boy when he pulled the sword out. It *knows* if you're the right, worthy person."

"You think it's to do with value?" Gwen exclaimed. "I'm being judged by a sword!"

"For what it's worth, Gwendoline," said Robin, steadily. "I believed you could draw it out."

"Thank you," she replied gratefully. "No good though, it was like trying to pull the head off a statue. It feels like the sword is part of the stone now."

"I believe in you too," Viola added.

"Do you want to try it, Viola?" Gwen offered, stepping aside. "I mean, Arthor was a duart. Maybe *you're* supposed to be here… maybe this story is about you."

"I don't think it is," her bodyguard said, quietly.

"From what I hear you're about to become a queen anyway." Old Meg had been watching the struggle and subsequent deliberation, and now stepped forward, her grey-blue eyes piercing through the layers of defeat and doubt. "An empress, no less, with no requirement for a demi-god blade. That's a great deal of responsibility, Gwendoline." She drew herself up the steps and gestured around the chamber with her staff. "The worst people who came here trying to pull it out all had at least one thing in common. I've seen them come and go, and most of them were not happy with the immense power they already had and came looking for more. They always get the angriest when they fail." She stepped between the group, studying each of them in turn. "Apparently, the world owes them success. That fallen tree there was hacked down in a pique of frustration by a chap named Edgar of Glendale… He's dead now."

"And the best of them?" Gwen asked. Meg seemed far away for a moment, but then responded.

"Oh, the best of them come looking only to protect those weaker than they. It breaks my heart to see the looks of hope in their eyes, to hold my breath along with them and believe, just for a moment, that they will be the one who can solve the riddle of the sword." She was now standing beside the blade itself and gingerly reached out a finger to press against its cold pommel. "When they fail… as everyone does… it hits them far harder than that first lot I told you about. The self-entitled lash out at a world that won't give them everything their little hearts desire. The selfless have nowhere to look but within, nobody to blame but themselves." She withdrew her finger and shook herself a little, tracing her way carefully back down the steps to stand by the archway that led out.

Gwen glanced down to Robin at the foot of the steps. That look on his face she had not been able to place earlier might just have been a potent blend of envy and admiration. In fact, it was one she had received from many people throughout her life, though she had been too focused on her own business to notice, and besides, there was more in Robin's expression that she couldn't place. It was clear to the Princess that this young duart once stood where she had just now.

That new and unusual squeeze on her heart grew tighter as she looked at him.

Tuesday Afternoon

In the afternoon sun things had become somewhat more tense. Robin was laying out elaborate plans to Oberon to convey their ransom demands for the Princess and fifteen hundred gold through a dozen proxies, the difficulty being the time that would take.

Gwendoline sat lazily in the sunshine reading one of Old Meg's books. Viola was perched nearby, eying her in a worried fashion. Every glance the Princess stole at Robin across the pages made her small companion fume. Robin had noticed and, at around three o'clock, sauntered over.

"Okay, we've worked out the most balanced way to get the ransom through," he told Gwen. "It's a compromise of safety and speed, we don't want to sacrifice too much of one for the other. But it's looking like we can get you home on Thursday afternoon. Do you… do you mind waiting that long?"

"No," Gwen said, magnanimously.

"Yes," Viola interrupted. "She minds, the Princess minds greatly. What a question!"

"No, Viola," Gwen interjected. "I *don't* mind spending some time here. Only… do you think we might explore a little more of Celador than just these ruins?"

"Absolutely not," Viola said firmly. "There's roaming gangs all over, and Akka. This is where the worst of them still live, you know. The kind that weren't even civil enough for London."

"I am right *here*," Oberon pointed out.

Viola rolled her eyes. "Oh yes… there *you* are."

"Your friend really is…" Robin said to Gwen. "Well, I was going to say 'extraordinary', but I'm going to go with 'extraordinarily unpleasant to spend time with'."

"She's normally fine with me, I assure you all," Gwen said, attempting to smooth things over. "Look, Viola, see reason here…"

"*Reason*?" Viola protested.

"With Oberon with us I don't think we have that much to fear," Gwen offered.

"We have *plenty* to fear!"

Oberon stood up, shaking with frustration, and finally weighed in on the subject. "Do you want to know the great crime the Akka committed which made the Duart hate us so much?" he asked the room. "Why they're so afraid? Anybody? Anybody want to be *filled in* on why we're such a bunch of untrustworthy thugs?" He looked around at his small audience. "We saved… *every single one* of your lives!"

Viola folded her arms. "Oh, yes, here it comes."

"Yeah, here it comes, do you know this story, Princess?"

Gwen shook her head. "Not the *exact* story you're about to tell, I'll warrant."

"Figures," Oberon retorted. "Your nanny wouldn't be too keen to give you an *accurate* history lesson. Those Drakes that Arthor was so good at holding at bay when he was alive, about thirty years ago they came back. Started ravaging the Southlands." He gestured wildly. "This whole countryside here was a Drake playground, they cooked and ate whatever and whoever they wanted. And what did *you* have? Huh? What amazing maajik did *your people* have to call upon for your defence?" Viola said nothing, so Gwen replied for her.

"Fire."

"Absolutely right, *fire*. Against a flying lizard with a gut full of it and unburnable skin. The Duart were absolutely screwed." He drew himself up, grimly and planted a finger on his chest. "So then *we* came along, the Akka, through a portal much like the one we came through early this morning. We were fleeing Hannoth, our own realm, and we brought with us a different maajik… *Ice*." There was a gleam in his eye now. A fierce pride. "Our shamans, who had harnessed icecasting, were all recruited by you, by your dukes, to head up your armies and drive the Drakes back to the Northlands."

"But you didn't take the trouble to *kill* them, did you?" Viola snapped, her eyes narrowed.

"No, you insensitive little shit," Oberon replied. "We didn't manage to kill *many* of them because it's goddamn hard to kill a drake!" His tone changed as his mind ran over this confluence of events. Now his rage was threaded with regret. "And that being the case, many of our shamans lost their lives in pushing them back."

"We were dying too." Viola interjected.

"But *we didn't have to*," said Oberon. "We could have just left you guys to burn. Moved across the green sea. We fought and died to protect you."

"Only in exchange for land." Viola turned to the Princess. "Don't let him play the hero here, Gwendoline. His people were *mercenaries*, plain and simple, and after we finished the fight they weren't happy with their pay

145

and they've been nipping at our heels ever since, trying to take more."

"We were promised *fertile ground*, somewhere secluded and with room to grow again. We were promised a future. They gave us marshland and waste ground. They gave us slums in Londinium. You promised us life but delivered purgatory."

Viola got to her feet. "Alright, I've heard enough of this slander. Come on, Princess, we're leaving."

"What?" Gwen said, startled.

"Wait," said Robin.

"Yes, wait," repeated Gwen.

"No." Viola shook her head firmly. "I've played along with this out of fear and tried to convince myself I was doing right by you, Gwen, but this ends now. I'm taking you home. We'll have to walk it and for that I'm sorry."

"You're not going anywhere," growled Oberon.

Viola clenched her fists. "Don't test me, you have no idea what I can do to your minds."

"May I suggest a compromise?" Old Meg put in.

"Gwen, please listen," Robin beseeched.

"Viola, darling."

"Shut up, all of you," Viola replied. "Gwen, you have one more chance before I have to drag your complicit body away by force." She turned to Oberon, and her voice became still more venomous. "Stand aside, akka."

"Oh no, you don't," said Robin, who had sidestepped into position behind Viola while she was shouting at Oberon. He managed to get one hand over her mouth, and her muffled shouts emerged from behind his fingers.

"Let go of her!" Gwen cried, reaching for Robin, who pulled Viola away.

"I beg both your pardons but I daren't," Robin said, then added to Viola, "It seems like you need your hands free and mouth uncovered to cast your maajik, and you were about to do something that was going to leave everyone unhappy."

Oberon moved across to Robin. "Alright, now what do we do?"

"I hadn't thought that far ahead."

"Bag?"

"Bag. It may be unoriginal, but it's effective."

As Oberon opened and lowered the bag over her, Viola went limp, and then sprang into action, jamming her foot down on Robin's calf and biting his fingers. The split second he drew his hand back instinctually was all she needed. They were on the ground with the bag to one side. Oberon had grabbed at her, but she cried out and directed her fingertips.

"SLEEP!" she snarled.

"Viola!" Gwen shouted, but it was too late. The scent of lavender filled everyone's nostrils and Robin and Oberon lay in a daze on the ground, not completely unconscious but very much bewildered. Viola charged forward and away from them, gripping Gwendoline's hand in her own, which was still emanating blue smoke trails. The outlaws began picking themselves up and staggering after the two women. Old Meg hung back, far enough away to be unaffected by the spell detonation, shaking her head and tutting.

"Viola, stop! Stop at once I say!" Gwen called, sleepily.

"CONFUSE!" shouted Viola. Gwen cried out in fright, then groaned as she tasted an unsettling combination of creamy milk and strong black pepper. The spell had hit its mark in the centre of her forehead and, reeling with blue and red lights invading her vision, the Princess stumbled drunkenly after her frantic companion. They rounded a corner and found more eroded hallways to traverse. Close behind, Oberon was gaining on them.

"BLIND!" Viola yelled, launching a black, inky wave in his direction.

Oberon careered unceremoniously into a ditch, wailing as he fell, and choking on the overwhelming taste of boot polish. Robin skidded after them, scrabbling across the overgrown paving and blinking back the remnants of Sleep to focus.

"Please wait, it's not safe in the forest!" he called after them, truthfully.

"It's not safe anywhere in this cursed land. SILENCE! CONFUSE!" Viola shouted.

Robin dodged the Silence spell and grinned, realising that there was a certain physics to these. They could be avoided. The Confuse hit him square in the chest just as Gwen was returning his dopey grin. His eyes crossed and he doubled over, moaning, uncertain as to what his name was or why he was now face down in the dirt.

"Come… on… Princess…" Viola sounded distinctly weak now.

Gwen was laughing deliriously. "Hahahaha… Viiillla… Y've x'austed y'self."

As the pair of them passed under the portcullis Viola found herself pushing against an invisible wall. She dived this way and that, battering her little body against empty space as Gwen sat on the ground, but it was no use. Around them they could make out a shimmering bubble. The duart slumped down, panting. Gwendoline smiled lopsidedly and pointed to the little pouch on her friend's belt.

"You… need… barley… sugar…" Gwen said brokenly.

Viola nodded glumly and fished a sweetie out of her pouch, popping it in her mouth and offering one to Gwen, patting her hand as it was accepted.

"I'm not giving up… on this…" she panted. "I just… need to rest… and eat… then you and I are absolutely walking out of here."

As Gwendoline lay on her tummy and gazed down to the dark moat below the drawbridge, Robin, Oberon and Old Meg drew up, the former pair rubbing their eyes.

"Please…" said Robin, "For the love of Jumping Jehoshaphat, can you not do that again?" He propped himself against a wall with one hand and tried to regulate his breathing. "I am currently… sick as a dog and Oberon can barely see."

Gwen's reply was slurred, but giggly. "You get why she's my bodyguard now?"

Chapter 10: Nagging Doubts

Tuesday Evening

At six bells Mortimer strode into the Mad Bull inn. She tossed down several coins and said, with cheer, "A pint of your least uriney beer please, good sir."

"Right you are, Mortimer," the hairy bartender, Morris, nodded. A pungent fellow sidled over and leered into Mortimer's cleavage.

"Alright, darling," he slurred.

"Bloody hell, one second, that might be a new record," she muttered.

"I'd best leave her alone if I were you, Garlic," Morris advised.

"What do I get for ten copper?" Garlic persisted.

"A smack in the face," she replied smartly, "and the arduous task of removing ten copper coins from your own anus." This drew a ripple of raucous laughter from the patrons around them.

"Alright, calm down, you mouthy slattern," Garlic snapped, his ego somewhat dented.

"Also, barkeep," Mortimer said, leaning forward and planting a finger on the bar. "Can you tell Stoat to get his donkey-buggering, penny-farthing-seat-sniffing carcass down here, tout de suite. Use those exact words."

"He's not going to like me saying that," Morris replied.

"He'll know who sent you," she told him. "I promise he won't hit you any harder than I will if you don't move *exceptionally* fast."

Garlic snorted. "She's a brave little snatch, isn't she?"

There was a sudden snapping sound, accompanied by a sharp, male scream, and Garlic disappeared from view below the bar. Mortimer sipped her beer with her free hand and twirled a strange device in the other.

"Be thankful I left you the other testicle," she said, without looking at the man on the floor. "Stoat, please," she repeated to Morris.

The bartender blinked, picking over the previous occasions when Mortimer had visited, and how much grislier her actions were becoming. He shook himself out of this trance and nodded dutifully. "Right away ma'am."

Shortly thereafter, Garlic now carted away, Mortimer's beer standing partially sipped as she cleaned her gelding gun, Stoat emerged from the basement. He wore a scruffy trilby and an oily demeanour.

"Mortimer, as I live and breathe." Stoat held out his hand, which she firmly ignored.

"Stoat, as I live and try *not* to breathe in here. It's mostly farts."

"You charmer," said Stoat. "I especially like how you maimed a bloke for mouthing off at you. Luckily he already has children."

"This is me breathing a sigh of relief," Mortimer replied. "Oh, I wish I hadn't done that. I have to breathe in again now."

"What do you want?" Stoat asked.

151

"I've been gathering information all day about this missing princess. I've traded banter with all manner of dandiprats, munz-watchers, mutton-shunters and windy-wallets. Figured I'd come and find out what the Knives have got."

"You were trying to find out if we'd done it," Stoat said.

"How perceptive of you."

"I've heard the reward is a thousand gold."

"Just between us…" Mortimer glanced around and lowered her voice. "I've been offered twelve hundred. That's why I'm trying to keep this one quiet."

"What have you got already?"

"You first," she insisted.

"Oh, for God's sake," Stoat sighed, rolling his eyes skyward. "I ain't got time for this. The Watch have already been here looking in our basement and every cupboard for this kidnapped bint. Things got pretty hairy, but all we told 'em is what we knew. It was probably the Knives or the Hoods wot done it. And between you and I, since I know it wasn't the Knives, that leaves one organisation worth investigating."

"The Hoods wouldn't be stupid enough to keep her in London. Too many eyes and ears," Mortimer muttered, shrewdly.

"So they moved her north or south or they went through the door."

"I heard a rumour today that one of their old hideouts was in Camelot Forest. Worth a look?" Mortimer asked.

Stoat was silent for a moment as he considered her proposal. "Alright, we'll do it. Now let's talk numbers before we go. I can get fifteen boys inside of an hour."

Mortimer frowned, thinking. "Much more than that and we'll attract attention from the Watch. I'd still say go through in three groups."

"You want me and fifteen men, we get eight-hundred of that twelve."

"Four hundred," she countered. "If anyone's pulling this off it's me. I can go on my own."

"Seven hundred. You don't know how many Hoods are in the forest."

"Five hundred. I can handle them."

"Plus fifteen of us on your tail," Stoat pointed out with an evil grin, "because we're going now, whether you like it or not."

Mortimer raised an eyebrow at him. "Six hundred."

"Deal." He spat on his hand and held it out. She shook it distastefully. What Stoat knew was that he and his gang would have deliberately struck at the heart of the Hoods for absolutely no reward. What Mortimer knew was that she would have gone as high as eight hundred before killing Stoat on the spot.

***

Back at Camelot, the little band sat around Meg's table while Oberon sullenly doled out bowlfuls of something brown and steaming.

"Here," he said, putting a portion down in front of Viola. "It's a stew."

"I'm not hungry."

"Then by all means, don't eat it."

"Oberon, there's something I need to know," Gwen asked. "I think it will help me understand your people a little better, and I'd like to."

"Why our skin is green?" he asked bitterly.

"No…" Gwen frowned. "Why did you leave Hannoth? Really."

Oberon looked at her for a moment before answering. "You know what mindshadow is?"

"I know it afflicted your race, once. Believe it or not Viola has not been my *only* source of information growing up. I've had a lot of Duart history fed to me over the years by my tutors… and my father, only…"

"Only *now* you're not sure how much of it is true," Oberon chimed in.

"It's more the half-truths I'm worried about," confessed Gwen.

"Mindshadow is contagious," Oberon said.

"Right," Gwen nodded.

"Wrong." He shook his head. "It's hereditary. Passed down through families."

"What a surprise," Viola put in. "Brutality runs in the…"

"Viola, shut up!" Gwen was now scowling at her companion, who actually appeared visibly shaken by this reproach. Oberon continued.

"She's right. In a manner of speaking. Not a lot of Akka made it out of Hannoth. It was an exodus. Those who wanted to make the journey to Celador and who didn't have this… this defect."

154

"And those that you had to leave behind?" Gwen asked, sympathetically.

Oberon lowered his head, pursing his lips. "They weren't the people we wanted to be," he said, in a low voice. "Their hearts and minds had… gone. They had lost what it meant to be Akka. All they did was survive and fight." He sat back and rubbed his tired eyes. "I don't even know if that world has a population any more, certainly not one capable of thinking for itself. They may simply be *animals* now."

"Like the Barghest," Gwen realised. "Oh, that's frightful. How do you know if an akka is born with this?"

"You don't," Oberon admitted. "My brother, Ajax, was one of the smartest kids I've ever known." A fondness entered his voice. "He was so quick, so creative. He was… he *is* an artist."

"Your brother…" The akka's shoulders drooped. Gwen wondered whether it would be proper to lean across the table and lay her hand upon his. "Oh, Oberon."

"It started when he was about seventeen years old," the akka continued. "He had these dark flashes where he would lose himself and forget where he was. Good days, I would tease him about it, but the bad nights…" Oberon lightly touched a faint, ragged scar beside his right eye. "That was many years ago. I look after him now… in fact, Robin, I'm going to need to come with you when you go back, I haven't checked up on him since Monday."

155

"You're a good man…" said Gwen, immediately aware that her words weren't doing the conversation justice. "A good akka – to stick beside him."

"Yeah, he's a lucky guy…" Oberon said, then looked at Viola. "Savage brutes as they were, I don't like that we left our afflicted behind. We were in very real danger of being wiped out, but it always felt like giving up to me. I don't do that. It looks like we have something in common after all, purple-eyes."

"Viola…" said Gwen with a warning in her voice. "The nice akka is speaking to you." The Fool shut her eyes so that she didn't have to catch the glances of the others in the room.

"I… wasn't aware of some of those things. I don't know what to say."

"Best not say anything then," Robin retorted icily. "Don't eat, don't speak, just be judgemental and sulk."

"Robin!" Gwen exclaimed. He had been silent so far and this sudden, acidic reaction unsettled her.

"It's right in front of your goddamn eyes, you pampered clown," he continued scathingly to Viola. "How can you stubbornly hold onto these beliefs?" He put his hand on Oberon's shoulder. "The greatest lie ever told by our people is that theirs are *beneath* us." Now his eyes had narrowed as he leaned in for the kill. "It's comforting not to think of what a bunch of greedy, duplicitous cheats we've been!"

Viola glared at him and sat back, folding her arms. "This, coming from a thief."

Robin shook his head, radiating self-righteousness. "I take back from those who won't give fairly of their own accord. I'm looking out for the people at the bottom who have *less* than nothing. If nobody pushes back, then that boot will just keep pressing down."

"Can you smell burning martyr?" Viola sneered. "You must sleep soundly at night knowing what a bloody hero you are."

"I sleep *phenomenally* well," Robin spat and turned back to Gwen. "Now if you'll excuse me, I have to go and arrange to have your worthless arses handed back to your despotic tyrant of a pretend father!"

"'Worthless… pretend'?" Gwen repeated, slowly, genuine hurt in her voice. There was a long silence as Robin picked over what had been said by all, and more specifically, how.

"I… Gwendoline, I just…I meant…"

"No, that's fine," she interrupted, raising to her feet and speaking with a measured, if tremulous, dignity. "You're right. Go do what you have to and we'll be out of your hair forever in a few hours." She turned her back and walked to the door. "You can carry on being a hero." And then she was gone.

Robin screwed up his face, bounced his forehead off the mahogany surface and departed himself, stalking into Meg's study, to find a book, a distraction, anything. Oberon sat with his head in his hands and Viola blinked, dumbstruck. The silence was eventually broken by the pink and purple duart picking up her spoon and attacking the stew Oberon had made, guzzling down every morsel. She felt him glance at her but chose not to comment.

Gwendoline sat on the cold, mossy stone, with her back to the well, sobbing her heart out. Eventually she became aware that Old Meg was standing to one side. A folded handkerchief had been extended in Gwen's direction. She took it and blew her nose.

"Would you like to see an interesting horse before you go?" Meg asked.

Gwen laughed through the tears. "Yes."

"Then follow me."

Holding up her lantern, the crone led the young would-be-adventurer through the streets and passageways of Camelot, passing by darkened, sealed rooms, locked gates and some hidden things that were so secret even the sage was unaware of them. Eventually they reached what remained of the ancient banquet hall. Meg rapped on the flagstones three times with her staff and, sure enough, from the shadows emerged a horse.

Gwendoline had expected a fine thoroughbred stallion, or one clad in full armour to match the surroundings. Instead what loped towards her was an ordinary and exceedingly scruffy black thing. It had an arrogant look in its eye and was swatting lazily at imaginary flies on its mottled backside with an ungroomed tail.

"Oh... aren't you... a handsome thing?" Gwen said diplomatically.

"Piss off," the horse grumbled.

"Oh!" Gwen sputtered.

It ignored her reaction and continued. "I know when I'm being patronised. Meg, don't waste my time again this week."

158

"This is a Princess of England," the old woman told him. "Could you be *nice*, just this once?"

"Nope." The horse shook its head with a snort.

"It talks," Gwen exclaimed.

"Yes," Meg sighed. "If you succeed in convincing him to stop, tell me how."

"Would you..." Gwen addressed the animal hesitantly. "Mr Horse... I mean..." She was pummelling her brain for how to handle this meeting, but no measure of her equestrian training had included tactful conversation.

"Give him this," Old Meg suggested.

Gwen took the offering and turned back to the beast. "Thank you, Megan. Mister Horse, would you like this apple?"

"Red apples given to princesses by strange old ladies? No, I bloody wouldn't," he replied. "Do you have a sandwich?"

"I... I can fetch you some stew," Gwen replied.

"*Yummy.*"

"You really are quite a deceptively remarkable animal, Sir...?"

"Just call him 'The Nag'," Meg advised.

"Sir Nag," Gwen finished, with a small curtsey.

"That's going to stick," the horse sighed.

"*Black Beauty* was one of my very favourite books growing up, and if you don't mind my saying so, Meg, it doesn't seem like you take care of The Nag anywhere nearly as diligently as a beast of his intelligence deserves," Gwen gushed.

The Nag tossed his head. "*So* many backhanded compliments in there I don't know where to start."

"I have *tried*, time and again, haven't I?" Meg told her. "Be honest, Nag."

"She has," he admitted.

"He won't be brushed or groomed or ridden or have those rusty shoes replaced," continued Meg.

"Why ever not?" Gwen asked.

"I don't like being fussed over and I can take care of myself."

"Except when it comes to sandwich-making," Gwen noted.

"Except that."

"So how did you come to learn to talk?"

"Well… it's really a very remarkable story," the horse began. "You see, at an early age I was bitten by a radioactive linguist…"

"Nag!" Old Meg interrupted.

He snorted. "I'm just a talking horse, alright? That's about the most information you're going to get right now, you nosy porker."

Gwen was amused, although slightly offended by the porker comment. "Well, I… I like you, The Nag. And you've cheered me up."

"Then I've done my job," he said, baring his teeth slightly in what could have been an attempt at a smile but seemed slightly threatening on a horse. Then he shook his head and closed his eyes imperiously. "Away with you. I recall promises of stew."

"Yes, sir," Gwen nodded, pleased at the prospect of a miniature quest to divert her from the sombre path she had been on moments ago.

Gwen turned about and began to pace back towards the little house, with her wizened guide in tow.

"Do you know, Meg," she said thoughtfully. "For the briefest moment earlier today, I really did feel like I could have pulled that sword out."

"Did it fit snugly in your hand?"

"It did."

"It does for everyone," said Meg. "Everybody thinks they're special, deep down. Like they were *meant* to do something profound in a troubled world, and then this shaft of destiny is placed before them and they tell themselves, *'This is what I am meant to do.'* And then… when it doesn't happen… well, that's when things get *really* interesting." She smiled gently at Gwen. Her accent had softened. The rough, Cockney edges had become quite precise and eloquent. "Having power bestowed is a revealing process. It shows who you are. But even more than that, having power denied – being thwarted, frustrated, turned down and defeated by chance, by strangers, by enemies… by friends. When the chips are down and you lose resoundingly and repeatedly, *that* is when a person's true character comes to the fore."

Gwen looked around at the faded grandeur of their surroundings. "Did King Arthor fail?"

Old Meg nodded. "Of course he did. He and those around him were unable to make his dreams of peace a lasting reality. They were, after all, only human… well, I mean they were Duart, but it's an apt phrase."

161

"How did he die?" Gwen asked her. "I mean, really. Whenever I'd ask for specifics they would always move onto heraldry and the importance of the bloodlines that were severed at that point." Meg breathed deeply and closed her eyes.

"His final act after driving the Drakes northward was to confront his brother Morgan, a frighteningly powerful necromancer who had brought forth the beasts into Celador in the first place. It was Arthor's wizard…"

"Merlin," Gwen piped up.

"*Merlene*," the old woman continued, "who used that same cross-dimensional maajik to bring the Akka into our realm, to act as allies in exchange for a new home, much as Oberon said. She thought… she *hoped* she could heal two worlds… She was wrong." Meg paused for a moment, opening her eyes. "And when Arthor fought Morgan, the brothers mortally wounded one another. The necromancer had been stopped, the portals closed, but at a price. We lost our king."

They had halted beside a great, columned archway and she now gestured through into the moonlit courtyard beyond. On a raised marble casket lay the carved figure of a Duart monarch, sleeping with his stone sword. Gwen sat down on the steps beside the tomb, drinking in this haunting sight.

"Arthor was brought back here," Meg said, quietly. "And here he lies, awaiting the day he is needed once more."

"Can he…? I mean will he *actually* rise from that grave?" Gwen asked, uncertainly.

The old woman rolled her eyes. "It's a *metaphor*, girl. Whoever pulls that sword has got to be worthy of the responsibilities he held. Flawed and proud and occasionally foolish as Arthor was, he was... my friend." She trailed off, but this was the last confirmation that Gwen needed.

"You're Merlene, aren't you?"

"Of course I am."

"I don't know what to say. Should I bow or something?"

"No, please don't."

"I'm sorry I got you confused with Merlin," Gwen said apologetically. "The accounts of your involvement were pretty vague."

Merlene shrugged unconcernedly. "Oh, I've been so many people, so many names, and to many I *was* Merlin. Look."

There was a flash, and in place of the old woman stood an old man; long grey beard, his head now adorned with a pointy hat.

"Now *this* is a form in which I've felt most comfortable over many ages, as you might imagine," s/he said, his/her voice now deeper and more measured. "I merely decided to harness female energy this time around. It felt like the appropriate course of action in this proud, masculine society. Being a woman felt... right."

Another flash and the form of the old lady returned, yet the hat remained.

"And I've gotten comfortable in these bones and in this old flesh in the ages since I made that decision," she added. "Not that I've held off dabbling in other forms every now and again."

There was a third flash and Gwendoline's eyes widened. Standing before her was a woman she had not beheld in close to a decade.

"Nanny M! Oh… oh my." Gwen gasped and started to cry. "Oh, I haven't seen you since-" She stopped as her head began to feel tight and painful. "I haven't seen you-" She struggled to recall. "Was I seven years old?"

Merlene nodded. "Yes, my darling. You flung a goldfish bowl at me and screamed to clean it up and rescue them before they died."

Gwen held her hands to her head, trying to shut out the pain as the memories returned. "Ohhhhh."

"And I left you there."

"And they died," Gwen said sadly.

"I am sorry, my child."

Gwen let the tears roll down her face without wiping them away. "Please… please don't say sorry to me. I am so ashamed. I was… I am… such a spoiled, wretched, worthless thing."

"Spoiled, yes. There's no denying that." She touched the girl's tear-stained face. "Wretched, perhaps a little, but worthless… no." There was a new kindness and a sympathy here. "Besides, a lesson needed learning that day and I realised I could not handle you at that time. So I came across Viola and…"

Gwen stared at her. "You sent her to look after me?"

Merlene shrugged slightly. "I *implied* that she may be able to put her talents to some good use."

164

"Oh, dearest Nanny M." Gwen looked down at her feet. "You must be so disappointed with me."

"Why?"

"You must have thought I could draw the sword or else I shouldn't be here," Gwen sighed.

"The thought occurred to me, but I am not disappointed. You shall make a *fine* queen… with a little more wisdom and humility." Merlene smiled. "I've known many good, young, occasionally foolish people try and fail to pull it."

"I've got this feeling that Robin has tried. He's…" Gwen closed her eyes in frustration. "Oh, he was so spiteful just now. I don't know how to think of him."

"You are right to be angry, of course," Merlene assured her. "His words were hurtful and ill-considered, but not, I think, born of anything beyond his own pain, and a protectiveness which sometimes falls beyond his control. That does not excuse his actions, though it goes some way to explaining them."

"So I should forgive him?" Gwen asked.

"You should consider whether forgiving him would be of benefit to you both," Merlene advised gently. "There is much you two can learn from one another-"

All of a sudden, Merlene leaned forward and extended her staff, striking the base against the ground. A shimmering bubble formed around her and Gwendoline, and a stun dart stopped in mid-air, inches from the Princess' shapely left breast.

(Damn… almost got her… Oh well, I suppose we'll have to do things up close and personal. By the way, the Knives and I had

just arrived at Camelot, in case that wasn't obvious –
MORTIMER)

Chapter 11: Nevermore

Still Tuesday Evening

All was uproar in Camelot. The moment the slinking thugs who had crept from the forest realised that they had been detected half a dozen of them charged in to grab at Gwendoline. Merlene pushed her aside and held out her staff, the end of which was now glowing with that familiar pale light.

"Get behind me, girl!"

"What can you do?"

"Hopefully enough to deal with this lot."

That same shimmering bubble formed around the pair of them and then burst, sending a shockwave through the stonework that flung several of the interlopers backwards. It was not a catastrophic fall for any of them and they began to pick themselves up within moments. Several more of the Knives took this cue to make a tactical detour and flank the pair, springing from the shadows to close in to around them.

Merlene took in the situation and realised how many of them there were. "Yes, this is going to be tricky," she muttered, "and I haven't prepared or had a warm-up stretch… so, ah… RUN!"

The two turned tail and fled through the crumbling veins of the fortress, Merlene leading.

"What we really need is a bottleneck."

"Hold your ground, I can fight them," Gwen gasped.

"You may have to, but let me protect you until we have no other choice," Merlene advised.

As they ran and called out to one another in the dark, Oberon, Viola and Robin emerged from Merlene's hut and sprinted towards the sound of their voices. The scene was chaotic as the only lights came from Robin and Oberon's torches, the wizard's staff, and the watchful moon.

"What the hell is going on?" Viola yelled as they approached.

"Some hooligans are trying to snatch me," Gwen called back. "Feel free to do your job now!"

"Oh, spiffing, absolutely *spiffing*," Viola muttered, then to Oberon, "With me, akka!"

Viola strode forward, flexing her fingers as energy began to crackle around them. Oberon squinted back in the direction Merlene and Gwen had come from and caught sight of several running figures with red bandanas tied across the lower half of their faces.

"Shit, Robin, it's the Knives."

"I'll take the Princess somewhere safe," said Merlene.

Robin nodded. "I'll go with you ladies."

"Of course you will," Oberon said, rolling his eyes.

"Protecting our investment. Now's the time to do the Akka thing."

"You're right, I got it."

"Go!" Viola yelled, losing her patience.

They left Viola and Oberon guarding the gate between the eastern and central courtyards, and Merlene took them through one of the inner halls and sidestepped through a window to emerge again into the night. Gwen glanced down at Robin, whom, it transpired, was barefoot and awkwardly hopping across the terrain.

"Excuse me?" Robin exclaimed. "I thought I was being rather nimble."

(It wasn't nimble. It was lurching like a drunken monkey –
THE NAG)

"Where are your boots?" Gwen demanded.

"Back at the hut, we left in rather a hurry, OW!"

(Your feet are all wrong. You should have hooves.)

"Even *you* wear shoes!" Robin retorted *(most unprofessionally. This fruitless bickering with his wise narrator was slowing the fleeing trio down and drawing further attention).*

"Come on," Robin said. "Throw me a bone, you petulant glue factory."

(Fine, Robin was jumping, with unparalleled catlike nimbleness, across the rocky terrain.)

"Thank you, OW!"

"You want to go back and get your boots?" Gwen asked.

"No, too many of them back there. Meg… can you please try to keep your light pointed to the floor ahead; I'll just have to dash between the smoother flagstones."

"Can you conjure up some boots for him, Merlene?"

"Oh, she's Merlene now?" Robin remarked. "I wondered if you were going to –"

"Do you have any idea how Maajik works, young lady?" Merlene interrupted.

"Well how the hell *should* I know?" Gwen snapped. "You're hundreds of years old and privy to god-knows what, the cards are pretty much off the table! Oh crap!"

Robin's piteous mewling over stubbed toes had indeed waylaid them for crucial seconds, allowing some of their pursuers to close in. A man with a cruel looking cudgel had swung at Gwendoline from an awning and was grabbing at her wrist with strong, cold fingers and pushing his weapon against her cheek. Gwen dragged him close and reflexively shoved him against the wall. His knee crashed into her ribs, more out of panic than judgment, and she was winded, but her response was to butt her forehead against his nose, which broke immediately, making him shriek with pain behind his bloodied bandana and crumple to the floor. Robin cleared the ground between them and reached her a moment after this.

"I could *absolutely* have taken him out," he assured her.

She glared at him and tried to catch her breath. "You know I'm… still very hurt from what you said earlier," she said, panting.

"I really am sorry about that. Your nurse was being atrocious and that fired up a part of me I find hard to keep silent," Robin said. "You're not worthless at all."

"You're semi-forgiven, but only because we're short on time."

"We have to move," Merlene prompted them.

"Thank you."

"You want his boots?"

"We have to *move!*"

"Those won't fit me. Most human shoes wouldn't."

"Hey!" Merlene yelled. "Both of you young prats need to *listen* to me. They're closing in. I can hold this doorway for as long as possible. There aren't many other ways through to the East Wing, so you're more secure over there."

"What about our friends?" Robin asked.

"They're doing their jobs," Merlene said pointedly.

"Oh, Viola. I wasn't thinking," Gwen held her hand to her mouth, her eyes wide. "Will she be alright?"

"If she's cunning and lucky, yes," Merlene ushered them through the nearby door. "If not, no. You can't help her now. Go. Get to flying and being less foolish."

Gwen and Robin nodded and rushed on through the black labyrinth as Merlene threw an iridescent gate across the archway and masked Knives began to emerge from the night. The wizard fixed them with a powerful expression of utmost determination and thrust her staff out in front of her.

"You know what I'm going to say, so let's just get to it!"

***

Back where they had come from Oberon was roaring with ferocity as he clobbered the interlopers who came within grabbing distance, breaking their bones and flinging them aside. Viola hopped nimbly around him, making use of the multi-tiered and uneven terrain to keep out of reach. She was carefully conserving her energy this time and relying mostly on low level Blindness spells which sent these men stumbling into uncertain footing.

She was beginning to tire already, and Oberon was actively avoiding contact. Had she not been fighting for her life she would have time to judge and consider her behaviour throughout their time together, but she was also proud and stubborn, so it seemed merely beneficial that this enormous creature was technically on the same side right now.

A vicious cudgel-blow slammed against Oberon's ribcage and he felt a crack, followed by several sharp cuts. He bellowed with frustration as he retreated, holding his side. The two Knives now closing in hefted their clubs, and one muttered to the other in a rasping voice. "Knock his tusks out next."

Viola slid away from the man with the broken arm who was still kicking at her and aimed a powerful Confuse spell at the speaker, who swung his arm out reflexively, connecting with the back of his companion's skull. As the struck fellow screamed in pain and surprise, Oberon leapt in to take advantage of their brief disarray.

***

Unbeknownst to the Hoods, Mortimer had encouraged the Knives to go for the swarm approach to keep the Princess' captors busy, anticipating that they would move their prisoner to more secure lodgings in their defence attempts. She had not expected so few of them, or for two powerful Maajik users to be among their number, but she kept her high vantage point and circled the arena in the outer shadows, watching the chaos unfold.

172

Now with just one outlaw and Gwendoline together she spied her moment to swoop in. All Robin saw was a purple blur, and then he felt a boot heel collide agonisingly with his exposed toes. The world went white and he doubled over with pain, only to be kicked in the face.

"Hello, Princess," said Mortimer with a grin.

Gwen turned to see what had happened but Robin was already over. A tall woman with black, braided hair and a bowler hat had just grabbed the Princess' hand and attached the cuff of a pair of shackles. Gwen snarled with fury and pulled her wrist back. Mortimer was slightly unbalanced but used the forward momentum to spring up and over Gwendoline's body and yank that arm across to her opposite shoulder, pulling on the cuffs.

"Ow, Jesus Christ!" Gwen yelped.

"Frightfully sorry," said Mortimer, sounding not at all sorry. "Lot of fuss and bother in the dark and I can't have you wondering off… Ow! Blast!"

Robin had picked himself up and, without checking his horribly bruised foot, had launched onto Mortimer's back. Mortimer was currently on Gwen's back and so Gwen sank to the floor groaning.

"Would you both get the hell off me, I can't breathe!" Gwen panted at them.

"You get off me, Duart," Mortimer snarled. "I have a testicle-removal gun with your name on it."

"Well, if you went to the trouble of personalising it for me, I shall accept it." He snatched the device from its holster.

"Hey!" Mortimer cried. "Right, I'm going to get that back and use it *twice*!"

Gwen tried in vain to throw them both off her. "Seriously, too heavy, I will roll on the pair of you."

Mortimer stopped trying to grab at the stolen gadget and seized Robin's wrist. "Loxley, I know how much I can get for you *on top of* her recovery, so I think…"

There was a click, and a latching sound.

"Oh, sod a dog!" Robin exclaimed.

"Did she just..?" Gwendoline sputtered indignantly. "Did she just *handcuff* you to me?"

"It would appear so," replied Robin, slightly sheepishly.

"Both… of you… get… OFF!" Gwen gritted her teeth and reared up, shaking Mortimer from her shoulders. As she turned, now more in control, she felt the weight of Robin swing out wildly on the end of the chain. The bounty hunter was picking herself up. Gwen fixed on her position, roaring and carrying the spin full-circle, raising her trapped arm with the wriggling duart on the end until he collided violently, sending Mortimer crashing back against the wall.

Robin flopped onto the stones, groaning in pain. "You are completely mad," he mumbled. "Don't ever use me as a morning star again!"

"I promise," said Gwen. Is she down?" A groan from the crumpled form in the corner suggested this to be the case, though it was too dark to see for sure.

"Yes, I think she's mostly unconscious," Robin nodded.

"Alright then," Gwen instructed. "Lockpick these cuffs."

"With the lockpicks that are in my boots," Robin replied drily.

Gwen rolled her eyes. "Oh, for f…" She broke off in an attempt to remain at least a little ladylike. "Well, you'll have to search her for a key."

"No way," Robin protested. "Like I said, she's only *mostly* unconscious. If I search her now she'll just wake up and steal my testicles."

"I have an idea," said Gwen. Her hand felt like it was about to tear off and made her yelp in pain as she yanked Robin off his feet again and over her shoulder.

"So, I just perch up here then?" Robin asked as she attempted a steady balancing act.

"Just hold the torch out and keep your head low, there are doorways to get through. Burn my hair and you lose that moustache." Gwen turned decisively, piggybacking the injured duart. She barrelled through the East wing, doubling back and retracing her steps several times, looking for a very specific chamber that she half-remembered the way to.

"No, it's the middle door," Robin told her.

"How do you know where I'm going?" she demanded, not turning her head.

"I've… had the same idea. I think," he said.

***

Gwen ducked under the final archway and put Robin down onto unsteady legs. The moonlight shone through the windows and large gaps in the ceiling and up above them at the top of the stairs stood the sword.

"Together this time," Gwen said.

"That was my idea too," Robin agreed.

The pair of them walked up, one foot after the other, through the moonbeams, their chained hands almost touching. Their steps were laboured with exhaustion and pain, and clumsy, with a childlike tentativeness.

They circled the stone and slowly reached out to grasp the hilt together. Their fingers tightened as they felt the blade give ever so slightly. Both of them gasped a little. Gwendoline gathered her strength, glancing down at Robin and they breathed deeply and pulled with all of their combined might.

Nothing happened.

The sword stood fast.

Gwen was crushed, and on the verge of tears again. "Oh."

Robin's face fell too. "I thought that would work. I really did."

"It just… made sense… why isn't it working?"

"Try again." Robin hopped up on the stone and planted his feet, gripping the crossguard and pulling up hard. Gwen leaned her full weight away, her fingers clinging to the hilt.

"Come… on… come on…" She gritted her teeth and roared. "COME ON, YOU BASTARD! WE NEED YOU!"

A long moment of intense, painful strain stretched out to be shouldered by both of them. During this time their frustration peaked, only to become overwhelmed by exhaustion.

"It's no good." Robin let go.

"No!" Her voice shook with fury. "It's not FAIR! I'm a princess, I want to be a hero and I need to protect you."

"I know. I was fine with sharing it,"

"We've done everything right, why won't it work?"

The pair sagged down and found themselves leaning back to back against one another. The sword stood above them, mocking their every intention. There was silence in the dusty space, broken only by breathing.

At the base of the steps, Mortimer stood, a tranquilliser dart gun in one hand and her electric prod in the other. Neither of them knew when she had stepped in.

"Well, for my part I'm glad it didn't work," the bounty hunter drawled. "It makes what I'm about to say a bit easier."

"You can knock us both out," Gwen muttered, bitterly, as they hauled themselves wearily to their feet. "And then enjoy dragging us back to a cart while whichever of our companions survived your many thugs out there comes straight for you."

Robin growled in kind. "OR you can just accept that you aren't going to win this one."

"I think I might have already won, though," Mortimer replied. "And do allow me to explain at gunpoint, because I feel like you're both liable to do something stupid if I don't."

"Fine," Gwen snapped. "Why have you won?"

"Well, it all depends on whether I've read this situation correctly." Mortimer turned to Robin. "As I am to understand it, Mr Hood, you snatched this lady up late last night, and if logic follows action you're looking to ransom her to her father?"

"Let's say yes, for now," said Robin.

"How much were you going to ask for her?"

"Yes, how much, actually?" Gwen asked.

"I need one thousand gold," Robin replied.

There was hurt on the Princess' face. "A piffling thousand! That's all I'm worth to you?" she said incredulously.

"It's not a reflection of your actual worth. It's just what I need for my purposes," he explained weakly.

"Which are?" she demanded.

"Well… that's very complicated, you see my friend owns this factory…"

"I'm being paid *two* thousand to bring the Princess home," Mortimer cut in.

"I don't *need* two thousand," Robin countered. "We're trying not to be greedy here."

Mortimer shook her head, hoping this nitwit would catch on soon. "If I split my take down the middle we both walk away with a cool grand." She motioned extravagantly with her weapons. "You do what you want with your half, I'll spend mine on whatever naughty things I like."

"Excuse me," Gwen began, but Robin cut across her.

"Yes, that does actually sound eminently sensible," he agreed.

"And safe," Mortimer added, "since I'm not extorting anyone."

"What about the bounty on my head, and my companion?" Robin asked. "How come you aren't after that?"

"*Excuse* me."

"Two reasons," Mortimer said, counting on her fingers. "Firstly, my army of lackeys appears to have been unable to defeat them, and clearly can't offer me the manpower required to catch and transport you Hoods. Secondly, I've been offered a bonus if she's in good spirits on her return. I prefer finesse to blunt force, not to mention biting off more than I can chew," she continued. "So, if you're agreeable, Princess, then the bonus should cover the heads of your new friends."

Gwen's fury, both at their discussion and the fact they were ignoring her, had risen to breaking point. "EXCUSE ME!" she roared. "I am not a bloody flag to be passed around to improve the standing of the bearer!"

"...I never thought of you that way," Robin insisted.

Gwen looked piercingly at him and put her hands angrily on her hips. "Alright then, you tell me what the thousand is for, right now."

"Fine," Robin snapped, then said in a low voice, though Mortimer still craned in and caught nearly every word. "It's to improve the prospects of a business that gives child labourers a fair wage and reasonable working conditions. It's to prevent our competitors who are actively *exploiting* those same children from running us out of the market. None of that gold goes into my pocket, if that's what you're thinking!"

"I didn't… I mean…" Gwen faltered, her self-righteousness deflating somewhat.

Robin pulled up his green hood over his head and irritably flicked his bowstring. "Robin Hood, *remember*?"

"How *astonishingly* noble," Mortimer said with a slight sneer. "I think I'm going to be sick."

"It does sound like a good cause when you put it like that," Gwen admitted.

Robin sighed and addressed Mortimer. "Alright, purple pantaloons, what if we say no and clobber you together, which we might still be able to do?"

"Well, for starters, I've already studied your weaknesses which means you'll be dreadfully sorry you said no and attacked me," Mortimer assured him. "And also, good luck dealing with the Archduke. He's really very… *very* cross about all this. I would wager my whole two thousand that you won't see copper piece number one from him. Most likely you would be found and clapped in irons, then executed before you can say 'This has all been a big misunderstanding'."

Gwen nodded decisively. "Alright, your first plan makes the most sense," she agreed. "Provided you're not trying to double-cross us."

"Which she almost certainly is," Robin pointed out.

"You're just going to have to *trust* me," Mortimer said with a wink.

"I have one condition," Gwen returned.

"What?" Mortimer and Robin asked in unison.

"That we wait until *Friday* to bring me back. I should like to… see a bit of London first. We shall disguise ourselves once more and you will give me the holiday I desire," she said imperiously.

"I don't think you really know what you're asking," Robin said to her.

"Yes, I do," Gwen replied fervently. "If my return to the life that has been laid out for me is going to be of benefit to people I would most likely never meet, I would like to change that and meet them first."

Robin shook his head. "It's a huge risk. *So* much could go wrong."

"I'm fine with this," Mortimer commented, aware that she was becoming less relevant to the conversation. "Just as long as you both understand I'm sticking to you like glue."

"Please Robin," Gwen said solemnly. "I need to- I need to know the world properly, so that I can make good decisions when I wear the crown."

Robin looked into her wide, blue eyes and despite his aching feet, twisted wrist, pounding head, and semi-dislocated arm he felt a new pain in his chest.

"Alright. But you stay close to me and accept that I know more about this city than you do, so my advice is pretty much gospel."

"I'll listen to you, but I'm going to make my own bloody decisions," Gwen countered.

"Fine," Robin conceded. "Can you unlatch us please, Mortimer? We need to go and help our friends immediately. While we've been bargaining one or all of them could have been badly hurt or captured or killed."

"Right you are, squire," Mortimer nodded, and pulled out a small key.

Their hands were freed and swiftly rubbed to alleviate the pain, as the uneasy trio left the sword behind to seek out the others. While neither Robin nor Gwendoline was entirely happy with the new situation, both told themselves it was for the better.

Chapter 12: New Skills

Wednesday Morning (Four Days Left)

Oberon rose early and went to wander the ruins in the dawn light, his eyes surveying the ground. He saw a set of knuckledusters that were too small for him lying on the stonework, the previous owner having dropped them during the scuffle the night before. The knuckledusters went into Oberon's knapsack. He ventured further, relishing the clear, cold air of the place.

His ribs, left thigh, right shoulder, and the fingers of his right hand still ached from the vicious brawl of the evening before. The cuts to his body were dressed and mending but he would have to go easy on them. There were a few too many times where he had been overcome in the dark and had to go to a place in his mind that would be overwhelming enough to his attackers to save him and his diminutive companion. It was a savage place and not one Oberon liked. But what disturbed him more was how naturally he could reach that state of mind, or indeed mindlessness. A reliance on instinct and action over conscience. It haunted him.

Near a bloodstain on the wall he found a small, discarded bag, containing a few coppers and an unimpressively plain ring. Whoever the thug had been planning to propose to imminently may have to wait a while longer. The bag went into Oberon's bag. He hesitated over a discarded shoe. Dark brown leather, scuffed with a buttoned flap that had been ripped open during the brawl. The shoe went into Oberon's bag. He chewed his lower lip with annoyance as he proceeded.

Not all of their attackers had lived through the night. The dead Knives had been taken away by those still living, on firm instructions from Merlene. From the baleful tone of voice she had used with them and the tingling in Oberon's skin he was well aware some Maajik was at play. What Oberon did not know was how frightened those men would be for the rest of their short lives every time somebody so much as mentioned the word 'Camelot'. The specificity of events would never return, only a great and terrible dread of what lay within the forest.

As a result, Merlene now frightened Oberon. Anybody with that level of power contained in such an unassuming frame was worthy of his respect but seeing her work her will upon these crude men he became more acutely aware of the chessboard on which he now stood positioned.

He had, knowing previously of her hidden identity and mythical significance, considered her to be the queen of this particular game. The piece who could move as she pleased and the possessor of power well beyond the pawns she had sent fleeing in the small hours. But now in the light of day things were clearer. Oberon flattered himself that he may be a rook, but it was increasingly more apparent that she was the player moving the pieces.

He stopped in at the horse. Sprawled on the flagstones in the middle of the stables, bathed in the sunlight pushing through the nearby glassless window frames, a dark-coated man lay dead. His hat was discarded some seventeen feet across the room, his head at an obtuse angle.

"He had an inkling…" said a voice, as The Nag stepped from the shadows and approached the akka, "To rustle this particular horse in the dead of night." A stalk of wheat was dangling from his lower lip.

"His intentions towards the rest of us were unsavoury," said Oberon. "So… thank you."

"Nobody forces me to carry them."

"I had come to brush you down."

"I don't need it."

"You don't *want* it?"

"Never did get that stew I was promised."

Oberon shook his head. "We had kind of a busy night."

"And nobody came to check on me," The Nag said woundedly.

"I'm here *now*," Oberon pointed out. "And, oh look…" He produced a soup flask from his knapsack. "Leftovers."

"So that's what I'm to be given to dine on, leftovers," moaned the horse. Oberon glared at him.

"Listen, I'm not going to tell any of the others I came to see you, so you can either eat this delicious, cold stew I made and accept a brush down or I can walk out of here and you can stay dirty and hungry. Either way, I'll remove the *corpse* from your living area."

The Nag stared at him for a long moment. "I will take you up on your offer. Brush away, but *don't you look at me!*"

Oberon began his attendance of the horse, smoothing down the rough, matted and clumped coat with a pair of firm brushes that were a little too small for his great Akka hands and had to be delicately gripped between his fingertips. The Nag contented himself with staring straight ahead. Each of them felt the warmth of the other as Oberon worked at the knots of tension in those mottled flanks. Eventually, to break the tension Oberon asked, somewhat self-consciously, "So… uh… you doing anything this weekend?"

"No talking."

"Fine by me."

***

On that same early morning Merlene found Viola in the guest bedroom of her cottage, sorting through the provisions the little band would be taking back to London.

"Viola Heartstone…" the wizard began, but the duart cut in without waiting for her to finish.

"Listen, if this is about my behaviour at supper, first of all I've already sort of apologised to the akka, second of all I think it's actually rather important to adopt a healthy sense of paranoia when one's position is a *bodyguard*." There was an angry, defensive edge to her voice. "It's my job to expect the worst from people! Those in my position who give everyone the benefit of the doubt end up with dead charges, and you *know* that at the very least two realms would be in turmoil if that happens. If she dies, or if anything happens to her, I-"

She faltered, tripped up by the panic that rose in her throat. "I would have failed utterly in my intended task. So if you're here to scold me about prejudices, you can take your sermonising elsewhere."

"Are you quite finished?" asked Merlene.

Viola nodded sharply. "That's all I have to say right now."

"I came to ask you about that maajik you employed yesterday."

"Ah." Viola looked away from Merlene's penetrating gaze. "None of that hit you, did it?" she asked, a little more respectfully.

"No, I had a shield up the whole time. In fact, I believe you encountered my extension of that on the drawbridge."

"That was yours?" Viola said, impressed.

Merlene nodded. "That was my signature move, yes."

"Can you teach me?" asked Viola eagerly. "They might come in handy the next time the Princess is in danger... which should be around teatime today."

"Sadly, no, that wasn't actually a spell, more of an *ability* I'm currently in possession of, so it's not something that can be taught. I do have a few other tricks up my sleeve, but I must confess that some of what you were flinging out eludes even me. Where ever did you learn that?"

"Oh, I learned those a *long* time ago." Viola waved her hand dismissively. "My teacher is gone now, you couldn't find her to hold her to account."

Merlene frowned and folded her arms. "The maajiks you wield *are* forbidden, child, but not by me. You needn't be so *insufferably* defensive."

Viola's shoulders sagged. "I'm hoping you fathom me here… what it's been like, spending half my life hiding what I can do. Knowing that if those men found out the truth I would be shamed, excommunicated, banished, executed… my name would go down in history as a traitor to our race."

"Of course I fathom. You and I, our station is to stand quietly in the shadow of the powerful. The uncharitable or short-sighted might consider our actions manipulation. The wise would understand that with the vast movements taking place, our charges have the blessed benefit of being able to make catastrophic errors in judgment, affecting countless numbers. Our task is to see those outcomes in the road ahead and steer them away. Would that be accurate, Viola?" The duart said nothing. Her voice caught in her throat as she stared at Merlene. "And it stands to reason that sometimes when a bright outcome, advantageous to many, presents itself, our charges may also need our gentle steering to guide them to the *new* road." Her expression was unreadable, but Viola's nodding continued. "That being said, I hope you will forgive the form I once used to steer *you*."

In a flash Merlene had transformed again to the woman Gwendoline had referred to as Nanny M.

Viola's mouth fell open. "You!?" Another flash and Merlene had returned, nodding. "That's some parlour trick."

"It's a glamour," Merlene said proudly.

"Do you use deception often?" Viola asked, narrowing her eyes slightly.

"Viola, I have one or another of these spells working on some level, *every second* my feet are in contact with this Earth. I'll warrant that if you or anyone else could perceive my *true* form I'd never be able to have an engaging, adult conversation with them again. It's not deceit, it's… etiquette."

"Can you teach me those?"

Merlene smiled at her. "As a matter of fact, I can."

***

There then followed several hours of training montage that is difficult to represent outside of a visual medium. It began with nearly an hour of mistakes and bungled attempts. She made her own nose disappear, gave Merlene purple skin and gave everybody enormous feet, but after these fiascos Viola's skill in other spells resurfaced and she began to get the hang of these subtle new arts.

The thing about a glamour is that it is only really the final ten percent of an illusion. The other 90% is down to the clothing and behaviour of the person the spell is cast upon. If they are charging around screaming obscenities and this is not the natural behaviour of their target, they will be seen for who they are, not their intended disguise. So if one were to, say, wear the face of Dame Judi Dench but the clothes and behaviour of Dame Edna Everage, the Glamour would only serve to confuse and draw further attention to you. Viola had to see it as more of a costume that an actor wears. The mind of the observer searches out faults in appearance and can reel and trigger alarm bells when something is off. The spell, when cast correctly, muffles those bells, distracts with the everyday, rejects scrutiny like a cat held up to its reflection.

Viola learned this over the day. The clothes and behaviour had to fit the identity, and if those were in place and the face fit the rest of the body, the illusion, to the trained maajik user, would be simple and subtle enough to keep operating in the background of their mind. It might necessitate only the attention required of, say, keeping the lyrics of a song playing constantly in one's head. With practice, it could become as natural as breathing, and the range away from the spellcaster could span great distances provided Viola could fix on a clear image of them.

She succeeded in making Robin look like he was dark-haired with a brown coat and a full, bushy black beard obscuring his features. She made Gwendoline look like Lady Tilly, a friend of hers from court, but mainly because Gwen was good at affecting Tilly's mannerisms. Viola made herself look like Captain Baltus but quickly switched back because being in his head-space was making her feel nauseous. Finally she managed to make Oberon look like a lumbering, ginormous human being, which quite took everyone aback, considering the level of detail involved, not least of all Viola herself.

It was well into the afternoon when Merlene allowed them all to depart and prepare for their journey back.

Wednesday Afternoon

In the main courtyard, Robin was instructing Gwendoline in how to comport herself on the streets of London in their new guises, utilising purloined clothing from the Knives.

"This jacket smells of beer and sweat," Gwen said, wrinkling her nose.

"Good," replied Robin. "It has to make you somewhat repellent, but not so foul smelling that people remember you."

"I'll never get this odour out of my skin," she scowled.

"Well, you can have a luxurious bath when you get back."

"Mmm," Gwen said. "Do you take baths? I mean you smell lovely… I mean you smell alright… I mean most of the time. I mean when we were in the trunk…"

"Yes. Yes, Princess, I take baths." Robin smiled. "Even the impoverished can occasionally muster hot water. Now tie your hair back and hide it under your collar, it's far too beautif…" He stopped himself. "Too eye-catching to leave out on display. We need as few things as possible for Viola to have to hide."

Gwen did as she was told. "There. Now if I pull this cap all the way down I look plain and ugly and boring."

Robin smiled again, but tried to contain it. "Nope, you're still radiant, even if we grime your face up. Your posture just makes you stand out. Show me how you walk?"

Gwen adopted various stances as she moved, complete with some subtle flourishes and gestures. "Do you mean at court, or to my horse, or greeting a dignitary, or in addressing a crowd? I have six different walks, Master Hood, all of them perfected over years of hard practice."

Robin shook his head. "Just show me how you walk down a street."

"Well… I suppose it's not dissimilar to walking to one's carriage, here." She stepped with elegant strides, holding her head aloft.

Robin folded his arms and shook his head. "Okay, now you've just been mugged."

"Well, *you* show me, then," she replied with slight exasperation.

Robin adopted a slower pace, hunched his shoulders and allowed his left-right movements to pull him into a natural lope that suggested resignation to defeat.

"That's *not* how you walk though," she said. "I've seen you." She rushed in front of him and strode past, swaying her hips in a swagger, flashing him a grin as she sauntered past. "You walk like you own the street. As though if someone were to stop you they'd get either a joke or a fight or a… kiss."

"That's when I want to attract attention to myself," he replied. "When I want to charm someone, or annoy them, or intimidate them. It's very much in-control. It's the Artful Dodger, and right now, you want to be thinking Oliver."

"Who is Oliver?" Gwen asked.

Robin's eyes widened. "Oh, by Thrale Copperhelm, you're reading the wrong books."

"I read all sorts of wonderful books," she replied haughtily.

"Have you read *Nicholas Nickleby*?" Robin asked.

"No, have you read *What Katy Did*?"

"This isn't a competition, have you read *A Tale of Two Cities*?"

"I've read *Frankenstein*," she snapped.

"That doesn't help us," Robin said. "We can't have you lurching around London like The Monster."

"I can walk like Victor."

"Better, but he's still not your common, everyday street urchin that the world chooses to ignore," Robin reminded her.

"Right…well, I can try walking like Oberon."

Robin stared at her. "Listen to me, the people of London, the ones we're going to be walking among are not in control of their lives. They want to be, but they know they aren't. Your walk has to reflect that… you need to feel like there's a weight pressing down on you and a rope pulling you forward. You keep moving so that you don't collapse and die in the gutter. The ones with pride attract attention to themselves, we can't be that right now. So just do this."

He loped again, kept his head down, kept his movements slight, adopted something of a scowl.

"Good Lord, how do they find the energy to get out of bed in the morning?" Gwen asked.

"If they want to feed their families they find the energy," Robin replied. "Simple as that. So, no more swagger. Not until you're back home."

They paced past one another several more times until Gwen's demeanour was suitably lowered and her sashay had transformed into a waddle. They stopped and stood beside the cart, Robin looking up into her face, Gwendoline looking down into his. Robin's moustache twitched.

"Much better," he said. "It's as though you were born on the street."

"Thank you. I've spent my life reshaping my behaviour for the benefit of others, so I'm quite used to that sort of thing by now," she observed. "Nearly all of my mind and body is on loan."

"What do you keep for yourself?" he asked, his voice low.

Gwen straightened up, her lip curling as she studied the duart. "That's a secret."

Robin breathed deeply to find, unavoidably, even through the vapours of sweat and beer, that he had caught the scent of her hair. He took a step backward.

"Wonderful. I think you're ready for the real London. Go find your bodyguard and we'll hit the road again."

Gwendoline frowned and turned on her heel, walking with that accomplished state of defeat as she sought out her nursemaid.

Chapter 13: The Empty House

Camelot

Robin winced, turned and chewed the wooden side of the cart as a tall, slender figure emerged from the shadows and approached him.

"You two really do make a delightful couple," said Mortimer. "You remind me of a fox being petted by a hippopotamus in a wig."

"We're underway in a few minutes time," he replied, pulling himself together. "Are you ready to go? Got all your gizmos packed?" The woman slid up beside him, serpentine and smiling, as she played with one of her braids, wrapping the dark hair around her deadly little finger. "That's a little too close," he cautioned.

"It's close enough for what I have in mind," she said.

"Consider having something else in mind then, I'm practically *wearing* you."

"I do look good on you though," she persisted.

"You look fabulous. That's never been at issue. What do you want from me?"

"I'm curious," she said, her head tilted. "You didn't defend her when I said she had the dimensions of a river-dwelling hulk. That to me suggests either that you see her in purely monetary terms or that you're afraid to show me just how deeply that smitten little heart of yours has fallen." She locked eyes with him. "So which is it? Cash cow or turtle dove?"

"What she represents," Robin said, choosing his words slowly and carefully. "Her title, her position, could bring a better life to so many."

"Ahh, but she could bring a great deal of happiness to just *you*, and haven't you earned it?"

"I don't know how many lifetimes worth of good work I'd have to perform in order to deserve…"

"Shhhh, just think about it," she breathed, her own atmosphere of scent and presence now surrounding him. "Living wild and free, with that smile, those eyes, those hips. And knowing every day you woke up together that there is a queen beside you, that nobody else can have."

"Why are you so fixated on what I…"

Mortimer's tone became business-like, although it did little to undermine the persuasive nature of her expression. "Because an awful lot of *my* gold is riding on this royal hog being returned to her pen, and I don't want you screwing the whole thing up because you can't stop thinking with *this*."

Robin coughed. "*My* gizmo is none of your business."

"Oh, but it could be." Her voice was silky. "Consider your options, Robin, there are so many more *appropriate* girls for you out there. Girls whose lifestyles run parallel to your own. Girls who will truly understand what it means to be on your side of the law."

"I know," Robin said, coldly. "And I'm going to bring her back, just as we've planned. That hasn't changed. Take your hand off me."

"Then you might want to consider hurting her…" Mortimer's eyes were cruel and danced with golden fire. "Badly… so as to leave her in no doubt that her place is on the throne and marrying that fine, upstanding duart lord. Do what you do best. Rob her of all affection for this life of the wild rogue she so clearly craves." Her expression was cold and resolute. "Break her heart now, to save her further pain. And get your head back in the business of robbing from the rich."

***

Gwendoline re-emerged from Merlene's hut with their companions in tow to see Mortimer pressing Robin against the cart. The bounty hunter leaned forward, sliding her smooth neckline close to Robin's lips as she turned to walk towards them, dipping into a theatrical bow.

"Majesty, your chariot awaits."

Gwendoline felt a breathtaking pain in her stomach which twisted up and drew immediate tears to her eyes, which she blinked back fiercely. Her teeth ground together as she glared at Robin and trembled uncontrollably, even as her back straightened and her head raised.

Why had she not listened to Viola? Why had she been so stubborn in her ideals? Something had been broken here, and it was easier now to think herself a reformed fool, resolving to be wiser in future, than to return to her previous obliviousness.

Alright then, if that was the stuff these parasites upon civilization were made of, she would prove her material sterner. As the words came they took out of her, like little souvenirs, the hopes that she had fostered in this remote and ancient retreat.

"Very well, take me to London," she said, raising her chin defiantly.

Robin stepped past Mortimer and approached Merlene, avoiding the eye of the Princess. "Are you sure you won't leave Camelot?" he asked the wizard. "It's clearly not safe anymore."

"I come and go from time to time," said Merlene. "It's not like I'm stuck here. But I always have to return. My place is with the Sword."

"Well, until *she's* back on the throne," Robin suggested, gesturing without looking. "You might want to consider going wandering and leaving this place a ghost town."

"I'll consider it… but who else is going to look after The Nag?" Merlene asked him.

Gwen now turned to the old woman. "Please take care, Merlene."

"Go, be off with you. I shall be fine."

"Will I see you again?" Gwen asked her.

"How should I know?" Merlene replied, shrugging vaguely. "I have six or seven timelines actively playing out right now, in three of them we do meet again, in three of them we don't. In one of them we're *lovers*, but I have no idea what I may say or do in future to make that happen, and it sounds disastrous."

Gwen laughed sadly, unsure of how to assimilate or even comprehend this information. "You are one of the most extraordinary people I've ever met. Thank you for everything you've done for us… Nanny M."

"You're welcome…" Merlene's tone was grave as she surveyed the group, nodding at Viola and frowning at Mortimer. "Good luck on your journeys."

"I suppose if I do have good luck I must be on one of the better timelines?" Gwen piped up, uncertainly.

"Are we done with all the temporal mechanics, my poor little brain is hurting," Mortimer cut in sardonically.

Gwen turned, and stalked past, calling over her shoulder. "I'm not sure I understand much of this at all, but let's get this show back on the road. Viola, my bags." Her nursemaid retrieved a rather heavy sack of clothing and oddments and began to drag it towards the cart. "Give them to *him*." Gwen added, "It will keep his hands busy." Viola blinked and dropped the sack beside Robin, hurrying after her companion. Loxley clapped his hand over his eyes as Oberon and Mortimer followed.

Wednesday Evening

At five bells they concluded their journey back to the centre of London. The clouds had gathered, the buildings rose up around them, stretching in pillars and points up toward the grey sky, and they all became painfully aware of the innate purity of the air they had previously been breathing.

Gwendoline had not spoken a word to Robin during the journey, but sat in the back with Oberon and Viola, the latter of whom had been working on concentration techniques that allowed her to maintain their new faces throughout the ride. They were all aware of who each other was beneath the obscuring facades. It wasn't anywhere near as crude and simple as a mask, but ephemeral and mundane, convincing in wholly different ways. When people glanced over, their features clearly bored the onlookers to the point that they found other things to be interested in soon after. They kept their shoulders slumped, their tone resigned and their movements slight.

Mortimer was sat beside Robin, and he found her the hardest to ignore. She cut rather a dashing figure; capable, cunning and commanding, and superficially speaking, every bit his equal. Had they met a week beforehand he would no doubt by now have been engaged in a merry fencing match of tongues with this impressive creature, but today this undeniable draw between them only served to make Robin more frustrated and saddened over the imminent releasing of the Princess.

He was well aware Gwendoline could feel his eyes on her when he looked back there, so he kept them to himself. However, as they headed south and she really began to *see* the people, to not just observe their presence in the world but to comprehend their place in it, the slump of those shoulders became increasingly less of a pantomime.

The smells hit her as well. It was not just the air, and the absence of that ancient woody atmosphere that Camelot was steeped in, but the antithesis here; a soup of coal fumes. Often not having kitchens of their own, the poor relied on cookhouses for their food, and the whiff of meats no sane person would ask the origin of travelled down the roads and past their noses, along with the reek of the Thames, a near-visible rancour, like salted rubbish, the stamp of horse shit, piling up on street corners for the turd-wardens to carry away for the fields, the nervous, filthy tremors of wet, desperate dogs peeking from their alcoves, the blackening of cheap sweet-chestnuts, and the sharp nip of gin on the breath of passers-by. For someone who dealt in nothing but the most refined, palatial air, it was overwhelming.

"They're so thin," Viola muttered.

"I'll bet you didn't think Akka could get that emaciated. Robb and I are lucky to be able to pull together the meals that we can."

"Why don't they just get better jobs that pay them more money?" Gwen wondered aloud.

"Some of these people have *three* jobs," Oberon corrected. "Lot of mouths to feed at home."

"Well, why not just have fewer…" Viola broke off abruptly, realising that what she was about to say was unfair.

Oberon looked at her, but this time it was without fury. What was in his eyes was actually closer to pity.

"Children?" he said.

"I was going to say…" She trailed off. "Nothing… there's nothing I *can* say."

Gwendoline decided to diplomatically move the conversation to something more positive. "So you and Robin steal from people like us and give to people like this?"

"We started out just giving to them directly," Oberon explained. "And we still do that with those who badly need the food or a few coins to live. But what our partner Scarlet figured out was that they really needed an industry that was on *their* side, not one that considered them to be biological cogs in the great machine. To be easily replaceable. We have a fundamental problem with that way of thinking."

"And here we are," Mortimer said, gesturing to the building they were fast approaching. "This is my place, you can all come on up and hide here for the night. We'll get this one back home tomorrow."

"I think I still want to stay a few more days," Gwen said icily. "You don't mind, do you Mortimer?"

"If you want to gawk at wastrels for hours on end that's no skin off my nose, my old bucko," Mortimer shrugged. "As long as I still get my cut at the end of it you consider this palace your new home."

They pulled the cart into a side alley, stabled Carrots, and climbed the wooden stairs up to Mortimer's apartment, which was actually a large Tudor house.

Oberon stooped, and spent the next few minutes ducking beams as they found themselves being led through empty corridors, past many vacant bedrooms and an expansive, cold parlour. Mortimer's so-called 'apartment' would have comfortably housed twelve families from this area of London.

The moment they were through the door Viola breathed out a sigh and their false identities melted away. Without asking, she hopped up on the kitchen worktop and began raiding Mortimer's cupboards for sweet things.

"Oh, help yourself," Mortimer said, incredulously.

As the bounty hunter conducted her house tour with a brittle smile, Robin took note of the lavish weapons rack in her well-stocked workshop, the dusty glasses on the shelves in her finely appointed, echoing kitchen, the one dish on the draining rack, and the elegant yet redundant dressing screen in her master bedroom.

He spotted a framed photograph of Mortimer stood beside a man bearing an enormous, bushy moustache. Perhaps a lover, though her gloved hands still obscured a possible wedding ring. However, the way they both held their heads aloft in that haughty, esoteric manner suggested a familial bond. A brother? He was clad in exploring gear and clearly had not troubled himself to put down his glass of port while the photograph was being taken.

On one of the parlour walls, opposite an impressive set of mounted moose antlers, hung the oil painting *Titania and Bottom* by Henry Fuseli. Robin had seen the original at the National Gallery and told Mortimer truthfully that this was an excellent reproduction.

"Oh darling," she said with a grin. "It's the Nash that have the reproduction… *that's* the original."

Several facetious comments about she and Oberon crossed Robin's mind but he found none of them worth uttering this time. Her boast aside, this painting's very

203

presence in this house began to tell him more about their new hostess.

Mortimer terminated the tour with unpractised abruptness, and after starting a fire in the grate she sat down on her couch next to a small table that was home to a single book. The rest of them stood far back from this lonely queen of the fairies.

She looked so small.

Chapter 14: All Manner of Pain

Thursday Morning (Three Days Left)

By ten bells the next morning, the Princess had still not risen from her slumber, and Oberon was pacing the floor, which is hard to do when stooping as well.

"Robb, can I just go alone?" he asked. "How is it safer having her with us?"

Robin shook his head. "I know how these things work," he insisted. "If we go to check on your brother that's when Mortimer betrays us and frogmarches Gwendoline back to the palace to claim the full reward."

"I'm heartbroken that you still don't trust me," Mortimer said, not sounding in the least bit heartbroken, or even surprised.

Robin ignored her and continued. "Or that's when the Knives who've been watching this house…"

"Nobody knows we're here," she insisted.

"…Or they see one of us randomly exiting the building, that's when they strike. I want to be together when that inevitably happens."

"You're rather agitated, Mister Loxley, if that is *indeed* your real name."

Oberon scowled at Mortimer. "You know it's not."

The bedroom door opened and Viola stood there, fully dressed and glaring at them.

"She's up."

"At last, get her ready to go," Oberon sighed, putting his hood up.

Gwendoline's voice drifted through from inside the bedroom. "Tea, Viola. Earl Grey, hot."

"Yes, your highness," Viola called back over her shoulder.

"And for breakfast I shall have cake. Cake please, Viola."

"Yes, your highness."

"And crumpets. I want two crumpets with honey and scrambled eggs."

"*Yes*, your highness."

"No black pudding."

"No, your highness."

"Quail's eggs or pheasant?" Robin called.

"Ooh, pheasant sounds nice."

"I'm being sarcastic," he said with forced pleasantry, not missing a beat. "Please get up, we're all waiting to go and check on Oberon's brother!"

"A princess must have her breakfast," Gwen retorted. "And I shall see London in my own time."

Oberon turned to the door in frustration. "I'm leaving now."

"There may be trouble out there," Robin cautioned.

"I'll go," Viola said quietly.

Robin turned to her. "What?"

"I'll go with him," she repeated.

"Why?" Oberon asked, visibly surprised.

"Because I don't want to wait on her hand and foot this morning, and she seems in no mood to make haste, so I'm not going to push her. But I fancy a walk and frankly I need a bit of a break from this place." Robin blinked, stunned. She locked eyes with him. "Guard her.

Don't let her leave the house. We'll be back in a jiffy. You're in charge." As she said the words, she glanced at Mortimer whose eyes narrowed. She and the akka left through the front door, not speaking to one another.

"Pheasant eggs!" Gwen called from the bedroom.

"Do you have any…" Robin began, turning to Mortimer.

"Of course not, she can have chicken eggs or she can go out and catch a bloody pheasant!"

***

Oberon and Viola approached the Hogwell Smotes Timber Mill, still ensconced in awkward silence. Over the sound of saw blades and heavy loading mechanisms the breeze was threaded with screams and roars. The akka broke into a run and the duart was forced to sprint after him, readying Sleep spells whilst maintaining their disguises, which was akin to simultaneously patting one's head, rubbing one's tummy and turning the pages of a book with one's toes. She realised as they entered the mill that the workers would need to be able to recognise her companion so his Glamour melted away as they passed into the work yard.

They entered a scene of devastation. An akka who looked not dissimilar to Oberon, only larger, with darker green skin, was roaring at the frightened humans, Duart and Akka around him. Two of his own kind were attempting to flank him and grab his arms. A human lay still and face down on the ground with blood trickling from his forehead. Nobody could reach the fallen man without coming within grabbing distance of the disturbed akka.

Oberon gasped as he took all of this in and charged forwards, his hands up.

"Woah, there, buddy," he called as he approached. The other akka was howling in confusion and anger. "Look, Ajax, your friend Evans is hurt. We have to help him!"

Ajax clutched at his head and stepped backward, his eyes closed, panting hard. He howled again.

One of the workers cried out, "We have to put it out of its misery."

"*No*, I've got this," Oberon insisted. "I'll take him away from here."

"If Evans is dead, he's got to face the hangman. Law of England," another worker snapped back.

"He's not dead," Oberon maintained, then pleaded quietly, "Come on Evans, get your ass up."

The foreman finally stirred, as Oberon, never taking his eyes from his brother, gently pulled the human upright and moved in between, to shield him. Viola, who was standing at the periphery, twinkled her fingers in a *Reverse* Sleep spell. Evans' eyes opened wide, he tasted mint and gasped.

"Get that… thing… out of here, now," he screeched.

"It's what I'm doing," Oberon assured him.

The terrified akka's hands were now trembling over his face. Oberon approached and leaned forward to gently touch his shoulder and Ajax reacted like a rocket, grabbing his brother's throat and roaring. Viola stepped forward and held her breath as she sent out the reversal of a Berserk spell. Oberon, far from fighting back, gently stroked the enormous, green arm. With his free hand, he fished about desperately in the internal pockets of his knapsack until he found what he was searching for, raising an object up into his brother's field of vision and tilting it in the light. It was a lovingly crafted carving of a Kuvasz dog.

Oberon spoke soothingly, though fighting back tears. "It's okay. It's fixed. We're going home together, buddy. You and I."

Ajax felt the effects of the spell and his flared, fierce glare softened with sudden concern. Oberon sensed the maajik in the air. A now increasingly familiar sense of taste though no food had touched his tongue; this one was liquorice. His gaze moved to Viola and for the first time, she smiled at him reassuringly. As Ajax released his brother and nodded sadly, confused but amiable, there was a tiny shift in the immense weight on Oberon's shoulders. Gently, indicating exactly what he was going to do, Oberon placed his palm in the small of his brother's back, and handing him the dog to hold, he led him from the factory to the lodging.

Behind them the stunned workers muttered with fear and loathing in their eyes. Viola followed in the tracks of the akka, a stone in her gut. She felt a strange mix of wretched regret and a glow of kindness.

At the empty lodging house, lined with bunks of three different sizes but utilitarian uniformity, Ajax found his trunk with his belongings. Before they left he pulled from under his mattress a length of dark mahogany. It appeared to be beautifully sculpted furniture until Viola realised what she was looking at. Ajax handed the artefact to Oberon.

"Brother," he said in a low voice.

It was a war club, carved with graceful, strong, sure curved lines. The headpiece was distinctly canine in shape. Oberon took it and turned it over in his hands, lost for words.

"It's your best work yet, buddy," he said softly. "I'll be keeping this with me from now on."

"It's magnificent," Viola breathed. Ajax grinned a little bashfully and glanced at Viola. Oberon stared at her too and found himself returning that smile from earlier.

"Now, we gotta beat it," he said to his brother. "You'll have to forfeit your last week's pay. I have to take you to stay with Scarlet until we can figure out a good home for the two of us. Viola, they're probably going to be looking for... for Akka on the street, can you mask us both?"

"I'll make you both very boring humans," she nodded firmly.

"Are you saying I'm interesting?" Oberon found himself saying, playfully.

Viola looked up at him sternly. "Let's not go loopy. That goes double for you, big fellow." She glanced at Ajax. He nodded, and within moments the two apparent humans and their allegedly dull duart companion quietly left the spartan lodging house of the Hogwell Smotes Timber Mill.

***

Ignoring Viola's warning that they should stay put, Robin, Gwendoline and Mortimer were currently traversing the slums of Whitechapel. Gwendoline had dined grudgingly on bacon and hen's eggs, toast and English breakfast tea, and then demanded that Robin show her London. He had, of course, refused.

"Out of the question."

"You told me I would have the holiday *I want*, that's where I want to go and I'm ready now," she replied petulantly, hands on her hips.

"I'm fine walking her around for you," Mortimer put in. "I once had an Old English Sheepdog she reminds me of. Though this one is a sight hairier."

"You must miss having another old dog around," Gwen responded coldly. She turned to Robin, ignoring the look on Mortimer's face, and continued. "Are you coming?"

"I promised Viola…" he protested weakly.

"But you promised *me* first," Gwen reminded him.

"You're the most famous woman in England. That spell of Viola's isn't on any of us right now."

"I'll wear my fighting disguise," Gwen persisted. "I'll keep my scarf up and my hat on. Nobody will care. You can call me Lady Katherine."

"Lady Katherine?"

"I used to have an imaginary friend I'd have tea with… before Viola. I called her Lady Katherine. I remembered her last night. Ow!" Gwen clutched her head briefly. "Seems like as good an alias as I'll get."

Robin shook his head. "It's broad daylight, this is madness."

But the Princess would have none of it. She went to her bedroom and came back bundled in her wool coat, scarf and hat. Robin sighed deeply and popped his hood up as Mortimer held the door open, her expression unreadable.

And now they walked among the impoverished and homeless of London and Gwendoline's bluster had melted away. The gaunt houses towered over them through crooked, cobblestone streets, scattered with filth. The thick, rank air rang with coughing and cries. Light came in grey panels and the cloudy sky beat down through the latticed architecture hanging above.

Robin's pace had quickened. His expression and manner was all of a sudden, serious, almost business-like. He bade Gwen and Mortimer wait outside Emerson's pie shop and emerged after a few minutes, holding several cast-iron bowls. He made a beeline for an old lady who was sat leaning against a lamp post, her gaze somewhere in the middle-distance. She was wrapped in filthy rags and her face was sunken and misshapen. He spoke with her for a minute or two, gave her the pie which she immediately began to eat, then nodded and patted her shoulder as he stood and moved to the staring man huddled in the gutter. His hands were bound and fingers splayed this way and that, injury or palsy having reduced them to shaking uselessness. Robin pulled the fellow into a sitting position and gave him the second pie before moving onto the two children peeking out of a nearby alley, skeletal and pale with malnourishment, their teeth blackened. They got a pie each.

Gwen did not hear what was being said, but she saw the slightly wary look on the faces of the destitute, and how that melted into relief as they began to eat. It was not an extreme of emotion, they were not beaming with joy or clicking their heels, their lives had not been saved, nor changed permanently, but the worry about where their next meal would be coming from had been answered and this act of charity seemed to have had some small impact. Soon people had begun approaching Robin to ask about a pie and in another moment, they were all gone. He walked back, wiping gravy from his gloves.

"I told them to return the bowls to Emerson and they'd get three copper back. Might pay for a bit of supper, too," he added.

He was not smiling or swaggering. A familiar look had come into his eye; unspoken worry. What he did not vouch to the women here, what he would never say, was that being so close to those at the very bottom of society actively *hurt* Robin. His mind filled with the myriad ways he could help them and each of these acts that he did not perform was a reason to chastise himself.

But conversely, after following through on any of them, feeding someone, slipping them the coinage they requested, he was then faced with more hands, more mouths, more sets of despairing eyes looking blankly at him, asking for just a little more. The tiniest hint of satisfaction from an act of kindness was so soon chased away by the swift, miserable assurance that he could never help them all. He could only try his best to do some good… and *some* good was never enough. In the bitter cold of winter was when this debilitating empathy struck him the hardest. Feeling the icy wind on his skin, he sharply pictured a struggle to stay warm without shelter, stay sane without hope, as hunger gnawed at his weakened frame and sapped his strength. Walking the poorer streets of London in January was enough to leave him a wreck of a man.

Now, beggar children scattered around them. Little outstretched hands filled their vision. A cynical and canny voice awoke in Robin, and though his heart was open, he opened his eyes wider and watched the collective pockets of his companions for small, encroaching fingers.

"Mortimer…" Gwen said quietly. "I appear to be without a purse. Could you lend me yours?"

Mortimer shook her head. "I only have silvers in mine."

"And?" Gwen looked at her pointedly.

"*And*, they're not worth giving real money to. Straight down the gin shop they'll go."

"I want to give them something, I want to… do something for them," Gwen said haltingly.

Mortimer started to call her "Princess" but caught herself just in time. "Lady Katherine, this is just a bitter taste of the poverty that our country is gripped by. You can't achieve anything helping individuals. It's best to ignore them."

Robin glared at Mortimer and handed Gwen a wallet containing copper and silver. "Here."

As she walked Gwendoline placed a coin in the hand of every child she came across. Every little *thank you* she heard, every *god bless you, ma'am* had the dual effect of massaging warmth into her heart and spurring her to cultivate more gratitude. The hands got older as more flocked to the trio and Robin began to get extremely nervous. His wallet was emptied and soon so was Mortimer's.

"That's all I have," Gwen said to the crowd. "No, I'm sorry, there's none left. I'm sorry, I'm so sorry miss. Yes, my name is Lady Katherine." She turned to the others. "We need more money."

"Don't look at me, I've just seen my next few meals go into the bellies of wastrels," Mortimer replied sharply.

"Would you like to do something to feed them directly?" Robin asked. "Something like the pies, but enough for a lot more of them?"

Gwen's eyes widened. "Yes," she replied breathlessly.

Robin turned and called out to the assembled crowd. "Any of you who can get to the Lampwick Kitchens on Old Montague street, be there at six bells for soup and a bread roll."

"Tell everyone you know that Lady Katherine is going to feed the poor of London," Gwen added.

Robin winced. "Christ!" The implications of this statement rippled through the crowd and the whispering began. He pulled 'Lady Katherine' through the streets and away from the growing mob to a quieter avenue. The Lady had begun to feel lightheaded and stopped in a doorway to catch her breath.

Mortimer stared at her. "I knew it," the bounty hunter muttered. "She's caught some vile malady off these urchins."

"I'm fine, I-" She covered her eyes with her hands and screwed up her face as waves of pain began to set into her head. "Oh... Oh my, that's powerful. Oh my-" She draped sideways and Robin steadied her.

"What's wrong? You've gone so pale."

"It's my head." Gwen's voice was slurred now. "I have these... fits. Might kill me one of these days. The pain of this one though. I'm seeing spots of light that can't be there. And then there's my old friend, the grey angry wall of fog closing in. I need to lie down."

"Not here," Robin told her. "Not in the street. We're exposed."

"Then take me to bed," she replied woozily. He shook his head, opened his mouth, but could say nothing as he attempted to help her to walk. "Take me to bed, Robin, please," she repeated.

He looked at Mortimer. "We need to get her to a friend of mine. At the Thirsty Hog in Fulham."

"That's miles away!" Mortimer objected.

"We'll take a cab. I'll send for our things and our horse, but I need to get her somewhere that I know is safe and we should have gone yesterday instead. Sorry for not trusting you as a host."

"That's fine, but I'm coming with you," Mortimer insisted.

Robin sighed. "I figured you would. Come on, 'Lady Katherine'."

"Where are you taking me?" Gwen asked.

"We're going to meet my friend, and then you're having a lie down," Robin told her firmly.

Gwen smiled sleepily. "Oh, good."

The trio pitched up at the Thirsty Hog some twenty minutes before Oberon, Ajax and Viola. In that time Robin quietly let them in the back and past Scarlet, who had her sleeves rolled up and was sat at the kitchen table next to a steaming mug of beef tea, poring over her map of London. Behind her reading spectacles her face fell as she caught sight of the unsteady Princess.

"Is that who I think it is?" she asked.

Gwen nodded dreamily. "I am who you think I... is."

"Blimey, is she alright?"

"Attack of the vapours," Mortimer said with mock concern. "Have you a fainting couch or a chaise longue at your disposal?"

"You can use my room," Scarlet replied. "Where's Oberon?"

"He's visiting his brother," said Robin. "You and I need to talk."

"Yeah, we do, who's this?" She jerked her chin in Mortimer's direction.

"This is Mortimer," Robin said, gesturing to the bounty hunter, who bowed theatrically and held out a hand.

"Charmed to meet you, Miss...?"

Scarlet's mouth fell open. She hastily folded up her map. "What in the name of Bonaparte's balls is *she* doing standing in my kitchen?" the akka said with a growl.

"I know, I know," Robin replied apologetically. "My head will be crushed for this, I deserve it, but think of her as an accomplice."

"A co-conspirator," Mortimer said with sardonic glee.

"You two talk, I'll get this one her nap," Robin said.

"What's that smell?" the Princess asked, raising her nose to sniff the air appreciatively.

"Oxtail soup," Scarlet replied.

Gwen breathed deeply. "It's lovely."

"Thank you, I'll make you some."

"Have you got a few more oxtails back there?" asked Robin, innocently. "I need to get some soup arranged at the Lampwick."

"For how many?" Scarlet asked.

"Oh, about… a hundred," Robin called back over his shoulder as he walked Gwen up the stairs. "Have fun, I'll be down in a bit."

"I'm going to pulverise your bones!" Scarlet shouted up to him.

"With good reason!" Robin yelled back. "But I think we may have our shipping contract." Scarlet was left alone in the kitchen with Mortimer, who sat down, daintily at the breakfast table.

"I'll have some soup too, please," she said, steepling her fingers. Scarlet's eyes narrowed.

***

As Robin hauled Gwendoline up the narrow, winding, wooden staircase she clung to him and tried to make her feet work properly. Eventually they reached the bedroom and she sank down into the bed which smelled of beeswax and sandalwood but was comfortable and spacious. Robin made sure she was properly positioned and turned to go. She still had hold of his hand and laced her fingers together.

"You're kind… to me," she said, softly. "To everyone."

"I'm not that kind, I'm just courteous, there's a difference."

"Robin…" Gwen gently drew him closer, bending him towards her. "You can go… if you like." Her voice was warm. She slowly let go of his hand.

"Will you be alright?"

"I'll be fine," she whispered. "I'm a big, tough girl."

He regarded her for a moment, unable to pull away. The Princess reached up and laid her fingertips on the back of his head, gently pulling Robin down into a kiss. She gave a little sigh.

A dozen things came into Robin's head as the kiss ended. There were flip remarks he could try to make, to hide his trembling and drown out the beating of his heart. He could not shake the feeling that he was taking advantage of her current state of mind. There were courtesies and professional notifications regarding bringing her soup and cold water and leaving her to sleep that would put him back to the distance he was required to keep. There were words dancing around that might express how he was actually feeling, how this pull on his being had never felt as strong. Instead he simply sat and they looked at one another in silence, stretching out the moment as long as they possibly could until merciless reality would intervene.

Before that could happen, Gwendoline sat up, and this time Robin pulled her towards him and into a second kiss, his fingers running through her hair as they clutched one another closely. The pounding pain in Gwendoline's head intensified and threatened to overwhelm her senses, but right now she didn't care. She simply knew that she loved him, and that this rush of fierce feeling, as though all was finally right with the world, was entirely worth the agony.

Chapter 15: Shattering Illusions

Thursday Afternoon

Meanwhile, their friends had entered the Thirsty Hog downstairs and Oberon was negotiating with Scarlet for his brother's safekeeping.

"I'll take him," Scarlet whispered. "But look at how things went at the timber mill. You've got to be here every day to look after him. Can you do that? Can you always be there?"

"Yes," Oberon replied firmly.

"Not like you have that many options," Scarlet continued. "I don't know what else you could do. There's no human or Duart institution that will accept someone like him. We took that responsibility ourselves."

"I won't send him away. Forget any plans that involve that." Oberon's face was resolute.

Scarlet frowned. "You're not going to like this at all, but it's got to be said, Oberon, considering where we came from and how. If… If he *kills* someone. If he harms someone and you're not around. I'll take him out myself."

Oberon was aghast. "How can you say that?"

"With great difficulty." Her expression was grim and hard. "But you and I have to be deadly serious about this and use our brains, not only our hearts. That akka is a genuine threat to everyone in this room." Her voice lowered. "He's getting worse and whether we accept it or not, he represents the sudden, unexpected snuffing out of other lives."

"Okay," Oberon looked down, breathing hard. "You're right… I hate that you're right about *this*. But let me promise you, once this princess business is over, I'll take him and we'll go away together."

"Where will you go?"

"Back to Celador, then head south over the Green Sea. Follow in the footsteps of the Akka who went that way. If we find a new home where we… if we find a place where he won't be too much of a danger to those around him, where there are strong enough Akka, maybe we can live out our lives there."

"And if not?"

"Then we won't." He looked up at her sharply. "But I'm the only one who needs to be responsible for him. I won't burden others with that."

Scarlet nodded slowly. "Are you going to tell Robin?"

Oberon shook his head. "I'll tell him before we leave, but he needs his head in this game right now."

Scarlet nodded again and gently touched the scar beside Oberon's eye. "You're a great brother to have," she said softly.

Oberon touched her shoulder and turned back to Viola who was sat across from Ajax and Mortimer, wolfing down a bowl of soup and chunks of treacle from the larder.

"Hey Tiny," he said. "Thank you for your help this morning."

"Just doing what I do, preventing calamity," Viola said nonchalantly, her mouth full. "Don't thank me."

Thursday Evening

The afternoon passed slowly. Robin emerged from upstairs, and the events of the past few days were discussed with Scarlet. He then departed for an hour with a small bag of silver to make arrangements at the soup kitchen, and Oberon went to retrieve their belongings from Mortimer's house. Viola spent a while playing indoor quoits with Ajax. Mortimer sat alone with nothing to do but read her book and clean her weaponry. Gwendoline alternated periods of unconsciousness with crying and laughing. Scarlet set up a sleeping room in the basement for all assembled and conversed with various Hoods who passed through the Thirsty Hog as to the word on the street. Apparently East London was abuzz with news of a mysterious, masked, coated lady with beautiful, blue eyes who had offered to feed *everyone*. Many suspected this to indeed be the missing princess. Viola ground her teeth. Robin, on his return, paced about but did not confront her.

When the hour approached, Gwendoline came downstairs to the waiting pub full of assembled Thieves.

"Shall we go, then?" she asked.

"Consider just staying here," Scarlet said. "Let them eat soup, but don't show your face. It's far too dangerous. People are going to be looking for you."

"Nonsense," Gwen said, dismissively. "The whole point of why I'm doing this is to engage with the people. To stop separating myself from them, and to be around them when they aren't on their best behaviour. I'll never get that as a princess."

"I agree with Scarlet here," said Robin. "This is too much. And you *know* how much a muchness has to be for me to say that."

"It's not about what you want or what you think is best for me." Gwen reminded him, and indeed the entire room. "I want to do this, you can accompany me if you wish."

"You know in some kidnappings it's customary for the kidnappER to give the orders." Muttered Mortimer.

"This isn't a kidnapping anymore," said Gwen. "In fact it hasn't been since minute one. This is a rite of passage for me. Now all of you, stop blocking my passage!"

***

They split into groups and travelled far apart. Robin took the first cab with Gwendoline. Viola and Mortimer followed behind, and Oberon, Ajax and Scarlet came third. Viola was now focusing on making Gwen look like a plain washer woman, since her earlier disguise had now made her infamous in a different way. Robin, with the appearance of a short chimney sweep, sat alongside her. They did not speak, but regarded one another through the masks as London drew past the window.

At six bells as they reached the Lampwick Kitchens. The cabs had to stop short, because the street was jam-packed. They went in the back way and approached the cooks who were being assisted by various Hoods in doling out the soup. Robin had arranged for several cauldrons and raided the nearby bakeries for rolls.

In her washer woman guise Gwendoline was afforded no politeness, and the crowd shoved past her. She was elbowed and kicked absently. Seeing her discomfort Robin stepped in front to at least shield that angle, but the Princess had a plan.

Gwen decisively retrieved her tricorn hat from a bag she was carrying and placed it on her head, pulling her scarf over her lower face and gesturing for Viola to drop the Glamour. The little duart shook her head, pleadingly. In response Gwen defiantly cried out.

"Are you all enjoying your soup?"

Her strong, refined voice carried. She got the attention she had been looking for. Two hundred eyes locked on her position behind a steaming soup cauldron.

"It's her!" someone shouted.

"Can you see who she is?" came another voice.

"Get her scarf off!"

"No, leave her alone!"

Gwen had been beaming, but the tide had turned in the past few moments. The difficulty was in getting everyone to disperse and allow others through to get their food because everyone had been searching the room for Lady Katherine. Now she had revealed herself nobody was leaving at all and the momentum became a shoving match towards the soup. What had begun as a charitable gesture had now warped into a chaotic circus. There were not enough Hoods to keep order and the Watchmen were already muscling through from the outside.

Robin was knocked to one side and Gwendoline lost her grip on his hand. The Princess began to panic. She had never seen so many people all crammed into one place before. Viola hopped up onto Oberon's shoulder and shouted at him over the din to push forward to Gwendoline. His human mask had melted away and he was now clearly an akka in a room full of violently shoving humans. One of the cauldrons was knocked over and people began to trip and fall on the hot, slippery floor. Oberon was punched and kicked from all sides. He buckled and the little duart toppled forwards. He grabbed for her but she had disappeared into the melee.

"Out the way!"

"Kill the Greenskin!"

"Get 'im down on the floor!"

"Move!"

Over the clamour, he heard Viola scream with fear and alarm as Darkness descended on the room.

Oberon roared, then lurched forward, barging bodies aside until he saw a flash of pink and made for it, getting a glimpse of horrified, purple eyes beneath a pile of heaving bodies. He snatched at her jacket, hauling her up high above him.

"We're leaving," he announced loudly.

But it was too late. In her fall, Viola had let go of the spells on Robin and Gwen, and through the haze of maajikal darkness, people were now looking at the shabbily dressed princess and crying out in amazement, delight and fury. Men surged forward to grab her. Women clawed at her hair. The hat was torn off, as was the scarf, and her face was laid bare for all to see. Gwendoline cried out in dismay.

226

Scarlet appeared behind her and grabbed the Princess, pulling the girl through the kitchen and into the back alley. Oberon had hold of Viola and Robin as he followed suit and they found Ajax and Mortimer waiting for them. Viola had cast a blanket of Confusion as they left and now, from the horrific sounds coming from behind the door, she wished she hadn't.

"So that's what this was all about for you?" Viola panted. "You wanted London to love you! You wanted to stand in the middle of an adoring crowd and be their Queen of Hearts. Well, I hope you're happy!"

"Of course I'm not!" Gwen sobbed.

"The Watchmen will be combing Whitechapel for you soon," Scarlet growled. "We've got to get back to the Hog and regroup."

***

The band made their way east, stealthily through the back streets and alleyways. Gwen removed and discarded her coat, and without a word Robin offered her his. She took it gratefully and pulled the hood down low over her face. As they journeyed Viola continued her admonishments.

"How many times have I told you about how rotten it is out here? Did you not listen? Did you not believe me?"

"I *couldn't* believe you," Gwen gasped, taking giant, panicked breaths. "How was I supposed to be Queen of a country like the one you painted for me? I wanted… I wanted to do something nice for people."

"But you wanted recognition?" asked Robin.

Gwen stared at him. "Yes."

"I understand," Robin replied, with no air of condemnation.

"Thank you, Robin," she breathed. "I'm so sorry for this, all of you."

Mortimer tossed her head. "No skin off my nose. I already despise the proletariat."

"Is everyone else alright?" Gwen asked.

"Just bruises," replied Viola, still shaking.

"Some bastard punched me in the head," said Robin.

Oberon put his hand to his side. "I think my stitches have burst."

Scarlet looked worried. "We need to see to those, quick."

Gwen screwed up her face. "Ugh… I hate this feeling so much."

"It's frightening, isn't it?" Robin commented. "They're not the same people anymore." She nodded. "They never will be again," he finished. His tone made it sound less like information, more of a curse.

They had stopped in an awning close to a water pump while Scarlet looked for the least crowded way through. Several human children were approaching with buckets, and an akka girl was making her way over from the opposite alley. Her presence drew glares and sneers from the men drinking on one of the doorsteps.

"Oi, why don't you go 'ome? Eh?" one of them jeered at her.

"Get out of it, there's no water for your kind," snarled another.

Things had turned extremely nasty, extremely suddenly. The men were now up on their feet as the akka child waited patiently in line, clearly trying her best to ignore them. Their expressions in the lamplight were scowling and fierce. Gwen began to step forward. Oberon stopped her.

"This is just what we have to deal with," he whispered. "The kid has survived so far, we can't take another chance tonight. You stay."

"No, I *can't*," Gwen hissed back. She could see a genuine pain and indecision on everyone's faces now, and she was determined to be the one to make the right choice.

"You've already shown your face in London," Scarlet said firmly, setting her jaw. "We literally cannot afford any more attention. Listen, after those people over at that awning move, we go on through and up that lane."

"Don't you dare lift a finger," agreed Viola.

Gwen shook her head. "This is so hateful."

A bottle shattered on the stone, a foot from the akka child. The humans in front of her scattered away and fled, leaving the pump alone. The men were roaring at her now.

"Oi, Greenskin, you deaf?"

"No water. No 'ome for you."

One or two of them had noticed Ajax, Scarlet and Oberon standing in the shadows.

"What is this, a whole family of 'em?"

The first man called out to the group. "All of you clear out of London, there's no room! There ain't enough work for real people, and there's nothing for goblins. You hear me, no room for you!"

Mortimer stalked in the direction of their escape, waving the rest of them along. The way wasn't clear yet, but it would have to do. Scarlet began to move, pulling Ajax and Oberon with her. Gwen and Viola, heads down, started to follow.

Robin remained. He was walking towards the loudest of the men. The outlaw's face had gone pale and stiff, his eyes flared, breathing ragged as he fought for control. He walked past the largest man who was clearly getting ready to take a swing and approached the child as she filled her bucket.

"Sweetheart, would you like me to carry that for you?" he asked.

"Thank you," the girl replied.

"Robb!" Oberon called out to him.

Robin ignored this. "You're very brave," he said to the girl. "But this is too dangerous. I'll help you get the water home, but is there another pump you can go to?"

"Robin," Gwen shouted.

"The other pump makes people sick," the girl replied. "The nearest after that is worse than this. I'll be alright. Thank you again, sir."

"Loxley!" yelled Viola. But the cries of his companions, thirty feet of wet pavement away, did not draw Robin's attention as the men closed around the pair.

The loudest of the thugs towered over Robin and the girl, staring down with jaundiced eyes, breathing fast, ready to lash out. Robin's entire demeanour changed, along with his voice.

"Alright lads," he said in a thick, natural, South London accent. "This is done, don' worry 'bout it, she's goin'. I'll take 'er off yer 'ands."

"I don't think so, son. She's taken Human water," growled the first man.

"Don't muck about now," Robin said. "You know it's everyone's; we gotta share. Come on, lemme get 'er 'ome."

The man shook his head slowly. "No 'ome for this kind in London. Give us the water back."

The akka child took the bucket from Robin's hand and poured the water out on the street. Then with a defiant eye she turned to go. Robin's companions had almost reached the pump.

"You cheeky little slit," snapped the first thug. "Get your arse back here."

"No!" Robin yelled in fury.

There was a sudden, devastating flash. The man had lunged past to grab at the girl's ponytail and Robin had sidestepped only to be grabbed by another of the men. His shirt collar was yanked back, along with his left hand. His right flung forward and punched at the first man, but it was accompanied by a burst of flame which immediately set the fellow's hair and beard on fire, burning the skin off the right side of his face.

His frenzied screams filled the alleyway, high pitched and uncontrolled. The men around them fled as he staggered backwards and fell to the ground, twitching and convulsing. Scarlet leapt to the pump and yanked the handle, spraying him with water and extinguishing the flame, but his wailing still cut through the night air.

Gwendoline and Viola stared at Robin, aghast, as the lamps went out and they were shrouded in darkness. His expression was filled with disgust, fury, and self-revulsion. The Akka child had fled.

"Leg it, now," Scarlet hissed.

The group split up. The Akka went one way, the humans and Duart went the other.

They eventually made it into cabs and returned to the Thirsty Hog where Gwendoline bodily pushed Robin up the stairs to Scarlet's room again.

The sharp memory of their intimate connection here hit them both as she demanded:

"Tell me the truth, who are you?"

Chapter 16: Hidden Identities

The Thirsty Hog, Upstairs

Robin, or rather, the duart who had claimed that name, stared back at the Princess, his fingers knotting and unknotting.

"You know, you don't have to tell me," she said.

"I want to," he replied after a brief pause.

He spoke again in the voice she had heard by the pump. Rough and common with no shred of artifice, theatricality or affected manners. This was his real voice, she knew now.

"My name is Benjamin Wessex… Ben. My father was a cobbler," he said. "Made boots and shoes until his hands gave out, then he just fixed them. My mother worked for a candle maker, and we were shit poor." All of this information came out in a flat and matter-of-fact manner. Not coldly, but without a hint of nostalgia. "When I was nine I decided I couldn't be his apprentice and I came to London."

Gwen continued for him. "Whereupon you found some education at some point, met Oberon, and struck upon the idea of being thieves and taking the mantle of Robin Hood."

He nodded. "Yeah, obviously."

"You're missing out everything important," Gwen said. She reached out and gingerly took his gloved hands. "I don't care a jot that you're from common stock. What I care about is that you immediately went to defend that girl. Knowing they would attack you. You weren't trying to impress me, so why? Who are you really? Underneath all this."

Ben's face darkened. "No," he said.

"No?"

"No, this is too much for you. It's horrible and I don't want you focusing on it, on me. I need to get myself away from you."

"Please don't leave yet," Gwen pressed. "We don't have time. I want to know who the man I love is."

He stared back at her, caught off-guard and too tired to know how best to react.

She nodded. "Yes. It's a fact, I know this to be true. I love Ben Wessex, or Robin or whatever you want to call yourself. This heart, right here." She gently laid her hand on his chest and then withdrew.

He gazed at her, unsure of where to begin. "My father was a monster," he told her, slowly.

"Alright." She nodded in acknowledgement, determined to accept everything about him.

"No, not alright," he exclaimed, a strange look coming to his eye. "You have no idea what it's like to be afraid of your own protector like that. You don't want to know about what he did to me and my sisters. What he did to my mother."

"It's okay, it's okay," she soothed, squeezing his fingers. "Please, I just want you to know you don't have to lie to me anymore, or ever again." He pulled his hands away and sat back. She maintained her stance. "I accept whatever you had in your past, what you have now."

"He used to get us in a corner," Robin said, his eyes unfocused, his tone quiet. "That was his way. Nowhere to run. Make us feel as small as he could, then stamp on us."

"Oh, God."

"My mother had grown used to it years before my older sister Joanne began fighting back." His eyes were glazed now. He was somewhere else. "I think I was five and Jo was ten when she first hit him in the gut. He gave her a black eye for it but she just kept fighting him and screaming." Robin's posture had changed, he had hunched and drawn inward, seeming smaller than she had ever seen him. "I was guarding my baby sister Lisa at the time. He would let me take her away from the worst of it while my mother tried to calm him down." He was trembling now.

"When Jo was eleven she tried to run away. She was going to… she was going to find work and get me and Lisa a place to live as well. He caught her. He went out into the streets after her and dragged her back. Broke her nose against the wall and…" The words caught in his throat. "I remember this, she turned back to him, Jo, she said he was a pathetic creature and she would never stop trying to escape from him, and she would never stop fighting him. She smiled through the blood pouring out of her nose as she said those words and I have never admired anybody more in my life. She was so strong. Stronger than me by far, all I could do when he beat me was cry and tell him I loved him, praying that it would make him stop."

Gwen was longing to hold him, wishing she could wash these horrors away from his life. But every time she leaned towards him he flinched. So she held back.

"I think he may actually have hit me harder than her for cowering. Like he respected her defiance a tiny bit more. Somewhere I think he attributed her strength to himself and didn't understand why it wasn't the same with me. I was his disappointment; she was his achievement." Robin's breathing was slow and laboured, his gaze was cast down, his fists clenched. "That was, until he killed her."

Gwen gasped and began to cry. "Oh no, please, no."

"Just… one too many times, the wall and her head. She just dropped that last time and the light went out of my world. Just gone."

He crumpled, visibly and Gwendoline reached out for his shoulder. This time he did not pull away. He no longer had the energy.

"She was twelve. I would have been seven, so Lisa was four. I had to take Jo's place. I *had* to. So every time he went after Lisa I got in the way." Reaching up, he held aside his shirt collar to show a ragged, white scar across his shoulder. "Bread knife." He pulled off his left glove and flexed his fingers. "That one broke three times, that one twice." He pulled his coat off and revealed his back, which was lined with thin scars and pockmarked with tiny dents. "Belt buckle." He sat back up and covered himself. "But my mother saw what was happening and I think it woke something in her." Anger was creeping into his tone. "She'd buried Jo. Lied to our neighbours about the accident on the stairs and now she was watching me go the same way." His breathing was shallow. "So, when I was nine and Lisa got another black eye from the old man, he and I were going to have a proper fight for once. Mum got in the way and he broke her jaw." He held up his hands and studied them, curling into fists and back again. "That's when the fire came out of me."

Without realising, Gwen had moved the tiniest amount away from him, "Oh."

"You're safe… I think," he drew his hands in. "I can control it unless I get very, very angry, which is why I am… like I am." As he spoke now, his voice changed back to the smooth, mocking tone she was familiar with; the effect was quite unnerving. "I have to find the black humour in even the worst of situations," And again it dropped back down to Ben's quiet, sombre tone. "Because that anger is down there, and I can't get rid of it."

She looked inside for how to react and found that how she had felt on that first night still rang true. "I feel safe around you," she said, and moved closer again. "That hasn't changed. I… I just thought you had to *learn* maajiks like that."

"Nobody told you about this?"

"Just that male Duart are the only ones born with the potential to make fire."

"It's a gift." He smiled mirthlessly. "Only *some* of us have the ability to conjure flame, but the maajik is all in *controlling* it," Now he was looking back and inward again. "Which of course, this being my first time I couldn't." He made two fists and gritted his teeth. "I lashed out at him… and the fire came too. It came straight out of my anger. I hated him so much." He was shaking now, and Gwendoline was faintly aware of a new odour in the room. As though someone invisible had entered and begun striking matches. She did not look at his hands, but she suspected that tiny smoke trails were curling up from them. "But of course, I was nine," he continued, and his shaking stopped. The smoke was still there, but his voice was flat once more. "I had no control. I burned him. I killed him. I burned my mother, our house burned down, the neighbour's houses burned down."

"Did your mother…?" Gwen gasped, terrified of what the answer would be.

"She lived. So did Lisa," he replied. "But I ran. I never looked back. I couldn't. And I haven't even told you the worst yet."

Gwendoline breathed deeply and focused herself. "What is the worst?"

"I didn't feel bad about killing my father." He admitted, his shoulders drooping. "I felt… happy… justified." For the first time in a long while he met her eye, and the look was riven with self-disgust. "That's completely the wrong mindset for a murderer, a murderer *child*… it made me feel like even more of a monster." He reached down and pulled his coat back on, seemingly for warmth. "So I didn't want to be *me* anymore. I didn't want to be *that*. And then tonight…" He glanced at her. "I went back there again." He blew on his fingers and the traces of smoke eddied around the room. "I'm so sorry. Darling, I am SO, so sorry I did that."

"Don't apologise," she told him, carefully. "I know *exactly* what you were doing, and why." That unsettled certainty she had proclaimed before was reforming, stronger for its upset. "I think I finally understand you now… Robin." She watched his face carefully to ensure her understanding of that name was felt.

He sighed deeply as he felt the full weight of this incumbrance shifting a little. The two of them sat together quietly, neither demanding anything of the other. Their companions downstairs left the pair alone for the night and eventually one thing led to another in that warm, dark bedroom, and Gwendoline made love for the first time in her life.

Afterward they lay staring out of the window at the stars, whenever the clouds parted long enough to see the actual night sky.

Chapter 17: On the Uses of Hatred

Friday Morning (Two Days Left)

With the events of the day playing out as they had Gwendoline awoke with Robin in her arms, and a sense of rightness hit her heavily.

His blue eyes opened. He smiled. He still had not said "I love you" in return.

"Robin, darling," she whispered. "It's all so clear to me now."

"What's clear?"

"This compulsion I've had to live free with you," she admitted. "I need to follow it. I can't be Queen. I don't want to and I'd be rubbish at it. And I certainly don't want to marry Lord Aaron."

Robin felt a thrill run up and down his spine. This was something he'd not dared to dream might become a reality. He hadn't allowed himself this indulgence. He was speaking in his theatrical voice again, but she gladly granted him this comfort.

"You want to be with me?" he asked hesitantly.

"Yes. More than anything."

"Where would we go? We can't stay in London."

"Anywhere! We can explore." She chuckled. "We have *two* worlds to chart. We could go to the Americas, or we could go back to Celador, see what's over there, on the continents the Duart are too afraid to tread."

Robin smiled and held her close. They made love once again for luck. Afterwards they lay and stroked one another, as both of their faces slowly went from those smiles to the blankness of realisation.

"We can't," Robin said softly.

"I know."

"I'm sorry," he added.

"I know," Gwen said again.

Robin was silent for a moment. "Can you list the major reasons why not?" he asked her. "It might make us feel better."

"Well, let's see." She propped up Robin's hand and counted on his fingers, still smiling to prevent herself from crying in front of him. "One – it's very dangerous."

"But I laugh in the face of danger."

"Two – we'd have to bring Oberon and Viola."

"The more, the merrier."

"Oh, very good," Gwen replied. "Three – we'd be hunted for the rest of our lives."

"And that's a huge difference for me, *how*?" he asked.

"Point. But it would be a huge difference for me. Four…" And at this she paused, and shame tinged her voice. "I'm honestly missing the comforts of the palace right now."

"Oh." Robin looked away, a little crushed.

"But not as much as I would miss *you*," she added hurriedly.

"Yes, you're going to miss the hell out of me. I'm still waiting for a reason we can't work around, though."

Gwen caressed his thumb. "Five – my… father, Coriolanus, all of his plans for the coming years revolve around my being there as Queen. Without me…" She stopped, considering "Do you know, I don't even know what his plans would be, so that's…"

"That's the main one, isn't it?" he said, softly. "Maybe you could just… ask him for a reprieve."

Gwen shook her head. "No, that wouldn't happen. I know him. His mind is set on this."

"You'd disappoint your future husband."

"I think… I think I'll be doing that whatever my choice." Tears were threatening to spill forth. She bit them back. "Remember what Merlene said about more than one different timeline?"

Robin nodded.

"Well, we're at a fork in the road here." She splayed her hands out. "In some worlds I'm going to choose to defy my father and stay with you. I will choose to run."

Robin looked at her expectantly. "…But…"

"But not in this one."

His gaze fell. "Of course."

"I don't know how the other versions of me are thinking when they make their opposing decisions, but in this world, I'm going to choose to stay. I'm going to marry Lord Aaron. I'm going to be Queen."

Robin nodded, as supportively as he could manage.

"My father is cruel," she continued. "He puts the happiness of the people well below the state of order and control. He believes that their continued survival and the strength of the system that holds them together is the real basis of their wellbeing." She considered for a moment, picturing the man in her head. "Aaron is no different. If I'm Queen I can help… steer the ship." These words were flowing forth, a sense of moral assurance, interwoven with well-worn pain, that seemed sharper now that she had been given the chance to relieve it. "Coriolanus has pledged to cede to me as Empress when I'm married to Aaron. That's influence I could never have anywhere else." Her tone was deadly serious as she locked eyes with Robin. "It's a gift. I have to use it responsibly. If I can be wise and just and strong I can use that influence to save lives and make things better. Unite as many as we can and get these worlds back on their feet."

Robin breathed deeply and held her hands in his. "Honestly, I think you'll be a *wonderful* empress. I wouldn't want anyone else in charge... and... maybe you can pardon me."

Gwen beamed, and only a single tear betrayed her. "Maybe... If you can be good."

"Meanwhile," said Robin, his face darkening. "The people who nearly tore you to pieces last night get a kinder person in charge of them. I'm sure their lives will all be improved."

"Well, why do *you* do it?" Gwen demanded, not accusingly, but searchingly. "Why do you give back to them? Why do you sacrifice your life for people who don't know and don't care?"

"Because..." The trace of bitterness subsided as quickly as it had come, and his face went blank. "I don't know how to do anything else."

"Well, there you have it," Gwen said. "That's as good a reason as any I could come up with."

The two of them crept quietly down the stairs, hoping not to wake anyone and steal some breakfast. As they opened the door into the kitchen they saw the others gathered around the table, staring back at them with various expressions.

"Did you have a good sleep?" Viola enquired sweetly.

Robin made his way forward and sat down with the others. Viola, Scarlet and Oberon scowled at him, Mortimer appeared aloof and disinterested, leafing through the Times. Ajax smiled in faint recognition and touched elbows with him.

As Gwendoline stood before the expectant group it became clear they were waiting for her next decision.

"Right then," the Princess began. "I suppose today is the day Viola and I return to the palace. I assume Mortimer here is just going to walk us through the front gate."

"That was certainly my plan," the bounty hunter remarked. "I'll negotiate a settlement, have the gold brought to the bank for me and then later on I can slip you people your half. Anyone else – sorry, any*thing* else you'd like to do before then or shall we head out now?"

Gwen refused to rise to the bait. "Miss Scarlet?"

"Just Scarlet," the akka corrected.

"Scarlet; Robin and Oberon mentioned your factories," Gwendoline pressed. "Would you mind if I toured one of them to ascertain how they're run?" Scarlet's eyebrows had already raised and she was clearly getting ready to politely refuse. Gwen pushed on. "I should like to see how the money for my return will be spent. In disguise, of course, and I promise you solemnly that this time I shall keep a low profile."

Scarlet considered for a moment, then nodded. "I can take you through Wool and Cloth," she agreed, then shot Gwen a piercing look. "But you muck about and I'll hand you straight over to her." At this she indicated Mortimer who smiled, primly.

Gwen shook her head with resignation. "My days of mucking about are over."

"Alright," sighed Scarlet. "Let's just finish breakfast and…"

There was a banging on the front door and everybody froze.

Scarlet wordlessly indicated the basement and Robin, Gwendoline, Viola, Mortimer, Ajax and Oberon all swiftly and quietly filed down the stairs, closing the shutter behind them. Scarlet covered it with a hessian mat, crossed to the front door and opened up. Captain Baltus marched in with a contingent of eight Watchmen. The Hood behind the bar continued to clean glasses nonchalantly, but those others sat having breakfast froze with their food in their mouths.

"We're just about to open," said Scarlet, to the Captain. "But I can get things moving faster since you're clearly in a hurry. Bacon and eggs all round, is it?"

Baltus stared at her balefully, and when he spoke, the threat was palpable. "Is she upstairs or downstairs or out the back?" He had locked eyes with her. "If you tell me the truth now, you'll escape the hangman's noose."

There was a long silence. Scarlet gazed down at the duart, grimly.

245

"You know of whom I speak," Baltus said, when she did not reply immediately.

"I can only assume you mean our missing princess," she said eventually. "Since that's all anyone will talk about this week."

"Correct. What is your name?" the captain asked her.

"Gillian Oberman," Scarlet replied without hesitation. "Same as it says on the lease for this place. You can check all my records."

"Not many Akka run businesses in London."

"I'd like to think I'm one of a new breed of intrepid entrepreneurs. We had businesses back on Hannoth, you know. How else could we have gotten by as a civilisation?"

"If you like to call that 'civilisation', then of course you did."

Scarlet didn't react to the implication. "What I don't know is why you might believe she's hiding in my pub. Now can I get your men a drink?"

"Let's save that little nugget about what I know for a little while, after I've said my piece. Will you please sit down, Miss Oberman."

"Do you mind if I eat?" she asked.

"Please do."

Scarlet slowly and deliberately retrieved a plate of food, sat before Baltus and began to eat with measured movements, keeping her eyes on him at all times.

"You know…" he began. "When we first arrived in London – the Duart, I mean – we were apprehensive as to the reaction of the humans." His demeanour had shifted somewhat. He leaned back in his seat as though

246

happy to be furnishing her with this background detail. "Certainly, we dealt with their barghest, but we were presenting them with an iron hand of governance. I wondered why they welcomed it so readily. I mean, do they *want* to be so ultimately powerless in the course of their lives? That was until I realised the masterstroke of the Dukes. Do you know what it was?"

"Tell me," Scarlet said.

"It was bringing *you* with us," the Captain stated, a thin smile on his lips. "It will come as no surprise to learn that you Akka *disgust* the Duart. We in the gentry thought it was only us to begin with, but the greater population of Duart citizens confirmed our feelings with a matching sentiment. In the years since you first plagued our realm, everywhere you have gone, the people who live in those lands develop this disgust as a natural reaction, and that means of course that the humans shared it." At this Scarlet said nothing and shovelled down a spoonful of scrambled egg. Baltus continued.

"Your species inevitably dropped to the bottom of the ladder, and theirs accepted our supremacy because we had given them *someone new to hate*." His voice rang with a note of triumph. "I assure you, there is nothing more that a working man needs in this life than a few coppers from those higher than he, a roof over his head and a family who lives on his street that he hates. Because you see, without that detestable *someone*, the man has nowhere to direct his hatred than upwards. He must live to protect his family and he needs an enemy to protect it from. So you see…" He leaned forward, conspiratorially. "We killed the barghest and you filled the black vacuum left behind."

***

In the cellar, directly below this discussion, Robin was staring up through a crack in the floor, a sliver of light crossing his face. Gwendoline held him tightly, Viola was shuddering with rage, Oberon had his hand over Ajax's mouth and this time even Mortimer's forced smile was beginning to show cracks. Why had she come down here with these reprobates instead of hightailing it out the back and over the rooftops? They huddled in the dark and attempted to subdue every sound.

Captain Baltus continued as Scarlet chewed impassively. "So, I want to thank you here today, warmly, sincerely, thank you," Baltus said. "For *giving* us England."

Scarlet finished her mouthful and said, flatly, "You're welcome."

"You know what?" he responded, cheerily, in a way that quite chilled her blood. "We *are* welcome, aren't we? And what makes me even more amused is that I am sitting here, symbolic of the highest a person can climb in our society, a decorated, military Duart man, champion of the people of Skygrail, born in the lands of Telemeron. I stand above nearly all Duart men, who stand above all Duart women, who stand above all human men, who stand above all human women, who stand above all Akka males, and at the very bottom of the ladder, barely able to separate themselves from the endless oceans of sludge beneath, are the Akka females. You." He stroked his beard with caronite-plated fingers.

"I'm curious as to how your people even get through the day," he remarked. "Do you hate rats or cockroaches with the same volition as we hate you?"

Scarlet fixed him with the steadiest gaze she could manage, and said in a measured, careful tone, "We know what the bottom feels like, and that every rung up that ladder feels better than the last. That's what keeps us going."

"But of course, with so many others locked into place above you, you must surely realise there aren't many rungs you can climb before you are stopped in your tracks."

Below, Oberon felt a hand on his forearm. He glanced down and found to his surprise that it was Viola. She did not look at him, her head was lowered with shame and rage, but he felt the fingers squeeze.

"Now let us return to what you said I may know," Baltus announced. "For you see, *you* have no way of knowing how much I *do* know. It is for you to suspect the very worst but pray to whatever totem pole you worship for the very best… that I know nothing about you or your business or what you do when you are not tending bar here." Baltus smiled mirthlessly and splayed his fingertips upon the surface of the table. "Now, what I offered before still stands. If you tell me where she is, you will escape the noose, but may I add a few cherries to the best cake you are ever going to be presented with?" Scarlet shrugged but said nothing.

Baltus continued, apace. "I have a particular fascination with the mental processes associated with torture." At the last word, Scarlet's eye twitched and Baltus leaned in closer. "I don't so much enjoy the infliction of pain, although I am able to do that without it bothering me, what interests me is how desperate people become when they have that one piece of information I want, but wrestle with their abilities to conceal it throughout their ordeal. Almost always they confer it to me in the end, but it fascinates me what they will endure under the mistaken apprehension that somehow my nerve is not as strong as theirs, and that I will stop… I never do."

Baltus picked up a fork from the table and turned it in his hands carefully. It began to smoke ever so slightly and Scarlet could smell the heating metal.

"But the worst suffering is for those individuals who do *not* have that piece of information that I want. Those who do not know why they're on my table, perhaps those who know many things but don't know *which* to say. Their suffering is far worse because they have nothing to focus on holding back." The fork was now glowing orange and Baltus ever-so-gently burned four thin black lines across the table-top. "My *point* is that right now, for all you know, I may believe, truly that you are in that first camp. That you know something and you are holding out against me because you think that I will stop. You could well be willing to suffer for what you know." He pressed down hard and moved his hand away, leaving the burning brand standing upright. "However, if you really do have nothing to hide, then it is even worse for you, because you are in the second camp… You do not know what to say to make me stop."

Baltus turned to his men and nodded. The eight armoured Firecasters proceeded behind the bar, into the kitchen and up the stairs. Below, Gwen's eyes widened as she cast her mind back to the bedroom. Had she forgotten anything of hers up there?

"You cannot affect what I know," Baltus said firmly. "You cannot tell me any lie that will eclipse what I know. You can do nothing to remove me, or these Duart men who stand so far above you, from your home."

The hessian mat was turned over and the cellar shutter was pulled back, letting a flood of light into the underground sanctum.

"All you can do is tell me everything right now. That is the only way you can be sure of your fate." He slid his fingers together and propped his chin up, glaring directly into Scarlet's eyes. "So, what say we do away with all this uncertainty? Uncertainty that you now know will only lead to your suffering."

Four Watchmen proceeded down the stairs and began turning over tables. Baltus continued to glare at Scarlet over the smoking fork as a growing dark patch began to pool out from it.

In the cellar the Watchmen approached the false wall the Thieves were hidden behind. Oberon spotted Mortimer very slowly and quietly cocking two different pistols. Robin's face was straining. His hands were starting to smoke. If they caught aflame or the Watch detected the traces of that on the air…

Viola blinked, thinking as fast as she could. Since the Watchmen were actively searching for hidden people she could not cast a spell strong enough to mask their presence and make them see farming equipment as she had done with Gwen and Robin in the trunk. That was a tough enough spell to manage with only two people to hide from a single slow-witted border inspector looking for fruits and vegetables. There was no point disguising them as six random, boring humans hiding behind a false wall. They would still be arrested for doing just that.

Darkness would do no good, the Watchmen would suspect something was up or bring more lights. She didn't have the strength to cast Sleep on eight guards at once, effectively – *maybe,* if nobody else was around her and she could see them all. But her companions in close proximity hindered her here. Confuse, Berserk, Silence, none of these could get them out of this cleanly.

A Watchman approached the wall and prodded it with a gloved finger.

Gwendoline squeezed Viola's arm hard.

Viola's mind went back to that spoiled little girl on the day they had met.

Suddenly she had it.

Viola cast a strong Silence spell across the whole room. There was a shift in the air. All four of the guards in the cellar straightened up and sniffed. Each of them could taste bacon strongly, the side-effect of the maajik that the little duart had just recalled. Viola's vision blurred as the spell took its toll, but the Watchman in front of their false wall licked his chops.

"Nothin' here Captain," he called up the stairs. "How about that breakfast?"

"Yeah, I could do with a sandwich," replied the duart behind him.

The men exited through the cellar door and good to her word, within a few minutes Scarlet had fried them twenty-seven rashers of bacon and a crucible of scrambled eggs. The entire time Baltus sat behind her, watching like a hawk.

Chapter 18: Goodbyes

Friday Afternoon

When they finally left, Scarlet was in no doubt that there was someone nearby keeping an eye on her establishment, so she waited until the lunchtime rush to smuggle the disguised outlaws and royalty out of the door and across to the Hoods' wool and cloth factory.

"We shan't be bringing you back there again, Your Highness," she told Gwen firmly. "This will be one of your final ports of call."

Gwendoline had been trembling with a mixture of confusion, doubt and anger for hours now and walking in an open space was what put her back on firm footing, as it were.

"My first order of business as Empress will be to *fire* that captain," she said haughtily. "He's beyond vile."

"I could have told you that…" said Viola. "In fact, I believe I have."

"The way he treats people…" Gwen continued. "I had no idea things were this hard. I'm so sorry, Scarlet."

"It's why we do what we do," the akka replied.

Scarlet walked them calmly and quietly through the sunlit factory, up and down several stories of workers beavering away at the spooling and weaving machines. Their labour was not much fun, but Scarlet took pride in their safety, their cleanliness and her remit not to exhaust them. She outlined the history of the industrial system for Gwendoline, the horrendously skewed distribution of wealth across the hierarchy of gender and species, with nearly everyone below the middle classes treated like a combination of livestock and machine. But here was a place, said Scarlet, where human, Duart and Akka were treated equally regardless of gender or age, a trend she was hoping would catch on.

Gwendoline stooped to pet a tabby cat that was making its way through the bales of wool, hunting mice, no doubt. Crouching down there the Princess spotted some workers watching the tour party with interest and before she knew what she was doing her hand was up and waving gracefully at them. It was what happened ten or twelve times a year whenever they went shopping and her carriage rolled through the pretty and grandiose streets of Knightsbridge, or whenever there was a Trooping of the Colour, or some other event where she was paraded before the public. Muscle memory jump-started conventional memory which immediately formulated into the makings of a plan.

"I've had an idea," Gwen said, her eyes lighting up.

"I believe we're still recovering from your *last* one of those," Viola reminded her. "And the one before that, and the one before that…"

"Viola, this concerns you," Gwen said.

"It certainly does," Viola replied.

"No," Gwen said. "I mean you have to take a part in this. Remember how I get you to pay guards like Simon to fight me?"

"Y-yes?"

"Well, why don't we just sneak back into the palace, say it was all a game and nobody kidnapped either of us, then you get me two thousand gold and we'll sneak it out to Robin and Mortimer?"

Viola's face fell. "I'm afraid that's not going to be possible, Gwen. The amounts I deal with are just golds and silvers. I can get the bursary staff to alter the pay grades of the guards a little, and you've seen the paperwork I have to fill out for that."

"But what about when I go shopping?" Gwen asked.

"It's a different place." Viola shook her head. "Everything has to be accounted for."

"Yes, but if we're clever we could move small amounts around where they won't be noticed," Gwen persisted. "See, I'm getting good at this skulduggery."

"We don't have *time*." Viola turned to the rest. "When did you need this contract?"

"*Wednesday*," Scarlet, Oberon and Robin replied simultaneously. Gwen looked momentarily crushed.

"Could I steal you a tiara or something very valuable from the palace? I'm sure Viola could cause enough distraction for me to pilfer enough to fetch a thousand. I've got all sorts of jewel-encrusted eggs you can just *have*. I don't want them."

"Two thousand!" Mortimer corrected.

"I've got fences who can deal in that stuff," replied Scarlet. "But not by Wednesday, not without taking some serious risks. And the only people who want sparkly eggs in London are... well, no offence ma'am, but people like you. And they want them from posh... uh... *reputable* places."

"Oh, well, Mortimer can *you* lend them a thousand?" Gwen asked, determined not to be thwarted yet. "Just until they can make that money back in trade?"

"No, I bloody can't." Mortimer looked entirely affronted at this.

Gwen narrowed her eyes. "Can't or won't?"

"Pick one," replied the bounty hunter, folding her arms firmly.

"Oh God, there are so many things that can go wrong with this," sighed Gwen.

"Believe it or not, these are better odds than we usually face," Robin told her. "Although there have been quite a few unforeseen... complications." His hand brushed against hers as he gestured.

Gwen stared at him for a long moment. "Alright... I'm ready... Take me back to the palace. We'll go with the reward plan," she said resolutely.

Robin's brow furrowed in concentration. "There's just one more thing we have to do. Scarlet, could you take Ajax back to the Thirsty Hog please?" She nodded and moved to the exit, gently but firmly nudging Ajax along with her. He turned before he left the factory and raised his enormous green hand to Viola. She looked a little stunned and raised her own in response.

Robin led them through the back alleys to a safe house he believed was secure and ushered them up to the attic bedroom. All aside from Mortimer, who was asked to stand in the kitchen and keep watch.

"What's going on?" Oberon asked, looking around the group. "Are we not taking her back yet?"

"Can you wait here for a bit, old boy?" Robin asked.

"What?"

"I just need a word with the lady, if you know what I mean."

"Oh God, fine!" Oberon grumbled.

He turned his back and directed his gaze towards the skylight. Robin nodded to Viola and left the room with Gwendoline who was glancing behind her with worry, her hand trembling in his. Oberon tasted lavender and turned in surprise as a hard Sleep spell hit him squarely in the face. He tumbled to the ground and Viola scurried forwards to check him. He was groaning so she gently pressed her fingers to his temple and whispered several words. The sleep became deeper and Viola began to shake with the onset of weakness.

***

A minute later she limped from the room, closing the door behind her.

"He's down," she whispered. "Took a lot out of me, but it's powerful. Should be out for about ten hours."

Robin kept his voice low as well. "Thank you."

"You two planned this?" Gwen asked incredulously.

"Listen, do you trust Mortimer?" Robin asked her.

"Not in the slightest," she replied.

"Well, if she double-crosses us, I don't want *him* to suffer for it, nor Scarlet, nor Ajax or anyone."

"Well, why do *you* have to do this?" Gwen demanded.

"You know why, and nobody else is going to swing on my account."

"For the record I approve of this sensible course of action," Viola put in, as she made for the stairs to leave them a final moment to themselves. She joined Mortimer in the kitchen, who glanced at the duart's little shaking hands and then up the stairs behind her.

"I smell maajik," the bounty hunter said slyly.

"I had to lay out the akk- *Oberon,* to keep him out of this."

Mortimer nodded slowly, her face a mask of concern. She leaned back against the counter and her coat draped aside, revealing her holstered pistol.

"Do I have to worry about you screwing up this deal, little one?"

Viola controlled her breathing and searched herself for some strength. She popped a piece of toffee into her mouth and glanced up.

"Not in the slightest," she replied flatly. "What I want most in the world is for Gwen and I to be back at Buckingham Palace. Safe and sound."

"Really… the rogue's life doesn't appeal to you?" Mortimer asked.

Viola looked down at the floor. "I'm a jester."

Mortimer studied her critically for a long moment. "Yes, you are." Viola's guts twisted up and she fiercely fought to maintain control of her face, her body and what was behind these feelings of everything being so very wrong.

***

Gwendoline stood before Robin in the dusty upstairs hall, uncertain of how to say goodbye to him, or whether she was capable of doing so at all.

"Listen," he said, choosing his words carefully. "I have one thing to say that I want to get said." He breathed deeply. "I have acquired a reputation in recent years for being something of a ladies' man."

"*That* I had heard," Gwen relied.

"I want you… no, I *need* you to know that on that first night, while I was dabbling in flirtations, I was genuinely very much enamoured of you… but over the days that followed that infatuation turned into something more, and last night…" He cleared his throat. "What I'm attempting, very *poorly*, to say is that… you were never a *prize*."

Gwen looked away. "Robin, I am betrothed to Lord Aaron. On Sunday night, he was to make me a woman… as is tradition." She sounded matter-of-fact. "At some point, I decided very firmly and clearly that I wanted to take that journey with you instead. This was my choice… *you* were my choice. And the fact that we won't…" She broke off with a slight choking sound. "I shall miss you, Robin."

"I shall miss you too," he said. "But you know, this is fine. We had an exciting week for us both to remember, and you got that holiday you wanted. I should have liked to take you to the French Riviera; it's going to be a lot prettier once all the monsters have gone."

"Oh, it sounds enchanting," Gwen replied.

"It is. I mean, I hear it was. I've never been off this island… in *any* dimension, come to think of it." He shrugged amiably.

"Then shall we agree to meet there together, someday," Gwen said, seizing on the chance to end it on this.

"Agreed," he smiled.

"Keep an eye on what I'm doing."

"I will."

"Try not to steal away any more girls," she advised. "We don't like it. It's creepy."

His smile faltered a moment. "I'll never steal another."

She laced her fingers into his and kissed the top of his head.

"A fine thief you turned out to be," she whispered.

***

Less than an hour later Gwendoline and Viola stood before the gates of Buckingham Palace as they were hastily opened. Mortimer had taken up the head of the triangle between the Princess and the Duart as they marched purposefully back, but as they crossed into the courtyard Gwen sidestepped and quickened her stride to steal her place in the centre.

The Archduke approached, his eyes wide and blinking in the sunset. He stopped before her and she knelt to embrace him in his hard, edged armour. His broad hand caressed her head.

"You are home, child," he proclaimed.

Back in her room, Gwendoline sank down on the bed as a flurry of medical professionals, courtiers and attendants moved about her, undressing, checking every inch of her body. Gwendoline stared at the ceiling the whole ordeal. Her skin was scrubbed clean, anointed with oils, and the physical aches were massaged out. All traces of the outside were washed away. She could no longer smell him around her.

Gwen fixed on Robin's face throughout, swearing to herself to keep those eyes in her mind, something to call upon in the future when the world was unbearable, when she was not required to speak but simply look pretty, when Lord Aaron was pressing himself down upon her. Eventually she was left alone to rest for the big day.

After some hours Viola entered her bedroom.

"Vi?" Gwen was surprised. She had assumed they would be separated now.

"I'm… I'm permitted to stay as your companion." Viola said. "For the time being."

"And after the wedding?" Gwen asked.

"I don't know. Coriolanus thanks me for keeping you safe. He's just finished dealing with the bounty hunter."

"Vi… be absolutely honest with me," Gwen begged. "Did we do the right thing?"

"I think we did the right thing… for England," Viola replied.

"So from this day forth… I am to close my eyes and think of England."

Viola laid a consoling hand on her arm. "It would appear so, my darling."

Friday Evening

Across London, some hours later, Robin stood in an alley not far from Mortimer's house. He chewed his lip and drummed his feet. He could see Gwendoline's face so clearly in his mind, that sad, hopeful strength he intended to project to the people he helped in the coming weeks and months of what was very likely to be a short life.

He spied the familiar lithe figure of Mortimer stalking towards him down the darkened street, carrying a small chest, and his mind raced back and forth along his journey back to Fulham with this coffer concealed under his cloak. Could he ask her to accompany him for protection?

He did not see her face in the shadows before he heard the clanking of the Watchmen.

There was a brief second while he weighed up his odds.

They were behind him at the other end of the alley.

Could they simply be patrolling the street?

No, too many.

And behind Mortimer, as she turned, more of them.

He was boxed in.

Robin sprang up against the right-hand wall, rebounded to the left and careered upwards, zigzagging through the air as a roar went out to open fire. The alleyway filled with flame and as he reached for the rooftops Robin heard Mortimer shout out not to burn her.

His fingers found the edge of the roof and he scrambled up to freedom, only to be confronted by a consortium of roofbound Grabbers, lightly armoured for stealth. They seized his arms and hauled him up, holding daggers to his neck. It was all Robin could do to grimace a smile through the sudden bolts of fear shooting through him.

"I'm just walking home from work, officers," he said, smoothly. "Is there something I can help you with?"

One of the Watchmen pushed the tip of his knife against Robin's throat. "Shut up. You're not getting away this time."

"Getting away?" Robin asked, trying not to let his coursing fear show. "Just what am I being charged with here?"

Captain Baltus strode across the roof towards the point Robin of Loxley stood pinned. He held up a wanted poster next to Robin's face. The illustration was an alarmingly good match.

"Let's start with robbery, burglary and evasion," Baltus growled, softly, triumphantly. "Then add kidnapping, conspiracy and *treason*."

Part 3: Hanging Heavy

Chapter 19: Revelations

Saturday Afternoon (One Day Left)

Saturday passed with alarming speed for Gwendoline. She was re-fitted for her bridal gown, well-fed, and given back all the comforts she had been missing. She visited with Aaron and Coriolanus, but all they spoke of was the wedding; nobody seemed to want to know where she had been, nobody was dying to unravel the riddle of the web of thieves hiding throughout London. It was all focused on the future; the past was behind her now.

That afternoon she sat nursing an iced lime sherbet in her bedroom, Sebastian licking her spoon as she did not seem interested in doing so herself. She stroked his lovely, furry head and wished she was as blissfully ignorant to the troubles of the world.

She checked herself. A week ago, she had been exactly as ignorant. Was she wishing all that hadn't happened?

Viola entered quietly and stood in front of her, eyes alarmed, tone slight and muted.

"Come with me, right now," she said.

"Where?" Gwen asked, sitting up straight.

"The library."

Figuring what this meant, Gwen put on her slippers, grabbed a lamp and followed her bodyguard to the secret tunnel, checking to ensure they were not spotted or followed. Viola led her a different way this time, turning to the left and left again until a few shafts of light piercing through from the adjoining room told her they were beside her father's retiring quarters. The voice of the Archduke filtered in.

Gwen recalled coming this way many years ago and spying on him. She had nestled with Viola in this dusty alcove, alive with anticipation as to what secrets she might hear. An hour later, after words like 'finance' and 'tariff' had been said many times, she had realised she wasn't actually all that interested in the politics he dealt in. Coupled with this was a gathering feeling of guilt for her eavesdropping. She knew she ought to respect his privacy, even at that early age, and the thought that he might return the favour and spy on she and Viola alone in her room made her uncomfortable. So, she had abandoned this post and returned to bed, only to sneak back a handful of times over the years to catch a glimpse of her father in repose when he had shut himself away for what she felt was too long.

Now, she felt his true mindset pertaining to her return would be rather important, and the look in Viola's eyes was making her very nervous. Another voice could be heard. It was Lord Aaron's.

"And how many ships for the September fleet?" her betrothed asked.

"One hundred, but these will not be warships," Coriolanus replied. "The Spanish Navy is most definitely depleted. These will merely be transport for a third infantry unit. Once again we shall bolster their ranks with appropriately attired humans."

"I am cautious of spreading our Firecasters too thinly over Spain," Aaron remarked. "Even after we have called our remaining forces through the gate, the British Isles will effectively have to be emptied of fire units. I fear an uprising on our own shores."

"I shall replace our firecasting prelates in the counties with non-maajikal officers," the Archduke told him. "Now that the barghest is all but extinct on this island there is little cause to station valuable weaponry across such scattered geography. It is a bluff the English will not call us on. This campaign turns on the axis of a *threat* of force."

"And if there are uprisings in France, or if Prussia anticipates our intent?" Aaron queried.

"Then it is as I said," Coriolanus responded calmly, "we shall have to strike with unyielding and merciless violence, enacting a battle so horrific, so far in excess of what the humans have come to know from their history as the bloodshed of war, that none will choose to engage in another."

"An unpleasant picture to paint for the sake of fealty."

"I do not like to think of war as punishment – it is the peak of a man's ability to affect the world – but occasionally, as with tomorrow's execution of the Hoods, an example must be made."

"I said it was unpleasant, but I *do* understand its necessity."

Gwendoline had heard enough to make the blood freeze in her veins. She stumbled away from their hiding place and back through into the library.

"Attacking the people of England? Execution of the Hoods?" she gasped in horror.

"I overheard before I came to you," Viola told her. "I had to see what the outcome with that bounty hunter was." Her face was grave and ashen. "They've taken the Thirsty Hog. Scarlet and everyone connected with her is now in the Tower of London." Gwen held her hands over her mouth to keep from screaming in alarm. Viola continued, her breathing shallow. "They caught Robin last night at the handoff of the reward."

Suddenly Gwendoline was moving. This was too much of a nightmare to stand still and absorb. She ran from the library and along the empty corridors and staircases of Buckingham Palace, straight to the Archduke's quarters. Two guards began to stop her walking in but her expression was so fierce that they held back.

She burst through the double doors to confront Coriolanus and Aaron, who stood poring over a map of Europe. It was dotted with models of ships and armed battalions. Gwen knew enough to recognise an occupation.

"Pardon them!" she shouted abruptly. Coriolanus looked up in surprise.

"What?"

"Pardon the Hoods immediately," Gwen demanded. "I was the one who orchestrated the entire kidnap and you're not going to put *me* to death, so pardon and release them."

Beside the Archduke, Lord Aaron's face changed from a look of shock to an indulgent smile. "You're all flustered, sweet pea," he soothed. "Those vagabonds have addled your poor mind even further, so that you wouldn't talk to me earlier. I was rather hurt!" He took a step towards her and held out his hands. "How about after your father and I finish our discussion, you and I go for a nice ride on our ponies. Get some fresh air. I'll ensure we're heavily guarded so this won't happen again."

Gwen did not even look at Aaron but kept her eyes laser-focused on those of the Archduke.

"Father?"

Coriolanus gave a long sigh. "Lord Aaron, Viola, may we have a moment in private, please."

Stunned, Aaron set his brandy and cigar down, and still trying to catch Gwendoline's eye, left the room. Viola backed out slowly, riven with worry for her princess, and closed the doors.

Once they had both disappeared and he was certain they were alone, Coriolanus spoke solemnly and carefully. "I'm afraid, Gwendoline, that I cannot do what you ask."

"Why not?" she cried.

"The Hoods are a nest of vipers," he stated. "They have sought to constantly undermine our rule, and this fiasco of your disappearance was the last straw."

"But I ran away," Gwen insisted. "I wanted a moment's reprieve from this marriage, this whole future you have set up for me."

"Regardless," he maintained. "It is for their mountain of previously allotted crimes that they shall be put to death." His posture shifted and his eyes narrowed ever so slightly. "Now, I am told by those who inspected you…" he said, "that your maidenhead is gone." There

270

was a pause, as his gaze rested upon her, unwavering. She glanced away. "I will not ask you how or why, but Lord Aaron will need to be informed so that he is prepared for tomorrow night." There was a silence between them. "To protect your honour, you may construct an acceptable falsehood about an accident that robbed you of your virtue. Nobody else need know."

Gwen turned this over in her mind, racing back and forth between her window of opportunity and her inescapable obligations. "What time are they executed?" she asked.

"What does it matter?"

"What time?"

"Eight bells in the morning," the Archduke replied. Gwen's face, which had been a picture of fury, crumpled into sorrow. He took a step towards her. "Were you thinking," he asked. "That as Queen and Empress you could pardon them yourself in my stead? Save their lives?"

Hope was draining away. Gwen changed her approach. "I ask you for this one sweet favour," she pleaded. "You need never do another thing for me."

"Considering you ask me for favours every week, I highly doubt that," he countered.

"I swear, this will be the last thing I ask of you."

"Gwendoline." There was a touch of gentle insistence in his voice now. "It makes no rational sense to reprieve them. It makes us look weak, permissive."

She shook her head, and then made a decision and composed herself. "Alright then, if you won't spare their lives, then the moment I am Empress I shall change everything that you hold to be of import. I shall start by firing Captain Baltus. He is a black-hearted lunatic and he makes all Duart seem beastly. I shall then commence the relieving of all the prelates in all the counties and giving England back to the humans." Her eyes flashed. "And you can forget about sending an armada to Europe. We shall trade with them, but our Empire will be short lived, I shall see to that." She paused, allowing her statements to sink in. "Or… you could simply spare the Hoods."

Coriolanus folded his arms and stared at her. "You will abide by our wishes and plans?"

Gwen closed her eyes and sighed. "That I cannot promise. I am weary of cruelty."

"So…" His voice was now cold, hard, metallic, even resentful. "You seek to dismantle the foundations of Duart culture, destabilise our place in this world and our own?"

"I seek justice and fairness!" Gwen's voice raised to meet his in righteous indignation.

"I see."

Gwen was shaking with adrenaline. She had stood up to him before, but never about anything remotely as important as this. She had never made a threat so complex and powerful, never put so much on the line with all her heart behind her words. It felt tremendous… and terrifying.

"Well?" she asked.

The Archduke went to the bookshelf, selected a leather-bound copy of *The Count of Monte Cristo* and retrieved from within its pages three pieces of folded parchment. He then walked to the desk and took from its drawers a legal document she had seen before. He slid the folded parchments towards Gwendoline.

"Read these for me, please," he said dispassionately.

He was so calm in his request, so steady and stern that Gwen did not protest. She took up the first sheet, unfolded it and immediately recognised her father's handwriting.

Sixth of March 1873, by this new world's reckoning; the fourth day of exploring the new Londinium, or London, as the natives call it. They are strange and curious. Taller in stature than we, but weaker in constitution. It was while patrolling the markets of Spitalfield and burning out a nest of what they call the Barghest that I found a native child. Filthy, unkempt and half-wild, I had to prevent Lieutenant Baltus from destroying her. It was from this youngster that we learned the difference between infected and unmarred natives, as she had no orange eyes. After I had her cleaned up she was able to tell me her name was Katherine Laydon, daughter of two bakers, for whom she had been searching for some months.

Gwendoline reached the end of the paragraph, broke off and looked up at him, confused.

"Now read the following legal documentation to me," he said. "Paying specific attention to the names of the children of Edward VII."

With a rapidly sinking heart and a growing sense of panic, Gwendoline read through the lengthy list of names.

"Albert Victor Christian Edward, born 8th of January 1864. George Frederick Ernest Albert, 3rd of June 1865. Louise…" She stumbled slightly and then continued. "Louise Victoria Alexandra Dagmar, born 20th of February 1867. Victoria Alexandra Olga Mary, born 6th of July 1868. Maud Charlotte Mary Victoria, born 26th of November 1869. Prince Alexander John, born 6th of April 1871, died… 7th of April 1871." Gwen paused and swallowed. It always saddened her to read the name of her brother, who had lived for only a day.

"And who is missing?" Coriolanus asked her.

Gwendoline said nothing. The Archduke slid another document under her vision. It was the parchment he had retrieved from his drawer and was identical to the one in her hands save for only one additional name.

"Gwendoline Amelia Gertrude Victoria, born 1st of April 1866." She stared at him. "You falsified my existence."

"Yes," he replied simply. "When she departed London, Queen Victoria had 24 grandchildren. The panic over the Barghest was so great that precious few were keeping track of numbers. By the time the palaces had been retaken and you were in line for the throne, all those of royal blood had been brought on board or silenced, and there was nobody who could challenge your lineage. I have often feared, over these long years of your ascent, that someone would emerge with irrefutable public proof, and would give me no time to act to suppress this information… but nobody has. What does that tell you, Gwendoline?"

"That you killed far too many people to keep this secret," she replied through teeth gritted to keep herself from crying.

"Perhaps. But more pertinently, England *wants* you as their queen. They desire you in this palace. We came in with heavy armour and an iron fist, but as we did so I gave them a bird in a magnificent, gilded cage. It is you who prevents them from falling into despair. You give them hope, Gwendoline. *You*… are the beautiful lie." He gazed at her without anger. "A despairing people have nothing left to lose and they are liable to do dangerous things that upset the balance. And I'm afraid since you threaten our people's continued wellbeing with this newfound sense of what you perceive as justice, then the day has finally come where I must give up that lie and slam down harder still with this burning, merciless iron fist." As he said this he slowly closed his raised gauntlet and held it so, before opening it once more. "That is of course, unless you agree to keep telling it. Keep the songbird singing. Preserve this fragile daydream."

Gwendoline could not speak. She simply stared down at the journal page and the real list of those she had, up until this moment, believed to be her half-brothers and half-sisters. The next name he said snapped her attention back to him.

"Robin of Loxley." There was a measure of understanding in the Archduke's voice. "I can tell you feel for him. I could let him go as a kindness to you, to spare you pain." He laid his fingertips upon the desk between them. "But I implore you instead, whatever occurred between the two of you, let that be the dream.

Let him go tonight, let him die tomorrow and you will be wed to Lord Aaron, and live in comfort in a world where *you* are the dream, you are the Madonna, and what they wish to be is *real*. Save them, Gwendoline," he urged, quietly. "Save them from *me*."

Gwendoline stared at him. Her shoulders slumped, her eyes filled with tears, and she sank at last into her father's red leather writing chair. Coriolanus approached and clasped her hands. His words were soft and gentle, though his armour was not.

"If you are in agreement, then let me spare you the pain in another way. You shall see Doctor Marcus immediately. I will have him brought here to the palace. He can help you forget this thief. And then, my daughter, you shall truly be free."

Slowly, quietly, Gwendoline nodded, raised herself to her feet and went to her chambers. Soon Doctor Marcus was in her room, speaking to her in his clipped tones, his metronome ticking away.

***

The next morning in the great courtyard of the Tower of London, at one minute to eight bells, Robin Hood looked up into the cold, clear sky from his place atop the gallows. Four miles west, up the River Thames, Princess Gwendoline was married to Lord Aaron, unifying the houses of Skygrail and Saxe-Coburg.

She became Queen of two realms.

Chapter 20: Captives

Atop the Fourth Wall

"Wait a minute, that's not at all what happened," said The Nag indignantly.

"No, I think you'll find everything you've read just now did in fact *happen*," Merlene assured him.

"Is this the alternate timeline thing again?"

"I have no way of knowing for certain, but in our timeline, Gwendoline marries Lord Aaron."

"And Robin dies?" The horse shook his head and snorted angrily. "Why did you have us tell them all this awful story?"

"Would you like me to take over the next bit?" Merlene offered. "Secret and mysterious things took place that need a steady hand and stern constitution to describe."

"Be my guest," said the horse. "This is too upsetting for me."

Saturday Morning (One Day Left)

It was just after midnight as Friday passed into Saturday. Robin hung chained to the wall, his muscles partway between atrophied stone and agonising fire. His trial had been so fast he had barely registered the barrage of accusations and conclusions, nor had he been allowed to represent himself. It was the kind of legal proceeding

London was famous for, and he had expected nothing more or less.

The heavy, iron doors of his chamber now opened and he half hoped it would be Baltus alone, come to gloat over his prize acquisition. The Captain was so humourless, so lacking in even the most basic of relatable characteristics that Robin recognised the kind of person he could goad and frustrate, verbally poke at the anxieties of, until all he could do was lash out and lose control. Robin knew his sort well.

The other half of him, however, prayed it would *not* be Baltus. Something about the self-assured clinical appraisal of torture accounted for back at the Thirsty Hog frightened Robin to his core, and every moment that went by and brought him closer to his death, the more he struggled inside. His heart kept leaping as though in shock, and time after time, while hanging from this cold, impassive stone he experienced sudden wakefulness, yearning for this to be a dream, believing it might be, feasting on the possibilities of the alternate life he may be leading right now that he would return to after this dark delusion had passed away.

It did not, and every consecutive hour brought more fear, quite unbecoming of one so wily and apparently courageous. In consequence, the prospect of adding torture and mutilation to these final hours lent a sharp, frantic desperation to proceedings, and so he retreated to his fantasy of simply annoying the psychotic Captain, spearing his dignity. That would be their only exchange before the scaffold.

As Baltus entered, he was followed by a multitude of Heavies, pushing figures Robin had prayed not to see. The Hoods filed in, their hands and legs bound by loose chains that allowed them a clanking shuffle but not the simple act of walking. Factory workers came too. Robin saw humans of every ethnicity, a few Duart and Akka of similar variety, most of whom he knew by name. Some were so young he could not bear to see their terrified eyes or hear their sobs. Robin recognised the Dragusha family, even little Lavinia, and he writhed in anguish at the unfairness of this situation. He saw no sign of Oberon, but was that a comfort, or had something worse happened to him?

Scarlet came last, her chained hands on the shoulders of Ajax. Robin could hear her speaking soothingly to him, holding the poor fellow in a state of relative calm. Ajax looked around unhappily, definitely sure he didn't want to spend the day here. Scarlet was limping. Robin could see the punishment she had taken to hold Ajax together during their capture. Why? Why not just go down in literal flames and try to take as many Watchmen out as they went? Was she planning to appeal for mercy? Hoping for reprieve or rescue? Simply clinging to the last few hours of life she could sustain?

Baltus stood as the prisoners were chained to the walls in a long line on either side of Robin. He watched them without smiling, a stiff expression on his face.

"Congratulations, Watchmen, you have done your countries proud," he declared. "Tomorrow we cleanse the filth from the crevices of this city."

Robin thought hard about how he could bring up Baltus' filthy crevices, but his heart wasn't in it. They had taken away Robin's boots and the cuffs that bound every one of them all were fitted, he had found to his chagrin, with Strode locks, near-impossible to pick. The shackles themselves were constructed of the same caronite metal of Firecaster armour. It was so resistant to extremes in temperature, that if he employed an erratic fire, born of his fury, he would melt the very flesh from his own bones before he could warp the frame of his manacles enough to escape.

Baltus continued. "As for the rest of you, think on your sins, beg the Greatfather for forgiveness and perhaps you and your brethren shall not spend *all* of eternity in the eight hells."

"You shall not crush us!" A voice came from the darkness behind him, delivered in a thick Devonshire accent. "Heroism ain't something you can kill. Nobody will forget the shadow of the Black Shuck, and how it struck fear into the hearts of…"

"You're still here?" Baltus interrupted him, clearly surprised.

"I am the thing in the night that creeps into your…"

"Why is he still here?" Baltus asked, turning to an under-administrator. "Iain, he was supposed to have been executed on Wednesday!" The Captain had removed his gauntlets to sign the admission papers.

"Beg pardon, Captain," said Iain in a very deep and gravelly voice. "But nobody turned up… and you said he was supposed to be made an example of, so we thought that we'd save 'im for the big day and kind of like you know, add 'im on at the end. Sort of like an after-dinner mint."

"*You* have after-dinner mints, Iain?" Baltus asked, genuinely curious.

"We has an extra strong peppermint," Iain nodded. "Settles the palate, and it's good for your stomach. See, I learned all about that when the wife got the lurgy and the doctor said…"

"There will be more like me!" the Shuck broke in. "There shall be a reckoning and the rooftops of London will clatter with the sound of hobnail boots!"

Robin piped up at this in a matter-of-fact tone. "You know, Baltus, the eccentric vigilante is right. It doesn't matter how many of us you publicly kill off, when London sees us up on that scaffold there are going to be people who want to take up our mantle. You can't control that."

"And if they do," Baltus turned with a scowl. "We shall catch them and execute them too."

"So what's the point of making an example of us?" Robin queried. "Surely killing us quietly here gives you all less work in future."

"Oh, you'd all far prefer the noose, let me assure you," Baltus said darkly.

Robin stared at him for a moment. "You *can't*… can you?" The outlaw's eyes lit up. "It's against the rules, and you just *love* those rules, don't you, Baltus? You get a tingly sensation in your manhood when those rules get followed to a tee." He grinned wickedly. "So what was it, Baltus? Strict nanny? Did she smack your bottom?"

"Be quiet," Baltus said, his teeth gritted.

"Was it your Daddy? Was he cold and aloof? Hmm? Critical of your every mistake? Only ever praised you when you followed those rules?"

"Shut up," Baltus hissed.

"Or was it not even that?" Robin persisted. "Did he… did he just never say anything nice to you at all? You just *hoped* he might if you…"

"SHUT UP!!!" the Captain roared, wheeling around and slamming his fist into Robin's stomach, causing him to buckle in pain, coughing out his victorious conclusion.

"Oh," he laughed, keeping his smile in spite of the agony. "I'm sorry Baltus, really I am. I sympathise." He locked eyes with the duart, panting. "It sounds like your father and my father should have gotten together once a week, to play a game of bowls."

"My father raised one of the finest exemplars of Duart culture in our times," Baltus snarled, his voice low and dangerous again. "Your father raised nothing but wretched waste… a cullion, forgotten after the morrow."

"Maybe he did…" Robin breathed. "But I still feel like I got the better end of the deal," His voice was dry and serious, still mocking, but also searching. "Have you ever loved someone, Baltus, *truly* loved them? Ever been loved back?" The Captain glared at Robin with pure hate in his eyes. "You know, I didn't think so… and you're *married*!" Robin continued, having spotted the wedding band before Baltus' had replaced his gauntlets. "So… that's really a shame."

The Captain's next blow tore a deep cut in Robin's chin that would scar if it ever had the time to heal. Head ringing, white pain flashing through him, Robin focused as best he could and nodded.

"Yup… I still wouldn't swap places with you," he said with a nod and a crooked grin.

Baltus leaned in close to him and said in a dangerously low voice, "We'll see if this foolishness still stands when the world falls away on Sunday morning. I shall watch you dance a gallows jig. I'll be looking into your eyes, and I'll know the exact moment you would switch places with me. I look forward to it."

He turned and marched out, shaking with rage and more, followed by a portion of the guards. The rest took their posts and watched the prisoners dully, allowing them to converse, simply because these exchanges were all that differentiated the days and nights in the tower for these guards, especially Iain, who was not a spiteful fellow and actually spent most of his time doing small things to ease the anguish of his captives. At this point in the evening for example he had released the tower cat, whose name was Squire Trelawney, to dispatch the rats who were making their way hungrily towards the toes of the hanging prisoners.

As the door closed Scarlet raised her head and looked piercingly around the darkened chamber at dozens of slumped forms, hanging from chains, quietly groaning, cursing or weeping.

"Alright everyone," she called out. "Here's the awful reality. Someone… someone I believe is present among us now… shopped us in. I know that having betrayed his or her friends and co-workers they almost certainly ended up thrown in chokey with the rest of us, since the Duart in charge don't give rewards to criminals, and whoever it was, was probably too thick to know that." She paused to let the insult sink in. "Now they're holding their tongue because they don't want the rest to find out it was them but here's why they should speak up and admit their treachery." She surveyed the many hanging faces along each line. "Because everyone here is wondering who it is and we're all going to the noose with that on our minds, unable to fully square away and exonerate *any* of the people we are supposed to trust. Now I don't know about you lot, but if I'm going to die, I want to do it among friends. So, whoever it was, say it now and give everyone peace of mind. I mean, we'll all *hate* you for doing it, but what are we gonna do besides that? None of us can move."

She waited to see if anyone would speak, and when none did, carried on. "What you did was terrible, unforgivable and our blood is all on your worthless 'ands. But if you're feeling any amount of that wretched regret you *should* be feeling, you can give us the gift of this courtesy, by way of recompense."

Her eyes roved over the pitiful captives around her until they fell on a tall boy she remembered. He was crying.

"Jack," she asked, not unkindly. "How are you doing, mate?"

"I'm… I'm…" he stammered.

"Got anything to say?" Her voice was still gentle.

"Yeah, you got me, I done it." He whimpered, his head drooping.

"I don't need to ask why," she said. "Reward that big."

"Well, you shouldn't have brought the Princess to the factory!" he cried out, indignant now. "Waving at us like that, we saw through her disguise. It's like bringing a cake trolley round a bloody orphanage!" Petulant and defensive, his tone frustrated Scarlet, and a note of sharp sarcasm crept into her voice.

"You're right, how could you possibly resist?"

"I'm sorry, alright, everyone? I'm so, so sorry," he sobbed. "I wish I'd never done it. I regretted it even as I was doing it. So just… you can all hate me. Just like she said."

"Alright," Dashurie, the Albanian matriarch, spat. "We *will* hate you."

"*I* don't hate you." The Black Shuck was looking over at young Jack with a nod of understanding.

"He didn't betray *you*!" Scarlet sniped indignantly.

"You remind me of *me*, young sir," said the Shuck, ignoring the akka.

"What?" Jack seemed surprised.

"Weight of the world on your shoulders," the Shuck continued, almost sagely. "Angry young man. Misled by weakness. Terrible, frightening, black city. You does what you can to stay alive."

"I was just sick of being so hungry all the time," Jack said. "Sick of feeling…"

"Worthless," the Shuck finished for him, his voice reflective. "You felt small and worthless, right?

Insignificant. So, you do big, frightening things that you pray will make a change." He paused and looked down at his feet. "But it didn't turn out like you hoped."

Robin looked up at these words and smiled dryly through cracked lips. "No, it didn't," he said.

"No, it didn't," Scarlet repeated in a low voice.

"No, it bloody well did not!" Jack confirmed.

"Jack," called Robin. "I'm sure if you could go back and change what you did, that you would. And you, Black… Shuck, was it?"

"Gregory… my name was… My name's Gregory," said the Shuck.

"Gregory, I'm sure you would have done things differently," Robin continued. "But for me, I don't know. I'm looking back on what I've done now, and why, and I feel an odd sort of comfort. I don't think I *would* have done much of anything differently. I'm proud of the things I did with the past few years of my life." He looked over at Scarlet. "You should feel the same."

"I do," she assured him.

"And certainly, these past few days for me… I felt like I was in the right place." He paused and glanced around him, contemplating. "However, having said all that, I suppose the one thing I would not have done is to trust that blasted Mortimer."

"Me neither," replied Gregory glumly.

Chapter 21: The Precipice

Saturday Evening

Some sixteen hours later and several miles west, in Buckingham Palace, after having confronted her father and learned the truth, that she was born with no responsibilities whatsoever and would face a return to that state should she make the *least* bit of trouble for those planning to conquer Europe, Gwendoline sat before Doctor Marcus. His metronome ticked back and forth as he questioned her on the events of the past few days.

"I heard word," he said chidingly, "of someone calling themselves 'Lady Katherine' in London this week. Would you know anything about that, Gwendoline?"

"Just a name I thought of," Gwen replied softly.

"Bringing back imaginary friends is deeply unhealthy," he warned. "We'll get rid of her again."

In the periphery of her blurred vision Gwendoline saw a little girl she used to know crossing her bedroom to sit at the table and share a pot of tea.

"Any sickness? Headaches? Fainting fits?" the doctor was asking her.

She nodded absently. "I was passing a… bakery and caught such a strong scent of freshly cooking bread. My breathing got quick and that's when my head exploded. Oh, it hurt so much."

"Yes, it's all these unhelpful memories of the past that set you off. We have to put them away or you won't stay well."

"My mother… my father…" she muttered. "I still haven't found them."

"They're gone, girl," Doctor Marcus told her firmly. "You know that. Edward is gone. Miss Hathaway is gone. Trying to find them is a pretence unbecoming of such an important monarch. Don't entertain such fancies, focus on your adopted family. Now, look into this grey light."

Gwen met his gaze. "No."

"No is not a word a lady uses," he said firmly. "Now, let me work." He lit a portable oil lamp he had brought and her vision was filled with a dull, muted brightness which peeled away her strength in layers. "Look into this light," he commanded, "and remember who you really are."

The world was spinning, the fog had closed in, her breathing was cold, and she was alone. Marcus' voice came booming through the curling mist. "For Queen and country, Gwendoline," he intoned. "For Queen and country. Your participation is required."

She held onto her anchor. The thing keeping her mind in the present. "Robin!" she said.

"One of England's greatest heroes," Marcus countered. "And he died a thousand years ago. A legend, to be sure, but nothing more than that."

To bring the words forth was a struggle, but Gwen persisted, knowing how heartfelt and true they were. "No… he was real… he… I loved him."

"A daydream, girl," Doctor Marcus contended. "A fantasy you must now wake up from. Remember who you *really* are."

The grey mists parted and Marcus stood there in her mind. Stern, authoritative, implacable, he towered over her.

She was seven.

She was Katherine.

She was Princess Gwendoline.

Then, from behind Marcus, a Duart boy stepped into view. Ragged clothes, bare feet, blonde hair, blue eyes. He spoke.

"For what it's worth, Lady Katherine, *I* still believe in you."

With a cry, Gwen leapt forward and grabbed Doctor Marcus by the collar. The mists rushed apart and his face was suddenly painted vividly with alarm.

"I remember who I *really* am!" Gwen cried, angrily and triumphantly.

With her free hand, she punched Doctor Marcus sharply in the face just as Viola crept in through the bedroom doors. The guards, dazed from a light Confuse spell, began to turn just as he cried out. Viola spun around, holding the door partially closed to obscure what was happening in the room.

"No disturbing the Princess, this is very delicate medical work. Back to your posts!" she said firmly, shutting them out. Gwendoline beamed at Viola. She still had hold of Marcus' collar, though he had slumped down onto his knees in a daze. Viola dived into Gwen's arms.

"Oh, sweet Viola, had you come to rescue me?" Gwen held her close.

"Yes, I was gearing up to be all heroic, but you appear to have done it yourself," Viola observed. At that moment the doctor groaned and started to come around, then went to shout, but Viola cast a whip-quick Silence spell, causing his yell to emerge muffled and barely audible. "Listen here, doc," Viola snarled, moving in very close to him. "I've never known exactly what you do to dear Gwendoline… That's the truth, my darling," she added, turning briefly to Gwen. "But I've suspected for a long time that your finagling with her brain is what was making the pain *worse*, not better."

"I want it all gone," Gwen said resolutely from behind her. "Do you hear me, sir? All of it. All the fog, all the blockage, all the pain. I want my mind clear."

He tried to object, but his voice was still stifled by the Silence spell.

"Let me get that for you," Viola hissed, leaning forward. "But call for help and I'll cast a Silence spell on you so deep you'll never speak again."

She swiftly undid the spell, and there was a long pause while the doctor coughed. "But you must understand," he insisted. "You are asking me to undo a decade of exceptionally complex mental rearrangement. It's like asking me to renovate a mansion in an afternoon."

"Try," Viola said coldly.

"I may not be able to bring everything back," he quavered. "I may not be *able* to entirely get rid of the pain."

Viola turned to the Princess. "Are you sure about this, Gwendoline?"

She nodded. "I'm sure. I want to remember my past without fear, without others meddling."

"Very well," Marcus replied, as he shakily retook his seat. "Miss Heartstone, I suggest you step back and try not to get too involved. You could do more harm than good."

The metronome came on again. Over the next hour, Marcus stepped stealthily through the mind palace of the girl who had been named Katherine and cleared away artifice and supposition, scoured out untruths and clarified half-truths. Gwendoline sat, eyes open, gaze firm. Her bodyguard watched her with an unsettling blend of admiration and pity.

Somewhere in the middle of it, Viola had a brainwave and called in one of the guards for a quiet discussion.

When Marcus was finished he surveyed the mind palace hallway one last time, stepped out of the front door, and closed it behind him, never to return. The gardens were free of fog and the Woman who would be Queen sat quietly and comfortably at long last.

Viola bade Marcus go and lie on the bed, casting a hard Sleep on him when he did so. It was imperative that he neither hear or see what was about to happen. The little duart took several sherbet lemons from her pouch and sucked them furiously.

"Gwen? Are you alright?" she asked, with her mouth full. "Ow – I cut my tongue!"

"I am," said Gwen, breathing out deeply.

"What did we do over the past few days?" Viola asked her. "Simon here would like to know." She indicated the guard Gwendoline had fought a week ago, and many times before that, and who was standing to attention in the room.

Gwendoline described all the events in detail, rather *too* much detail at times, and Viola had to hurry her through the sexual congress. Viola was satisfied; Doctor Marcus had done his work as promised and this was the Gwen she knew.

"So what's your plan now?" the duart asked.

"What time is it?"

"Just gone six bells."

Gwen got to her feet. "Good Lord, Robin will be dead in fourteen hours. We have to break him and the rest of them out of the Tower of London. Simon, can you muster enough guards loyal to me to do that?"

"It's patrolled by firecasting Duart, your Highness," he replied, shaking his head. "The human soldiers I might get together would be burned to a crisp in moments."

"Could we sneak in?" Gwen asked.

"If I may, your Highness," Simon interjected. "I believe Viola has a rather irregular plan."

"What is it, Vi?" Gwen turned to her, impatiently. "Every minute we waste is one less chance. I have to get dressed for battle now!"

"Where are you going to go?" Viola asked her. "Who can we ask for help?"

Gwen though for a moment. "Well, let's see now. There's Oberon, it's possible he escaped capture, and we should get to the Thirsty Hog too, and see if he or anyone else is still there. And, now that I think about it we really should call on…"

"Merlene," Viola suggested.

"Merlene," Gwen agreed decisively. "It would *definitely* be advantageous to have such a powerful wizard on our side. But we have to hurry. Let me get dressed while you tell me *your* plan."

She crossed to the wardrobe and pulled on her favourite riding clothes, which gave her freedom of movement as well as looking rather fine. She finished it with her favourite red coat and then took out her toughened blue leather gloves. She paused over these for a moment and then, smiling to herself, snipped off all the fingers in honour of Robin's mitts. Pulling them on she thought to herself, *These are the gloves of a Thief.*

She turned back to Viola and Simon and got the shock of her life. There, sat on the chair she had been in before, wearing her dressing gown, sat Princess Gwendoline.

"Oh!" Gwen's hand flew to her throat in surprise. There was no sign of Simon, and Viola was smiling proudly. Gwendoline moved forward and crouched before her doppelganger in amazement. It spoke.

"I've studied the way you move and the way you speak," Simon said earnestly. "I think I can do a pretty good impersonation for a day or so." His voice was a little higher than usual, metamorphizing more as he talked, until he sounded eerily like her.

Gwen was overcome with gratitude. "Simon… you are the sweetest man I have ever known." She leaned forward and kissed herself on the lips. It was an odd sight that Viola had difficulty making sense of, like a mirror that wasn't behaving itself. "But are you sure?" Gwen asked him. "Once this disguise drops, which could be any time, you could be charged with treason."

Simon shook his head. "No, your 'mind-witch' manipulated me into doing all this, remember?"

Gwen looked across at Viola who shrugged.

"I'm already going to be branded a traitor," she sniffed. "So, I suppose in for a copper, in for a gold."

Viola closed her eyes in concentration and the real Gwendoline's face began to change, the jawline squaring up as her curvy body drew itself into masculine lines and the person standing there resembled Simon. The Gwen doppelganger spoke once more.

"That's uncanny!"

"Wow…" Gwen looked down at her new Simon-shape. "I rather like this body."

"Come on, Princess, get going," Simon urged her. "Take my hat. Save your outlaw."

"Grab *him* on the way out," added Viola, pointing to the doctor.

Gwen-posing-as-Simon straightened up, and with little difficulty lifted the sleeping form of Marcus from the bed. She barged through the doors and Viola shouted at the remaining guard outside in rapid bursts of information, giving him no time to object.

"The Princess only went and punched his lights out. Her fits are getting worse. I'd let her sleep if I were you. She's very nervous about this wedding tomorrow.

Anyway, we need to get this man some smelling salts, so we'll be back shortly."

And with that, Gwen still cradling the slumbering mesmerist, they made their way to the library, and escaped through their most secret of tunnels.

Chapter 22: A Long-Awaited Clash

Saturday (One Day Left)

Oberon awoke with a start in the early hours of Saturday morning. All was quiet and black outside. The safe-house was deserted. His first feelings were confusion and disorientation, for there was very little available to indicate what time or indeed what day it was, or exactly what had transpired during his long sleep. He began to wonder if it was in fact just a very boring and dark dream. His next response was anger and indignation at being deliberately excluded from proceedings, followed by intense worry that something had gone horribly wrong.

Oberon hauled himself groggily to his feet and lumbered downstairs to the street. For a moment he considered making his way over to Mortimer's house to see if the band had regrouped there. Perhaps Gwendoline and Viola were still with them, but his concern for the Hoods overrode that unlikely scenario and he made his way slowly across London to The Thirsty Hog. He saw no light in the windows, which was unusual for Scarlet, who tended to run things round the clock, with Hoods passing in and out during the more shadowy hours when dark deeds were afoot.

He went in through the back to find the whole place had been turned over. Chairs and tables flung aside, windows smashed, cellar gutted, false wall uncovered, bedrooms awry and not a soul inside. There were scorch marks here and there, it was frankly miraculous the pub had not been burned to the ground.

There was no Robin, no Scarlet, no Hoods, and no Ajax.

Oberon sat in silence for a long while, surveying the carnage, before picking up a table and chair and putting them back to their places. The rest of the furniture followed and the broken pieces went into the yard out back. He slowly, methodically cleared the place, and all through the quiet hours, as the world outside went from charcoal to grey to blue and the sun began to rise on Saturday, Oberon tended to the restoration of the Hog.

Then at nine, when he considered himself finished he cooked a breakfast, consumed it mechanically, and went out into the city to attempt to glean as much information on the events of yesterday from whomever he could find.

Oberon learned that the reward on his own head had gone up considerably and had to evade the Watchmen several times, resorting to a very bulky collection of rags for a disguise.

He learned that the Princess had been returned in exchange for a handsome reward. He learned that Mortimer was not at home today and nobody had seen her. He learned that Robin had been taken into custody nearby, summarily tried and convicted within an hour, then brought publicly to the Tower of London, marched roughly down the street for all to see.

He learned that the Hog had been taken shortly afterwards by Captain Baltus himself. Someone had ratted them out for a reward, that much was obvious.

The factories had all been closed down over the past few hours, and all the workers taken to the Tower as well.

He learned that many of the craftsmen in the city had been summoned there, along with carts full of timber, and that right now enormous, multi-tiered gallows were being constructed in the execution yard, the better to hold as many Hoods as possible to dreadful example.

Worst of all, when he made it down to the Barge moorings on the Thames, he learned that the Albanian family, the Dragushas, were no longer there. Word was that their newest little girl, Lavinia, had possessed a particularly fine doll that had been spotted in a market by the young Lady Imogen, daughter of the Marquis of Chiswick. There had been a terrific row, which the Dragushas had come off the worst for, and all seven of them had been rounded up and taken to the Tower as well. Fortunately, Veronica had been returned to her original owner, so justice, in this case, was served.

**

By sundown he had taken about us much bad news and despair as a person can and found himself back at the Thirsty Hog. Inside, he lit the lamps, opened the doors and slumped down at a table with several flagons of mead, becoming increasingly bitter with his subsequent inebriation.

Around seven bells he was joined by a familiar, lithe figure who had poured herself a glass of fine Old Pulteney Scotch from a bottle she had been surprised to find nestling behind the bar of such a humble tavern.

298

"Why the long face?" Mortimer drawled at Oberon, who did not look up. "Nothing? Oh, surely I can say something in the next few minutes to ring your bell?"

Oberon sighed quietly and took another swig.

"You know…" she continued. "I have a brother, Calvin. He's a jolly sort. He and I used to be inseparable; twins, you know. I could always depend on an intelligent conversation with him. We explored all of Surrey together. None of the other children liked us," she added bitterly. "Last I heard he'd reached the rank of Commander and went off to explore the Americas. I do miss old Cal. So I can understand why you might miss your friend… or your brother." She glanced at him over her glass. "I can reunite you if you like. The bounty on your head is pretty hefty and since you seem intent on drinking yourself to death tonight we may as well come to some arrangement that would be mutually beneficial."

Oberon finally looked up at her, but all she saw in those eyes was sadness and regret.

"Oh, come on you great lunk," she snapped angrily. "*I'm* the one who sold Robin down the river, profiteering from his capture, surely you want to strike me dead on the spot. Come on, I can take it!" She paused, waiting for some kind of reaction – *any* kind of reaction – from him. "No? Nobody here appreciates the dubious merits of a good strangling?"

There was another long silence, broken only by Oberon knocking back more mead and the tiny sloshes as Mortimer turned the whiskey in her glass and dully studied its fiery colours. Eventually she sighed, knocked back the drink and continued.

"Truth is, I didn't know I was being followed and by the time I realised it was happening, they were surrounding us." Her tone was quieter now, reflective. "My mind must have been elsewhere. There's no chance they could have got the drop on Mortimer Wilson a week ago." She paused again, struggling to get the words out. "But I've come back to see if there's anything I could do… and now *we* could do." She looked at him hopefully once again and saw that his green, furrowed brow had not moved. Her own lowered in frustration. "However, I can see you've entirely given up, so I suppose I'm going to have to run this suicide mission all by myself, as per bloody usua…"

She broke off as a fist slammed her face to one side.

Oberon gave a start as he realised they were not alone. Gwendoline and Viola had entered the Hog behind them and Gwen was now grabbing Mortimer by the scruff of the neck.

"You treacherous bitch!" Gwen yelled at her. Far from being frightened, insulted or overwhelmed, Mortimer cackled right into her face.

"Ohhhhh, that's more like it!" The bounty hunter stood and shoved Gwendoline backward, wiping a trickle of blood from her scarlet lips. "Come to avenge your Merry Man? I can see he's made quite the impres-"

Gwendoline cut her off with a roar, grabbed her by the coat and flung her across the pub. Mortimer twisted in the air and bounced nimbly from the wall, rebounding to kick the Princess smartly across the face, landing in a complicated spider-like manoeuvre which entangled their legs and sent Gwen crashing to the ground.

Mortimer rolled on top and began to beat down on her opponent. Gwendoline trapped the bounty hunter's arm and flung her sideways, smashing a heavy table in the process. It happened to be the table Oberon was sat beside but he kept a firm grip on the flagon as the wood fell away. Viola had perched beside him and he offered her a swig.

"Are you going to intervene?" he asked.

"Oh, heavens no," Viola replied. "She only wanted me to give her red hair tonight to conceal who she was, that's all I'm doing."

The brawl spilled out into the street as Gwen flung Mortimer towards a horse trough.

"You scheming, heartless, money-grubbing, two-faced snake!" the Princess bellowed.

"You obstinate, clueless, condescending old sow!" Mortimer shouted back. An array of gadgets came out of her coat but were swatted and kicked aside until she managed get a good jab in with the electric prod, laughing maniacally.

"Owwwwwww, did you just..?"

"Hahahahaha!"

"I will shove that thing up your-"

"How are you two back here again?" Oberon asked Viola calmly. She explained in swift detail what had happened since yesterday afternoon.

"We went to find you back at the safe house," Viola said. "Dropped off an evil hypnotist while we were there, then reasoned you'd come here."

"I'd had enough of sleeping," he commented coolly.

"So, you figured you'd start *drinking*?" Viola observed, somewhat acidly.

He shrugged. "The situation looked hopeless."

"'Looked', as in the past tense?"

Oberon slurped from the flagon and conceded, "There may be a little hope for us, now." The dead end he had been stuck down now seemed only *mostly* dead.

***

In the street Mortimer used a grappling hook to fling herself up towards the rooftops, but with an almighty leap Gwendoline caught her boot heel and sent her crashing to the pavement, where they continued to roll around slamming against one another.

"Augghhhhhhh!" shrieked Mortimer, hitting the floor. "Why don't you get your nursemaid to put me to sleep, just like she did that green haystack?"

"I'm frightfully sorry about that," Viola said, now standing in the doorway of the Thirsty Hog beside Oberon.

"Hey, I'm still *here* because of you," he admitted.

"Slothful truffle-pig!" the bounty hunter sneered. "Always hiding behind your oh-so-special friends!"

"At least I *have* friends, you twisted spinster!" snapped Gwen.

"I have *plenty* of friends!" Mortimer roared.

(She didn't – THE NAG)

"No wonder you couldn't pull that sword. So very erroneously convinced of your own moral superiority."

(Gwen was.)

"But I know the truth you don't want to confront." Mortimer pulled hard on Gwendoline's hair and scratched her face, making her yowl in pain. "You and that Loxley chap were both putting on grandiose theatrical acts, convincing the world of your purity and altruism, when really you know deep down, that everyone is just as selfish and greedy as the next person."

"Owwwwwww!" Gwen seized Mortimer's braid and yanked on it, pulling her head back. "That's the difference between us," the Princess thundered. "When I come across the tiny pockets of people who *aren't* greedy and selfish… *now* I can finally recognise that as *precious*! So, you know what, you mouthy tart…?" And at this she let go and stepped back as they stood before one another panting heavily and staring with wide eyes. "I actually feel sorry for you."

Unfortunately, this show of sympathy did not go down at all well. Mortimer screamed in utter fury and threw her weight against Gwen, slamming them into the nearby wall as she commenced with pounding her body. But Gwen was more than used to this kind of treatment and now the wiry lady was within the Princess' grip she could overpower her with sheer strength.

However, she could also feel that old stamina problem creeping back. She had to grit her teeth to keep going, kneeing Mortimer in the crotch and gut-punching her to knock the wind out. The bounty hunter used the reeling back motion to un-holster her pistol and press it to Gwen's forehead. The two locked eyes; Gwen's fierce and bright, Mortimer's hurt and scared. Viola gave a start forward. It seemed like this madwoman might actually pull the trigger.

Gwen's voice rose to a furious howl. "You were always going to betray us!"

"But this time, *I didn't*!" Mortimer screamed back at her.

Curtains had been pulled aside in the houses around them and people were peering out of windows and gathering on the street corners to watch these two furious women grapple so spectacularly. There were already mutterings about Lady Katherine being back, but clearly it couldn't be the now-returned princess, so who was she? The Watchmen had been called and were approaching.

Her chest heaving violently, Mortimer slowly lowered her gun. "I had *every* intent of handing his share of the reward over," she insisted. "I frankly don't need the extra money anyway, who do you think I spend it on?"

"Yourself, that's all you care about," Gwen spat.

"Poppycock!" Mortimer countered. "I'm standing here, offering my help to you, *for free*, for the first time in my life. That's what I was saying to that great green oaf before you came wading in with your big fists and your giant tits!"

Gwen turned to the akka for confirmation. "Oberon?"

He nodded. "She's telling the truth; at least she *thinks* she is… and if not, she's just plain crazy."

"So… you'll assist us in our rescue?" Gwen asked.

"*Just* that," Mortimer clarified. "Just so we're square and you can stop blaming me for what went wrong."

"Fine," snapped Gwen.

"Thank you."

"But we're not coming with *you*," the Princess asserted. "You're coming with *us*. We've less than thirteen hours left now." There was a pause as they straightened up and composed themselves.

"Time enough... ow... to see my private physician," Mortimer winced. "I'll pay for your treatment; he's a good man, and thorough. We won't get far if we can't get these wounds cleaned and dressed and bones reset."

"I... ow! Is he far?" Gwen asked.

"No, follow me," said the bounty hunter, gesturing to them.

Oberon quickly closed down the Hog, glaring back at the scene of renewed devastation in there, and sighing as he blew out the lamps. Then he, Viola and Gwendoline followed Mortimer on swift, quiet, limping feet, through the London streets to the house of her physician, who was indeed a good man, and thorough.

***

Later that night, they passed through the gate, posing as farmers, and Oberon led an unfamiliar horse, Carrots having been repossessed by the Watchmen, down the dark roads of this other world once again. This time Viola and Gwendoline were unafraid. This time the forest, no matter how tangled and intimidating, was a place of sanctuary. This time the ruins of Camelot were their last, desperate hope.

Gwendoline hopped down as soon as they drew to a standstill and yelled into the night.

"Merlene! Please, please still be here."

Chapter 23: Unspeakable Power

Early Sunday Morning

The Princess' voice echoed out through the remnants of archways and the overgrown halls. Taking a lamp, she proceeded shakily to Merlene's hut, but nobody was home. Embers burned in the grate but the owl was gone from its perch.

They fumbled through the ruin, chasing noises, but always coming across more forgotten pathways, until they stepped through a final atrium and found themselves once again, inexorably, standing before the steps of the sword. At the top of them the wizard lay crumpled, her eyes closed. Gwen rushed forward.

"Oh no, Merlene!"

The old woman awoke with a start.

"Blast it, I ain't dead yet! What do you want?" she snapped.

Gwen cried out in surprise, and then again with joy. "Oh! Oh, Merlene, Nanny M." She flung her arms around the old woman.

"Get off me girl!" Merlene growled irritably. "My bones are made of dry old clay, you'll crush me."

"What were you doing?"

"Sleeping… or trying to," Merlene replied, narrowing her eyes.

"She never even finished the bedtime story," said a voice from the shadows with a hrrumph. The Nag stepped forward, his black eyes glowering in the lamplight.

"Why are you sleeping here?" said Gwen, puzzled.

"I told you, my place is with the sword," Merlene exclaimed. "You really don't listen much, do you, Missy?"

"We don't have any time…" Gwen pressed. "How do I explain this? Robin and his gang have been captured. They're to be executed at eight bells and it's nearly dawn now. We need to rescue them and you're the most powerful and wise person I know."

"Where are they being held?" Merlene asked her.

"The Tower of London."

Merlene shook her head. "Can't be done."

Gwen's face fell. "No…" she said in disbelief. "No… You *must* help us. You have powers, you can…"

"You could have spent the past few hours sneaking in with disguises," Merlene interjected. "What can *I* do for you, aside from shield you from flame?"

"You could…" Gwen stopped, unsure how to continue.

"You *know* why you're back," Merlene said sternly, "and it's not for me."

"No, it really is for you," Gwen insisted.

"You want one more go at pulling the sword," the old woman said, simply.

Gwen stared at her in growing frustration. "The *sword*? No, it doesn't work! I tried it three times, twice with Robin's help. It doesn't…" She broke off, then added quietly, "It doesn't *want* me."

"Has your manner of *thinking* changed since last we met?" Merlene asked. "That often helps with these binding spells."

"My manner of thinking has changed insomuch as I don't want the bloody thing either!"

Merlene gazed at the girl for a long moment. "Do you want to know what these symbols really mean?" she asked her, finally, gesturing at the intricately carved glyphs beside them.

Gwen shook her head in disbelief and panic. "I haven't got any more time, Robin's…"

"The ones on the blade say 'Might is Tyranny Without Wisdom'," Merlene interrupted. "I didn't come up with that, whoever made this sword did, but it's rather appropriate. Now the inscription on the stone itself is rather more complex, you see…" She turned to indicate the symbols, but Gwen cut her off.

"I don't care! Don't you hear me? My father is going to keep crushing down on that city, and that country and everywhere else our people go. Now he's a wise man, but he's also tyrannical, so I'm sorry, but whoever carved those runes onto this sword was talking absolute *bollocks*!"

She had been stamping around the stone as she said this, and at the last word she pulled at the hilt angrily. The blade came out of the stone and everyone stepped back, aghast. Gwen regarded the sword, hefting it in her hand.

"…Oh…"

There was a sudden blinding flash. Her arm shot skyward, holding the Archenblade aloft as lightning

309

clattered down around them. Her hair and coat whipped about in the shocking hurricane. Her blue eyes shone, and a new and titanic strength rippled through her form as ancient knowledge passed from the orb into her mind.

Merlene rose up and stood before her, voice booming over the thunder and the unseen choir that were chanting for the return of a demi-goddess as she intoned the words from the inscription on the stone.

"They that seek true power shall never hold me. They that understand it, I shall hold them."

The Nag reared up behind Gwendoline, shaking his mane which became pure white as two immense, feathered wings unfurled from his flanks and a long, sharp, golden horn sprouted from his forehead.

Gwendoline lowered the sword as the thunder rolled back, the wind subsided and the light reduced to a twinkling pearlescent glow from somewhere just above her.

"Holy Mother of God!" she gasped. "That was…" She promptly dropped the sword with a clang and the light went out. Gwen staggered forward, suddenly weakened. The Nag, however, remained in his winged form.

"Woah there, young lady," Merlene cautioned. "Pick that thing back up."

Gwen groped around, found the blade glowing in the darkness, its runes flickering with golden fire. The moment her fingers touched the metal her strength began to flood back, and as she grabbed the hilt again the light reappeared.

Viola gaped at her. "Wow… Gwen… you look a little bit amazing," she stammered.

"I'd follow you into battle," Oberon concurred.

Mortimer cocked her head on one side and looked at Gwen appraisingly. "So… can *anyone* have that power if they grab the sword now? Say if she were to drop it, and maybe get kicked in the face?"

"You dare even think that!?" Viola snarled, turning on her.

"Would you like me to bite her whole head off, Gwen?" the akka asked.

Mortimer rolled her eyes. "I'm *joking*… good Lord… you people have no sense of humour."

Oberon scowled at her and turned back to Merlene. "And what about The Nag here? Is he drawing this new form from the sword?"

"Nay," the horse replied, shaking his mane.

"A long time ago, this one's name was Nightwind," Merlene told them.

"You heard the girl," 'Nightwind' cut in. "We haven't time to discuss exactly how I came to choose this form, but I have agreed to help you today… help you a smidgen. I'm only carrying *her*." He inclined his head in Gwen's direction and tapped the ground with a hoof for emphasis.

"Well…" Gwen said, close to speechless, but acutely aware of their task. "Let's go now."

"Hold on," Merlene cautioned. "Don't you want to know what you can do?"

"Time!" Gwen snapped.

"*Preparation*!" the sorceress rejoined.

Gwen looked skyward and clenched her fists. "Fine!" She closed her eyes for a moment. "I feel very strong… like, *ludicrously* powerful, like I could jump a mile in the air."

"You can," Merlene said, quietly, with a little smile. Gwen's face lit up with obvious excitement, and Merlene nodded and rolled her hand over. "Go on, get it over with."

Gwendoline crouched low and then erupted upwards sailing high into the dawn sky.

***

The air shot past her and the world fell away. Her view adjusted and she beheld the cresting sunlight illuminating this expanse of wilderness. Far ahead of her she saw other forests, just as dark and mysterious as the one beneath, and behind them, high mountains, little rivers and nestled villages of duart people just waking up to see a shining red speck ascending towards the clouds.

It was everything she had hoped for and more, a wild and dangerous land. Human eyes had rarely, if ever, taken in so much at once. She was suddenly and acutely aware of the temperature. It was cold on the ground, but windy up here, and so quiet. The rushing feeling as she was propelled upwards made her heart float as she reached the apex of her jump and inhaled deeply.

Then Gwen began to fall, panicking as she was propelled downwards far faster. Did this strength make

312

her invulnerable too? Why would Merlene tell her to jump if… But it was too late, the ground was hurtling towards her and she curled up and braced her legs, shouting in exhilaration and fright.

The Princess impacted in the centre of what had once been a specialised gathering hall for Knights to show off their new, colourful and finely enamelled armour. The catwalk had long since rotted away and it was into this area that the crater around Gwendoline was created in an expanding, circular wave of tumbling stone. The others rushed in from one of the doorways.

Gwendoline's legs hurt, about as much as you or I might feel after walking halfway down the stairs and then jumping the rest of the way. She had that same lingering sense of "shouldn't have done that" which we get in the aftermath, which is our brains telling us how to survive longer whilst conducting physical checks.

Viola approached Gwen and smiled proudly. "Were all the lands laid out like an embroidered blanket?"

Gwendoline beamed at her. "They were," she panted.

"Nobody but you can access that power by holding the sword," warned Merlene. "But they *can* take the sword itself from you. As long as you hold it you are strong, and fast, and to a degree, very hard to hurt, but underneath, you are still human, you can still get tired. Watch yourself, girl."

"I will," Gwen promised. "Nag? Nightwind?" She was hesitant, not sure what to call him now.

"Nag," he replied decisively. She gazed at this proud, beautiful, yet still slightly disgusting steed. He was more magnificent than the unicorns she had seen in picture books, yet his eyes had that canny, defiant quality that separated him from everyday horses.

He was actually rather frightening to stand beside. Anyone who has gotten close to a horse can tell you of their musculature and strength, and how intimidating it is to sit high up on their back for the first time. Now add a very pointy erratically moving horn and enormous, powerful wings; recall, if you will, that old adage about a swan being able to break a man's arm, and fathom how much bigger than a swan this creature actually was. Take the fear of falling and multiply the distance by ten, twenty, even a hundred times. Then increase significantly the speed that this animal could achieve. Even as an experienced rider who just received a limited invulnerability, Gwen's knees were shaking at the prospect of mounting him.

"Nag, may I climb aboard you and fly?" she asked politely. "We haven't much time at all now."

"Get on," he agreed. "Put your legs behind my wings."

Gwen clambered on, with some difficulty. "Sorry, there isn't a saddle. Whoops!"

"Ow… no… what part of "behind" do you not understand?" he snorted. "And by thunder, you're heavy!"

"Can you take me?" the Princess asked.

The horse nodded and grunted. "Yes, it's just… been a while."

"Go, Gwen!" urged Viola.

"We'll follow and try to get there in time," Oberon promised.

Merlene patted The Nag's neck and clapped at Gwen's back, approvingly. "Keep hold of that sword. It's part of you now… until the day you die."

Gwen looked a little disappointed. "I can still die?"

"Damn right you can!" Merlene's face was grave and solemn. "Arthor died, just as sure as every mortal will."

"Then I'll try not to die!"

Nightwind beat his enormous wings and rose up. Gwen's whole body leapt to attention and she clung to his neck, wrapping his mane in her free hand and gripping with her strong thighs. They pulled away from Camelot and soared out over the forest and the plains beyond. The winding road along which they had come was so far below now.

Gwen could not help herself. She cried out in absolute joy as the thrill of flight coursed through her. The black alicorn said nothing but she felt him go faster, spurred on by her enthusiasm. They swooped low, hurtling towards the road and as the border guards dived for cover, threaded through and into London, where Nightwind again took to the air and flew high above the buildings, dodging spires and weaving through chimney smoke as they sailed over the rooftops.

The Londoners just emerging from their homes caught sight of this strange pair crossing their skyline. Many had been granted the morning off work to attend the wedding and were filing across to the Tower to watch the executions first. Gwendoline's hair, now golden again, was recognised, as was her face as it rushed by. The word went out that Lady Katherine was back, and on a winged horse at that. But to what purpose?

***

Robin stepped out into the dawn light a few minutes before eight bells. He screwed up his fists, gritted his teeth and thanked fair fortune that his captors had allowed him to retain his warm, green coat.

For their part it was not an act of kindness. His dangling outlaw form, so very recognisable, would make a clear statement that the reign of the Hoods was over. But it shielded him from the morning chill which would only exacerbate the tremors of fear coursing through his whole body that he was fighting to control every second. They had even permitted him his boots back, though they had been thoroughly checked and had the lock-picks and concealed blade removed. All the better for him to shortly fill this same footwear with effluent.

That was of course the most undignified aspect of this whole process. The voiding of one's bowels at the frenzied and terrified moment of death. Robin attempted to smile defiantly in a manner the hundreds of onlookers around the base of the scaffold he was climbing might find noble, prepared to die for what he believed in, perhaps even beatific. He looked down at their upturned faces. In some eyes he saw hate, jeering, assurance that this wrongdoer was getting his just desserts. In others he saw curiosity; they only wanted to say they saw Robin Hood die.

He was still so afraid. This was all wrong. He was sorry, he would make amends. He really hadn't hurt anyone who didn't roundly deserve it, had he?

A flash of anger hit him. Nobody knew about his firecasting; he could hurl himself from the scaffold, a burning ball of retribution for the gawkers in the front row.

No… no, he resolved. He would simply try his best to shit hard in their direction as he swung.

Scarlet and the rest of the Hoods were being led out behind. The magnitude of this finally hit him hard. Were he simply a lonely man about to die, that would be bad enough, but to die with all one's friends gathered together and dying as well… for people to see. Considering the hope and well-meaning nature of the crimes these people had committed, this was an appalling shame. Scarlet had been wrong, and so had he. They had lost this game and the good people of London would suffer far worse for it.

There was anger in the crowd now. People were pushing, protesting, crying out for the freedom of the prisoners. Robin saw the lines of Watchmen assembled and imagined the flaming bloodbath that would occur if they came into ferocious contact with these unarmed Londoners.

He thought about shouting out something inspirational, but he was unable to trust his voice to remain strong and not quail mid-cry. Scarlet took the position next to him and they exchanged final glances of solidarity. Her head was held high even though the jeering became unbearably raucous at the sight of this uppity akka.

But some had recognised her. Hands were over mouths and upon hearts.

Scarlet would say nothing, so Robin must. This was his only chance. All of a sudden, he was yelling out to all that would listen.

"Find other heroes!"

As he uttered these words an executioner's elbow collided with his gut, knocking the wind from him. As he buckled, he saw, in a way that stilled his heart for what would surely be the second-to-last time, the traces of tears in the crowd. There really were people crying. Those soon to die would be missed. They were valued. He had achieved *something* in this muddled, violent, flawed and semi-fictionalised existence. *That*, surely, was the truth he needed, the reassurance.

He thought of Gwendoline, very soon beginning her new life.

His last hope was that it wouldn't be half as bad as she had feared.

Let her just be happy… happy enough.

He prayed.

He was ready…

No, he wasn't ready, but it would have to do.

The hangman hefted the noose to place around his neck.

***

In the great courtyard of the Tower of London, at one minute to eight bells, Robin Hood looked up into the cold, clear sky from his place atop the gallows.

He saw a rapidly approaching winged horse with what appeared to be a Valkyrie riding atop it.

Her hair was virtually aflame in the sunlight, and she brandished a sword in her hand.

He realised it was Gwendoline around the moment that she bodily leapt from the horse in mid-air and dived in his direction.

He also saw her look of sudden horror upon discovering that she could not steer herself much in the air.

***

"What are you *doing*?" The Nag shouted.

"Improvising!" Gwen called back as she flung herself outwards. "OH, SHIT!!!"

"Oh, *perfect!*" cried the horse, as Gwen hit the scaffold like a chunk of masonry fired from the largest siege catapult in the world, devastating the hard work of all those London craftsmen, and sending prisoners, executioners, onlookers, Watchmen, wood and curses flying.

Chapter 24: The Battle of the Tower

Sunday Morning (No Days Left)

Robin's eyes opened and he found the Princess' body wrapped around him, protectively. They unfolded and struggled to their feet as bits of wood scattered from their clothing, amid the settling dust.

"Hello," he said softly.

"Hi."

"What the devil are you doing here?"

"Saving you," she responded. Around them the scaffold began to tumble down as Gwendoline pulled him into a passionate kiss. Both of them were flooded with a powerful cocktail of relief, and adrenalin. "Now, let's free the others."

"I'm a little tied up at the moment," he pointed out. "Would you get that jailor's keys for me please? The one over there."

"As you wish!" She collared the terrified Duart and snatched his keyring away. Robin freed himself and they set about picking up the Hoods and factory workers and unlatching them swiftly.

The sound of clanking armour and footfalls was growing closer and guards began pouring in from all sides of the scaffold as the roar of the confused crowd became all the more agitated. These were Heavies, not marked with the firecasting livery, but that meant reinforcements would not be far behind.

Gwen had half a second to react as one barrelled towards Robin, brandishing a keen short-sword in his gauntlet. She lurched forward and kicked out hard. The guard felt as light as a football under her boot and flew backwards with a yell, pancaking against the stone wall of the tower with a sickening crunch.

Everybody froze and gawped at this mess and then back at Gwen who had her hands up to her face, eyes wide and mouth agape with somewhat awkward surprise.

"Uh…" She hesitated, not sure of her next move, then cried out to the other Heavies. "I suggest you all get back and let these people alone…"

Before she could finish the command, Gwen was grabbed from behind, and suddenly, armoured Duart were swarming her. She clutched at the hilt of the Archenblade and shrieked with frustration as their hands pulled at her hair and coat, dragging her downwards.

She had trained mostly in fighting single opponents using wrestling, boxing and her own personal style developed from combining those two disciplines with street fighting and several forms from South America. However, the crushing bodies in heavy armour, all attempting to roughly subdue rather than injure, were overwhelming, and far too many for her to cope with. Hearing the clink of cuffs and remembering the ordeal of being fastened to Robin in Camelot, she gritted her teeth and strained upwards, feeling her newly acquired might destabilise and move these men.

It was strange, she could feel great strength, but it was tiring her too. Gwen angrily swatted away a helmeted guard pulling himself on top of her and realised that her gloved hand had connected with the sharper edges of his armour in doing so. There was just enough time to inspect her stinging appendage to find that it was not bleeding, nor was her skin damaged, and it became apparent that she could merely punch them aside *through* their armour and not be badly wounded in the process.

A miniature eruption of soldiers rose up and Gwen smashed and kicked her way free, retrieving Robin who had been trying to pull the Watchmen aside to get her some space, and was receiving a fairly savage beating for his troubles. They retreated from the guards and in the next few moments had time to unlatch more prisoners who were rushing towards them for aid.

"You pulled the sword from the stone then?" Robin panted.

"Yes," Gwen shot back. "The trick was understanding how unbalanced power really is… that and not giving a damn about having great power myself."

Robin shook his head in disbelief. "Of *course* that's what it was. Why didn't I think of that?" He glanced back and forth at the guards closing in on them. "Feel free to go ahead and use it!"

"How?"

"Poke them hard with the sharp bit."

"I'll kill them!" Gwen protested.

"I know," he replied. "And if we weren't already at a public execution I'd be happy to debate the morality of it, but we are!"

Gwendoline was now aware that she had already probably killed a man; the stain on the wall spoke of someone at the very least with only a few unbroken bones in his now crumpled body. Her unspeakable physical power became all-too-apparent. She could most likely snap these Duart in two within their armour. Oh, it would be horrible exertion, dangerous and messy, but the confinements on capabilities and possibilities were now broken open. The processes of effective slaughter could easily become as natural as those performed in her sparring matches.

She felt sick inside and resolved on the spot to avoid going too far in her efforts to stop these oppressors.

She grabbed at the oncoming guards with her free hand, flinging them at the splintering wooden beams.

At each other.

At anything softer than a stone wall.

The Princess barged against them with her shoulders and swiped their legs out from under them, knocking the wind from their lungs, anything to prevent the weapon in her hand from tearing through their flesh. Hardy and rough though they were, it would be all too easy to part them from their spark of life with this fiery, golden sword.

The pommel, though, that thick bit at the bottom designed to balance the blade, made an excellent tool for smashing against their chest-plates and helmets. These blows, each pulled at the last moment to avoid bursting their hearts, sent them to the floor roaring in pain and surprise, very much out of the fight but apparently not mortally wounded. Gwen panted and choked with laughter at her successful, if frantic, attempts to take them down, but again could feel her energy draining away with every mammoth blow. The Princess was tired and aching and needed to rest. If they kept coming there was no telling how long she would last. She caught glimpses of the assembled Londoners as she turned this way and that. They could see her fighting; many were even cheering, conveying ripples of much-needed energy.

And around her, the Hoods had been freed and were dispatching Watchmen, tearing off armoured helmets from the Heavies and purloining weaponry as they did so, until all had something to defend themselves with.

Gwen caught sight of Scarlet and Ajax, the bartender from the Thirsty Hog and Latika, the Punjab lady who had helped free them from their captors that first night, as well as a curious fellow clad in black, brandishing a broom handle and bellowing something about midnight's champion being here to claim them all. She also recognised a lot of workers from the factory, though not being fighters they hung back behind the Hoods, hoping for protection.

More guards were rushing in as the wildly leaning wooden frame around them began to collapse. As the Hoods pulled the last few captives from the wreckage the scaffold gave way, falling inward, and before them stood Captain Baltus, his face a mask of cold fury. Flanking him were two dozen Firecasters, all primed and ready, their grim features obscured behind those caronite helmets. Behind *them* were an equal number of

Heavies, standing not far from the madding crowd, holding them back.

Baltus roared at the Hoods. "Cease this dissent or I shall have my men open fire!"

Gwen cried out and stepped in front of the outlaws. "Captain Baltus, it's me!"

He started at the sound of her voice and looked her up and down. "Princess… What is the meaning of this? You are supposed to be marrying within the hour."

"I came here to prevent this mass execution," she replied. "There's been a huge misunderstanding. These people are innocent of kidnapping me and I pardon them of all their previous crimes. Do you hear me?" She turned to face Hoods and workers alike. "I pardon you all!" Her voice was cracked and though the crowd could not hear her over the din, they did see her standing her ground against Baltus. Word spread quickly that this was the Princess, and that she and Lady Katherine were indeed one and the same. Now many within the throng of Londoners began to jostle forwards to reach her, crying out as they were pushed against the line of steadfast Heavies.

"Stand down, your Highness," Baltus urged, harshly. "Come with me at once to Westminster."

Gwen stared at him for a moment. "I…" She raised her chin defiantly. "I will do so if you let everyone behind me go free. Grant them passage back into the city."

Baltus was enraged at this attempt to negotiate. "I will *not* do that," he snarled. "They have been tried and convicted. To contravene the law runs entirely counter to my station. You demanding this of me makes you and these conspirators *all* guilty of treason against the realm. This ends now." His tone was growing more vicious as he spoke. "You will stand down, girl!

Gwen cried out to the gathered crowd, waves of exhaustion gripping her, dizziness threatening to overwhelm. "Everybody go home! Get out of here. Get back to safety! I stand with the Hoods, and the people of London!"

More heard her this time. There was louder cheering, and Baltus' face darkened further.

"Last warning, girl," he snarled. "You are sheltering outlaws and the penalty is death. Ready, men!"

The Firecasters all ignited in a line. The smell, like burning paraffin, filled the breeze. Gwen thought of the poor, captive barghest, pictured them roasting alive and screaming, hanging from their bonds as their existences ended in agony. There was nothing she could do. If she surrendered herself, her companions, these innocents would all still be incinerated where they stood.

The people had realised now that their Princess was in danger and some were pushing all the harder against the ranks, screaming in protest to do her no harm.

"Firecasters," Gwen called out to the Duart Watchmen lined up behind Baltus. "I am Princess Gwendoline Amelia Gertrude Victoria of the house of Saxe-Coburg and Gotha. I order you to put away your flames and escort these citizens to safety," Not one of them wavered. The flames licked over their gauntlets as the crowd wailed. Baltus had taught them well. 'Queen and Country' fell by the wayside when Queen threatened country.

Gwen turned back to Baltus. "Please Captain, I am begging you. *Do not do this.*"

His face was locked, his eyes flared. There was no mercy, no humanity within that frame. As she looked into his black eyes the Princess became desperately afraid. How could someone be so evil? So intent on killing for an ideal?

Gwendoline searched the skies for any sign of Nightwind, but as she had dismounted from him, mid-air, he had fled. Of course, this was as far as he could have taken her. The Nag would never suffer having those magnificent wings burned to help others. Coward though he was, she felt an odd sense of relief. Something would survive this terrible day.

She looked back at Robin, seeking the strength to stand.

As she gazed into his eyes Robin struggled hard to withhold his own overwhelming despair. He had made peace with his death, but not hers. Now at the last moment he could feel the familiar and dreadful burning sensation begin to grip his hands; the one element guaranteed to make their situation somehow worse. There was no fighting this fire with what he had.

For a moment he considered pleading with her to give up, to go with Baltus, to not die with them here right now. And yet here she was, of her own volition; she had already returned to her palace and that life, and it could not hold her. Suddenly suggesting she surrender in order to live another day in service of the kind of rulership that would allow this imminent atrocity seemed an unforgivable insult. So Robin held his tongue.

Gwen's mind raced. She prepared herself to rush forward and stab Baltus through the heart. It may not prevent the onslaught of fire, she may die in doing so, but this despicable tyrant needed to be gone from the world, and there was the tiniest possibility that doing so might stun the Watchmen into compliance to her will.

"FIRE!" Baltus screamed too early, and there was no time to reach him.

***

Gwen beheld the flames begin their slow movement across the scene of devastation. The crowd were all lit up, their faces horrified. It occurred to her that she could jump straight up, grabbing Robin as she went. Why had she not thought of this earlier? She could jump them both to safety, they could disappear into the wild. Leave everything and everyone behind. Even as these thoughts burrowed their way through her mind she knew she could never have run from here, but the anger at herself for not leaping upon Baltus and slaying him sooner burned hotter than the oncoming wall.

Those slowly moving flames were now spreading up and overhead, arcing across an invisible bubble as Merlene, riding Nightwind, hurtled in from the sky, throwing up an enormous, translucent shield as she came.

Gwendoline registered this in a dreamlike daze and all she could comprehend was how magnificent was the sight of this aged enchantress upon that jet-black stallion, framed as they were in a wreath of flame. Time returned to normal as the inferno ebbed away and the Watchmen and Baltus flinched as it rolled back in their direction, dissipating as it went. Mercifully these fireproof sentinels acted as a barrier before the Londoners, but they were still bowled off their feet by the force of the blast.

Baltus began a call again for another volley, but was suddenly silenced as Viola, Oberon and Mortimer charged in behind Merlene, their cart practically airborne with tumultuous motion; the spellcaster perched atop the horse and aiming her gloved hand at the Captain with a triumphant cry as he tasted bacon.

***

Immediately all was uproar. The Hoods surged forward and began attacking the Watchmen. The barriers broke and the crowd rushed in as well, and the interior execution yard of the Tower of London became a heaving mass of bodies, armour, screaming, blood and fire.

Gwendoline had pushed through towards the spot Baltus had stood. There seemed little better or quicker way to end this than by ending *him*, but there was no sign of the Captain and too many people were jostling around her. The available space filled up frighteningly fast and she was being shoved past and grabbed at.

Panic set in; lights flashing, head pounding. Gwen lifted her hands in defence and the sword was suddenly gone.

She was punched in the mouth and dropped to the ground, strength bleeding away, desperately searching around her, hoping to see where it had fallen.

The coldest reality made itself known. The Archenblade had been taken.

Gwen got to her feet again, pulling up out of the choking darkness of limbs and curses and looked around desperately.

Some thirty feet away, now far beyond reach, was a Heavy Watchman, brandishing her sword. He was swiping it at some humans and screaming at them to get back. There may have been some knowledge of its immense value and power, or he may simply have been desperate for survival enough to take it for defence, having lost his own weapon. Either way Gwendoline struggled forwards and pulled herself towards the nearest edge of the scrum. He was nearing the gate. She looked around frantically for aid.

Gwen spied him on the ramparts grappling with three bowmen who had been taking pot-shots into the crowd. The third of these men tumbled down as Gwendoline screamed out for help.

"RO-BIN!!!!!!!"

Robin of Loxley saw her unarmed, and his heart leapt. He had about six seconds to act. Grabbing a discarded bow and nocking an arrow, he squinted off into the distance, his arm tense and shaking. There was no way he could be sure of hitting the escaping Heavy from up here. There was too much shadow and too many people milling about nearby. Besides which, even if he got in a lucky shot and hit him square in the back, the caronite armour would most likely deflect his arrow. Robin hopped forward onto the descending steps and focused with all of his might on the bright, hanging oil lamp just ahead of the fleeing soldier.

Robin felt a flare of fierce, protective joy. He would get this princess' sword back to her. The end of his arrow ignited as he focused on its burning point.

Time slowed as he let it fly, arcing across the courtyard, leaving a smoking, orange fire trail over the heads of the crowd, thundering through space until it pierced and shattered the lamp, spraying burning oil into the path of the fleeing guard, who reeled back in fright, dropping his prize.

Gwendoline had cleared the melee and was hurrying towards the blaze, her eyes now on the fallen sword. The world jerked backwards as she felt a vice-like grip on her left wrist. A Firecaster pulled her towards him, purposely stepping on her coat-tails and planting his elbow on the back of her neck to bodily force Gwendoline to her knees. She reached around for a weapon, a discarded helmet, a stone, anything.

"Stay down," he growled, viciously.

Robin saw what was happening and began to run. His fire could not hurt this Duart, his arrows were unlikely to pierce that armour and the high chances of hitting the struggling Gwendoline were dire. This would have to be up close.

He rushed down the steps and ran as fast as his short legs could carry him.

A purple-coated figure now stood beside the sword. Mortimer turned and glanced over at the fallen princess, smiling with cold satisfaction as she lifted the ancient artefact up to inspect it. Gwendoline's jaw dropped in horror.

"Hey, BOOM-Hilda," Mortimer called out. "Catch!" The bounty hunter lobbed the sword in Gwen's direction and it slammed into the Firecaster's shoulder, lodging firmly and deep. He screamed and let go of Gwen who twisted around, grabbed the hilt and gasped as her power returned, drawing the blade out forcefully and perhaps by mistake relieving the caterwauling Watchman of his arm in the process.

Robin reached her seconds later as Mortimer approached, reloading her guns.

"Thank you, *both* of you," Gwen said.

"No time for chit chat," Mortimer barked. She cracked off a shot into an area immediately behind Gwendoline, blowing the hand clean off an attacker, just as another tore in from Mortimer's right and was himself suddenly snatched away as Nightwind swooped overhead, bashing in many thick Duart skulls with his thundering air-superiority, and expertly smashing that particular Watchman high overhead with a single swipe of his wing.

He had not been idle this battle. Instead, he had been prancing through the sky and drawing the flames to himself, dodging nimbly out of the way as he wheeled and circled, rationalising that while their gaze was on the heavens and aiming to bring down this magnificent, black beast, they would not be on the ground, flambeeing peasants. But on several occasions, this being one of them, both to thin out the troops and to reignite their interest in him, he swooped low and met them hoof-to-helmet.

Merlene, meanwhile, rushed from one group of Hoods or Londoners in danger to another, shielding them from harm, bowling over the strongest of their attackers and crying out battle orders. She was less concerned with evacuating the crowds and more focused on tactically placing the right people in the right places to break up the Watchmen units and drive them back onto unsteady footing. Some of the Duart in the melee raised on stories of King Arthor and his wizard began to become demoralised.

If the heroes of their past were on the opposing side, what did that make them?

Those Duart defending the humans and Akka, however, felt a surge of fresh inspiration. With a new Arthor and an old Merlene, they might actually win this one.

As the battle raged on, Oberon had finally found his brother.

Ajax was fending off two Watchmen, the primal rage that might have proved so helpful for survival somehow not surfacing here. His eyes were frightened and his blows were panicked and unfocused. Oberon swung in with the deadly weight of his beautifully carved new club, entirely beheading one of the attackers, a sight which frightened the other away.

Behind them huddled the Dragusha family.

"Brother," Ajax called out to Oberon. "Your club. I make." He slapped his own chest and pointed proudly.

"Ceiling breaker," Dashurie greeted him. "This is your brother?"

"Yeah, he is," Oberon smiled. "Can you guys take him out of here? He shouldn't be in a place like this, and neither should you."

Lavinia stepped forward. "No, you cannot stay! They'll kill you!"

"I'll be fine. There's some people I've got to help." He knelt down beside the girl. "Can you do something for me?"

"Whatever you need," she said, sniffling.

"Can you take care of my brother? He gets scared sometimes, so you have to keep him happy and calm, okay? Be a big sister to him."

"But I am *tiny*," she said, bewildered. "Is this one of your jokes?"

Oberon shook his head. "You have to be big inside, because inside *him*, he's littler than you."

She nodded. "Ahhhhh, now *that* I understand."

Oberon lifted Lavinia up and placed her in Ajax's arms, then indicated the Southern gate. It was a narrow choke-point that seemed far off amid the chaos.

"Ajax, buddy, you keep this one very safe, keep the bad people away from her and stay with her family. I'll meet you all back at your boat, now go!"

"Goodbye," said Lavinia, biting back her stubborn tears. They began to move and Oberon turned to dive back into the affray.

Mortimer and Robin had taken up positions around Gwendoline, allowing her to be the heavy hitter while they picked off strays.

This was a triangle that had been noticed. Captain Baltus, glaring down from the watchtower above Traitor's Gate, marked their position and began to make his move. The Princess would not leave this place alive.

Baltus was spotted by Viola, who had been trying to make her way to Gwendoline, guarded by Merlene's shields as she cast Darkness and Confuse on every man in uniform. She was beginning to flag now, and Merlene had rushed to the aid of some children who were being muscled towards a pit by a particularly brutal jailor.

Viola was alone, weaponless.

Baltus, flanked by four Firecasters, was making his way across the yard towards Gwen.

In this moment, Viola realised that it was time to fulfil her task as a bodyguard at all costs.

Over the distance between them, she cast a spell with pinpoint accuracy upon the Captain.

"Sleep!"

He stumbled and turned; furious, but woozy. "The deceitful buffoon," he growled. "Kill her!"

"Sleep!" she yelled again.

The Firecasters flung scorching bolts in Viola's direction, which she ducked and weaved around, casting more Sleep spells at Baltus, one after the other. He dropped to one knee as Oberon appeared with a roar and barged through the four casters, yanking off their helmets and dislocating their arms. Baltus aimed a vicious firebolt at Viola which narrowly missed as she closed the gap between them, limping now.

"Sleep…" she gasped, visibly weakening with every incantation. "Sleep… SLEEP!"

Each spell hit Baltus square in the chest and he crumpled further, down to both knees, thrusting forward and lashing out to grab at Viola.

Oberon saw this and wrestled his way forward but was held at bay by heaving metal. Viola choked as the Captain gripped her throat savagely, tearing at her jacket.

The taste of lavender in his mouth was now so overpowering that bitter, black bile rose up in his throat and trickled forth as he screamed.

"DIE!!!!!!"

Viola's voice was barely audible. She had almost nothing left.

"*Sleep.*"

On this last spell, Viola's two fingers to his forehead, Baltus' eyes rolled back into his skull, while his eyelids remained open, his face drawn wide in shock as the cumulative effect of these spells hit home. His consciousness retreated back so far into the depths of his mind that it would never return. His lungs forgot how to work, his heart ceased to beat, his mouth fell open and his tongue lolled out, seconds before his face crashed, chin-first, against the stone floor.

Viola coughed and struggled out of his twitching grip.

She pulled herself halfway to her feet and smiled in gratitude at Oberon.

"Weaker sex…my tiny arse!" she mumbled, before collapsing.

Chapter 25: The March West

London Town

Viola was weakened to the point of death, and Oberon rushed in to catch her.

He searched her face and brushed pink hair aside with his enormous, green fingers, feeling for a heartbeat and a breath with his thumb. Her eyes flickered open and she could not speak but gripped the dark leather of his coat.

"No... Don't you go," Oberon said, in a low voice.

He reached into his knapsack and retrieved the crumpled bag of cinder toffee he had purchased during his wanderings around London the day before. Gingerly, he knelt and supported her as the battle still raged around them, breaking off a small piece of the honeycomb and placing it to her lips. She sniffed and bit into it, crunching down the confectionary with tiny laboured movements. She swallowed with difficulty and was able to eat a little more as Oberon looked around frantically for a safe spot. Viola's eyes eventually opened and she smiled faintly, but as sensibility returned and her memories of cruelty to him over the past few days trickled back, she could no longer meet his eye.

"It's okay..." He was gearing up to say something forgiving, feeling a tiny glow of pride that he had retained the toffee for just such a scenario, but that pride was offset by a great relief that she was alive.

***

At this exact moment, several hundred yards away, they saw the Dragushas' path towards the exit being barred by pike-wielding Watchmen. These Heavies jabbed at Ajax who turned Lavinia away from them, shielding her with his back and bellowing in pain as the points stabbed into his flesh.

Oberon roared in dismay, and still cradling Viola he pulled himself to his feet and charged across the battlefield, readying his club with his free right hand.

Gwen, Mortimer, Merlene and Robin joined them as they went.

As one, they tore into the spearmen, splintering their weaponry and laying waste to their bodies in a hail of blows, bullets, fire and spells. Their movements were chaotic, but there was finally some semblance of coordination; an irregular pattern of erratic turnabouts and ferocious retribution.

Robin and Mortimer dodged and weaved about, confounding the Heavies and targeting their vulnerable areas, aided by Viola, who had regained enough strength for distraction casting, and protected by Merlene. Gwen and Oberon flattened and broke the men, bodily flinging them far out over the quayside and into the Thames, clearing the pathway so that everybody could escape the Tower. At least two of them were hideously gored to death by Nightwind's golden, armour-piercing horn.

Since Baltus had entered his eternal Sleep, and with the last of the Watchmen at the gate now thoroughly gone or dead or surrendered, the battleground began to clear and the group regarded one another, the weight of

338

this effort threatening to overcome their exhausted frames. Oberon broke first and, still holding Viola, he rushed to Ajax who was sitting on the ground, his eyes screwed shut, clutching at the wounds in his back.

"Easy big guy," Oberon said gently. "You did real good. The family are all alive."

"Hurt," Ajax whimpered.

"I know buddy, we're going to help you."

"Oberon…"

Oberon looked up, surprised to hear his own name. "Yeah… it's me."

Scarlet had been ushering people out of the front gate, but on seeing the wounded Ajax, she stepped over and knelt beside him.

"Go easy," she said. "Ajax, can you roll over this way please, and hold your hand *here*. I need to attend to this now."

"Owww," Ajax howled as he followed her instruction.

"I need bandages, alcohol and needle and thread," Scarlet said sharply.

"I'll find them." Robin rushed off.

Scarlet shook her head. "My fingers are shaking, I can't hold a Duart needle." She glanced around and saw Mortimer hovering nearby. "You!"

"Me?"

"Yes, *you*, you're going to be my hands."

"Here." Robin had returned with a basic medical kit from the guardhouse. He held it out to Mortimer, and they all noticed her hesitancy.

"There's no time to waste searching your soul for a shred of moral decency," Scarlet barked. "We need you now."

"I'm a professional findsman and an assassin," Mortimer snapped, grabbing the kit from Robin. "I can bloody well see to an injury." She angrily fished inside the kit and placed the bottle of alcohol on Scarlet's outstretched hand.

"Brilliant, you're hired," Scarlet said, pouring the clear liquid over Ajax's wound.

Together they set about tending to the hurt akka, Scarlet cleaning him up and soothing his fears with a professional air as Mortimer, grumbling quietly, closed up the tear. After he was bandaged, the pair, who had been joined by the few present with appropriate medical skills, moved onto others who could be saved.

***

Gwendoline surveyed the ground, littered with bodies. Duart, Human, Akka, their still frames armoured, decorated, clothed in trousers and coats, clad only in rags. They had been beaten, burned, stabbed, choked or crushed. None of these differences seemed to matter now. The main contrasts that hit her hard were the stark line between the living and the dead, and the hazier one between those injured, and those hovering on the cusp.

"This cannot be for me," she murmured under her breath.

"What cannot?" Merlene turned to look at her. Gwen shook her head.

"I will not have *this* be the way of things."

"If you choose to oppose your father," Merlene said gravely, "people are going to die, no matter what."

"Well then, I shall have to find a way to minimise this." The Princess waved her hand towards the casualties.

The wizard nodded slowly. "Then I shall do what I can to help you."

"Merlene, this sword," Gwen said hopefully. "Does it mean…? I mean I didn't even really think about it too much, I was so intent on saving Robin, but am I Queen of Britannica now?"

"No."

"Oh…" Gwen's face fell. "Oh dear."

"Strange women living in ruins distributing swords," Merlene explained, "is no basis for a system of government."

"That's what I thought." Gwen nodded sadly.

"What I was guarding," Merlene continued, "was the literal power it would bestow. That's why I placed such a complicated enchantment on it. Arthor was already the heir of a king. You, baker's daughter, are not."

Gwen stared at her. "What am I, then?"

"You tell *me*, young lady," Merlene responded, not unkindly.

"Right…" Gwen placed her hands on her hips and raised her chin. "I shall, then."

***

341

Not far from where they stood, Robin found Mortimer and handed her some more needle and thread.

"So, I've been told…" he began hesitantly. "That you didn't betray us."

"Impossible to talk now," Mortimer replied curtly, not looking at him. "Holding this fellow's spleen in my hand."

"Would you like some help?" Robin asked. She glanced up at him over her spectacles.

"Well… *obviously*," she retorted.

So they set about saving a few more lives as the ravens circled the ramparts, their eyes on the unfortunate dead who would become their next few meals.

***

Oberon sat between his brother and Viola, who had propped herself against the wall with the bag of cinder toffee in hand. She offered it to Oberon and Ajax, and they quietly crunched upon its contents, feeling a glimmer of comfort and their strength returning.

Viola spied Gwen marching out before the crowd that had assembled in front of the tower, made up of survivors from the brawl and newly arrived Londoners who had filed in from Lower Thames Street to see what the commotion was. Nightwind flew down to walk beside the Princess.

"I'm going to Westminster Abbey," Gwen called out, her voice echoing around the ancient Norman stone. "Who else fancies a walk through London?"

About four hundred hands went up.

*****

They marched the three miles west down the bank of the
Thames. The journey took an hour and over that time
they accumulated more and more locals to their cause.
The streets had already been packed with people on their
way to the wedding, hoping for a glimpse of Gwendoline
and the newly entitled *Prince* Aaron.

No Watchmen attempted to stop them as their
numbers had become daunting. Gwen was spurred on
by this, and part of her began to believe that a great
change was beginning here. Maybe she could save
London from tyranny without being Queen at all.

Officials had been spotted hurrying ahead and by the
time they reached the wedding itself the Archduke
would be waiting. She sat astride Nightwind who took
his place at the tip of the spear, making for a
breathtaking figurehead. The air of that morning was
crisp and invigorating and she drew as much strength as
possible from this brief moment of purposeful respite.

To her right walked Robin, and Oberon who was
carrying Viola. Next to them limped Ajax, holding his
bandaged side. Scarlet, with Lavinia now perched on her
shoulder, walked by the Dragushas at the front of the
line. To her left was Merlene, radiating an air of silent,
sober determination which had proved infectious
throughout the group. The scattered Duart and a few of
the Akka among them were whispering about the
possibility that this could indeed be the great wizard

from out of their distant past. The sword was here, and the Princess was showing many traits of the fabled powers of Arthor. What did this all mean? It was rich and fascinating information to deliberate, and very conducive to hushed chatter.

Beside Merlene strode Mortimer, rifle slung over her shoulder, once again refusing to look at Gwendoline, who was now not sure how to feel about this woman. Twice she had lent her aid entirely voluntarily and without promise of coin, behaviour most unbecoming of a mercenary. The second time had saved Gwen's life, along with many around them, but the Princess could not shake that suspicion. She was so rude and aloof and selfish and shallow… and lonely. But then so was The Nag. And yet here they both were, walking with her, straight into the heart of danger.

Gwen could not kid herself that what followed would be anything less than a standoff that would affect millions of lives, very possibly in the dire negative. She would have to choose her words so carefully and be so sure of where she stood.

Now the real fear set in, and she resorted to her hard-practised resting serene face, so that barely a hint of what was tumbling about beneath the surface would show. She looked across and saw Oberon glance down into Viola's face, studying it with concern. Her friend perched within the crook of his arm and entwined the leather strap from his knapsack around her bare wrist to steady herself. Gwen felt a little jolt of wordless excitement at this unusual measure of trust.

They turned right at the clock tower, beside Westminster Bridge, moved down The Queen's Walk and came up against the crowd that had already gathered round the Abbey, proceeding as those assembled parted before them, onto Broad Sanctuary at the end of Victoria Street.

It was twenty minutes after nine bells. Gwen had heard Big Ben chiming a while back as they travelled. At this point, had things gone differently, in another timeline she would now be emerging into the sunlight with Aaron by her side, unhappily married.

At this exact moment 'Princess Gwendoline' emerged from the doors of Westminster Abbey, Aaron by her side, her face a picture of composure, radiating happiness. The two Gwens locked eyes and Simon's heart leapt, ever-so-slightly smudging his Glamour, which Viola had been holding the whole time. Both had performed their roles magnificently, even as Viola collapsed near-dead back at the tower, even as Simon said the words "I do".

Prince Aaron looked at Gwen astride a black, winged unicorn with what appeared to be half of London at her back.

He glanced at the Gwendoline by his side and bellowed, "What is the meaning of this?"

Chapter 26: The Confrontation

Sunday Morning

Viola stepped down from Oberon's arms, cast a gentle Sleep spell upon Simon and lifted his Glamour. The strapping fellow in the beautiful white wedding dress crumpled forward drawing shrieks of alarm and babbling clamour from the assembled, now-hysterical gentry. On the ground, immobilised, he was far less likely to draw direct aggression for his crimes.

Merlene spoke up. "That fellow was an innocent pawn." Her voice boomed out over the din, silencing everyone. "The woman in red who stands before you is the one you have all come to know as Princess Gwendoline!"

Aaron looked down at the man he had just married, and then glared at Merlene, Viola, Robin and the Akka beside him, and his face darkened into a snarl.

"Witchcraft…" he growled.

Merlene rolled her eyes. "*This* again."

"Thou shalt not suffer a witch to live!" Aaron screamed. "Guards, seize the pink one and the grey one!"

"That may not be necessary… yet," came a voice.

Archduke Coriolanus had exited the Abbey after the happy couple, and now stepped in front of No-Longer-Prince Aaron to take charge of the situation. He looked down at Simon, studied Gwen, comprehending her movements over the past day, recognised the

Archenblade and Merlene, assessed the numbers of the rabble behind them, along with their lack of weaponry, armour, training and coordination, weighed it up against the assembled guards he had immediately at his disposal, added the wild cards of a legendary wizard and King Arthor's abilities which Gwendoline now presumably possessed… and nodded solemnly.

He removed three folded pieces of parchment from his pocket and ensured that Gwendoline saw them. His largest risk here was that she would simply kill him on the spot.

Gwendoline indeed saw the parchment, considered what her own options were and, for the first time, counted forward a number of days after deposing and maybe even killing Coriolanus and, if she was lucky, the remaining six Dukes spread across England and Britannica.

Who would be in charge then?

With a sinking realisation she knew she could not coordinate a takeover bid on this scale herself, without grievous loss of life, even with the help of all of her assembled friends; even with Merlene, whose political experience was probably centuries out of date for the world they now stood in.

She could not do this.

Not like she'd hoped.

It would mean disaster.

"I caught word of the assault on the tower just under an hour ago," the Archduke told her. "Though the true identity of the woman on the horse could not be ascertained, I suspected it might be you."

"And you allowed me to marry an imposter in the meantime!" Aaron shrieked at him. "I married a man! What does that make me?"

Coriolanus ignored him and continued to address his words to the Princess. "There was also a high chance that this was still my Gwendoline. I must say your duplicate was wholly convincing, so I allowed this to play out."

"I can't believe this!" Aaron ranted. "I shall be remembered for nought but *embuggerance*!"

The Archduke finally turned and glared at him. "Lord Aaron please, you had no idea."

Aaron shook his head violently. "I kissed him… I put my tongue in his mouth!"

"In your defence, my *Lord*," piped up Robin, from Gwen's side. "For a man, that is an *extraordinarily* pretty specimen. I'd probably kiss him too."

"Robin, know when to shut up," Scarlet hissed at him.

"Gwendoline," Coriolanus went on, as Aaron continued to gape and sputter, wordlessly. "I have already sent for the regiments stationed at Stratford and Shoreditch. They shall be here soon. One thousand Duart soldiers, and a great contingent of their numbers are Firecasters." He surveyed the crowd behind her. "These unarmed commoners will all be killed if they continue their revolt. You can prevent this matchless slaughter. You have one final chance to take this man's hand in marriage." He gestured towards Aaron.

"I'm not sure if I want to now," the noble Lord said, petulantly.

"Trust me, you want to," the Archduke said, his voice low and laden with warning. "Alternatively, Gwendoline," He tilted his head and held a gauntleted hand to his breast, the parchments within his grip. "I can speak to this crowd. I have several rather pertinent things to say."

Gwen's heart pounded, her body would not stop trembling, and she felt giddy with the enormous pressure weighing her down more than ever before. She looked at Viola, standing side by side with Oberon, looked at the purple-clad freelancer working for free, looked into the blue, inspiring eyes of Robin and felt her shuddering subside in favour of a strange new calm.

Merlene nodded. "You knew what you were coming here for, girl, and it was never to steal a throne."

Gwendoline whispered to Nightwind and he rose up, slowly beating those great black wings of his. Viola took a deep breath and cast a powerful Reverse Silence upon her. Merlene held up her hand and a translucent shield formed in front of them, walling off the Archduke, Lord Aaron and the guards, temporarily preventing anyone from directly harming those assembled.

And at last Gwendoline spoke to London. Her voice was commanding and strong.

"Ladies and gentlemen. Duart, Akka, Humans alike, citizens of England and Britannica. It is time you were given the truth." She glanced back through the barrier at the Archduke who for the first time appeared surprised. This was manifestly not what he had intended. Yet he did not stir to intervene. "Going forth with this new knowledge you may all decide how best to respond,"

Gwen continued. "It has come to my attention in the past few days that I am not the woman I thought I was, in *every* possible respect of that phrase. But most importantly for you all, I am not Gwendoline Saxe-Coburg, granddaughter of Queen Victoria. I am, in fact, the offspring of two bakers from Spitalfields Market. My name was Katy Laydon.

"I remember… my mother singing." She gave a gentle laugh. "Her voice was screechy so I always knew it was her. I remember playing with the cats on my street, the smell of fresh bread at our bakery, my best friend, Tom with the wonky teeth, who used to find cloth in the abandoned houses for repairs. I remember shillings and pennies, I remember we could only afford to eat meat once a week and it was always beef, my father drank beer because the water was so bad, my sister… Molly, she *died* from drinking the water from the pump. I remember all of it.

"I'm a Londoner, born with nothing to my name, found and taken by chance alone at the age of seven by the Archduke of Buckingham, and told the same fairy-tale that you all were; that I was your Princess and would one day be Queen. And somewhere back then I forgot Katy and I only just remembered her." There was a shift in the crowd. Nobody spoke up, but it was clear this was just as unexpected for them.

"Several days ago, I was taken, but not against my will, by thieves who convey their ill-gotten gains to the impoverished and the needy. Help those who would otherwise be slaves find honest work. I saw what true nobility was at last. But I have also seen division and segregation. I have seen what we do to one another when our fear of outsiders or people we perceive as being *unlike* ourselves, what those fears can do to us… to them.

"And this sword, The Archenblade," she hefted it and the sun bounced off brilliantly. "I pulled this from the stone in Camelot, but not because I was the rightful ruler of anywhere. It came to me because I can now *fight* for you all and know exactly what I'm fighting against." She pointed the blade behind her, directly at the Archduke and Aaron. "But right now, I ask that you all return home. I will go from here with my new knights, this collection of vagabonds. Nobody else will be harmed today on my account. I do not seek war between our people. We did not come here to seize control, but to let the truth be known. Today there is no alternative to the rule of the Dukes, but there will be… in time." She looked briefly back at Coriolanus. "The ruling Duart must forgo their lust for a re-forged British Empire and focus instead on their current dominion. They must work *with* this world, not attempt to conquer it."

For a moment she was silent, as she came to a realisation. "You know I used to be obsessed with the idea of freedom. I wanted to go where I pleased. But I am not sure if we can ever be *truly* free, in the empirical sense, when we depend on one another."

She looked at her companions, then surveyed the faces in the crowd, men, women, children of all species.

"Let us not fight for freedom," she beseeched. "What we should seek is *fairness*… and with that, a greater unity than we have ever known.

"I am *so* sorry that I could not be the woman you need me to be. I shall not be your Queen, today, I do not deserve it. But I can bloody well try to. And in time we are going to find a way to live… together."

The crowd did not erupt into universal, grand applause as she had hoped they might, but neither did they collectively begin to jeer and throw things as she had prayed they would not. Instead, she heard *some* supportive cries dotted through the masses, some hatred for her betrayal, a lot more for the Dukes in general. It was, in fact, a roiling body of discordant murmurs as they beheld that the show was now over and began to filter away to their homes in a varied range of moods, from disgust to inspiration.

Over the coming weeks and months that talk would turn the attention of the city towards the oppression and imbalance perpetrated by their short overlords. Deceit would be added to the list of wrongs, and the people of Britain would begin to speak very candidly of revolution.

Nightwind alighted on the pavement, and Gwendoline stepped down and addressed the Archduke.

"I shall meet you back at the palace," she said, in as commanding a manner as she could muster after this speech, the bent of which, she felt, must have appalled him. "There is a discussion that needs to happen."

Coriolanus slowly and decisively folded and pocketed the parchments and nodded in response. Simon, who had regained consciousness in time to see Gwen's speech, walked across the barrier that Merlene was now lowering, to join them. Gwen hugged him hard in gratitude.

"That was far above and beyond the call of duty," she told him.

"Well, it was better than being punched in the kidneys," Simon confessed.

"We'll get you an annulment."

"Oh, thank God," Simon sighed.

Seeing this, Lord Aaron's nostrils flared and he suddenly lunged forward, unsheathing his sabre.

"You've denied me two Kingdoms, you wretched peasants!"

He nearly reached them but found a golden and very pointy horn neatly jabbing against his breastplate.

The Nag scowled. "You've lost nothing that wouldn't have been stolen... And you call *them* thieves."

"She stole my *dignity*," Aaron snarled. "Ow!"

"Kissing a man doesn't make you any less of one," the alicorn told him firmly. "Refusing to take your defeat with good graces most definitely does." He gave the lord a hard prod and turned with a snort, cantering down the road towards St James's Park, and beyond that, Buckingham Palace.

Gwendoline turned to Robin, offering him her hand in accompaniment. He smiled and took it.

"I love you," he said.

"With good reason," Gwen replied.

Chapter 27: The Parting of Ways

Sunday Afternoon

The entirely knackered companions sat in Buckingham Palace, later that afternoon.

There aren't really words adequate to describe the supreme awkwardness of the scenario, but I shall attempt to do so nonetheless.

Robin was sat with his feet up on an ottoman from the Ottoman Empire, a gift from Sultan Abdul Hamid, head propped up on hand, marvelling in a dazed fashion at his strange reversal of fortune.

Oberon slouched to his right with arms folded and boots outstretched. He was perching upon a sturdy table that had been put in place there for him, since shamefully, there had never been call for chairs in the palace that could accommodate an akka's frame. Even being made of English oak, his table seat groaned periodically.

Ajax sat beside him upon a matching table, eying his brother carefully, and attempting to mimic his demeanour.

Next came Viola, with her hands together, avoiding the eyes of the palace staff and casting very light Sleep spells on herself from time to time, purely as a measure to calm down.

To *her* right was Scarlet, who had taken the opportunity of being there at the pinnacle of sumptuous excess and requested that the staff bring her the finest foods and wines in the land. She ate standing up, deftly shovelling down the fare from the serving dishes brought to her. Nobody else felt like gorging themselves on lamprey pie and lemon cake so she was the source of the only sounds in the echoing hall.

Beside Scarlet, Mortimer was attempting to keep her head high and disdainfully brushing off the crumbs and meaty chunks that scattered onto the lapels of her coat.

Then there was The Nag, his wings and horn now hidden once more, stood, scornful and irreverent, looking *astonishingly* out of place in this great hall, swatting at now-imaginary flies with his filthy tail. Every so often he would whinny, his hind quarters would shudder slightly and he would raise that tail, causing the attendants to rush forward with a large, porcelain pot. Each time they did he would glance at them slyly and lower it once more, snorting with contempt.

And finally, there sat the great wizard, leaning forward on her staff, wondering how in the eight hells – including the one reserved for those who let their dogs crap in the street without picking it up – she could possibly steer this unhinged gaggle of miscreant outcasts away from at the very least a dozen impending disasters.

***

Upstairs, Gwendoline stood in her father's chambers, as she had done the day before. She had not rested in the interim and had gone through so much exertion and trauma that every physical fibre of her being, and a large portion of the mental ones, were crying out to her to just call a halt to this discussion, stagger to her bedroom, slump down on clean, Egyptian cotton sheets and sleep for a week. But she stood her ground, arms folded, sword still gripped in her hand, and stared this great leader down.

"Alright, let's negotiate," she said finally.

"You know, Gwendoline," the Archduke sighed. "Your appraisal of the landscape of all things political is deeply simplified and childlike."

"I know what's right and what's wrong," she retorted. "And you may as well call me Kathy; we both know everything about me is a lie."

"Believe it or not, child, that wasn't a criticism," he said. "I was once idealistic myself. In fact, it was my lifelong desire to *save* the people that brought us to this point. A part of me wishes things could be as you see it. With compassion and fairness on one side and tyranny and oppression on the other. The truth, as I found over long and painful years, is a grey and treacherous sea of compromises and the constant ebb and flow of power struggles.

"We may go forth from here," he continued gravely, "and you may fight against me and the house of Skygrail in some altruistic attempt to, as you put it, 'free the people'. You can stand against injustice where you see it. But you must know, there is no steady, experienced political leadership at hand to take our place should the Duart retreat from England tomorrow. There would be the same chaos that we encountered a decade ago when you were a feral vagrant. Worse, because we would be taking our dependable social structures with us.

"But deeper than that," he went on. His tone was not patronising or mocking, or even triumphant; it was simply clinical and factual. "More unavoidable a prospect, if you look back on the history of this world, of our own world, and I daresay countless others, you will see common factors in the manner by which people are led. The natural way of things is not expanding freedoms, spiralling outward making each person their own individual sovereign state; it is *order*, and weakness following strength. These people *want* to be ruled.

"Oh, don't read me wrong, they do not wish for cruelty to be visited upon them or their families, I would be quite mad to suggest that. But they do seek leaders who will be cruel, they do rally to banners of those who can crush their enemies. Like it or not, Gwendoline, the natural way of things is free of the complications of individual liberties."

Gwen glared at him. "Give me one good reason why I shouldn't kill you on the spot right now and claim England for myself," she said calmly. "Nobody could stop me, and if the people respect that wresting of power you speak of, they will not only *not* mourn your passing, they will rally to me."

He shrugged. "I cannot give you a reason. Tactically it is, as you say, the wisest course of action."

She was silent for a long moment, trying to contain her fear. "If our roles were reversed," she said quietly, "would you kill me?"

There was a long pause. "No."

"Why not?" Gwen asked. "If you live by this code of power above all else?"

"Because, Gwendoline," he said, "I am, though this was not expected… so very proud of you."

She could feel her legs trembling as she studied him. He stood still and resolute, unarmoured for the first time she could remember.

"And I *will* continue to call you Gwendoline, because for all my layering untruths onto your history to position you as a princess that you absolutely have no right to be, this person who stands before me, this strong, fierce warrior… she is what you have made of yourself."

Gwen felt a wave of emotion and battled for control, her thoughts racing for how to respond. Forceful tears were welling up in the corner of each eye that left her afraid to blink and send them rolling down her face. Holding herself rigid, she smiled grimly.

"Then I have three requests before I walk from this palace and do not return," she said. "That is, unless I have an army at my back. Do these three things for me and I will not strike you dead in this room."

"I shall need to hear them before I agree," he replied.

"First, I want full pardons for everyone. Everyone downstairs, every Hood, everyone connected to them that is currently classified as a criminal, I want them cleared and freed…"

Coriolanus shook his head. "They will all almost certainly return to a life of crime immediately. I cannot stand by and watch London and England fall to that. This one I cannot agree to."

"You didn't let me finish," Gwen countered. "For *one* week. That is all I ask. After that they can choose to do whatever they wish with their lives and you can respond within the laws you lay down. Pardon them and do not hunt them for one week."

He considered for a moment. "Done. Next."

"There are too many hungry and impoverished in London," said Gwen. "I have seen their faces, looked into their eyes. It is an existence I would not wish upon anyone. You will set up charitable concerns for their shelter and feeding."

His lip curled and he shook his head once again. "These are leeches, they provide us with nothing."

"Providing for them provides *us* with humanity," Gwen insisted. "You can afford inexpensive, nourishing food and a bed for the night, and it may surprise you what positive outcomes are achieved."

"After this week, nothing shall surprise me," said the Archduke, without humour. "Very well, I will do what I can within the boundaries of practicality."

"You will do it from now on," she added. "You don't cut this expense to fund the military, this is a constant, ongoing project for *you* personally."

His voice was low. "You are truly testing my limits, child."

"If you are as proud of me as you say, then use me as your inspiration, don't just make those empty words, meant to curry my favour. You *show* me how proud you are."

"And… the third?" he asked.

At this, Gwendoline blushed and approached him, still holding tightly to the sword, before stating her third demand in a quiet, clear manner. He studied her and nodded.

In the vestibule, Oberon now paced nervously, looking around and through into the palace rooms. Robin approached to stand with him.

"This place is pretty... scary for me, Robb," the akka confessed.

"It really doesn't feel like we should be here, does it?" Robin responded.

"No, and nobody's stopping us going anywhere. This is... I'm not sure if I can handle it."

"We'll be alright. She'll be back in a short while and whatever happens next... I suppose at least we'll be together."

"No, Robb, you don't understand. I'm having difficulty *handling* our new situation." Oberon looked meaningfully at his knapsack.

"Oh... Oh!" The message finally got through to Robin. "Well... what have you got there?" he said sympathetically.

"I'm just admiring these sabres on the walls and that tiara that *was* in that case over there and now..." He tapped his knapsack.

"I understand, old boy. I'll put it back for you."

Oberon slowly, reluctantly, opened up, reached inside and pulled out a gold tiara, glittering with rubies. Robin admired it for a second, crossed to the display case and then stowed the tiara decisively within the pockets of his coat.

"Hey!" Oberon cried indignantly.

"I take your condition very seriously," said Robin, "but I *am* still a thief after all. This will make a fine present for her." Oberon stared at him and then slowly smiled. It was great to have his friend back.

***

Simpson, the butler, came to the entrance reception hall and called out to all within earshot.

"Ladies and gentlemen, I present to you all for the last time, Princess Gwendoline Amelia Gertrude Victoria of the house of Saxe-Coburg and Gotha."

Robin's brow furrowed and he hurried to the foot of the stairs to see what this meant. The rest of the outlaws joined him and waited expectantly, their eyes searching the top of the grand white marble staircase. And then she appeared.

She wore crimson silk gloves that extended to her elbows. Her neck and shoulders were bare and her hair was up and intricately styled above an exquisite, matching corset with a delicate lattice across the front and complex, curling silver patterns shining across its surface. Below this was a many-layered gown, cut specifically for Gwen's figure, to accentuate her height and hips. Its outer layer was blue silk, its under-layer made up of many frilled petticoats, each one nearly as light as air, and shimmering in different shades of lilac, pearl and periwinkle that played in the light, so that as she moved she attained the ethereal lustre of an oil painting come to life. In her hand, like a sceptre, she held the Archenblade, its golden runes glowing and the orb at its crossguard pulsing a deep red.

She made her way slowly, elegantly, down the stairs to meet them, head held high, serene and noble, but a half-smile breaking out on her lips as she saw Robin's expression. He gingerly stepped up and passed her, standing slightly higher and turning so that their faces were level.

She was quiet and unsure. "We don't have time to dance," she said apologetically. "I'll change back into my action clothes, I just… I just wanted one chance for you to see me like this."

He broke forward and kissed her, shaking a little as he brought his hands up to lightly cradle her face. He had not said anything, simply because at that point all words faded away.

As kisses go, this one was pretty spectacular.

***

Later, Gwen and Viola stood in her bedroom, bidding her cats goodbye. Simpson stood politely to one side.

"You will look after them, won't you?" Gwen asked. "I mean, there may not be anyone in the palace who wants this many cats running around after I'm gone but… Oh, Sebastian, I'm going to miss you. There's just no way I can take you with me. You're too old and soft to be out there travelling." She pushed her face against his warm fur to wipe away the tears.

"I shall ensure that Sebastian finds a home," said Simpson. "Doubtless there will be someone who favours the old and soft kind of cat. Certain staff were, after all, despite his more trying moments… very fond of him."

"Goodbye, Simpson," Gwen said sadly. "You've always been a perfect gentleman, polite, discreet and kind, even though you thought nobody would see."

He coughed lightly. "Well, it was simply an honour to serve you, your Highness." Gwen drew the butler into an embrace, quite ruffling his shirt as she held him tightly.

***

As Gwen, Viola and their companions walked out of the front doors, far behind them, up the stairs, Archduke Coriolanus watched his only daughter, now his sworn enemy, leave. In his silence and seclusion, he allowed himself, for the first time in far too many long years… a smile.

Chapter 28: The Journey On

Monday Morning

The next day, after marching from the palace and losing themselves in London, sleeping in a pair of safe-houses and proceeding out toward the reassuring darkness of Camelot forest, the group of briefly reprieved criminals convened for their first council of war.

It took place on the site that a Round Table had once been, its timbers wasted away to nothing. Gwendoline stood in the spot where Merlene informed her Arthor had sat, took a deep breath, and surveyed her allies.

"The house of Skygrail," she said, "headed by the Dukes, intends to martial their forces and spread out to conquer Europe. With me gone, that takes away the Royal pageantry my fa– that the *Archduke* of Buckingham founded his plans for an empire on, which means he will have to take these countries by force.

"The French Empire, Spain, Prussia, Austro-Hungary," she went on. "These are all places where the people are weakened and struggling to survive. There are barghest over there, countless in number, impeding trade and travel, making them very dependent on England. It will not be too difficult for the Duart to act as both their salvation and an ever-present threat. They haven't a chance of repelling a serious attack. So, we need to *give* them some kind of chance. Are we all in agreement on that?"

All assembled said yes, with varying degrees of assurance.

"And are we all in agreement that as things stand, we can't possibly take down the house of Skygrail on our own?" Gwen asked, and again they all concurred in their own way. "Very well then," she said, turning to the wizard. "Merlene, what are our options?"

"As I see it," the crone replied, "our possible courses of action are either to return to London and continue Robin, Scarlet and Oberon's rebellion, expanding it to a full-on revolution. In this manner we attempt to confound the control of the Duart and give the Londoners a chance for a better life." She shifted her staff to the other hand.

"*Or* we stay in Celador and journey over the Green Sea. We follow in the footsteps of the Akka tribes who made their exodus south, and travel through those uncharted wildlands. We then try to recruit as many of their icecasters as possible and build an opposing army that way."

"Uh, I have something to say." Oberon cleared his throat, and everyone turned their attention to him. "Whatever you guys choose, I volunteer to head south. Ajax and I will do our best to get you all the help we possibly can. But… we're going to be on our own."

Robin stared at him. "What…? Nonsense, old boy, I'll come with you."

"No, Robb, this is a journey we have to take alone. Ajax is sick. You know that. He's been a danger to all of you, even though you've been so welcoming."

"Uhh," Ajax said uncertainly.

"I know, buddy, you wouldn't do any of them any harm on purpose. But it's your head. Something up there isn't safe. And I have to keep you alone and away from people you could harm until… until we can find folks just like us who can take it."

Gwen started to shake her head. "Oh, Oberon you don't have to…"

"No, I do…" he interrupted. "And this is something I've been living with for a while, and I haven't told any of you.

"See… about six months ago I blacked out. Lost an evening. Woke up next to the carcass of a cow. Its blood was all over my hands, my jaws…" He lowered his eyes. "I couldn't even remember killing it. Since then I've had flashes. Little ticks where I have to remind myself where I am. I've been angry for no reason. I've lost what people's faces should look like. I've… I forgot my name. Thought it was John for a while."

"No." Robin's face was pale.

"And yes," Oberon continued. "I find myself stealing things for no good reason. Useless, random things. It's like this guy right here when he was younger. That's how it started with him." He rubbed Ajax's shoulder. "I haven't been able to face up to it. I didn't believe I had the strength until the past few days when everything seemed like too much to get through, and yet here we are, still alive." He held out his hands in grateful disbelief.

"What this means is that I'm showing all the early signs of mindshadow. I don't know how much longer I can be around… safely. I just know that if I hurt any of you…" He looked hard at Viola who had both hands over her mouth, her shoulders shaking a little. "Life would become unbearable."

"There must be a cure, surely," Viola blurted out.

"There's no cure," Oberon replied flatly. "And it's going to get worse… a *lot* worse. So, we're just gonna go.

"We'll be fine, Ajax and I. It'll be good to be out in the fresh air, just walking the world, seeing what we can see. But I want you all to know it has been… well, not the *best* time of my life, some of it was terrible, but look at what I've got to choose from. This last week has helped me focus on what was important. And I wish-" He paused for a long time, unsure how to put this last part into words. "I just hope I don't forget you all."

Robin got to his feet. "Oberon, I will stay with you."

"No," Oberon said firmly. "You can't understand what this means. I won't put you through it."

"If you want to leave because you really need to be alone," Robin interjected, "you can go and be alone, but I'm not letting you walk away just to protect me." His accent slipped slightly, traces of his older, rougher, South London one becoming more evident. "Listen, my whole life, every moment of my day is dangerous and foolhardy. If I have the option of being with my friend while I'm doing that, then so be it. Plus, I'm pretty fast, you'll have to catch me." He cleared his throat, and the more theatrically heroic voice returned. "And I'm prepared to do that for the rest of my life." He glanced at Gwendoline. "But I won't ask you to do the same."

Gwen regarded him steadily, her voice even and determined. "This week," she said. "I have lost my house, my job, my virginity and my cat, and I *just* got hold of the two of you. I'm not letting you go."

Viola looked at Gwen with new eyes, lowered her hands, breathed deeply, and spoke quietly, but decisively. "I know for sure now that I can help… I'll stay with you too."

Scarlet chose her words carefully. "My place is in London," she stated. "What Gwendoline said about us giving those people a chance is what I've devoted the past ten years to. I've got so many more who need and depend on me. But I'll find us a new hideout there and keep the home fires burning, and you and your brother… the lot of you… will always have a place at my table."

It was Merlene's turn. "I can't possibly promise that I'll be there at all times," she said, her voice grave and measured. "But for now, you can rely on my counsel and my shield."

Nightwind harrumphed and stamped a hoof. "You provide me with those rub downs every few days and find me some *tasty* food, and I suppose I'll grace you with my presence… but only because hanging around this castle bores me now."

They all turned to regard Mortimer, who had remained silent for most of the past day.

"What?" she asked incredulously, then shook her head. "I'm not sure what you want me to *say*. I mean, this is heart-warming if you're that sort of person, but I'm not.

"I don't *dream* of Prince Charming. I don't *gather* round with the family on Christmas day and watch the

368

little ones open their presents. I don't *see* why giving up my life of luxury to go wander in the great beyond with someone… *two* people who may lose their marbles and attack me at any minute, is such a capital notion. Quite frankly I think you're all off your rockers for saying you will." She looked around at their faces for the slightest sign of agreement and found none. Mortimer Wilson collected all of her dignity, prepared her most cutting of departure speeches, and then sighed.

"But after all… I suppose… Oh, sod it. Since London's about to turn into a war zone I might as well tag along with you bunch of prats for a quiet life. I may find a lucrative application for my skills while I'm doing so." She nodded abruptly and shut her mouth before any more insanity could burst forth.

"Alright," Gwen agreed. "But you betray us again, even by accident, and I'll kill you."

Mortimer smiled icily at her. "If it comes to that I think I can handle myself. I pulled my punches and *didn't* pull my triggers last time."

Gwen nodded. "Settled then. Glad to have you aboard."

"I don't know what to say," Oberon exclaimed. "This is… No one's ever-" He looked down at his hands again. "Thank you all."

"You don't need to say anything, old chum," Robin reassured him, nudging his arm. "Just stop talking about going off alone. You'll *never* be alone."

A peace had settle upon the group, threaded with a counterpoint of anxious apprehension.

"So it's decided then," said Gwen. "We go South over the Green Sea to find the Akka tribes and recruit an army of icecasters."

"If I may make a final point before we begin our journey," put in Merlene, "there is *one* task that we could achieve in addition, should we obtain their aid. Let's say we do muster a ragtag army. *That* many icecasters put together are a powerful force. So on our return, *before* we march on London, if we head North from here, through hundreds of miles of forests and mountains we will find the resting place of the Drakes.

"There we could finish King Arthor's work and put an end to those balefully cunning, fire-breathing beasts once and for all, thus making those lands safe for the Duart in England to return. That way, should we prove victorious or not, we will have saved this world from further destruction and given a home back to both those Duart who would otherwise seek dominion elsewhere, and the Akka who rightly deserve recompense for their sacrifice."

Gwen didn't look convinced. "Hundreds of miles is an awfully long way to drag an army that's already travelled so far – especially with only the promise of a fiery death to free up the land that rejected them for the benefit of their hated enemies."

Merlene looked stern. "If we do not, then when the Drakes awaken once more we shall *all* feel their wrath. Imagine if they got through to your world."

"I know," said Gwen. "It's something that keeps all of the Duart people up at night; what will happen when the Drakes eventually, *inevitably*, return, how can we defend ourselves? I know it's a threat we can't ignore. I know that if we do then everything we fight for will be in danger one day anyway…" She paused, looking around to make sure everyone was giving her their full attention.

"Which is why we're going to *recruit* the Drakes to fight my father."

***

Afterward, in the crumbling atrium, Robin waited for Gwendoline to emerge from a private conversation with Merlene. Viola came out first. They regarded one another for a moment.

"If you ever make her cry," Viola said, "I'll unravel your brain like a cat with a ball of yarn."

Robin shrugged. "Fair enough. You ever make Oberon feel like less than a prince and I'll donate all of your possessions to a dozen vagrants."

Viola gave a nod and a little smile. "Then we understand one another."

"Listen, Viola," he began. "I'm terribly sorry I kidnapped you and called you a pampered clown. Well, I mean that's not entirely true, I'm not sorry all this happened, but…"

"You're forgiven," she interrupted. "And I'm a teeny, tiny bit sorry I was such a beast to you."

Robin stared at her for a moment, formulating what he wanted to ask. "I've been wondering though, I've never seen someone who can do… *what* you can do. Firecasters, all over the shop and I once saw an Akka icecaster work their stuff, but this mind maajik is something else."

"Ah…" Viola looked away.

"It's forbidden, isn't it?"

"Yes. Deeply."

"Then wherever did you learn?"

Her lips drew into a crooked smile. "Ahhh, now therein lies a tale, and you're going to have to get me pretty bloody drunk to hear it."

"I know the worst place in town."

"Why and how does that not surprise me?"

At that point the prior princess finally appeared. Viola shot one more meaningful look to the thief and made her excuses. Their new leader stood, somewhat shyly, with the green-clad duart, both back in their outlaw outfits.

"So…" Robin asked her. "What am I calling you?"

"You seemed to know last night."

Robin blushed. "Well, yes, but I mean *now*. Is it Gwendoline, is it Katherine? Who are you going to be?"

"Are you going to carry on being Robin?" she asked, with genuine uncertainty. "Would you entertain the notion of going back to Ben Wessex?"

He shook his head.

"No," he said firmly. "I *chose* my new name. I purposefully abandoned that old life. Whatever I am now, I built with this new role. It means so much more to me, and it's a constant, daily reminder of what I have to do… what I *want* to do.

"Ben is a ghost, but… everyone knows *you* as Gwendoline."

"Yes, they do." She mused. "And if I'm honest, Lady Katherine was a mask, and the little girl I once was is always going to be there.

She placed her hand upon her heart. "But just like you… Gwendoline is who I am *now*, and when people look to me, that's who I want to be."

"But not a princess."

She was quiet for a long moment.

"No. And I've been considering that deeply too. I've thought of a name for our gang, far better than Merry Men, which will serve as a reminder of the greatest act of theft that England has endured under Duart rule.

They took from us, the idea that we had a right to govern ourselves. That's what we're taking back."

"So, what are we going to be called?" asked Robin.

"Well…"

Gwen took a deep breath.

These characters will return in The Christmas Thieves;
a little tale that takes place in the winter of 1882,
five months prior to the events of The Princess Thieves.
And after that, their journeys will continue on.

Epilogue

"Something new stalks the night in London. The Black Shuck Rises… and also Returns, to punish all wrongdoers, whatever wrongs they be doing. And now, tonight, he has a young ward with him. Someone to mould in his image and teach the ways of the brutal streets, and his name is *Shuck Puppy*!"

"Oi," Jack said irritably. "You said I was gonna get to choose my name."

"Well what d'you want then?" the Shuck asked him.

"I wanna be The Dark Wolf!"

The Shuck shook his head adamantly. "That sounds a bit *too* intimidating, you need to be about half as scary as I am."

Jack scowled. He'd had his heart set on the Dark Wolf. "The Dark Shuck then? That's *less* black *than* black."

"The Dark Puppy?"

"Blackjack."

"The Wolf Cub."

Jack broke into a broad grin. "No, I've got it – *Spring-Heeled* Jack!"

The Shuck thought for a moment. "Yeah, alright." He cleared his throat and began his declamation again. "The Black Shuck will avenge his probably-dead-now parents!"

"And Spring-Heeled Jack will make amends for his terrible wrong!" Jack added. "He will save as many lives as was lost for his greedy moment of stupidity."

"Let's go and liberate some Londoners," said the Shuck.

"We are the things what howl/spring in the night!"

From the Author

This book is dedicated to my daughter, Lyra Shaw, who became my biggest fan while I wrote it. Her constant support and enthusiasm provide brightness when all other lights go out.

It was penned and produced as an episodic audio drama podcast during that most foul Year of our Lord, two thousand and sixteen. A time of upheaval and cruelty, with madness in every direction. A time where both sides of the Atlantic were worn down by travesties of politics, where unity and progress were kicked aside in favour of misguided notions of supremacy through independence, segregation, rejection of the kindest of human values and the vilification of previously admired virtue.

I won't lie, I suffered about a dozen mini breakdowns over that time, and there were days when I woke to a grey sky and a storm of despair on social media and wondered whether I could write this story with the hope which it was originally conceived.

That it exists at all is testament to my amazing family, my friends, my readers and listeners keeping me going, reminding me that this ugly age was when the beautiful, stronghearted whimsy of Gwendoline, Robin, Oberon and Viola were needed most. We need fuel for our furnaces or else we burn out.

We need stories that tell us fighting is worthwhile when it is for something so inherently good.

And if we can make it through the darkest of nights and into a brightest of days it will be *together* that this is achieved.

-Alexander Shaw, October 31st 2017

Printed in Great Britain
by Amazon